SHADOW'S REACH

BOOK SEVEN OF THE TALES OF THE
TERRITORIES

PETER WACHT

KESTREL MEDIA GROUP, LLC

Shadow's Reach
By Peter Wacht

Book 7 of The Tales of the Territories

Cover design by Ebooklaunch.com

Published in the United States by Kestrel Media Group LLC.

ISBN: 978-1-950236-50-3

eBook ISBN: 978-1-950236-51-0

Library of Congress Control Number: 2024913372

❀ Created with Vellum

ALSO BY PETER WACHT

THE FALLEN KNIGHT SERIES

(Forthcoming)

The Death of the Dragon (short story)*

The Dragon Awakens

Duel With a Dragon

Beware the Dragon

The Dragon Returns

THE REALMS OF THE TALENT AND THE CURSE

THE LEGEND OF THE DRAGON LORD

The Painful Truth (short story)*

Stealing the Light (Forthcoming 2025)

THE TALES OF CALEDONIA

(Complete 7-Book Series)

Blood on the White Sand (short story)*

The Diamond Thief (short story)*

The Protector

The Protector's Quest

The Protector's Vengeance

The Protector's Sacrifice

The Protector's Reckoning

The Protector's Resolve

The Protector's Victory

THE TALES OF THE TERRITORIES

Stalking the Blood Ruby (short story)*

A Fate Worse Than Death (short story)*

Death on the Burnt Ocean

Monsters in the Mist

The Dance of the Daggers

Bloody Hunt for Freedom

A Spark of Rebellion

Shadows Made Real

Shadow's Reach

Storm in the Darkness (Forthcoming 2025)

THE SYLVAN CHRONICLES

(Complete 9-Book Series)

The Legend of the Kestrel

The Call of the Sylvana

The Raptor of the Highlands

The Makings of a Warrior

The Lord of the Highlands

The Lost Kestrel Found

The Claiming of the Highlands

The Fight Against the Dark

The Defender of the Light

THE RISE OF THE SYLVAN WARRIORS

Through the Knife's Edge (short story)*

* Free stories can be downloaded from my author website at PeterWachtBooks.com. My books are also available on Amazon and other online retailers.

SETTING THE STAGE

The Tales of the Territories continue the adventures of Bryen Keldragan and Aislinn Winborne as they travel across the Burnt Ocean to the Territories, what will eventually become the Kingdoms of *The Sylvan Chronicles*.

The events occur more than one thousand years before the happenings in *The Sylvan Chronicles* and take place in the lands far to the west of Caledonia that have been opened for colonization thanks to territorial grants sold by the deceased King Corinthus Beleron.

There Bryen and Aislinn will take on new challenges, make new friends and enemies, and continue to battle those who have turned to the Curse.

In the Territories, sometimes called New Caledonia, as in the other realms, the ability to use the Talent sets apart the person gifted with this unique skill. But being able to use the Talent is only part of the dynamic. For if a Magus chooses to follow a darker path, the Talent becomes the Curse.

The Sylvan Chronicles, The Tales of Caledonia, and *The Tales of the Territories* are a part of the larger world of *The Realms of the Talent and the Curse.*

1

STRANGE KIND OF PLEASURE

"One more time, Alister," Hakea Roosarian purred. Her voice was soft. Seductive. "Just so he understands."

The whip whistled through the air, slicing across Davin's back and leaving a hiss of static in the air, a few seconds of expectant silence following behind it.

Davin held his breath, gritting his teeth, his entire body tensing against the pain. He refused to call out. He refused to give the Governor of Fal Carrach the satisfaction that she craved.

He began to breathe again when the sizzle across his back slowly, excruciatingly transitioned into the slow burn that he welcomed. Relished, in fact. Harnessing it just as Declan had taught him. Using the stinging throb to strengthen his resolve.

The pain a palliative of sorts.

A reminder that he was still alive.

What he was experiencing now was no worse than any of his combats on the white sand.

It was all the same.

The pain.

The exhaustion.

The struggle for clarity.

But no fear.

Never fear.

Declan and his incessant training made sure of that.

This was just another contest.

A contest of wills.

He had never lost in the Pit.

He refused to lose now.

"Again, Alister. One more time. We want the Crimson Giant to remember this experience for however much longer he continues to draw breath."

Davin's expression didn't change when the whip bit into his back again. To maintain his concentration and his control, he needed to find a focal point.

With that in mind, he stared at Hakea Roosarian. His eyes cold. Dispassionate. Never revealing what he was truly feeling.

The Governor stood before him offering an imperious gaze and an arrogant smirk. She tried to avoid his eyes, but she couldn't. His frigid orbs catching her. And once he had her, Davin didn't let go.

He wanted to send her a clear message.

He wanted her to see only two truths.

The first, purpose.

The second, a promise.

Once he was certain there was no confusion between them, he gave her a small smile filled with a menace that made her take a step back.

Out of surprise, not fear. That's what Hakea told herself. Because the gladiator wasn't going anywhere. And he certainly wasn't in a position to make his promise real.

Davin stood in the same circular chamber from which he and Talia had stolen the vial of black liquid only a few hours before.

Behind him were the two cells draped in a deep pall. Yet

now they only contained the Stalkers that Roosarian had created. Just a drop of the Curse in fluid form all that was required for each horrid transformation.

The shadows hid the monsters' features, although Davin had no trouble seeing them in his mind's eye. During the last few months, he had become much too familiar with their razor-sharp claws, long fangs, and mottled black flesh that resembled melted wax. The only feature visible in the tenebrous gloom that nestled around the Stalkers, just as always was the case, were their brightly burning blood-red eyes.

Davin ignored the monstrosities. They were a threat, but they were not the immediate threat.

He forced himself to keep his gaze fixed on the source of his torment. The petite woman with a sword on each hip who took a sadistic pleasure from the punishment that she was inflicting upon him.

He hadn't noticed the rungs set in the floor the first time he entered the chamber, his focus solely on stealing the vile liquid that turned men and women into monsters. But he noticed them now. Those steel rungs allowed Roosarian to chain him and have her way with him as she was doing now.

The soldier tasked with whipping him gave Davin just enough chain so that he could stand to his full height. No more than that, however. Because of that limitation, he couldn't raise his arms or shift his feet more than a few inches in any direction.

He wore only his breeches and boots, the torturer removing Davin's leather armor before he began his less than tender ministrations. Davin's shirt now no more than a bloody rag, most of it shredded, just a few strips of cloth still keeping it across his shoulders.

Davin could no longer recall how many strikes of the whip he had suffered through to reach this point. He had lost count, finding the exercise of keeping track too tiring.

He had tried to retreat into his mind. To separate the physical punishment that his body was enduring from his spirit.

It was easier to do that at the beginning of this torture session. It had gotten more difficult for him as his pain and suffering intensified with every slash of the whip, the knotted leather leaving one bloody streak after another across his broad back.

"There is no point in fighting the inevitable, Davin Noname," smirked Hakea as she sought to re-exert her authority. She was impressed by his persistence. Nevertheless, she believed that it would only take him so far. "You will give me what I want in the end. You know it just as well as I do. So there's really no point in continuing to resist."

Davin did his best to ignore her taunt, somewhat discomfited because it held the unnerving ring of truth to it. Gritting his teeth to the point where he thought they might crack, he hardened his expression until his face resembled a stone.

He would not allow her to take from him who he truly was.

He would not allow her to make him into who she wanted him to be.

To that end, Davin stared right into Hakea Roosarian's eyes. Refusing to blink.

He would make this hard on her. He would make her understand that a gladiator of the Pit could not be broken.

He had fought men and women on the white sand. He had fought Ghoules and Echidna and Slayers. He had fought Stalkers. He had even fought a Bakunawa, which, thinking back, was not one of his better decisions.

Even so, he had survived each combat. Often when he didn't deserve to. Always ready to go to the other side.

His honor, his integrity, intact.

Because when it was time for him to journey to the other side that would be all that he would have.

She might kill him.

She probably would.

But he would not give her what she wanted.

That thought driving him, he refused to give her the satisfaction of knowing that she was hurting him. He would not allow her to shatter his strength of will.

Because that's the only way she could win. That was the only way that she could get what she wanted.

She needed to break him. And despite the agony that his back had become, that wasn't going to happen.

He would live with the pain.

He would savor the pain.

The more he hurt, the more he knew that he was winning.

The more he knew that he was still alive.

Hakea stared right back at Davin, trying to match his expression with her own. She would not be the one to give in during this battle of wills.

Just as she always did, she would win in the end. She was sure of that, her eyes sparking with pleasure as she took in the gladiator.

Her lips curled into a small smile while she studied him. Then she bit her lip.

He was tough. There was no question about that. Tougher than any person she had ever met before.

That only made what she was doing to him now all the more fun. All the more exciting. Almost intoxicating, in fact.

No one had done it before.

But she would.

She was the one who was going to break the Crimson Giant.

One way or the other, one of the most famous gladiators to ever fight in the Pit was going to do her bidding. Become her servant. Whether he wanted to or not.

"Davin Noname," she purred quietly. She knew that he still heard her even over the sharp crack of the leather whip striking his back with a frightening consistency. She shook her head then as if she were disappointed in him. Although she really wasn't. She was impressed. Even slightly aroused. "We didn't have to be here doing this. We could have been doing something else. Something much more exciting. Much more fun. Back in my chambers. Just you and me."

The gladiator didn't respond. His expression didn't change.

Davin simply stared at her.

She couldn't see a speck of emotion in his eyes.

She knew it was there, however. Just locked away for the time being.

She would worry it free soon enough.

Once she found the key to unlock him.

And she would find that key.

Because she was very skilled at getting what she wanted.

She mulled the gladiator's name as Alister slashed into his back in that steady, comfortable rhythm that the soldier had perfected, a bloody spray erupting every time the leather struck Davin's flesh.

She had been right when she first met the gladiator. The spark between them unmistakable.

It had been instantaneous. The moment their eyes met on the Carlomin dock.

There had been a promise there of what could be. Why the gladiator couldn't see that as she did, Hakea didn't know.

She would make him see it, nonetheless. She would make him understand why he should have left Talia Carlomin's service and joined her.

Why he didn't, she still couldn't understand. She couldn't quite come to grips with the strange sense of loyalty he demonstrated toward that blasted woman.

Most any other man would have acknowledged the precariousness of his position and acceded to her demands without a second thought.

The gladiator hadn't, however.

Why?

Why so obstinate?

As she thought about that, she shook her head in disappointment once again. He had been such a fool. If he had been smarter, they truly could have had so much fun together.

But now ...

Now it was too late.

He was too stubborn. Too unwilling to see and understand the larger picture that she had placed before him.

That lack of vision was going to cost him. More than he anticipated, in fact.

Although she did have to admit that she was quite enjoying this spectacle. This show that he was putting on for her.

Her eyes gleamed as they wandered over him. Every scar that crisscrossed his body told a story, and she wanted to hear each one. She wanted him even more than she had wanted him before.

But sadly, it wasn't to be.

Because the red-haired fighter who had been quick with a grin and a wink wasn't there.

She wasn't staring at Davin Noname any longer.

No, the Crimson Giant stood before her now.

Bloody and beaten, true, yet still defiant.

That's what she wanted. His recalcitrance gave her a thrill that she hadn't experienced in quite some time.

"Your loyalty is misplaced, gladiator," Hakea finally said very softly, as if she were sharing a secret with him. "You know that. Yet still you force this punishment upon yourself."

She didn't expect him to answer, although she was pleased when he did.

"You know that my decision is made. I will not do as you want. No matter what you do to me, I will not kill Talia Carlomin for you."

"So you'd rather die for her?" Hakea tsked, shaking her

head with regret. "That seems such a waste. She's going to die anyway. You know that. And there's nothing that you can do to prevent her death. Why not hasten it for her? Ensure that it's painless. Ensure that it's done quickly and correctly so that she doesn't suffer."

"Gladiators of the Pit are unique, Hakea," Davin replied quietly. He took advantage of the short break given to him as his torturer halted his labor at his mistress' nod. The soldier stepped back and flung the whip over his shoulder, fully expecting to put it to use again soon, working out the tired muscles in his arm and shoulder while he waited. "Death doesn't choose us. We choose our death. I will not kill someone who doesn't deserve it."

"Even if your death means you never leave this chamber as you are?" Hakea asked, enjoying ever so much the brief spark of fear that flashed across his face when he realized what she meant.

"Even so." Davin's voice wasn't as strong as it had been before. The whipping affecting him. The veiled threat more.

"I don't understand this loyalty of yours." Hakea stepped right up to Davin, making sure that his eyes were locked onto hers, before she began to walk around him. She trailed a finger along his chest as she did so before moving to his back.

"Obviously you have some useful skills. Perhaps you'd still be willing to use those skills for me without having to continue this game between us. Without having to reach the pointless end toward which you're forcing us."

She stopped for just a moment, taking her time as she traced with one finger a scar along his side that slid below his trousers, before she started walking around him again. "We could achieve a great deal together. We could be unstoppable."

She halted right in front of him then, giving him a suggestive look. When he didn't respond as she wanted him to, Hakea grabbed the chain attached to the collar around his neck and pulled his head down so that their noses were no more than an inch apart.

"All this could stop, Davin Noname. All you need to do to make that happen is agree to do what I want you to do. All you need to do is kill Talia Carlomin. Why is that so hard for you?"

She leaned up then, kissing him roughly. Hungrily. She allowed her lips to linger on his, relishing the blood and the sweat that she tasted.

When she pulled back, she smiled brightly and then laughed softly. She was beginning to understand the source of his rebelliousness.

"There's more than just loyalty between you and Talia Carlomin, isn't there?"

Davin kept his expression the same as it had been – strong, flinty, cold -- even as his emotions roiled within him.

"There's nothing between me and Talia Carlomin," Davin replied softly. "It's a matter of honor. Nothing more than that."

"Honor? Really?" She chuckled softly. "You killed how many? Hundreds? No, that's probably too low. It must be thousands. And despite that you're still not willing to kill one woman to save your own life and ensure a prosperous future for yourself? I find that hard to believe. No one can be so selfless."

"I've been forced to kill, that's true. I don't view myself as a killer."

Hakea laughed at that. "Then you're just kidding yourself. We're all killers, Davin Noname. When the circumstances require it."

Hakea pulled on the chain again, pressing her lips against his even more roughly this time. Her ardor intensifying.

Davin had no choice but to comply, unable to pull away because of the irons and the collar.

Hakea released his lips and stepped back, although not

before she gave him a painful bite on his lower lip that drew blood.

"You would rather suffer here for that fool Carlomin? I thought you were smarter than that, gladiator?"

"You're right. I am smarter than that. I already bet on the winning horse. And you're not it. My dying doesn't matter. She'll still beat you even after I go to the other side."

Hakea's eyes widened at his comment. Infuriated, she drew the dagger from her hip. With a lightning-fast slice, she cut across his chest, a thin stream of blood sheeting down his abdomen.

"You think you can stand up to me?" Hakea hissed. She wanted to cut him again. To make him flinch since he hadn't the first time. Her natural reaction to crush anyone who resisted her. Yet for some reason she didn't quite understand she held back.

"I already am, Hakea. You know it just as well as I do. Do what you will. You won't get what you want from me. I will never serve you."

"You're not afraid of much, are you?" she asked.

"Why would you say that?" Davin needed the distraction. The longer he could draw this out the more time he would gain to steel himself for when the whipping started again. Likely as soon as Hakea tired of this conversation. "I'm frightened by many things actually."

"Really? I would think that right now you were frightened only of me."

"Although I'm sure you'd like to hear that, no. I'm not frightened of you."

"Why not?" Hakea asked, more curious now than angry.

"Because you're not scary enough. You're predictable."

"I'm not scary enough?" Now she was getting angry. She held the bloody dagger in front of his face. "I could cut you again. And again. And again. I could cut you until you resembled nothing more than a slab of meat."

"You could, that's true. But again, where's the imagination in that? It's all very predictable. Just like I said." Before Hakea could interrupt him, he offered more of an explanation.

"Now spiders ... spiders are scary. For example, the widowmaker spider. You wouldn't even know that little nasty, which could fit easily in the palm of your closed fist, was there until you felt its bite. And then you'd only have hours left to live. In fact, one of the gladiators I knew in the Pit was bitten by one of those tiny monsters. He started bleeding from his nose, his eyes, his ears, and no one knew why until the physick arrived after he died and showed us that the widowmaker had nested in his armpit, eating its way into his flesh. That spider was going to use that gladiator to plant its eggs. Now that's scary. And then there's this centipede ..."

"Enough, Davin Noname," growled Hakea. "I am not interested in insects."

"What's the matter? You wanted to know what I was afraid of and why I wasn't afraid of you. That widowmaker spider ..."

"Stop!" shouted Hakea, having lost patience.

Now it was Davin's turn to give her a smile and a lift of his eyebrows, gaining the reaction that he wanted.

"I should have assumed that you would be difficult."

"You should have, yes," agreed Davin.

"Clearly you're familiar with pain. Clearly you're not afraid of Stalkers, because they are little different than some of the monsters you've fought in the Pit."

"That's true," Davin agreed.

"And you're not afraid of death."

"Right again," Davin said, trying to nod and not able to because of the chain and the collar. "Since we've worked all that out, there's really no reason to continue with all this. It doesn't help either of us."

"Maybe," Hakea replied, appreciating his attempt to extricate himself from his difficult circumstances. "Then again, doing what you don't want me to do doesn't have to be about you. It could be about me."

"I'm afraid to ask," Davin grumbled.

That comment brought Hakea's smile back. "You see, Davin Noname, if you haven't figured it out by now, I enjoy inflicting pain. And you have a very high tolerance. That just means that I have to try a bit harder, and that only will make it that much more fun for me."

"I doubt that you could do any worse than you've already done," Davin replied, although he wondered right after he said those words whether he was going to regret uttering them.

"I'll have my fun with you, Davin Noname, and when I'm done with you, I'll do what I need to do. What was that saying your friend had? You must do what you must do?"

Davin nodded, even though he tried to stop himself, becoming even more concerned when he saw how Hakea's expression shifted from menacing to almost barbaric.

"A very appropriate saying for our current intractable situation," Hakea continued. "Because you will do what you must do. But after I'm done with you, you will do it for me. Believe that. Think about that for the next little while. If your perspective doesn't change, then I will do what I must do."

It was then that she reached into her pocket and pulled out the small glass vial, holding it up so that he could see the roiling black fluid contained within it.

Davin steeled himself as best as he could. He feared it might come to this.

He had the tolerance for a great deal of pain. A great deal of suffering.

He knew that.

He knew that he could stand almost anything she might do to him.

He certainly didn't fear death.

But he did fear what one drop of that black liquid could do if it was forced down his throat.

"So this is how the Crimson Giant meets his end?" Hakea mused, her smile fiendish as she rubbed the glass vial against his cheek. A promise of a type. "The terror of the white sand. What a waste."

"Like I said ..."

"Yes, yes, yes, I know. Death doesn't choose you. You choose your death. Very trite. And it will mean nothing in the end." She stepped back then, slipping the vial back into her pocket. "One way or the other, you will kill Talia Carlomin for me. Because if you continue to resist, I'm not going to kill you. I'm going to turn you into a monster instead. You'll die. Or this part of you will die while the monster that's inside you will live. And you'll know it the entire time. Think about that for a few days and then tell me you're still willing to disobey me. Tell me you still refuse to kill Talia Carlomin. Because one way or the other you will obey me. You will kill her."

2

BLOOD AND MONEY

"Come on, you wenches," he muttered under his breath, shaking his large head in annoyance, his jowls flapping as he did so. "At least make it interesting. There's money to be made if you put some effort into it."

Torstan Sharperson closed his eyes, taking a few deep breaths in an effort to calm the irritation beginning to simmer within him. Leaning forward with his elbows on his knees, he ran his two meaty hands over his scalp.

Sweat trickled from his temple down the back of his neck, teasing the few bristles of hair along the back of his head and around his ears. He needed to shave the stubble again. Better bald than going bald, though it had taken him awhile to come to that realization.

At least he was exercising some control rather than waiting for the inevitable to occur. He didn't like the fact that he was losing his hair at a young age. He disliked even more not being able to do anything about it.

Because that's what he craved most. What he had always craved while growing up just a stone's throw from the seat of power in the Caledonian Duchy of Sharston.

Control.

It served as a stimulant for him.

An aphrodisiac of sorts.

When he didn't have control, he felt uniquely out of sorts.

Lost. Like a ship adrift at sea.

Just as he did now.

Worse, during the last few months, that feeling of addictive control, that all was well within his Territory, within the world that he was creating for himself, had dissipated to the point now where it evaded him entirely.

The duel taking place below him on the brown sand – not the white sand that he required and that his soldiers couldn't seem to find anywhere in New Caledonia -- was just another, smaller example of the struggles that he faced.

When the combat began, he thought that it would be a good bout. The two women, veteran soldiers, appeared to be well matched. Even better, both started aggressively, on the attack, seeking to gain the upper hand on the other in the first few minutes.

They demonstrated a cool ferocity, lunging and stabbing, slicing and swinging, spearpoints scraping against steel shields with an entertaining regularity that only served to liven up the somewhat sparse crowd.

That early savagery led to higher stakes, the spectators adding to the betting pool at a rapid rate.

A good thing for whoever won, and thus a greater incentive for the pair of women to put on a good show. For him as well, since he took a large percentage from every pot.

The two soldiers testing their luck as gladiators, and making some extra money for their efforts, both had served in different Guards in Caledonia before crossing the Burnt Ocean and coming to the Highlands. They had the wounds to prove their experience if not their skill. And, reportedly, from what his Captain told him, they had served with distinction upon joining the Highland Guard.

Well, perhaps not with distinction.

Torstan didn't believe all that his Captain told him. The man knew his moods, so Eliasin Hippolates tempered the information that he provided based on how he believed the conversation would play out on a particular day.

Torstan permitted the indiscretion because it often suited his purposes as well. Although he didn't appreciate not being told all that he needed to know, his Captain had other skills that he was more than happy to employ when circumstances demanded it. In particular, a very loose moral code that came in quite handy when certain actions at which others might balk were required.

Besides, Torstan didn't rely solely on what his Captain of the Highland Guard told him. Doing that would prove dangerous.

He had his own sources among his soldiers and in fact throughout the Stone. He had learned from his brother the importance of having a private network of eyes and ears. Better to get the truth that those who feared you or those who served you preferred not to share when it was their own skin on the line.

Thanks to his many other sources, he knew that these two women had worked their way through several different Caledonian Duchy Guards because they had no choice. Each had been dismissed by at least two for various offenses, ranging from theft to attempted murder. Each had a penchant for completing certain assignments with a gusto at which others might hesitate.

Who was he to judge?

Their stories were similar to the stories of most of the other members of his Highland Guard.

This pair struggling on the brown sand didn't serve with

distinction. They served themselves. And so long as his interests and their interests were aligned, they would serve him.

That only made sense to him. Another truth that he had learned from his brother Talus.

These two soldiers, just like all the others who made up his Guard, did what was required of them. No more, no less.

So long as he continued to pay them and he gave them opportunities every so often to wallow for a time in their baser, unsavory natures, whether that meant earning some extra golds in Torstan's version of the gladiatorial games or through some other more nefarious means, then all worked well in his world.

Unless they failed to do what he needed them to do when he needed them to do it. And right then, as they stalked around one another in the Little Pit, the two women were not doing what he needed them to do.

The fire they displayed at the very beginning of the combat had fizzled out like a flame smothered with the top of a pot. Now they were putting on a lackluster exhibition that was boring him and, worse, boring the crowd.

Neither could be permitted.

The arena he built specifically for these combats, which was supposed to be a smaller replica of the Colosseum in Tintagel and could seat fifteen thousand people, was barely a quarter full. That just wouldn't do.

Yet that was only to be expected with one desultory performance such as this one following right after another. He couldn't expect his citizens, the ones he needed to fill his coffers with gold, to make such an important contribution to his treasury if he didn't give them cause to hand over their hard-earned wages.

To do that, his gladiatorial games needed to be a true spectacle that couldn't be missed. Just as had been the case at the Colosseum in Tintagel.

What he was watching now, what had become the standard in recent weeks in the arena that was nestled in the peaks just a quarter mile from the Stone, was anything but.

Did these soldiers playing at gladiator not understand what he was trying to build here?

Did they not understand that their current efforts, which involved nothing more than circling around one another, scraping their spears across the other's shield every so often to make it seem like they were putting in a real effort, harmed his ability to do what was necessary here in the Stone and by extension all of the Highlands?

No, of course they didn't.

They didn't care.

All they saw was what they needed to do for themselves.

That was just the way of the world, wasn't it?

Me first. Me last. Me always.

For some, a disappointing perspective. For Torstan, a real-istic one.

That got him thinking, nodding to himself as the pieces of his current puzzle slowly began to fit together into a solution.

He should have realized this sooner.

If he was going to make his Colosseum what he wanted it to be, what he needed it to be, then he had to make sure that those fighting in the Little Pit concluded that they needed to put in the necessary effort.

Either on their own or with a not so gentle nudge, maybe jab, from him.

"Cowardly dogs," Torstan grumbled, motioning in disgust at the boring display slowly drawing to a close beneath him. "Enjoy whatever this is while you can, because it ends today."

After the first few minutes of frantic struggle, the two spear-carrying soldiers were less interested in winning and more interested in not losing.

Each one had several chances to take advantage of the

other's mistakes. If he had seen them, then he had no doubt that they had as well. But they had done nothing with the opportunities presented. Delaying. Hesitating. Playing. Not fighting.

The two women proffered little more than a lackluster effort, assuming that if they went through the requisite motions – a stab here, a slash there, a scream of anger, a little taunting, maybe a feigned slip now and then – their lack of any real desire to exert themselves or take a real risk wouldn't be noticed.

But he had noticed.

These two were schemers. He knew that now, and it jibed with what his eyes and ears in his Guard had told him.

Useful in other situations. A detriment in the current one.

He suspected that this pair had reached an agreement before the combat to share the purse that would be split between them if there was no clear victor.

Smart.

You made your money more slowly, but it guaranteed that you stayed alive and avoided serious injury.

He had to give them credit for that.

What really irritated him was that they were taking advantage of a mistake that he had made.

When the gladiatorial games took place in the Colosseum in Tintagel, the rules were simple.

Kill your adversary and you lived to fight another day.

Kill or be killed.

Torstan liked that.

The simplicity of it all.

Here in the Highlands, Torstan had adopted what he believed was a more enlightened approach that would ensure a more constant revenue stream.

Rather than force people to fight, he wanted to give them the opportunity to do so.

You could choose to fight in the Pit. If you won, you made good money. If you didn't, you had the chance to walk away.

There were accidents, of course. But usually a fighter who held a knife to his opponent's throat gave his adversary the chance to yield, hoping to receive the same mercy if the positions ever were reversed in the future.

A good system in Torstan's opinion.

Not as bloody when compared to the Pit in Tintagel. Still, he believed that he could make more money off the combats by having a regular stable of fighters that the crowd grew attached to and supported.

A bloody show of sorts with a regular cast of characters.

To that end, he limited each combat to no more than thirty minutes. If you didn't defeat or kill your adversary by then, you received a smaller cut of the purse and walked away, the bulk of the pot going to him of course.

If you won a combat, you took twenty percent of the take, which depending on the interest of the spectators, could be a massive sum. A hundred golds if not more.

If you didn't defeat your adversary and your adversary didn't beat you, then you both split that twenty percent.

The benefit being that more of his combatants lived to fight another day, which at the start of his version of the gladiatorial games was essential, because he didn't have many fighters willing to step onto the brown sand to begin with. Even when he offered reduced sentences to anyone imprisoned beneath the Stone for minor offenses.

He believed that his rules accommodated that reality and built interest in the games. And for a time it had worked fairly well, although not at the rate of growth that he wanted.

The combat that he was watching now certainly didn't help. A combat that was becoming a regular occurrence here.

Neither of the women wanted to do what was required to kill or at least defeat her adversary.

Neither wanted to risk a serious injury.

Neither wanted to die.

He shook his head in growing annoyance. The purse wasn't big enough for them to take a risk and the purse wouldn't increase if they weren't willing to take a risk. Not if they weren't willing to give the crowd the excitement and the blood that they wanted.

Clearly, his system wasn't working as he needed it to, which meant that he needed to change the system.

He would eliminate the shortcomings. He would remedy what was ailing what could become his primary source of revenue.

What based on current events he needed to become his primary source of revenue.

He thought that he could entice people to enter the Pit and put on a good show with the carrot, the lure of a large bag of golds too much for most hoping to make an easy killing – whether literally or not Torstan really didn't care -- to resist.

For some, that proved to be the case. They would do whatever was required for those golds.

For others, those not as greedy or desperate or with a more patient approach, they were willing to accept less if they could reduce the risk to themselves.

It was that latter group that was putting his entire enterprise at risk. They had learned to game the system.

Now he needed to game the system so that they no longer could.

He realized then that he had to adopt the more brutal approach that had proven so successful for hundreds of years in Caledonia.

He needed to make his Pit function just like the Pit in Tintagel did. Or had, until the Volkun led the rebellion that ended the Beleron dynasty and freed all the gladiators.

Lesson learned.

Torstan closed his eyes and shook his head in dismay as the two fighters danced around one another on the sand.

And he didn't mean dance in a good way. Half the time they just feinted at one another now, the sand running through the hourglass to mark the end of their combat almost having run its course.

It was as if they had choreographed the entire duel. He wouldn't have been surprised if they did.

The pair of combatants were just going through the motions now and the crowd was beginning to realize it, losing interest, the screams and shouts and demands for blood replaced by hissing and even a few boos.

This was ridiculous.

He would put the new rules in place for tomorrow's contests.

The free could continue to fight if they chose. Anyone currently languishing in the cells beneath the Stone would be forced into the Pit. No exceptions.

If a criminal won, Torstan would commute their sentence if he hadn't ordered them to hang. And the chance at freedom certainly would give them the incentive to put up a good fight.

The crowd would love it as well. Someone fighting for their freedom. That was a narrative that could put more golds in his treasury.

If the criminal was sentenced to swing from the gibbet and survived, then the Pit would be their life for however long he or she lasted.

Another narrative that would appeal to the crowd. And as Torstan knew, a happy crowd meant fuller coffers.

Simple.

And one other rule to motivate all the gladiators, whether free or forced.

He would adopt the stricture of the Colosseum in Tintagel.

Kill or be killed.

Two would enter the Little Pit. Only one would leave.

For the first time since the combat between the two soldiers had begun, Torstan smiled. Those few though necessary changes should liven things up on the brown sand.

He had no doubt that they would increase interest among the residents of the Stone. And that, in turn, would increase his revenue.

That was the key after all.

He needed to enhance the revenue that he earned from this venture because he was close to losing control over what had been his largest and most profitable revenue stream since he assumed his seat as the Governor of the Highlands.

That and the fact that for him, it was all about control.

Satisfied that he had solved a problem that had plagued him for too long, Torstan attempted to enjoy what was left of the combat. He couldn't wait to see the faces of this scheming pair when he told them what would be required of them on the morrow.

They would fight one another again. Both would walk out into the Little Pit. Only one would leave.

And if they refused, they would hang.

Simple.

And he liked simple.

Simple was clean.

Simple was best.

That thought made him smile, his eyes sparking viciously. His smile only grew wider when he thought of another consequence of his changes.

His new approach to the gladiatorial games would save him some money as well. It would help clear out the cells beneath the Stone on a more regular basis.

A little churn would be a good thing, because he wasn't concerned about those cells being empty.

He would find others to take the place of those forced into

his Colosseum in the Peaks. He always did. Whether they deserved to be there or not.

For the first time in several months, Torstan finally felt more like himself. Like he was doing something to solve his problems rather than just reacting to them.

He was exercising control.

That's what he needed now.

Because though he had addressed this issue, many others remained. Now it was just a matter of applying that same initiative to the much larger challenge that burdened him.

His plans that were so promising when he first assumed power in the Highlands had soured terribly in just the last year.

All because of the usurper.

The blasted rebel living within these craggy peaks who the people had proclaimed to be their rightful leader.

The thief who had appropriated the role that Torstan was supposed to play as the ruler and defender of these damned mountains.

The so-called and falsely named Lord of the Highlands.

He was the Lord of the Highlands, blast it!

Torstan Sharperson!

No one else!

Not some boy who was younger than he was.

Torstan smacked his meaty palm against the stone railing in front of him, shouting another curse that was lost in the tepid roar and not insignificant jeers of the crowd.

"Is it as bad as it looks, Governor Sharperson?"

"It is, Captain." Torstan didn't bother to turn around as Eliasin Hippolates strode into his private box, his leather armor immaculate as always. "I expected more bloodthirstiness from your soldiers."

"Can you blame them, Governor Sharperson? They're evenly matched. If they each faced a weaker opponent, they would put more effort into acquiring the larger purse."

"No, I guess I can't," Sharperson sighed, leaning back into his chair, thinking about what Eliasin said, even though at first he didn't want to.

That was good advice. He would need to put it into play as well.

Match a stronger opponent against a weaker one and tell the stronger to have a little fun before killing their adversary. Do that, work the spectators into a raucous fury before completing the deed, and he would pay the better fighter a bonus well worth their while.

That would certainly please the crowd. And a more engaged crowd meant more bets on the outcome of the combat.

That would please him, because it meant more revenue for his dwindling coffers.

Another decision made, Sharperson pulled his gaze away from the duel and locked eyes with the man he had selected to lead the Highland Guard. A man with a reputation for getting things done. No matter what was required. No matter the cost.

"Do I really want to know, Eliasin?"

"It's not all bad, Governor Sharperson. It's just not all good either."

"Start with the good."

"The Highland Guard is in place as we discussed last night. Three concentric rings of a mobile defense extending out into the mountains. Our soldiers are well trained and they're well provisioned. The rebels have no chance of getting past our troops and attacking us here at the Stone."

"Do you think the Highlanders would take such a risk? Come at us here?"

Hippolates considered the question before responding. "With the Wraiths a continuing threat, actually becoming more of a threat since the Murk is descending with greater frequency, no, I don't believe they will be. They can't risk being caught out from their towers, and they have no towers close to the line we've established."

"I agree with you on that," Sharperson confirmed with a nod. "And beyond the three or four leagues surrounding the Stone that we control?"

"That's the part you're not going to like, Governor Sharperson."

"Tell me, Eliasin."

"As you already know, we exercise little authority beyond where our most advanced companies are positioned in the mountains. The rebel Highlanders roam freely through the Territory unless we send out a large force. And doing that is useless."

"They just disappear into the wild or the brochs they've constructed. I'm well aware, Eliasin. That strategy clearly doesn't work for us."

"Agreed, Governor Sharperson."

"And there's little point in attacking those confounded towers. We can swarm over them all we want and still not take them. To go along with the fact that we can't tell which Highlanders are rebels unless they proclaim themselves to be rebels."

"Correct, Governor Sharperson. It's a waste of time."

"And to have any success would require actions on our part that would only serve to stoke the rebellion from a slow burn to a blazing fire."

"Exactly so, Governor Sharperson. Although I'm not opposed to implementing such methods against the general populace, it does little to help us in the end." Hippolates understood the Governor's frustration. He was frustrated as well. But that didn't mean that there still weren't a few options to consider that might help their cause. "Besides, with most of our soldiers positioned around the Stone, we don't have the resources to chase after the rebels. They'd love to lead us on a merry chase if they could."

"To say nothing of the fact that we still need to protect the handful of mines that are still producing the gold, silver, and metals that we require."

"Yes, very true, Governor Sharperson. Unfortunately, although not unexpectedly, even that is proving more difficult."

"The Highlanders have dared to attack our mines?" There was a hint of shock in Sharperson's voice that failed to mask his worry. He didn't believe the rebels had the strength to do that, but perhaps he was wrong. And if he was wrong about that ...

"No, Governor Sharperson. Not yet. Those mines are too well protected. Still, we are in a difficult position in that regard."

Sharperson nodded, understanding the dilemma Eliasin was placing before him. "Having a producing mine is of little value if we can't get the metals and other resources back here to the Stone."

"Exactly so, Governor Sharperson."

The Captain of the Highland Guard fell silent then, noticing how the Governor's very large head was slowly turning a bright red. Not just his face. His scalp and crown as well. Making him look like an overlarge ripe tomato.

That discovery worried Hippolates.

He had no desire to bear the brunt of Sharperson's fury. As he had learned through hard experience, better to leave the Governor be until he calmed himself down.

And that was proving to be a challenge for Sharperson. His rage knew almost no bounds.

He was incensed by this new example of his weakness as a ruler. Of his lack of control.

Control.

That's what he needed.

He had to exert some control if he was to have any chance of remedying what was quickly becoming a dire situation.

The usurper who was calling himself the Lord of the Highlands in many respects actually appeared to be the Lord of the Highlands. And as Sharperson knew, appearances could be just as powerful if not more so than reality.

The usurper could move freely in the Territory while he, the rightful Governor, the true Lord of the Highlands, could go no farther than a few leagues from his citadel without the risk of being attacked.

It was almost as if this Lord Kestrel had placed a noose around Torstan's neck and was slowly tightening it. That it was only a matter of time before he would be swinging from the gibbet rather than this rebel.

He smacked his large palms together, the pain he experienced giving him an added, necessary clarity.

This couldn't stand. Not any longer.

He was losing control of the Highlands to this infernal Lord Kestrel. He couldn't allow that to continue.

He had given Hakea Roosarian advice on how to deal with Talia Carlomin, the woman who was challenging her just as this usurper was challenging him.

He had told her to take her on directly. Don't work from the shadows. Use your larger Guard openly. Crush her.

Then use that example to demonstrate the lengths to which she was willing to go in order to solidify her authority as a warning to anyone else seeking to take her place.

His circumstances differed somewhat, so he couldn't do exactly the same. At least not entirely.

He could act more directly, but he needed to do so in a more surgical manner.

The Stalkers sent after this so-called Lord Kestrel had failed. To the best of his knowledge, all of them slaughtered.

His Guard when sent out in force had failed as well, unable to find the usurper. The rebel Highlanders refused to engage if a large number of his troops approached.

Unless the usurper wanted to be found.

And when that happened that was never a good thing for his soldiers. The rebels sliced and diced his larger force apart, cutting off a squad here and there, sowing fear within the ranks, building confidence within the countryside.

An effective strategy. And perhaps one that he could employ as well.

Torstan still had his other game in play. The longer game. One that was less certain, that was true. Still, he believed that it could prove successful.

If he could gain the result he desired, then all the better. And if not ... there was no harm in seeing how it all worked out because it cost him nothing in the end.

But there was no reason to place all his chips on that single bet. As he had seen with all his other strategies designed to eliminate the usurper, this Lord Kestrel had beaten the odds each time no matter how well he crafted the scheme.

When the bell sounded, signifying the end of the combat, Torstan gave the two women on the sand a reluctant nod. They nodded to him in return. He then shooed them out of the Pit with an irritated wave.

He had made money on the duel, although not as much as he could have if those two had fought to win rather than fought to survive.

He would allow them to count their earnings. Then he would send Eliasin to tell them that they would be fighting again tomorrow, whether they wanted to or not.

So there was no reason to allow their perfunctory performance to continue to bother him.

He had solved that problem.

Now he needed to solve the problem of the usurper. And to do that he required a strategy that would allow him to go right to the heart of the problem.

Or rather cut out the heart of the problem.

He would leave his longer play in place. If it worked, then all the better. And if not …

Well, there was no point in focusing on what could be. That wasn't exercising control.

He would put another piece on the board that might give him a better chance of success. A piece that would allow him to exercise greater control.

Even if his only real chance of killing the usurper was the game taking place in the shadows, he still needed to put on a show. Just as he was doing here.

He needed to be seen as the Lord of the Highlands. A man who put down any hint of rebellion harshly.

What he had in mind might not work. But he couldn't see how it would hurt.

"Captain Hippolates, you will select your best soldiers and form three companies that can move swiftly through the Highlands. And by best, I mean those soldiers you trust implicitly to do whatever is required of them without a second thought. No matter how bloody. No matter what might be demanded of them."

"I understand, Governor Sharperson. I have just the right men in mind for this assignment."

"Good, I thought you would. You will lead these companies yourself."

"My objective?" Hippolates smiled. He already knew the answer, and he was looking forward to the challenge. He would have his fun with the boy before he put him down for good.

"Find this Lord Kestrel. Kill him."

"Are there any restrictions I need to be aware of?"

Sharperson turned his predatory gaze back toward his Captain. "There are no restrictions, Captain Hippolates. You will use whatever means you believe are necessary to achieve your mission. You will bring me the head of this Lord Kestrel so

I can fix it to a pike at one of the entrances to the Stone, and if anyone gets in your way, kill them."

3

A NEW HUNT

"You're certain?" Declan felt a shiver run through him just looking at the roiling fluid.

"Yes, without a doubt," Rafia replied absently, unable to take her gaze from the black liquid that boiled angrily in the small glass vial even though no heat was being applied and there was a chill to the mountain air. It was as if the noxious fluid had a life all its own. And maybe it did. "This is a nasty concoction."

Captain Jennison had delivered the glass flask to them the evening before, finding them on the Isle of Mist right before they were about to lead several squads from the Blood Company back across the channel and into the Highlands.

The Magus was glad to receive it. Finally, with this small sample, Rafia's suspicions with respect to the Stalkers became fact.

"So your worst fears are confirmed."

"I'm afraid so. This liquid was created with the Curse. I have no doubt now that there's a Dark Magus working here in New Caledonia. Whoever it is, this person is responsible for birthing the Stalkers."

"And you're certain that it's a person? A Dark Magus?"

"You're worried that it could be a monster? Like the Ghoule Overlord in Caledonia?"

"Yes, which would only make the challenges we face here all the more difficult," Declan confirmed with a nod.

"A worthy concern, but in this case I'm certain. It's a Magus who has turned to the Curse."

"How can you be so sure?" Declan held up his hands, wanting Rafia to understand that he wasn't challenging her. Rather, he was curious. He wanted to make sure that they ruled out all other possibilities. It's just how his mind worked. "By the look in your eye, I get the feeling that you've come across a situation like this before."

Rafia gave Declan a wry smile. She wasn't offended. Actually, she should have expected this from him. He was much too smart for his own good. "I have."

Declan's expression changed then. He gave her a knowing nod. "You used to hunt the Magii who turned to the Curse, didn't you?"

"I did," Rafia sighed, dropping the vial of seething black liquid into one of the many pockets sewn into her cloak. "I never enjoyed the task. But it was one of my primary responsibilities as the Keeper of Haven."

"How many did you find?"

"Four all told during my time in that position."

"You were in that role for how long?" asked Declan.

"A decade."

Declan nodded, thinking about the odds involved. "Was four in ten years a large number?"

"It was," Rafia confirmed with a nod. "I thought the same thing you're thinking now."

"Why?"

"Exactly." Rafia knew what Declan was going to ask next.

"Any idea as to why so many Magii turned to the Curse during that very short time span?"

"A few, although nothing that I can prove. At least not yet."

"You didn't hunt Dark Magii on your own, did you?" asked Declan.

"Never alone. Always with another Magus. Sometimes more than one depending on who it was we were chasing. We couldn't allow them to roam free."

"Did you catch them all?"

"I did," Rafia replied, her eyes sad as she recalled several of those disheartening and quite disappointing victories. "The last one the worst of all. Such a waste."

"How so?"

"The Magii foolish enough to turn toward the Curse all had been quite promising. So skilled in the use of the Talent. They could have been so much more than what they became. But they all suffered from the same two failings, among several others."

"Arrogance, I take it," Declan suggested.

"Yes, the belief that they could ignore the risks of studying that corrupt power without consequence. Of attempting to make it their own without realizing that over time rather than you controlling the Curse, the Curse controls you. That was the subtle, insidious truth of that tainted energy that was always missed or ignored. Those Magii enticed by the Curse never believed that it was turning them toward its purposes rather than the other way around. They didn't learn that they couldn't escape the dangers of the Curse until it was much too late."

"And the other failing?" Declan prompted.

"Greed. The desperate need to acquire more power. An almost unstoppable urge that they couldn't resist. Often, they masked this weakness in the argument that the acquisition of new knowledge that could prove useful in battling the Curse required taking risks that they might not have taken otherwise.

Never considering, and likely never caring, how that knowledge might affect them."

"What was different about the last one?" Declan asked.

He hadn't missed Rafia's expression, how she lost herself in a memory if only for a few heartbeats, when she referenced her most recent hunt.

"The last one ... she led me on a chase that dragged on for months. I found the Magus right before she was about to escape. She seemed remorseful, regretting what she had done. But ..." Rafia shook her head sadly. "Once you've been touched by the Curse, you can't escape the Curse."

"Unless you're Bryen and the Seventh Stone merges with you," Declan murmured.

"Right you are," Rafia agreed with a heavy sigh. "She refused to surrender. We fought. I won." Tears began to form at the corner of Rafia's eyes. Declan didn't comment. He didn't believe that it was his place to do so. "I don't see how she could have survived, but I never found her body."

"And you liked to have the body just to make sure," nodded Declan, understanding. He was much the same way. He always preferred tangible proof. Needing to see to believe. At least when it came to bloody work.

"Morbid, I know, but necessary when hunting Dark Magii. With this last Magus, I never found her trail again. So I have no reason not to think that she's dead."

"Yet still you wonder."

"Still I wonder," Rafia sighed. She gave Declan a wistful smile. "It's strange how I tend to focus on the worst that has happened to me rather than the best. How memories like that tend to stick with me."

Declan gave her a sympathetic smile. "I know the feeling."

"You're much the same," Rafia replied, not surprised. "I assumed as much."

"I am," Declan admitted. "Now before you turn this conversation into another chance for you to learn more about me, let's focus on you."

"Me?"

"From your expression, I gather that there's more to that black liquid than just the fact that it was created by a Dark Magus," Declan coaxed. "That there's something else about the vial that has caught your attention beyond the fact that the Curse was put into a tangible form."

"You seem to know me quite well," Rafia replied, a small smile breaking out, Declan's comment helping to pull her thoughts back to the present.

"I'd like to think I do," Declan replied modestly.

"I'd like to think that you do as well." Rafia reached out and grasped his hand warmly, giving it a squeeze before letting go.

"Now back to the Stalkers." Declan wouldn't have minded if Rafia's touch lingered for just a little while longer, but they had work to do. "The Dark Magus used the Curse to create the liquid in the vial, and that liquid turns men and women into Stalkers. What is it that you're reluctant to tell me?"

Rafia started to reply then stopped, displaying a mixture of mild disbelief and disappointment. "I never expected that whoever did this would take such a risk."

"You mean beyond the fact that this Magus gave himself or herself to the Curse all with the goal of increasing their own power?" Declan's sarcasm was thick as molasses. "Shocking, someone wanting more for themselves and willing to do just about anything to obtain it."

"There's no need for your dry wit right now, Declan," Rafia told him with a raised eyebrow.

"Sorry," he replied, giving her a sheepish smile. Although he didn't sound all that remorseful. "But there's more than just the obvious going on here."

"With respect to how these Stalkers are made, you're correct. It's not just the Curse that we've come up against in the past. In several key ways, it's distinct from the power displayed by the Dark Magii I've hunted before."

"How so?"

"The tainted power used to make the Stalkers has an ancient feel to it. Mixed in, just a hint, so it's very subtle. Nevertheless, it's still there. It's the Curse, that's undeniable, but ..." Rafia lifted her arms in irritation. "I just don't know. I've never come across something like this before. I never expected to. In fact, I hoped that I never would."

"That's saying something," Declan nodded. "Should I be worried?"

"I don't know yet."

"You're not filling me with a great deal of confidence, Rafia."

"I know, I'm sorry. That's the best that I can do right now. When I was examining the tainted power infused within the liquid, it made me think of an evil that hasn't touched the Natural World in quite some time."

Rafia closed her eyes, needing to think. She had never believed that ancient evil could disappear entirely. Rather, she had hoped that it would remain dormant, a concern for another age. Nevertheless, she knew as well just how much hope was worth.

She should have given greater credence to her concerns. She had known that it was only a matter of time before this terrible threat sought to make its return. To reclaim what it believed was its right.

For just a second an irrational fear – what she hoped was an irrational fear – shot through her.

Could this be the beginning?

Was the dreaded moment approaching?

Was that ancient evil preparing to reveal itself again?

To touch the Natural World again?

And this nasty concoction was just one part of that larger objective?

"What kind of evil do you mean?" Declan asked, clearly uneasy.

"I'm thinking of an evil that hasn't touched the Natural World in millennia."

"You're not making this any better for me," Declan grumbled, not at all pleased.

"I could be wrong, you know."

"You're rarely wrong, Rafia."

"The way you just said that, I'm not sure it was a compliment."

"You're thinking too much, Magus. Either that or you're trying to delay."

"So we're back to Magus now?" Rafia offered Declan a raised eyebrow. "After all the progress that we've made?"

"You're delaying, Magus. Either you're gathering your thoughts or you just don't want to tell me what you're thinking. Better just to say it."

"All right, all right," Rafia said, raising her hands in surrender. "You really do know me much too well."

"Perhaps so. But putting that to the side ..." Declan motioned with his hand, wanting to hear more about what clearly was worrying her.

"There are some similarities to what we faced in Caledonia. However, if I'm right as to what went into making this liquid, then there's a greater peril here than just that."

"That doesn't sound good."

"It isn't. Because the Ghoule Overlord is nothing compared to the threat presented by this ancient evil."

"You keep saying ancient evil. You're not offering much in the way of specificity."

"I'm sorry, I'm just not sure. I haven't had as much time as I would like to study the sample that Talia Carlomin sent us. Until I do, then I'm really just talking in theories. I can't give you anything that's substantive."

Declan nodded, understanding why this was so difficult for her and why she was reluctant to provide anything more than a vague indication regarding her concerns. Still, the look in her eyes suggested that she was more certain than she was willing to let on.

"Tell me, Rafia," Declan said quietly but insistently. "You know what I was. You don't need to protect me."

"A Sentinel." Rafia smiled then. "You're right. I'm being foolish. If anyone can handle what I'm worried about, it's you." She sighed. "I have nothing to base this on other than a feeling, but I believe that the Curse contained within the vial is laced with the power of a more specific threat, much of what we know about it now blanketed by myth thanks to the passing of the centuries."

Declan didn't reply immediately, taking his time, mulling over what she was proposing. Others might scoff at the claim that Rafia was making. That was the most likely response. Arguing that a myth millennia old offered little in the way of the truth.

Declan knew better. In the last year he had fought against monsters that were supposed to be no more than stories. Or rather nightmares. So he never doubted that there was always a nugget of truth in every tale, no matter how much he wanted it to be no more than fiction.

And, of course, before that, before he came to Caledonia and now the Territories, he had been raised and trained to fight against the most terrifying myth of all. A myth who had conquered the Spirit World. A myth who sought to take the Natural World for his own as well.

A monster who supposedly was no more than shadow and shade yet was all too real. A monster against which Declan and his brother and father and so many of his forebears had defended against ever since the Veil separating the two worlds was ripped.

"The Ancient One."

"Unfortunately ... yes," Rafia confirmed.

"Do you believe that the Ancient One is an immediate threat?" When Declan asked the question, the world around him seemed just a bit more surreal. After he left Skaffa Falls, he never thought that he would ever have to concern himself with that terror ever again. But the world had a strange way of bringing you back to where you started, whether you wanted it to or not.

Rafia thought about Declan's question for quite some time, wanting to provide as accurate a response as she could. "I don't believe so. At least not right now. I get the sense that if I'm right, the Ancient One is not yet ready to play a more direct role in our world. That this evil wants to play at the edges for a little while longer. Allow his Disciples to do his work for him until the time is right."

"Almost as if he wants his Disciples and other servants to prepare the way?" suggested Declan.

"That was my take on it, yes."

Declan couldn't say that he was surprised. His father had been quite thorough with his training, ensuring that he and his brother were well trained in the tactics and strategies employed by the Ancient One and his servants.

If, indeed, the Ancient One was stirring once again, it would stand to reason that he wouldn't rush his attempt to conquer the Natural World. Having failed before, he wouldn't want to fail again. He would want to ensure that all the pieces were set on the board just so before he made his first move.

Declan came back from where his dark thoughts had led him. He would worry about that later. Now they had more pressing concerns. "If this really is the work of the Ancient One, and he isn't an immediate threat, we need to focus on what's right before us. We need to deal with these Stalkers before we worry about that crusty bastard."

"Agreed."

"And just to be certain, this is the last of the large packs hunting in the Highlands, correct?"

"Yes."

"Once we kill these beasts, if we leave a few companies from the Blood Legion here in the mountains, they should be able to eliminate the last few Stalkers still wandering among the peaks, correct?"

"Yes, I believe they could."

Declan nodded, pleased to hear that. One threat removed, which would allow them to move on to the next.

He was a Sentinel at heart. Just like his father and his father before him and his father before him going all the way back to the time of Henry Blackgard, the Lord of Skaffa Falls who remained true to his oath despite what it cost him personally. Declan's forerunner had sacrificed his family to ensure that the Ancient One didn't escape the Valley of the Dead the first time that monster sought to subjugate the Natural World.

So of course he was concerned that the Ancient One might have had a hand in creating the Stalkers. Nevertheless, that wasn't his primary concern. Not at that moment.

He was worried more about Davin. The young man was like a son to him. Just like Bryen was. Just like Lycia was a daughter to him.

Declan had done all that he could to ensure that Davin survived the white sand of the Colosseum. Thankfully, the Crimson Giant had.

And after all the trials and tribulations of the Colosseum, after all that had occurred after Bryen freed the gladiators and they took up the fight against the Ghoule Overlord and his Legions, after all that Davin had done against the Kraken and the Bakunawa, there was no way that Declan was going to leave him to the mercy of a supercilious Governor who wanted to use him like a playing chip.

Captain Jennison had provided as much detail as he could. Unfortunately, he didn't have much to offer. Only the barest sketch of what Davin had done to ensure that Talia Carlomin could share the secret of the black liquid with Rafia.

All of it very useful to be sure, but the Captain couldn't provide the one piece of information that Declan craved the most.

Whether Davin was still alive.

No one could.

Because no one knew.

Based on what Captain Jennison told him, Declan should assume that Davin was dead. If not killed by the rockfall he caused to aid Talia's escape then at the claws of the Stalkers hunting him.

However, Declan refused to assume the worst. He had faith in Davin, in his abilities, in his decisions, even when the young man didn't have faith in himself.

And just as Rafia had noted with respect to needing a body to confirm the demise of a Dark Magus, he took a similar perspective when it came to his gladiators.

He knew what they were capable of.

The lengths to which they would go to survive.

He wouldn't believe that Davin was dead until he saw his body.

The only way to do that was to storm the Rock. But he couldn't do that right then no matter how much he wanted to.

Because the Blood Company, or rather the Blood Legion as he was calling them since their ranks had swelled so much during the last few months, had taken on the primary task of ridding the Highlands of the Stalkers. By doing that, they gave Jakob Kestrel the chance to concentrate on removing the slavers and freeing those forced to work in the mines.

Therefore, before Declan could do what he really wanted to do, he had a job to finish here first.

The large number of Stalkers coming their way.

Davin after that.

"Then we stay on task," Declan said, a hint of reluctance still audible in his voice.

"Correct," Rafia confirmed, understanding where Declan's heart was leading him. "We'll deal with these Stalkers. Remove them as a threat. Then we can shift our focus to the matter in Ballinasloe."

"Thank you," Declan sighed, giving Rafia a nod of appreciation. That settled, he returned to the topic that had started this conversation. "Do you know how to find this Dark Magus? Once we deal with these monsters, we should think about going after the queen of the hive. Kill the Dark Magus, and we won't have to worry about any more Stalkers."

"Let me think about how we could do that. I like that idea. It goes right to the heart of the matter just as always."

"You can't follow a trail like you did with the Elder Ghoules?"

"Only if the Dark Magus makes a mistake," grumbled Rafia, not happy with the answer she gave Declan. "This Dark Magus hasn't made a mistake. He or she is masking themselves too well for me to find them."

"Talia and Jakob both believed that the Stalkers came from the north."

"Meaning?"

"Meaning that if they're right, Bryen and Aislinn might be able to find the answer for us. Maybe even kill the queen."

"They might. We can hope." Rafia shook her head in frustration. She didn't like hoping that they could find the answer. As Sirius had liked to say, hoping doesn't make it real.

She wanted the answer. Because she needed to find this Dark Magus. And when she did, she'd deal with this person, no matter who it was, as all Dark Magii deserved to be dealt with.

"How far away is the pack?"

Rafia extended her senses with the Talent. She smiled. It didn't take much to find these monsters.

In part because the scent of the Curse was so strong. Also because a handful of kestrels flew above these Stalkers as they raced through the Highlands, keeping an eye on them, the raptors that were so fond of Jakob Kestrel less than pleased that these creatures dared to hunt in their territory.

"Two leagues."

"They're coming from the direction that we want them to?"

"They are."

"Good. Let's get into position. We only have one chance at this, so we need to do it right."

~

"*I still don't understand why I have to be the one to do this.*" He lay behind a large pile of rocks atop a small ridge that cut through the forest of heart trees and gave him an excellent view of the wood that ran for more than a league to the very base of the snow-capped peaks to the west.

"*We've already been over this, Chesin,*" Declan replied in his gravelly grumble.

"*Why not Majdi or Dorlan? They like taking risks. I don't.*"

"*Small houses can't run, Chesin,*" Declan replied, a hint of exasperation in his tone. "*You can. Faster than anyone else.*"

"*That may be, but I really don't like this, Declan.*"

"*I never would have guessed, Chesin,*" the Sergeant of the Blood Company sighed, his sarcasm plain. "*Neither do I, but it needs to be done. And you're the best person to be doing this. You know it just as well as I do. So a little less chatter and a bit more focus. It will all be over soon.*"

"*What do you mean by that?*" demanded Chesin, his nerves getting the better of him.

"You know exactly what I mean," Declan almost shouted. *"So stop seeing shadows where there aren't any."*

"I really don't like this, Declan," the gladiator muttered again.

"You've made that abundantly clear, Chesin," cut in Rafia. She could tell that Declan was about to lose his temper. He didn't mind a complaint. A constant stream, however, only served to burn away his admittedly already limited patience. Yet just a little more patience was required then.

Rafia had used the Talent to connect to the gladiator so that all three could speak in one another's minds. In addition, taking a trick that she had learned from Jakob Kestrel that he employed with great success when battling the Wraiths in the Murk, she also gave Chesin the ability to see what she saw when she extended her senses into the forest. That meant that the gladiator observed everything that was occurring around him for more than a league without having to reveal himself.

Making it a great deal harder for him to be taken by surprise by the monsters coming his way. Assuming, of course, that he was paying attention. Because right then, he seemed focused less on that and more on complaining.

"I just don't like being the rabbit, Magus Rafia."

"I completely understand, Chesin. No one does. But what's done is done." Before Chesin could offer another complaint – and she could tell that he was about to – she continued, hoping that what she said next would put him in the right frame of mind for what was being demanded of him. *"Just remember, you have nothing to fear if you stick to the trail and keep your wits about you."*

Rafia heard him offer several choice curses in his mind, although none of which were directed toward her. Rather, much of it had to do with his fellow gladiators, none of whom were as fast in a footrace as he was.

She understood his anxiety. If their plan was to work with the bait surviving, it all came down to one key variable.

Speed.

Miss a step and Chesin was done. She knew it. So did he.

As a result, his grumbling was more the anticipation of what was to come eating at his nerves. He was done waiting. He just wanted to do what was required of him so that he could be done with it.

That was only natural. And he would soon get his wish.

"Besides, I will be with you the entire time," Rafia offered, hoping to put the young gladiator at ease. *"Watching over you."*

Chesin still grumbled in his mind, although more quietly this time. Not wanting to irritate the Magus.

"Do you see them?" asked Declan.

"I do," Chesin replied, his tone sharper now. A tinge of excitement in his voice. He was done with his complaints now that the game was about to begin. *"Have I told you that I really don't like this?"*

"A few minutes more, gladiator," Declan urged, giving Chesin the commanding voice that he used so frequently on the training ground. *"Just be patient."*

"Fine, fine. I'm done. No more from me."

"Can you see them yet without the Talent?"

"No, not with this dense undergrowth, Magus Rafia," Chesin replied.

In this part of the forest, the sunlight broke through more frequently. With the ridge scarring the wood, there was less shadow and more shrubs, along with the twisting roots of the heart trees, which only served to make navigating the scrub that much more difficult.

A good thing in Chesin's opinion, as that complication would give him more time to make his escape. A bad thing as well because it meant that he wouldn't see the Stalkers racing toward him until they were almost upon him.

"But I'm getting the feeling that I'm not alone anymore," Chesin added.

He was getting nervous, which he found ironic, since he

never got nervous fighting in the Pit after he won his first few combats.

It stood to reason, however. This was different. He wasn't in the Pit, an environment he had grown used to. An environment that he could control.

It had gone quiet all around him. The squirrels and other small animals that had been skittering about in the undergrowth had vanished. As had the birds, their warbles and cries that filled the wood with life no more. Even the wind that had been playing through the leaves that were larger than a shield had died away.

Chesin didn't need to see the danger to know that he was in danger.

"They're to your left side," Rafia whispered more out of habit than need, remembering after she had done so that it wasn't necessary.

"I know. Just two hundred yards away," Chesin confirmed. *"I'm having a hard time identifying individual beasts. How many?"*

"Seventeen," Declan offered in a matter-of-fact tone.

"Seventeen! I'm the rabbit for seventeen Stalkers? Are you kidding me?"

"It's more than we thought, true," Declan admitted. *"Still, you have nothing to worry about. The plan is still sound. The number of Stalkers chasing after you doesn't change that."*

"Is that so?" Chesin challenged. *"Declan, you're the one who told me that no plan survives contact with the enemy."*

"I did, you're right," Declan admitted. *"I'm glad that you were listening."*

"Declan!" hissed Chesin, his nerves almost getting the better of him. He was going to tell Declan and Magus Rafia how much he hated doing this, but what was the point? Magus Rafia was correct. What's done was done. He had only one path to follow – literally – to get out of this mess.

"Chesin," Declan said as calmly as he could. *"You have

nothing to worry about so long as you stick to the plan. The plan is still sound."

"*Chesin, focus!*" Rafia ordered. "*The first Stalker is coming right toward you at speed. It knows where you're hiding. Go! Now!*"

Chesin's eyes widened, all thoughts of continuing to gripe coming to a swift end as he glimpsed the black blur streak out of the forest below, the Stalker digging its clawed feet into the soft dirt and driving itself up the gentle slope.

His first instinct was to stand and fight. He wasn't worried about taking on one Stalker. He had faced worse in the Pit.

It was the sixteen other monsters that were now racing out from the wood below that concerned Chesin.

Pushing himself up from where he had been hiding behind the pile of rocks, he kicked out with his left foot once. Twice. And then a third time.

The largest rock that he had placed there specifically for this purpose refused to move.

Blast it!

It wasn't supposed to play out this way.

He kicked again, as hard as he could. Still nothing!

The small boulder refused to move.

With the Stalker less than thirty yards away, the monster already screeching in triumph for what the beast viewed as an easy kill, Chesin did the only thing that came to mind. He bent down, digging his fingers into the dirt beneath the boulder and lifting while also pushing with his shoulder and thigh.

That did the trick. And just in time.

The boulder, which was almost as big as Chesin was tall, was slow to get moving. But once the stone picked up some momentum, there was no stopping it.

After its third rotation, the boulder rolled down the slope at a bone-crushing pace, continuing to pick up speed as it went. Following in its wake came all the loose shale that Chesin had piled up in front of it.

The gladiator didn't bother to watch the result of his handiwork. Once the boulder started moving, he was down the other side of the slope and sprinting through the wood, dodging around, jumping over, and sliding under the heart tree roots that spread haphazardly across the forest floor like an unsolvable puzzle.

He didn't need to observe to know what damage he was going to inflict. The Stalker confirmed it for him when the monster's screech of triumph swiftly become a scream of rage.

Whether Chesin succeeded in killing or injuring the beast, he didn't know. But he did know that he had gained the time that he needed to build the lead that would give him a slim chance of surviving this ridiculous race that he had agreed to run against his better judgment.

For the next several minutes, Chesin relied on the training that had served him so well when fighting on the white sand. He focused solely on what he was doing. On the route that he had selected. On where he was headed. On where he was placing his feet.

He didn't look over his shoulder. He didn't allow the shrieks from the Stalkers that were drawing closer to him with every step they took to affect his concentration. He didn't think about what would happen if those monsters caught him.

And with every step he took, Chesin counted.

He was getting close. When he selected his hide, he had walked off the distance twice to ensure that he could make it back to the broch before the Stalkers caught him.

He should be able to see it just about now.

Glancing briefly to his front, he hoped to catch a glimpse of the stone tower that was his objective.

He realized his mistake the instant his front foot slipped out from beneath him.

He had counted the steps so that he wouldn't need to look

to know where he was, understanding the risk of taking his eye from the rough path, but he hadn't been able to help himself.

Muttering a curse in his head, Chesin fell on his backside and slid off the narrow trail he had been following through the wood, ending up in a narrow gulley that ran along the edge and split the heart trees for the next hundred yards.

"Chesin! Are you all right?"

"Yes, Magus Rafia. All good."

He was lucky. He didn't break anything. He didn't even twist an ankle.

Either of those injuries would have spelled his doom.

He was about to dig his way out of the vegetation and climb back onto the trail when Rafia's voice froze him in place.

"Hold!" Rafia waited a few seconds before speaking again. *"He's right above you. Can he see you?"*

Chesin allowed several seconds to pass before responding, catching the shadow just above him on the rim of the gulley. Hearing the growl and then hiss, he crouched down slowly, quietly, trying to burrow into the large, leafy plants with a faint and hopefully masking scent that he had fallen into without drawing any attention to himself.

"No," Chesin replied. *"But he's not going anywhere. He knows that I'm close, just not exactly where."*

"Let me see if I can help," Rafia replied.

Chesin didn't see what Rafia did from where he was hiding. Instead he heard it.

There was a whoosh right above him that sounded as if all the air had been sucked out of the gulley followed by a loud grunt.

For just a heartbeat, a deeper silence descended over the wood. The other Stalkers chasing him had stopped, trying to determine what had happened.

Chesin jumped back in surprise when the Stalker that had been hunting him fell into the gulley right next to him, a large, smoking hole right where the monster's chest was supposed to be.

"To the east! Now! Straight to the broch!"

Chesin didn't need to be told twice. Obeying Rafia's sharp command, he pulled himself out of his hiding place and sprinted down the game trail that paralleled the top of the ravine.

The Stalkers were after him again in an instant.

He could hear them.

He could sense them at his back.

The gladiator didn't care.

He knew where he was.

He knew what he had to do if he was to have any chance of surviving the last leg of this race.

Keeping his head down so that he didn't lose his footing again, he didn't look up until the gloom that he was running through faded to a welcome brightness.

When he did, the redoubt that he and the other gladiators had finished building just the night before towered in front of him. A surge of hope shot through him. He just might make it.

This was just one of several dozen brochs the Highlanders and the soldiers of the Blood Legion had completed in the last few weeks. The fortifications had proven to be highly effective in defending against the Wraiths. Chesin had no doubt that they would serve a similar purpose against the Stalkers.

Assuming he could get to the broch before his pursuers got to him.

He felt the Stalkers catching up to him. Their growls grew increasingly shriller, more insistent, more ravenous, giving Chesin an added burst of energy.

Even so, he couldn't increase his lead on his hunters. The monsters stayed right behind him, their hunger for blood and flesh driving them forward.

Thirty yards.

Twenty yards.

Now just ten yards.

A shiver ran down Chesin's spine. With one good leap the Stalker right behind him was going to dig its claws into his back.

He wasn't going to make it.

After all that he had been through, he wasn't going to make it!

Chesin already was cringing, waiting for the monster's daggerlike claw to slice into his flesh.

Strangely, thankfully, it didn't happen.

The Stalker's shriek of triumph that filled Chesin's belly with a cold terror was drowned out by the series of explosions that erupted behind the gladiator.

Chesin was still at risk, the Stalkers still coming for him, but he could breathe a little easier now.

He had gained a few extra yards, and that might be enough for him to make his escape.

Following the narrow game trail toward the broch took him through the field of magical mines that Rafia had laid out before the sun had risen that morning. Those mines, tuned to creatures touched by the Curse, let him pass without incident.

However, any creature tainted by the Curse caught within that blast was incinerated in a flash, not even having the time to scream.

The Stalkers closest to Chesin disappeared in a flare of power. Those trailing their brethren by a few yards were lucky. They escaped the brunt of the blast, only scalded by the energy or thrown off their clawed feet, though still alive.

In just seconds, the Stalkers lucky enough to make it through the minefield -- burnt, charred, and in a murderous rage -- were back after their prey.

Chesin paid no attention to his pursuers' misfortune, pleased by the success of the magical traps.

He hadn't doubted that this would work. He knew what Magus Rafia could do with the Talent. Rather, he had feared that he wouldn't make it past that point on the trail before the Stalkers caught up to him.

Yet even with the number of his hunters reduced, his concern about reaching the broch before the Stalkers reached him consumed his thoughts.

There were still a dozen or more of the monsters behind him and quickly getting back up to speed.

The thought of a claw digging into his flesh almost made Chesin stumble again. This time, however, he kept his head down, forcing himself to maintain his concentration, focusing less on what was behind him and more on what was to his front.

He really hated being the bait. If he survived this, he would refuse to ever do this again, no matter the consequences.

After just a dozen more yards, Chesin broke free from the heart trees and their curling and looping roots and raced into the small glade that was to be expanded into a large green.

He ignored the shrieks and screeches behind him that sounded much too close, only interested in the long beam that stuck out over the broch's parapet.

Sensing that the Stalkers continued to close the distance on him, knowing without having to look that one of the beasts had launched itself through the air with the goal of driving him into the ground, before it was too late Chesin leapt up and grasped the rope that swayed slowly in front of him.

As soon as he grabbed hold, with a hard jerk that almost tore his arm from his shoulder socket, Chesin was pulled into the sky. Swinging through the air, he gripped the rope with his other hand right before the wild jerking and spinning motion sent him tumbling to the earth.

The Stalker that dove for him smashed face first into the ground, tumbling across the dirt field until the beast finally came to a stop, smacking the back of its head hard against the stone tower.

Before the other Stalkers could reach for him, Chesin was already fifty feet above the ground and still rising, Majdi, Dorlan, and Jenus all hauling on the rope, bringing him swiftly up and over the balustrade that ran along the top of the tower that rose one hundred feet into the sky.

Although the sharp pain suggested to Chesin that he indeed had dislocated his shoulder, he didn't mind, appreciating his friends' rough diligence in getting him out of danger. Better that than a Stalker claw in his back.

When Chesin dropped to the roof of the tower, Majdi was there to help him back to his feet, clapping him on the back, glad his friend had made it. Chesin let loose a long stream of expletives as a mind-numbing pain rushed through him.

Majdi just laughed. Chesin had been hurt worse than this. "Nkia can put your arm back in place."

"I'll go find her when this is over," Chesin hissed, which was the best that he could do because of the pain. "Better this than being food for Stalkers."

"I couldn't agree more," Majdi said as Chesin leaned back against the parapet, the adrenaline surging through him making his whole body shake and helping him to deal with the aching fire in his shoulder.

"What's that smell?" asked Majdi, sniffing the air.

"Mint," Chesin replied, pushing himself up off the stone, no longer needing the support to stay on his feet.

"How'd you manage that?"

"Took a tumble," Chesin mumbled.

"A nice smell," Majdi murmured. For just a moment, he wondered if Nkia might enjoy a smell like that. She had mentioned that he needed to take more baths. He was about to ask Chesin where he had found the mint when Declan's shout drowned out every other noise on top of the broch.

"Gladiators to the wall! The Stalkers are coming for us!"

"Go see Nkia, Chesin," Majdi rumbled. "You've done your job. It's time for the rest of us to do ours."

The gladiator turned toward the parapet, knowing by the sound that Stalker claws were digging into stone and mortar and that when he looked over the side he would be greeted by the sight of blood-red eyes staring right back at him.

CLIMBING the stone walls with their sharp claws was an easy task for the Stalkers. It proved to be much more difficult for the monsters when they neared the top of the tower.

Majdi, Jenus, Dorlan, Caellia, and a dozen more gladiators of the Blood Company used the parapet as their shield, stabbing with their spears as the Stalkers hung from the stone, unable to defend themselves without fear of plummeting to their deaths.

The Stalkers never even got a claw over the wall, the gladiators sending them falling back to land heavily in the dirt, bones broken, leaking blood. Many suffered more than a dozen puncture wounds before they dropped away from the wall. A savage effort on their part to claim the parapet despite their obvious disadvantage. Also a doomed one.

The spears demonstrated such a brutal efficiency that Asaia, Kollea, Tehana, Nkia, and the other gladiators who made up the second line of defense had nothing to do other than watch the vicious and precise efforts of their comrades.

For that second rank of gladiators, it was almost disappointing. Then again, they couldn't really complain about their success. As Declan had taught them, the best combat was the one that they didn't have to fight.

Rafia was just as pleased as Declan. He stood next to her on the tower, watching the engagement, nodding with pleasure at his gladiators' efforts, every so often offering a sharp instruction when he saw something that he believed required correction.

Rafia not having to use the Talent in their defense demonstrated just how effectively the Blood Company was resisting the Stalkers. Although she understood as well that the skirmish wasn't quite over.

"More Stalkers are coming. That was just the first wave."

"How many?" Declan asked.

"A dozen. Maybe a few more than that. They're moving very fast. They'll be here in just a few minutes."

"Blood Company, hold the wall!" Declan ordered. "It seems that the Stalkers haven't had enough of us yet."

The gladiators quickly reformed their ranks.

"Spears, don't hog all the fun for yourself," Declan called. "The swords want to get into the action as well."

Declan's comment earned a laugh from the gladiators.

"We'll let one or two by," Majdi promised. "Just so Nkia and the others don't get bored." The gladiator waited a second before offering his last comment. "Or rusty."

"Who are you calling rusty?" demanded Asaia. The sharp-tongued gladiator, her whip held comfortably in her hand, stood next to Nkia, speaking for her. Nkia glowered at Majdi, which was all that she could do, needing to rely on Asaia for her words since she had lost her tongue when she was enslaved as a child. "I have thirty golds that says Nkia takes you down in the practice ring without breaking a sweat."

"I'd like to see that happen," Kollea replied. She stood on Nkia's other side. "And I'll add thirty golds to the pot."

"Finally, this is getting interesting," rumbled Dorlan. "I'll put my golds against yours, Kollea."

Declan smiled, leaving the gladiators to their bickering. An argument like this was common for them before a fight. After spending so much time on the white sand, little fazed the soldiers of the Blood Company.

"How do they know we're here?" asked Declan.

"You remember the Slayers?"

"Those beasties are hard to forget."

"Too true," Rafia nodded. "The Slayers hunt by scent. Not smell, mind you, but by scent I mean essence."

"Which was how they were able to find Bryen. They had been given the essence of the Seventh Stone by the Ghoule Overlord."

"Correct," Rafia confirmed with a nod. "My guess is that the Dark Magus who created the Stalkers modeled them after Slayers."

"Which means the creator of these monsters has a great deal of experience with the Curse as well as the monsters subservient to the Ghoule Overlord." Declan looked out beyond the tower wall, searching for any sign of movement at the edge of the wood. Nothing yet. Soon though. His gladiators had stopped arguing with one another, their focus on the treeline as well. They could sense the Stalkers coming for them just as he could. "Definitely a Magus from Caledonia then. Does that bring to mind anyone who might have gone down a path that he or she shouldn't?"

Rafia stared at the heart trees for a time. She didn't want to believe it, but after her previous conversation with Declan, she couldn't ignore the direction toward which the facts pointed.

She looked at Declan after she reached a conclusion that troubled her.

"I can't be sure," Rafia replied, her mind still working through her reasoning, seeking to poke holes in it. She couldn't afford to be wrong about this.

"But you suspect," prodded Declan.

"I thought she was dead," Rafia murmured ever so quietly, a touch of sadness entering her voice.

"Maybe she is. Maybe it's someone else. You said there were a handful of Magii here in New Caledonia and that you didn't know them all. It could be one of them."

"It could be ..."

"But you're not convinced."

"No ... it just doesn't feel like it could be anyone but her. Not after you got me thinking about Magii who studied the Ghoule Overlord and his servants. It feels like ..."

"We'll find the Dark Magus responsible," Declan promised, recognizing how Rafia was struggling. He couldn't be certain from where he was standing, but it appeared as if tears were forming in Rafia's eyes. He could only assume that her suspect was someone she not only knew, but also knew well. A Magus who had been close to her. They could talk about that after they dealt with these Stalkers, however. "Have no fear of that. So these Stalkers were sent against us specifically?"

"Correct," Rafia replied, thankful for Declan understanding that she wasn't quite ready to reveal all that she was thinking. Not until she had a chance to ensure that there were no other options for her to explore. "These Stalkers were given our scent just as the Slayers were when we were in Caledonia and making our way to the Sanctuary."

"Whose scent specifically?" wondered Declan. "With Bryen ..." He realized that he already knew the answer. He turned his gaze toward Rafia, who was giving him a small, reluctant smile. "You."

"Yes, me," Rafia replied. "The scent can be of the Curse or of the Talent."

"So the Dark Magus knows you."

"Yes, we have to assume so."

"You're fairly certain that it's someone who is close to you. Or was. Someone who you thought was dead."

"I am," Rafia confirmed. "But we can talk about that later. I need to think about it a little more."

"Fair enough," Declan replied, not feeling the need to push. "If you're right, that means …"

"Yes, this Dark Magus is worried about us."

"The Stalkers are coming through the wood from the north!" Majdi yelled.

Declan turned in that direction, catching a hint of movement in the shadows at the very edge of the forest right before several more of Rafia's magical mines exploded, the blasts so powerful that the Stalkers facing the full force of the Talent were ripped apart.

Only four of the dozen monsters seeking to come at the tower from that direction survived the trap.

The clash that followed offered little challenge to the gladiators.

Intent on completing the assignment given to them despite the loss of their brethren, the last of the Stalkers dug their claws into the stone and began pulling themselves up the tower.

They didn't care about the men and women waiting for them above.

They didn't care about what happened to them when they reached the top.

They only cared about killing the person their master had charged them with killing.

Whether they lived or died didn't matter to them. Not anymore.

Because what they had been was already dead.

They had no choice but to obey their master.

The one who had given them this task.

The one who had given them the scent of the Magus.

"Such a waste," grumbled Declan, a strange sorrow draping itself around him.

He stared down at the dead Stalkers scattered about the base of the broch. The battle against the last four monsters couldn't even be described as a skirmish. The gladiators had dispatched them in less than a minute.

No better than a slaughter.

True, the Stalkers were vicious fighters, the terrors of the Highlands when the Wraiths didn't claim that title, but as he looked down into the glazed expression of one of the creatures, there seemed to be something all too human about them in death.

Another emotion began to infringe on his sadness.

Anger.

At the Dark Magus who had done this.

At the fate thrust upon those forced to do that Dark Magus' bidding.

"If you're right about the Stalkers ..." began Declan.

"The only way to stop them is to stop the Dark Magus," finished Rafia.

"And how do we find this Dark Magus?"

"Let me reach out to Bryen and Aislinn. Perhaps they can start the search for us if they haven't already. In the meantime, we've got other business that requires our attention."

"That we do," agreed Declan, his expression changing in a flash. It was almost as if he was back on the white sand, his entire countenance becoming as solid as the stone at his back. "That we do."

4

THE NEXT STEP

"Anything to worry about? I don't care much for surprises."

"You know, I never noticed that about you."

"You don't need to offer your dry wit all the time," Lycia murmured, the tone of her voice suggesting that she was both testy and slightly amused. "Discretion is permitted on occasion."

"I'll remember that for the future," Jakob replied softly, only listening to what the gladiator had to say with half an ear.

More intent on the perspective provided by the four kestrels soaring above the three mountains that resembled a trident and rose right in front of him. It was slightly disorienting for him when the kestrels dove and curled tightly through the sky, allowing the air currents to guide them.

It was a small price to pay. His ability to connect to the raptors with the Talent and see what they saw gave him a viewpoint he couldn't have gained otherwise.

Their sharp gazes revealed the narrow, rough trail that led down through the forest to the hollow that fronted the central peak and focused on features of the environment that might have slipped right by him.

"Well?" Lycia prompted.

"Well what?" Jakob asked.

He was studying the approach to the only mine that was still functioning in the northwest section of the Highlands, looking for any hides or good spots for ambushes. There were many. All unoccupied.

If he moved forward with his plan, he would be exposing the hundred Highlanders with him to the risk of attack from behind. He wanted to avoid that. Because just like Lycia, he didn't like surprises.

"Is there anything to worry about?" Lycia asked again, her tone more demanding.

As they got to know each other better, Jakob revealed more of his personality. She learned that sometimes he liked to be difficult just to be difficult. And sometimes he was just distracted. At the moment, she didn't know which one it was.

"Nothing that I can see. Just give me a few more minutes. I want to make sure. If we're going to take this risk, I want it to be a calculated one."

He had confirmed already that there were no Stalkers in the surrounding area. He extended his senses for more than fifty leagues, all the way to the east and the coast, hunting for any monsters still lurking about.

Jakob was pleased to confirm what he already knew.

It validated his decision to work with Declan and the Blood Company and give them the responsibility for clearing the Highlands of the Stalkers since those monsters concentrated so much of their attention near the crossing to the Isle of Mist.

From what he could determine, there were large swathes of the Highlands free of those monsters now. And, in a few months, if all went to plan, the Stalkers would be an afterthought within the peaks.

Nevertheless, Jakob understood that achieving their objective wouldn't be as easy as he hoped it would be. Nothing ever went to plan. His father had taught him that. And he had experienced it too many times himself to ignore that lesson.

Thus his desire to ensure that what he had in mind for the Highlanders' attack on the mine was based on the reality of their current situation and not on what he wanted it to be.

Because there were still monsters that needed to be eliminated. It just so happened that here the bulk of those monsters took human form.

"It just seems a little too easy," Lycia said softly as she lay next to Jakob, hidden by the rocks, watching from the ridge that allowed them to look down upon the entire hollow.

From all appearances, taking the mine should be a fairly simple task. Based on the number of guards they identified, the Highlanders would face little resistance when they freed the slaves.

Yet, if that was so, then why was she so unsettled?

Maybe it was because the gladiator didn't trust what she saw.

As they journeyed between the peaks now at their back and approached the mine through the wood, they hadn't run into any patrols or guard posts. Perhaps the slavers were unconcerned because the mine was situated within the wilder terrain of the Highlands. Perhaps they were just lazy after several years of being left alone. Or perhaps there was another more dangerous variable in play.

Maybe Lycia's unease resulted from the fact that there was only one way to reach their objective, the heart trees so dense that they had to take the trail that led down from the mountains and through the small forest. It wouldn't require many soldiers coming at them from behind to block the path and trap them in the small valley, the soaring mountains around them offering few options for escape.

Shaking her head in annoyance, Lycia returned her focus to their target. The main entrance to the mine was located in the central mountain.

There were two smaller tunnels visible in the base, each one a hundred yards away from the opening that was wide enough for twenty soldiers standing abreast of one another to march through. There were no tunnels visible in the mountains on either side.

A small village had grown up around the entrance to the mine, a large dirt field separating the primary shaft from the first of the ramshackle buildings. A stockade curved around the hamlet. The crescent-shaped wall was anchored against the sides of the central mountain.

The wall was only fifteen feet in height. Easily scaled if the defenders atop the parapet didn't realize that they were under attack. And, based on the space between the soldiers standing atop the barrier, the Highlanders should be able to make it to the top and gain a foothold even if the alarm was given.

This mine really was no different than the others that they had scouted previously. In fact, the defenses here appeared to be weaker than they were at the other mines.

Maybe that was why things didn't feel right here.

The guards standing atop the wall appeared bored and disinterested. They were in a static position, not moving along the parapet, staring out at the wood and looking for any sign of intruders, though just as much observing what was happening in the compound. And there was a good reason for that.

Most people's eyes were drawn to movement.

There was no activity in the valley other than the slaves forced to work in the mines moving back and forth between the small village and the entrance.

This mine was in a remote location in the Highlands. There were no brochs within twenty leagues and those few settlers who attempted to make their way in the surrounding mountains already had been scooped up by the slavers.

"What's the matter?"

He was looking at Lycia now, his sharp green eyes capturing her gaze, her breath catching for just a few heartbeats. She shrugged, unable to give him a good reason for her apprehension. "It just seems too easy to me. There's something about all this that doesn't smell quite right."

"What are you so worried about?" Saraa lay hidden among the rocks on Jakob's other side. "We've been eliminating the Stalkers and pressing the slavers. Sharperson is afraid. He's terrified of challenging Jakob. He knows what will happen if he does. That's why the bulk of his troops are protecting the Stone. That's why we've got an easy task here if we're quick about it."

Since the combat between them, Saraa had adhered to her promise to treat Lycia with less animosity, although it was obvious that doing so pained her. She could barely contain her contempt for how Jakob permitted Lycia to play such a large role in what they were trying to accomplish in the Highlands.

Saraa believed that she was right. The gladiator didn't belong there with them. Lycia was a threat to what they were trying to achieve. Unfortunately, Jakob didn't see it that way. Only she did.

She couldn't do anything about that fact now. Not yet anyway. But she would when the time was right.

And who knows? Maybe her problem would work itself out all on its own in the clash to come.

"Don't you get the sense that they're waiting for something to happen?" urged Lycia. "As if what we're seeing now is just an act? It's almost like they want us to attack."

"That would mean that they know we're here," scoffed Saraa.

"Exactly right," Lycia affirmed.

Jakob nodded slowly as he continued to study the layout of

the stockade. "Lycia makes a good point. This mine is just as large and productive as all the others that are still functioning in the Highlands. Yet there are fewer guards on the walls. Fewer slavers walking about. Fewer workers in the village and going to and from the mine."

"The slavers and miners are probably in the mine," Saraa advised. "My guess would be that they don't need as many guards here since this location is so difficult to reach. Sharperson likely believes that we'll keep our focus on the coast. There's more work for us there. More to gain."

"And what of those tracks we saw when we were making our way here?" countered Lycia. "What we found on the trail hinted at a large party coming here during the last few days. Who are they? Where are they?"

Jakob nodded. They had picked out the signs as they worked their way down the trail and into the hollow. A few hundred people. Maybe more. It was hard to be exact because last night's steady, drenching rain had washed out a good part of the path.

It could have been more miners making their way here just as Saraa proposed. Or it could have been something else entirely. Something more worrisome.

"Don't look a gift horse in the mouth," argued Saraa. "That was probably just another gang of miners. Several, in fact. With what we're seeing in front of us, it certainly points to that. They've been letting the product pile up here rather than taking it back through the mountains. They waited too long. They need to get it out. Simple as that." She turned her gaze toward Jakob, her eyes almost pleading. "This is too good an opportunity to pass up, Jakob. We need to take advantage of what the slavers are giving us."

"That's the problem," Lycia challenged. "If I was looking to set a trap for us, this is how I would do it. Give us a target we can't resist and defenses that appear to be lacking."

"Is the great Crimson Devil frightened?" Saraa snorted in disdain.

Lycia, who had kept her attention on the mine below the ridge, turned her harsh gaze toward the Highlander. She didn't take insults well. She never had.

Before she gave free reign to her temper, she took a breath to calm herself. Saraa was simply trying to get a rise out of her. Rather than give her the satisfaction, Lycia smiled sweetly instead of snapping at her.

"Frightened, no. I'm not," Lycia replied. "But I'm not stupid." Before Saraa could poke at her again, she continued, making her argument one more time. "By all rights, yes, this should be an easy raid for us. Not as many guards as you would expect. Not as many people in the village as you would expect. A load of ore and other metals, maybe even some jewels, waiting for us. But I don't like it. I say we wait until we get a better sense of what we're facing here. Waiting doesn't hurt us. It will just give us a broader view."

"Wait?" hissed Saraa. "If we wait, we could lose this chance."

"What's wrong with waiting?" countered Lycia. "We know there are no threats around us. There arc no companies of Sharperson's Guard coming to bottle us up in this valley. What's the rush? Why not spend a little more time scouting before we make our move?"

Jakob ignored the bickering that circulated around him. Saraa and Lycia didn't have any more arguments to make for their differing perspectives, so it swiftly devolved into repeating what they had said already.

Frustrating, yes. Even more so because both offered good points.

Saraa was correct. This really was an excellent opportunity.

They were isolated here, and as Lycia had noted, they didn't have to fear the Governor's soldiers coming up behind them.

There were only five working mines remaining in the Highlands. If they eliminated this one, they'd be turning the screws even tighter on the good Governor Sharperson.

It would take them one more step – one very large step – closer to freeing the Highlands from his grasp.

Sharperson would become more desperate. Perhaps even make a mistake. Maybe even weaken his forces around the Stone and give the Highlanders the chance to make a play for his citadel.

Take his fortress and Sharperson would be on the run if they didn't catch him there. He would have to leave the Highlands. And if he wasn't in the Highlands, he could do very little to stop the Highlanders from claiming what belonged to them.

Unfortunately, Lycia was correct as well.

Much of what he was observing didn't feel right. He agreed with her on that. Maybe those tracks were workers coming to take back to the Stone the ore and jewels that had been dug out of the mine.

More than a hundred pallets on sleds were lined up off to the side of the main entrance. Many of them full.

The trails through this part of the Highlands were too narrow for horses and wagons. It made sense to assume that the workers who might have been brought here would be tasked with delivering those sleds to the Governor.

Which meant that the Highlanders could seize the mine, free even more miners than they anticipated, and prevent Sharperson from making use of the riches waiting to be transported back to the Stone.

That thought appealed to Jakob. Even so, Lycia's concern stayed with him.

It could be an opportunity.

It could be a trap.

Then again, it could be both.

It probably was.

Because he could hear his father's voice in his head telling him that this was all just a little too easy. Just as Lycia warned.

Wanting to get rid of his father's strident tone, Jakob released the stream of the Talent that connected him to the kestrels flying above them. He redirected his focus toward the mine and the mountains themselves.

He took his time, thorough with his evaluation. There were more men and women working in the mines than he thought there would be. Although that could be explained by the several dozen empty sleds waiting to be filled that were lined up next to those piled high with the natural resources that Sharperson relied upon.

However, if those people in the mines were the cause of the tracks that survived during last night's downpours, then why was he filled with such an acute sense of foreboding?

His concern now had nothing to do with Lycia's hesitation. There was something not quite right about the scene set out before him.

It didn't take him long to figure it out.

A large number of the people working in the mines weren't actually working. Rather, they were gathered together in caverns just off the main path that led deeper into the mine.

They weren't doing anything at all. Resting. Sleeping. Just waiting.

There was no maybe about it when he concentrated on the group closest to the main entrance.

Definitely soldiers, not miners. A lot of them.

Close to three hundred and more than enough to make the tracks they had seen on the trail.

Lycia was right to be concerned.

So what else could be waiting for them in the mines?

He got the feeling that it wasn't just the soldiers loyal to the Governor.

Jakob extended his search with the Talent, reaching deeper

into the mountain. Exploring the shafts that led a mile or more beneath the ground and that were free of both slavers and miners both.

Jakob nodded to himself. He should have assumed as much.

It was definitely a trap.

Although it was an opportunity as well.

But why here?

Why would Sharperson believe that he would come here?

Why order so many soldiers here?

There was no way around it. The Governor would have had to have known that Jakob was coming here and when. It was the only way to get the soldiers here before him. Otherwise, he was wasting resources that he could use elsewhere. And Jakob knew that Sharperson loathed doing that.

That question faded away for a time when Duff walked up the slope, waiting for Jakob, Lycia, and Saraa to slide back down through the dirt and shale before they stood up.

The Highlander had been coordinating the scouting that was taking place along the edge of the wood. He wanted to find any weaknesses in the wall that they could exploit.

Duff trusted Jakob and his use of the Talent. Even so, he liked to see things for himself. It was a habit that had been ingrained within him by the Blademaster, and he was reluctant to let it go.

"Are those two going to bicker all day?" grumbled Duff.

"Seems like it," Jakob replied when he stepped up next to the Highlander, whose ever present hammer rested on his shoulder.

The Highlander smiled at that, then crawled up to the top of the ridge so that he could survey the target before sliding back down.

"What did you decide?" he asked.

"We've got a surprise waiting for us."

"The tracks?" asked Lycia.

Jakob nodded.

Lycia gave Saraa a triumphant grin that only served to escalate the argument between the two.

"Even so, we're going to make a play for the mine," Jakob said, ignoring the tension between the two, "but we're going to go about it a bit differently than we discussed originally." His decision cut off the quiet wrangling between Saraa and Lycia.

"What did you have in mind?" Duff shifted his hammer from one shoulder to the other. "I take it that we have some unwanted visitors waiting for us in the mine?"

"We do," Jakob confirmed. "If we're fast, we could turn what they have planned for us against them."

"Sounds good to me. The lads and lasses want to make a try of it. They know how important this is to our larger effort."

Jakob nodded, understanding. He also relayed with a glance that after this conversation he and Duff needed to have another one. Just the two of them.

"A squad will advance first into the compound to get eyes on the mine entrance and eliminate any guards wandering the village at night. They will serve as an initial skirmish line before the bulk of our forces come over the wall and then move through the village."

"I want that responsibility," Saraa said.

Jakob nodded. "So long as you're careful."

"I'm always careful."

Jakob grunted at that, not entirely convinced. "While Saraa is scouting the compound and the entrance to the mine, the rest of us will take the wall. We'll keep a reserve here in the wood. Just a few squads. Just in case."

"It's a trap?" asked Lycia, already knowing the answer but wanting to hear it.

Jakob nodded. "But also an opportunity." That last mollified Saraa, who was about to offer a few choice words to rebut any argument Lycia might offer. "If we can turn the trap to our advantage. That's going to be the primary challenge."

"How do you propose to do that?" asked Duff.

Jakob took the next few minutes to explain. "Saraa, why don't you get your squad ready. It should be dark within the hour."

"With pleasure," she replied, scrambling down the slope and disappearing into the wood.

Jakob turned his gaze to his second in command.

"What do you need?" asked Duff.

Jakob explained.

"I'll do what I can," nodded Duff.

"Thank you."

"And the other matter?"

"It will have to wait. There's nothing to be done about it now."

"Fair enough," Duff nodded, although based on Jakob's expression, he really wanted to know what was bothering him. "I take it that you're going for the wall?"

"I am."

"Lycia will be going with you?"

"I will," Lycia replied before Jakob could respond, "whether he likes it or not."

"Good," Duff grumbled. "Hopefully she can keep you out of trouble. Because if this doesn't work the way we want it to, we're all dead."

"Thanks for the vote of confidence," Jakob deadpanned.

"I do my best," Duff replied, his ready grin breaking free. "Now let's get to it. One way or the other, this is going to be quite a fight."

5

PERSONAL TOUR

"So tell me, young man, have you really fought in the Pit? I've been told as much, it's just that ..."

"You expected a fighter who was a bit more imposing," Aislinn cut in, her eyes sparkling with humor when she caught Bryen's brief frown.

"That's right," Kendric agreed. "I was expecting a bit more muscle to be honest. No insult intended, young man, but I didn't spend much time at the gladiatorial games when I was younger, and in that environment I was always under the impression that size mattered."

"Yes, he doesn't look as you might expect," Aislinn agreed, giving Bryen a wry grin as she did so.

Bryen was tall, lean, wiry, and he carried his double-bladed spear with the confidence and surety of a man who knew how to use it. However, he wasn't built of the blocks of muscle as were several of his friends in the Blood Company.

As Aislinn had learned after speaking with Bryen about his experiences in the Colosseum, survival on the white sand didn't depend solely on strength, both physical and mental. Success as a fighter in the Pit, and by that he meant surviving a combat so that he could fight the next one and then the one after that – a never-ending, soul-draining cycle, relied just as much if not more on speed and cunning.

As he had demonstrated time and time again, Bryen lacked neither of those qualities. And he was now hoping to employ that cunning to gain a better perspective on what was really happening in Shadow's Reach.

On the surface, all appeared exactly as it should. Clearly he and Aislinn had come to a prosperous city that was expanding well beyond its original walls. Bustling marketplaces. New buildings rising all over town.

Yet after having only been there for a few days, Bryen sensed beneath that hum of activity an undercurrent that dismayed him though he couldn't say that it surprised him.

After what he had learned from Jakob Kestel and Talia Carlomin, he had expected the worst. As had Aislinn.

The question now was could they find the source of the taint that covered this city in a barely detectible blanket of corruption and decay.

"He doesn't, you're right, Aislinn. However, the scars," Kendric said, motioning toward Bryen's face and neck, "suggest that it's true. That the famed Volkun strides beside me."

"Guilty as charged, Governor Winborne," Bryen replied with a slight nod.

"Kendric, lad, when we're with friends and family. No need for formalities."

"Thank you, Kendric," Bryen replied with a brief nod. "I appreciate your kindness."

"It's nothing. Now for what were you sentenced to the Pit? It must have been a horrendous crime. Only the worst offenders are sent there."

Kendric often didn't pay attention to standard social boundaries. Having grown up as a Lord of the Southern Marches and now proclaimed a Governor of the Northern Territory, he had seen little need for them. He had learned quickly that because of his rank and power he could say and do what he wanted. There were few who would challenge him. Other than his brother ... and his wife, of course.

Catching the aghast look that Aislinn gave him, he realized that he had stepped over a line with his question. Before he could backtrack, however, he got his answer. And it wasn't one that he anticipated.

"I killed a Duke who asked too many questions," Bryen replied.

Kendric stopped abruptly upon hearing that. The young man's eyes were cold, his expression grim, and his voice carried not a trace of emotion.

He gulped, not knowing what to say. He felt as if he was standing in the Pit, about to take up arms against the greatest gladiator of the last decade.

It wasn't a feeling that he enjoyed.

The squad of soldiers walking around them stopped as well, having heard what Bryen said. Uncomfortable. Nervous. They didn't know what to do. A few even placed their hands on the hilts of their swords, on edge, and with good reason. Because the young man with their Governor's niece radiated a lethal competence that was unnerving.

Kendric's eyes widened the longer he stared at Bryen, unable to pull away from the frigid gaze that held him, beginning to wonder if he had actually done more than just step over a line, his habit of speaking before thinking taking him down a path from which he couldn't recover.

Bryen kept his eyes, which somehow became even colder, locked on Kendric's, not saying a word. Then, much to Kendric's shock and relief, Bryen laughed softly and gave him a wink.

It took Kendric a few seconds to realize what had just happened, his mind still reeling from the possibility that he might have put himself in a position to be challenged to a combat for his perceived insult.

"Oh, very good, young man," Kendric chuckled.

The soldiers around them relaxed as well. Though only a little bit.

None of them had any desire to cross blades with the man holding his double-bladed spear as if it were an extension of his arm. Even so, they kept their hands on the hilts of their swords. Just in case.

Satisfied that the spilling of blood had been averted, at least for the time being, they shifted their gazes away from the daunting visitor back to what was going on around them. They had little to fear from the townspeople who gave them a wide berth while they walked through the busy square and city streets.

"I have my moments," Bryen replied.

"Indeed you do," Kendric agreed. "How very droll."

"Yes, Bryen has quite the sense of humor," Aislinn explained with a raised eyebrow and a hint of pique. "He likes to push boundaries as you just experienced. Even when he's been warned that his humor isn't for everyone."

She punched Bryen lightly on the arm to register her displeasure. He shrugged in response and gave her a lift of his eyebrows, as if to say that he was who he was. Aislinn didn't appear to be satisfied, her fingers forming into a fist again.

"There's nothing wrong with that in the least," Kendric said, still chuckling. "A little humor can go a long way."

Kendric guided Aislinn and Bryen farther along the main boulevard that led away from the Shadow Keep and toward a large bridge that spanned the square and connected the citadel to a long, rectangular building that was covered by a swarm of workers maneuvering large beams into place. The massive structure's roof was well on its way to completion.

Kendric pointed toward a block of residences being built at

the very edge of the plaza. "Those are some of our newer homes. You'll note the unique construction. The narrowness of the windows. The steel wrapping the doors. The thick tiles on the roofs. Very distinctive, don't you think?"

"They are indeed," remarked Aislinn. "In some respects, they look more like gatehouses than homes. Aren't there some similar buildings in the Southern Marches near the Northern Spine?"

"Good eye, Aislinn," Kendric replied with a nod of approval. "And you're correct. I got the idea for them from those same buildings."

"Weren't those residences designed as places of safety for travelers? Somewhere to go for the night so that they didn't have to fear bandits or whatever else might come down from the mountains under cover of darkness?"

"Yes, correct again. These homes function in much the same way as those buildings along the Northern Spine. With a few enhancements that I came up with to improve upon what we had in the Southern Marches."

"And these houses are in response to the Wraiths?" Bryen sensed an opportunity to touch on a topic that he wanted to discuss.

Kendric took a moment before responding, his lips pressed together as he thought about what to say. It was obvious that he was irritated with himself for not anticipating the question.

There was no point in trying to avoid it, however. Aislinn and her Protector had wandered the city before appearing at the Shadow Keep. They likely had heard quite a lot.

"They are."

"Are they effective?" Aislinn asked. These homes did resemble those along the Northern Spine, and there also were similarities between these new constructions and the broch she and Bryen had visited while meeting with Jakob Kestrel.

"Quite effective," Kendric replied. "We wouldn't be building them otherwise."

"So the Wraiths have breached the wall?"

"What makes you ask that?" demanded Kendric, his tone sharp.

"We heard as much in the city. Rumors that the Wraiths have been coming over the wall and into the city. That they've killed some of the townsfolk while doing that."

"Rumors carry little in the way of truth," Kendric replied evenly, though his eyes blazed fiercely. From anger or shame, Bryen couldn't say. "Have you not been taught, young man, the danger of listening to rumors?"

Bryen gave Kendric a sad smile then, Aislinn's uncle confirming what he believed. The rumors were true, Aislinn giving Bryen a brief nod that she agreed with him.

Shame rather than any real anger, Bryen was certain. Kendric felt responsible for what was happening in his city. The fact that he had yet to put a stop to it upset him.

"I was taught that in every rumor there is a nugget of truth."

Apparently, Kendric had no good reply to that, so he chose to ignore it. "The rumors you have heard are false. We have held the Wraiths at the city walls. We build these homes simply as a precaution. As I said, defending this city is my responsibility as is ensuring that its residents can live their lives free of the perils beyond the walls. These new homes and some of the other projects underway are designed to do just that."

Kendric gave Bryen a fatherly smile. "As you'll learn as you get older, perception is often just as important as reality. What we're doing in the city gives the people the perception they need. The comfort they require. It's as simple as that."

Aislinn and Bryen paid little attention to Kendric's argument, unable to ignore the fact that her uncle was lying to them. The Wraiths had walked the streets of Shadow's Reach.

His vaunted Northern Guard couldn't stop the monsters in the mist.

"You're correct, Kendric," Bryen replied, "perception is often just as important as reality."

"But you have something else to say."

"Why would you think that?"

"It's a skill of mine, knowing when people have more on their minds than what they're revealing."

"Fair enough," Bryen replied, catching the hidden meaning carried by Kendric's words. "I was also going to say that there is a danger in trying to make your perception of the world into your reality."

"You think that's what I'm doing here?" challenged Kendric, a tinge of irritation marring his voice.

"I didn't say that, Kendric. All I'm saying is that based on my experience, those who decide to focus on perception rather than reality rarely do well."

"Is that so?" Kendric gave Bryen an arrogant look. "And with all your worldly experience young man, what happens to those who fail to shape reality in the manner they desire?"

"They get bitten in the ass, Kendric. Often worse. Every time."

Several uncomfortable seconds passed before Aislinn moved the conversation in a different direction, having gained a key piece of information. She and Bryen already suspected it. Her uncle had corroborated it for her with the vehemence of his reply.

"So tell me, Uncle," Aislinn began, "what was it like when you first arrived here?"

Kendric brightened at that question, glad to be off the topic that disturbed him so. His niece finally had brought up a subject that he enjoyed talking about.

"The city that you see now is twice the size of what it was when I first arrived. In the time that I've been here what we've accomplished is truly remarkable. We have turned a border town into the capital of a Territory. The construction all around us certainly testifies to that."

"The Shadow Keep?" prodded Aislinn.

"Yes, we began work on the citadel within days of my assuming the Governorship. What was there before was just roughly cut timber and poorly placed at that. Not much of a deterrent. It couldn't keep out a pack of wolves. After so many long years of work, the citadel is almost complete. It would have been already, in fact, but we had to delay for a time to focus our attention on the city walls."

"And now it appears that you are extending the walls."

"Correct, Aislinn. Many of my friends laughed at me when they heard that I would be assuming command of the Northern Territory. They viewed it as nothing more than a backwater. They didn't see the opportunity that I could see."

Kendric smiled, shaking his head slowly from side to side in pleasure as a memory took him. "Your father told me that he had no doubt that I could make them all eat their words. And that's what I've been doing. There is nothing but growth and opportunity here. Business is booming. Trade is expanding throughout New Caledonia and beyond. The future is bright."

"That is quite obvious," Aislinn agreed, choosing not to ruin her Uncle's moment by adding at the end of her comment "unless the Murk comes in."

"It is indeed," Kendric agreed. "We have made a great deal of progress in just the last five years. Although I'll be the first to admit that we still have a long way to go, I think I can say that based on what we've achieved here, under my leadership, the years to come hold nothing but promise."

"You must have overcome a great many challenges to reach this point."

"You have no idea, Aislinn," Kendric chuckled. "Your father as Duke of the Southern Marches understands the struggles of leadership. But when he assumed the seat of power in our family's Duchy, the Southern Marches was well established. The mechanisms of rule, of administration and governance, were already in place."

He made a placating gesture with his hands. "Now I certainly don't want to belittle all that my brother and your father has done as Duke. But I must point out that the circumstances I've faced here are nothing compared to what Kevan has dealt with back home. Here, all that you see, all that has been accomplished, has occurred because of me and your aunt. Without us, none of this would have been possible."

"Like what exactly?" She was hoping for specific pieces of information, deciding to try a little flattery. "I know you've had to deal with more than most in your position could be expected to manage." Aislinn was disappointed, as she didn't get what she wanted.

"The stories I could tell," Kendric laughed as he strode proudly along the edge of the square. "But I won't waste your time with those. Now, thanks to your aunt and me, we are down to the little things. In fact, did you know how difficult it is to acquire stained glass from Ironhill?"

"Stained glass?" asked Aislinn, not quite understanding.

"Yes, I ordered it more than a year ago, and it only just arrived. With this last piece, I can finally complete my audience chamber."

"No, I can say quite honestly that I did not know that."

"That's understandable," Kendric replied. "As I said, we're down to the little things."

Aislinn couldn't quite believe what she was hearing from her uncle. He seemed to be disconnected from what was going on around him. From the larger challenges that were plaguing his Territory.

That or he knew what was going on, he knew what the real

tests were, but he either chose to ignore them, couldn't address them, or didn't know what to share with her and Bryen.

All three possibilities concerned Aislinn, especially the first two. It was not the way to ensure a prosperous rule. Worse, it put at risk the people living in the Northern Territory.

Moreover, based on what she had learned from her father, it was a symptom of corrosion in what needed to be a strong, just, and fair governance structure.

Papering over the cracks only got you larger cracks.

"Now tell me true." Kendric's voice held the hint of an order as he pushed the conversation in a different direction. "How is it that you ended up in the Pit?"

"When I was a child I stole food to survive in Tintagel," Bryen replied, having listened with a great deal of interest to the conversation between Kendric and Aislinn, using their dialogue to broaden his viewpoint on their new environment. Much like the Pit, there was a danger here. Yet unlike in the Pit, the peril that he sensed lurked in the shadows rather than right in front of him. "The City Watch caught me."

"You were sentenced to the Pit for that?" Kendric was incredulous. "A child? You can't be serious."

"The Belerons' sense of justice was quite draconian."

"That's a kind way to describe it," added Aislinn.

"And my brother saved you from the Colosseum and made you Aislinn's Protector? A kind gesture on his part," he said with an authoritative nod.

"That's one way to put it," Bryen replied very quietly.

Aislinn cut in before Bryen could offer more of what he truly believed regarding what her father had done to him. "What my father did was wrong, Uncle Kendric. He admitted it and apologized to Bryen once he realized the mistake that he made."

"After the fact doesn't always help, now does it?" murmured Bryen.

"Maybe not," Kendric said with another nod. "Still, my brother did you a great service, did he not?"

Bryen looked at Kendric strangely. He was about to offer a pointed response. Aislinn beat him to it.

"He did indeed," Aislinn agreed. "If not for my father's error, Bryen never would have found me."

"Quite the prize," Kendric said with a proud smile. "You could have found no one better to be at your side than my niece."

"Quite the prize indeed," Bryen agreed, although the sarcastic tone of his voice suggested that he had a slightly different perspective on the matter, his humor earning a raised eyebrow and a pointed look from the woman he loved.

"I can see why you two get along together so well," Kendric said as he led Aislinn and Bryen through a market that had been set up in the massive square that surrounded the Shadow Keep, hundreds of vendors selling from their brightly colored and eye-catching booths anything and everything that might be required or desired by the residents of Shadow's Reach.

Whenever Kendric passed by a stall, the merchant never failed to bow his or her head in respect, honoring the Governor of the Northern Territory and the man who could slow or halt the wheels of commerce as was his desire or need.

"Why is that?" asked Aislinn, nudging Bryen with her shoulder, ensuring that he realized that she didn't appreciate his attempt at humor. "I'm not sure I agree with that statement."

Kendric chuckled then. "Because you both have strong personalities each in your own way. You challenge one another. Although not in a confrontational way. More as if your interactions bring out the best in both of you."

"That might be more perception than reality, Uncle Kendric."

"It is reality, Aislinn, and you know it. I can see that you're just trying to be difficult as you so liked to do when you were a child."

"I was very well behaved when I was a child," she protested.

Kendric laughed loudly at that. "You were anything but. The grief you caused your father and mother? Oh, the stories I could tell. It was so much fun to watch. Even better to rile you up before I returned you to them."

"Perhaps you could share those stories when we have a few hours to kill," suggested Bryen. "I'd love to hear them."

"Done," Kendric nodded. "You'll need a strong mug of ale as well."

"I'm looking forward to it," Bryen replied, nudging Aislinn with his shoulder and earning a grimace from her.

"Now as I was saying," continued Kendric, "how you two work together, that's a good thing. It bodes well for your future together. Your strengths are enhanced and your weaknesses disappear."

"Aislinn would say that she has no weaknesses."

"I would not ..." Aislinn tried to protest, Kendric cutting her off.

"You're right about that, young man. But it's not unexpected. What you and Aislinn have is much like what I have with Aislinn's aunt."

"And how did you meet Ursina, Uncle Kendric?" Aislinn asked. She chose to hold back several pointed comments that were on the very tip of her tongue that she believed would rectify what she viewed as an inequitable situation. Bryen gaining the upper hand. For a time.

Her question brought a broad smile to Kendric's visage. "It was a day that I will never forget. That I treasure even now. Ursina had just arrived in Shadow's Reach. The very same day she rode through the gates, she came to the Shadow Keep to pay her respects."

"Do most people settling here do that?" Aislinn wondered.

She found it strange from what she could piece together from her conversations while walking through the city that a woman with little means would make the Governor's residence her first stop. Unless there was a clear purpose in mind for doing so.

"No, they don't," replied Kendric, "which was why I was so glad that she did. When I saw her that first time, a bit rough around the edges because of her long journey, I knew that we were meant to be together. It was like being struck in the heart with an arrow. I was lost then. My heart was hers." Kendric looked across at Aislinn, nodding toward Bryen, who was walking just a few steps behind her. "Was it much the same for you and your Protector? Love at first sight?"

Aislinn snorted out a laugh at that, barely able to control herself. "Far from it. I thought he was just a thug."

"A thug? Truly? He seems quite civilized now," Kendric said, looking over his shoulder and giving Bryen a wink to tell him that he was fighting for him.

"A thug. He was a gladiator. I thought that the only thing he knew how to do was to fight."

"I guess that stands to reason," Kendric admitted reluctantly.

"It took me a while to realize that there was more to Bryen than just the fact that he was remarkably skilled with a piece of steel in his hand. But the truth of it was that my father forced Bryen upon me. I didn't want him as a Protector. He didn't want to be my Protector. So we certainly don't have the story that you and Ursina enjoy."

"Then how is it that you two are together now? With me and Ursina, we were inseparable from the moment we met. I couldn't live without her by my side. We were married a month to the day after she walked into my office."

"It wasn't that way for us. After spending some time together, Bryen and I came to an agreement of sorts. We needed to. With Bryen forced to wear the Protector's collar, we had little choice," Aislinn said, motioning over her shoulder to the silver torque around Bryen's neck. The power of the collar was no more, yet still Bryen chose to wear the artifact. A symbol with many meanings and important to both of them.

"That's quite right," Bryen replied.

He was studying all that was occurring in the marketplace. It seemed no different than any other square in any other city, yet it was. And he didn't know exactly why.

He frowned slightly. Some aspect of this place, of where they were in the city, felt off. It was almost as if that very faint trace of decay was centered here.

Yet why that was the case, he didn't know. He would need to speak to Aislinn about it when they were alone. "I can't tell you how many times I wanted nothing to do with Aislinn."

"The feeling was mutual. Yet despite all that, we became friends. After more time passed, after working together to over-come some of the challenges placed before us, we became more than that."

"For better or worse," Bryen grumbled from behind her.

Aislinn controlled her impulse to turn and give him another punch in the arm. "Much as you have discovered with Ursina, Bryen and I have learned that we are stronger together than apart. It just took us a little bit longer to get there."

"That I certainly understand," Kendric nodded. "I don't know what I'd do without my lovely wife. Problems that I can't solve she can with what seems like just the flick of her wrist. There is something about her that is just ..."

Kendric shrugged, his smile becoming bemused as he thought about it. "I don't know how to describe it. There's a power to her that makes me feel more alive than I ever have before."

"A power?" asked Aislinn, curious, beginning to wonder if

Kendric was referencing what she and Bryen sensed the first time they met the Lady of the Northern Territory.

"Yes, a power," repeated Kendric. "I don't know how to describe it exactly. A confidence? With Ursina at my side, I feel as if I can do anything. That no one can stop me. Stop us, I should say."

"That's wonderful to hear, Uncle Kendric. I look forward to getting to know my aunt while Bryen and I are visiting with you."

"I'm sure that Ursina would like that as well," Kendric confirmed. He looked back over his shoulder, catching Bryen's eye. "I wish I could have been there to help you during the rebellion. My sword would have been yours."

"That's kind of you to say. We could have used you."

"It must have felt good to kill the King."

"Not good," Bryen replied quietly. "Just necessary. I've never enjoyed killing. Even when consigned to the white sand."

"Music to my ears, lad. Music to my ears." Kendric stopped once they passed through the market, looking at Bryen out of the corner of his eye. He couldn't get a read on Aislinn's Protector.

He had heard of the Volkun and wanted to learn more. Thus, his decision to take him and Aislinn around the city and try to find out if there was more to the young man than just the obvious.

From what he had been told, never having seen the young man compete in the gladiatorial games, he was supposedly one of the greatest fighters to ever stalk the Pit. Because of that, he expected this gladiator to be a bit more bloodthirsty.

But Bryen was anything but. A conundrum that Kendric would need to continue to puzzle over. Particularly since his niece loved him.

"Once the Shadow Keep is completed, this one will follow," Kendric said, not wanting to think about why the Protector made him nervous and needing a distraction, pointing to the large building that they had begun walking toward. Hundreds of workers scrambled over the framework of a structure that when completed would be as large as a city block. "It will serve as a barracks for six thousand soldiers once done. Hopefully by the end of the year. Thanks to the bridge, the Highland Guard will have easy access to the Shadow Keep."

"You have need of a Guard with six thousand soldiers?" asked Bryen. Kendric governed a large Territory, that was true, but compared to the others in New Caledonia the number of residents was quite low. "That seems a bit excessive."

"It's necessary," Kendric said gruffly. "You experienced one of the challenges we face here. Bandits on the road. We have touched on the Wraiths. At all times you must remain cognizant of the fact that we are not in Caledonia. Travel just a few miles beyond the walls of Shadow's Reach and the land is wild and untamed. It hides dangers that are best avoided and, when that can't be accomplished, must be protected against. As I said before, that's what I'm doing here."

"I understand that," Bryen replied evenly. He wasn't trying to antagonize Kendric, at least not openly. Although based on the Governor's tone, it seemed like he had just hit on a sore point. "I think I can say with complete honesty that Aislinn and I are quite familiar with danger. It just seems that based on how those homes were constructed, what you're building here ..."

"You can say it, young man," Kendric urged, sensing the gladiator's hesitation. "Have no fear. I will hold nothing against you if you speak your mind."

"Fear is something that is distinctly lacking in Bryen," Aislinn murmured, thinking that she had said it under her breath, her uncle hearing the comment anyway and giving her a look of displeasure at the interruption.

"I haven't been here very long, so I don't want to speak on something of which I know very little. It just seems that ..."

"Out with it, young man," Kendric ordered, his impatience rising. "I don't take you to be one who exercises a great deal of diplomacy."

"Just so." Bryen grinned at that, giving Kendric a nod of respect. "It seems that you're worried about more than just bandits and Wraiths."

"What do you mean by that?"

"Nothing specific," Bryen replied calmly, locking his cold grey eyes onto those of Aislinn's uncle, Kendric actually taking a half step back from him when he did. "It's just a feeling, although based on experience I tend to pay attention to feelings such as this one. Having spent so much time in Tintagel and living within the shadow of the Colosseum, I see some similarities here to what was happening there."

"What do you mean by that exactly?" Kendric's tone contained a hint of pique that he couldn't hide.

Bryen shrugged his shoulders, trying to soften what Kendric likely would perceive as a blow. "I admit that I don't know you very well, really only your reputation. But from what I learned about you from Aislinn and others, you are not a man who likes to be on the defensive. You prefer to be on the front foot."

"You're correct in that regard."

"Yet what I see here with all that is being built suggests to me that ..."

"Have you ever heard the saying that you need to put forward a good defense before you can attack."

"I have," Bryen replied calmly.

"From whom? I wouldn't think that a gladiator would be trained in the art of war. I would think that a gladiator would be trained to specialize in single combat. No more than that."

"The Master of the Gladiators taught me many things, most of them having little to do with fighting on the white sand."

"Then all credit to the Master of the Gladiators. What you

see before you, what you see throughout my city, is me trying to implement that strategy. We are not strong enough yet to deal with all the threats that we face. We are building our defense. Making sure that defense is strong. Dare I say impregnable. Once that is in place, we will go on the offensive. We will remove any threats that get in our way."

"Our way?"

"Mine and Ursina's."

"Of course. And what is in your way?"

Kendric stared hard at Bryen, recognizing the challenge not only in the tone, but also in the look. "It is really quite simple, young man. My wife and I seek to make the Northern Territory into a land that resembles a Duchy of Caledonia. Doing that takes time. It takes hard work. It takes hard decisions."

"And if anyone gets in your way?"

"Then I will not hesitate to ..." Kendric stopped himself, realizing where Bryen was leading him. "I will not hesitate to do what might be required to ensure that the interests of the people living in Shadow's Reach and the Northern Territory are protected."

"A worthy objective."

"Indeed it is, and not an easy one as you've likely surmised."

"It is not," confirmed Aislinn. "Why so many stonemasons atop the battlements?"

They had wandered farther down the boulevard, past various shops and markets, through the square to a spot where they could see the northern wall just a few blocks farther on.

At first, Kendric hesitated, then realized there was no reason to do so. "As I just mentioned, I will do whatever is necessary to defend my city."

"The Wraiths," prompted Bryen.

"Yes, the Wraiths. Their clawed hands allow them to climb the stone walls with little difficulty. We are making some improvements across the top of the wall that I hope will make their climb more difficult. If these enhancements prove effective here on the northern wall, then we will put the same in place on the other walls."

"So you expect the Wraiths to continue their attacks," nodded Bryen, "perhaps even in greater numbers."

"It's inevitable," Kendric admitted. "Every time the Murk comes in, they come with it. And the Murk is coming more frequently now. The Wraiths will not stop until we stop them."

"What is it like to fight them?" asked Bryen.

"It's like trying to fight the wind, lad," Kendric whispered. "Barely seen. Never heard. There but not." Kendric lost himself for just a moment, his eyes taking on a faraway look. When he came back to himself, he gave Bryen and Aislinn a wistful grin. "Although I'm sure that it doesn't compare to the Volkun fighting on the white sand. I dare say that from what I've heard of you, you'd have little trouble in a combat against a Wraith."

"You're being too kind, Kendric. Every combat is different. You never know how it's going to end until it does. I have no doubt that you're well aware of that."

"Yes I am, young man. Well said."

"Speaking of combats," said Aislinn, "how would fighting a Wraith compare to fighting a Stalker?"

"A Stalker?" asked Kendric, Aislinn noticing a flash of concern passing behind his eyes that he locked away just as quickly as it appeared.

"Yes, a Stalker. From what I understand, they are vicious creatures plaguing the Highlands and Fal Carrach." She chose not to tell her uncle that she and Bryen already had some experience fighting those monsters.

"I couldn't say," Kendric replied evasively. "I haven't come across these Stalkers as you call them, assuming they're not just the imaginings of people spending too much time in taverns."

Aislinn knew immediately that her uncle was lying. Again. The tells were many and obvious. He had just said more than he possibly could have if he had spoken the truth, and that saddened her.

Before Aislinn could ask her next question, Kendric turned away and began walking back toward the Shadow Keep, clearly uncomfortable and having no desire to continue the conversation. "Why don't we head for home. I have some business that I need to attend to this afternoon before we sit down to dinner."

Aislinn followed her uncle. She saw her father in him. His build. His gait.

She saw as well some weaknesses that were not present in her father. Weaknesses that she and Bryen had been playing upon for their own purposes.

She didn't like doing this to him. But she needed to.

She and Bryen had to push him. The Blademaster's comment while they were aboard the *Freedom* sticking with her.

Aislinn knew her uncle when she was a child. A great deal of time had passed since then.

People changed.

He had changed.

It was obvious.

For the better or the worse, she wasn't quite sure yet.

"Did you see him?" asked Bryen, not looking to the left. Keeping his eyes on Kendric as he walked a few steps behind him.

"I did. Any reason he would be here at this time?"

"I can think of a few."

"None of them good?" asked Aislinn.

"None of them good."

6

OVER THE WALL

It was early morning. The last of the full moon provided what light there was, and that was hidden more often than not by the clouds drifting across the sky.

The torches burning atop the wall were down to their last embers and, with the sun expected to rise within the hour, the guards seemed to have little interest in replenishing them.

Saraa grinned maliciously as she and her squad of Highlanders snuck up against the stockade, staying out of the soldiers' line of sight. Getting into position had been much easier than she anticipated, the long grass hiding their approach. That and the fact that the men standing along the parapet were spaced more than one hundred feet away from one another and were more asleep on their feet than awake.

Seeking to take advantage of that lack of discipline, Saraa selected a spot that was halfway between a pair of sentries that she believed, after studying the wall for several minutes while still hidden within the wood, were the closest to falling asleep if they weren't, in fact, already dozing.

She was quite pleased by her squad's initial success. They were ahead of schedule. The extra few minutes that they had

earned would give her just enough time to perform the work
that was required of her.

"Quickly and quietly lads and lasses," she instructed,
having picked up the jargon that Duff used so frequently. "You
know what to do."

Mikan and Jorie moved into position immediately. Out of
the six Highlanders crouching against the rough-cut timbers,
they were the tallest.

Mikan extended to his full height and braced himself
against the fifteen-foot wall, arms spread to the side, hands
resting on the wood, leaning forward to ensure he didn't lose
his balance. After he gave a nod, Jorie climbed his back, setting
his feet on his friend's shoulders. Once in place, he was only
two feet from the top of the wall.

Jorie could pull himself over simply by reaching up if he
wanted to. But that wasn't his role.

The Highlander spread his arms wide and then gripped a
knot in the wood on each side to fix himself in position. Once
he was balanced, he looked down, nodding to Saraa.

Saraa didn't wait. She pulled herself up Mikan's back and
then right up onto Jorie.

She waited just a heartbeat, flicking her gaze to the left and
then to the right, wanting to make sure that the sentries still
weren't aware of their presence.

Neither of the soldiers on either side moved.

The Highlander wasn't there to start the fight. She would let
Jakob do that when he came after her. She had another task to
accomplish.

With that goal top of mind, she affixed to the wall a hook
that she had wrapped in cloth. Certain that the grapple
wouldn't move and that it wouldn't make any noise when it dug
into the wood, she dropped down a short length of rope.

That done, she climbed silently over the wall and
crouched on the parapet. She waited for several seconds.

Listening. Looking for any movement along the wooden walkway.

Neither of the sentries on either side did so much as flinch. Even better, no one came rushing through the small village, sounding the alarm, intent on killing her.

There wasn't a noise to be heard that suggested that the soldiers charged with guarding the mine had any clue that she was there.

Satisfied that all was well, she extended an arm over the wall and motioned for the Highlanders below her to come up. At the same time, she studied the small village that spread out before her.

Thirty huts and a few other buildings. A mess hall. Latrines. Maybe even a laundry. The layout was just as she had been told that it would be.

All was quiet. The only light came from the sinking full moon, still more shrouded in the clouds than not. It wouldn't be long before the sun began to brighten the peaks to the east.

As the other Highlanders settled down next to her on the parapet, she selected the route that she would take toward the main entrance to the mine. Toward where the torches burned brightly, although there was no activity to be seen.

The miners were in their huts, likely dreading the sun and the day to come when they would be forced once again deep into the darkness, while the sentries not on duty slept comfortably in the long barracks built against the mountain to the right of the wide track that led into the gaping maw of the mountain.

She examined the barracks for a few seconds more. Two doors. Exactly as she had seen when Jakob offered her a view of the compound with the Talent.

She glanced behind her when she felt the walkway dip a few inches. Mikan and Jorie had joined her. They were both tall, heavy men. But it was the steel bars they carried that made her want to get off the parapet as quickly as she could.

She had given the pair of giants the task of planting those steel bars into the dirt and fixing them against the doors to the soldiers' barracks. That measure might not prevent the guards from joining the fight for very long, but it should give Jakob and the rest of the Highlanders enough time to get into the clash before the trapped slavers did.

Sensing that the time was right, she locked eyes with every one of her fighters. She wanted to make sure that they were ready.

Pleased by the looks she received in turn, Saraa jumped down from the parapet. She landed without making a noise. Her Highlanders joined her just a few heartbeats later.

Jakob had told her that at least two guards would be making their rounds through the village. Since she didn't see them, she decided to take the most direct path to her target.

Jorie and Mikan stayed right behind her, carrying their steel bars over their shoulders. The other Highlanders spread out to either side, Sonia staying a few yards behind to act as a rear guard.

They were almost through the small village, the broad dirt field that separated the slavers from their captors growing larger in size with every step they took, when Saraa raised her hand above her shoulder, her fingers closed into a fist.

The Highlanders stopped. Listening. Their eyes moving from side to side. Looking for the source of the sound that had forced them to halt.

The soft voices came from just to their left, behind the corner of the last house on the narrow path. Those voices drew their eyes, except for Sonia's, who kept her focus on what was behind them. They waited as patiently as they could for what they knew was going to happen next.

Saraa didn't say a word. Instead, with her hand still raised, she opened her fist, flashing two fingers in the air.

Grenna didn't need to be told what to do. She was the

fastest member of the squad. This was her job to handle. And, all the better, she was the closest to the corner.

Moving on silent feet, she crept along the house's wall of uneven boards until she was just a finger's breadth away from the edge.

The conversation between the soldiers continued while she moved into position. Clearly, they didn't know that she was there.

Grenna waited for almost a minute more, listening to the discussion, building a picture in her own mind of exactly where the soldiers were standing. Once she was certain, she moved in a flash.

Dagger in hand, gripped for a backhanded stab, she hadn't even stepped around the corner completely before she heard the shocked gasp, her blade finding the throat of the soldier closest to the edge. She tore her blade free, the dying man slouching against the wall.

She ignored him, already bringing her bloody steel up and through the other soldier's chin, the man not yet even registering what had happened to his friend. She didn't end her motion until the hilt was right up against the bottom of the man's jaw and she punched the tip of the dagger into his brain.

Grenna held the dead man in place for several seconds.

Waiting. Listening. Wanting to find out if her attack had drawn the attention of any other soldiers.

She didn't see any movement. No one was coming toward her from across the dirt field. And she didn't hear anything other than the sad gurgle of the soldier as he slid down against the wall and settled in the dirt.

Nodding to herself in satisfaction, she pulled free her dagger and aided to the ground the first soldier who was gasping silently for the air that wouldn't come, the two friends ending up slumped against one another, dying together.

Her job done, she stepped back around the corner, nodding to Saraa.

The entire time Saraa and the other Highlanders hadn't made a noise. They hadn't moved an inch.

They trusted in Grenna's abilities.

Their discipline rewarded, Saraa motioned toward the dirt field and the barracks beyond.

~

"THEY'RE OVER," Lycia said.

She turned away from the wall that rose just fifty yards away and walked deeper into the wood in which she and the other Highlanders hid.

Jakob hadn't been watching. He hadn't needed to. Instead, he had used the Talent to track Saraa and her squad's progress over the parapet and then in among the buildings.

He sat on the curling root of a heart tree that for several feet resembled a bench. Lycia sat down next to him, hands on her knees.

Jakob and the Highlanders with him would wait a little while longer before making their approach. He wanted to give Saraa the time that she needed to complete her assignment. And when they did attack, he wanted the rising sun flashing in the eyes of the guards who would be tired, lethargic, and very much looking forward to the end of their shift.

"Anything to worry about?" asked Lycia.

Jakob took his time before replying. He didn't want any more surprises.

Using the Talent to search around them, he started at a distance of ten leagues and worked back toward them. Nothing.

Just as there had been nothing only a few minutes before. The Highland Guard wasn't coming their way and seeking to block the only entrance to the hollow.

Expecting that, he then searched the stockade and the village. His timing allowed him to watch Grenna perform the grisly task required of her.

He was impressed. He couldn't have done the work better or faster himself.

As Saraa and her squad moved stealthily across the dirt field and toward the barracks, Jakob pushed his search into the mines.

Nothing had changed within those dark depths. There were no new threats there other than the ones they already knew lurked within.

"No, we're good," Jakob confirmed with a nod. "You ready?"

Lycia popped up from where she had been sitting. She felt like she did right before she walked out onto the white sand, the sizzle of energy running through her giving her a greater clarity.

"Ready."

Jakob nodded and was on his feet a moment later. Duff stood a few feet away, right at the edge of the wood, his eyes never leaving the top of the wall.

"Tommie, you and the others ready to begin?"

"Yes, Jakob," she replied, the confidence in her voice quite evident. Offering additional confirmation, she placed her spectacles in the leather pouch that she wore around her neck.

"Do you anticipate any problems?"

Tommie shook her head. "No, the wind is light and it'll be coming from behind us. Easy shots."

"Just make them clean shots," Jakob requested.

"Done."

With that, Tommie moved into position, the other archers joining her. They spread out along the edge of the wood, staying hidden within the gloom. They already had picked out their targets.

"You're in charge now, Tommie," Duff said.

He and the other Highlanders found their spots right next to the archers. Jakob and Lycia joined them. All of them held a dagger in each hand. Swords, axes, and hammers strapped to their backs.

Tommie nodded, then raised her bow, arrow already on the string. The other archers positioned along the edge of the wood did the same.

She waited a few seconds. Then, judging that the wind was just as she wanted, she issued a single command.

"Go!"

Duff, Jakob, Lycia, and all the Highlanders standing beside the archers burst from the copse, benefiting from the grey gloom of the early morning and the cover of the long grass as they sprinted toward the wall in silence.

They kept their focus on the timbers rising to their front, the soft hiss of the arrows streaking above their heads barely registering.

Before they even reached the base of the wall, a few of the figures who had been standing atop the parapet grunted or groaned softly. None called out.

More than half of the soldiers fell over the wall to either side, landing with soft thuds that barely broke the quiet of the early morning. Several of the mortally wounded soldiers slumped against the parapet, bleeding out, taking their last breaths. The two or three who took an arrow in the shoulder or an arm rather than a more serious wound barely had time to thank their luck before another shaft streaked through the air and slammed into them.

In seconds, the wall was clear and no one was left to sound the alarm.

Jakob and Lycia led the way through the long grass. Trusting in Tommie and the other archers, they concentrated on scaling the rough-hewn palisade.

They didn't have need of a rope or ladder. Instead, they

raced right up to the wall. When they were only a few feet away, they jumped up as high as they could with one leg extended, placing a foot against the timber and then launching themselves up the barrier as far as they could reach.

Before they dropped back down to the ground, they drove their daggers into the wood. Coming to a rest only a few feet from the top, they placed their boots against the roughly cut timbers and climbed up to the top with their daggers.

Knowing that they had nothing to fear from the guards, they slid over onto the balustrade. A few of the Highlanders assigned the grisly but necessary assignment moved silently down the walkway in both directions, ensuring that all of the guards were dead and helping on their way those who weren't.

Jakob and the Highlanders with him waited. Wary. Watching. Listening. In less than a minute, Tommie and the other archers joined them on the balustrade.

He had never expected them to get this far without the alarm being raised. Not because he didn't believe in his Highlanders' skills, but rather because there was always something that you couldn't plan for that got in the way of perfect execution.

Another lesson from his father. And a good one.

Although apparently one that didn't apply to what he was doing now. At least not yet.

Even as that small concern wriggled its way through the back of his mind, Jakob didn't hear any soldiers racing from the barracks to defend the mine or retake the wall. They had breached the stockade with the guards none the wiser.

So far so good.

It was at that very moment that another of his father's many sayings decided to pop into his head.

Good luck was good, but good luck wasn't forever.

That thought filled Jakob with the urge to get moving. Nevertheless, he understood that he couldn't accede to that desire. Not yet. He needed to give Saraa a few more minutes to complete her task.

Not wanting to spend those next few minutes fretting, Jakob tried to distract himself. Although not in the way that Lycia wanted. She was crouched right next to him, her eyes continually running over the village that spread out before them.

"I'm sensing that the tension between you and Saraa is still there."

The gladiator didn't want to have this conversation. Not now. Not ever, really.

Lycia gave Jakob a look that made it quite clear that she had little interest in the topic that he had raised. Nevertheless, she refused to run away from it. It was just another combat to her, although a bit different from what she was used to.

"I've been trying to stay away from her," Lycia finally said, realizing that Jakob wasn't going to let go of the matter. She shrugged then, as if to say that there was little that she could do beyond what she had done already to ease the tensions between them. "She doesn't like the fact that you and I spend so much time together. She views me as a threat. Like I'm trying to get in between the two of you. There's nothing that I can do about that."

She was pleasantly surprised by what Jakob said next.

"I'm sorry. Saraa can be a bit stubborn at times."

"At times? And just a bit?" Lycia asked with an arched eyebrow. "Really?"

"All right, most of the time," Jakob admitted with a tight smile. "And more than just a bit." Even as he spoke with Lycia, he continued to scan around them with the Talent. He didn't expect to find anything that would give him any cause to worry any more than he already was. Thankfully, he didn't.

"I've spoken with her a few times." He was slightly distracted as he focused on what he knew was waiting for them in the mine, wanting to make sure that nothing had changed since that was the greatest threat that he expected they would have to face. "I'll talk with her again. Her feelings for me are getting in the way of what we need to do."

"Her feelings for you?" Lycia asked, not quite believing that he acknowledged the real source of the tension.

"Yes, she wants more from me than I'm willing to give."

Lycia nodded. She didn't know what to say. In truth, she was afraid to say anything at all. She never believed that Jakob would see the dynamics of what was going on between him and the Highlander, much less have the courage to talk about it.

"We've spoken about it," Jakob continued, "but it's been hard for us."

Lycia simply listened. She didn't know if she was supposed to say anything. And she didn't want to get in the way of what was a rare opportunity, since Jakob rarely revealed what he was thinking or feeling.

"Saraa wants something from me that I just can't give her. It's not that I don't care for her." He shrugged his shoulders, trying to communicate that he didn't quite understand why Saraa's feelings for him were so difficult to deal with. "I do. Just not in the way that she wants me to."

Lycia dared to ask a question when Jakob took a few heartbeats to gather his thoughts. "Why are you telling me this now? We're in the middle of an ambush here."

Jakob chose that moment to shift his gaze toward her, his green eyes locking onto hers.

Duff interrupted them, the worst possible time in Lycia's opinion. "Is this really a good idea?"

"Maybe," Jakob said, releasing Lycia from his gaze, giving her a warm wink as he did so that only served to confuse her. "Maybe not. It's too late now to second guess. There's only one direction for us to go."

"Thanks for filling me with confidence."

"I do what I can."

Duff snorted softly when he saw Jakob's grin. "I really hope this is worth the risk."

"It will be. If we do this right."

"Will it work?"

"There's only one way to find out."

Duff nodded, grumbling under his breath. He reached out, clasping hands with Jakob. "I'll see you on the other side."

"I'll see you on the other side," Jakob replied quietly.

With a nod, Duff walked silently down the battlements toward the south where the wall butted up against the mountain. Several squads and all of the archers followed him.

"You seem less than pleased, Tangsten. You don't care for the dark depths?"

"I've never cared for enclosed spaces, Captain," Tangsten replied in as even a voice as he could manage.

Captain Hippolates was correct. Tangsten hated being deep beneath the surface with thousands of tons of rock above him. He struggled against his almost paralyzing fear with every step he took down the tunnel that led from the mine's entrance.

But he would keep all that to himself. He didn't feel like dealing with the ribbing his friends would give him if they learned of his weakness.

In fact, the only reason that Tangsten had been able to make the trek down to where Captain Hippolates was waiting was because the information he brought would help to ensure that he would be able to leave the mine within the hour.

"Fall down a well when you were a child?" Hippolates chuckled softly. "You couldn't make it back out on your own?"

"No, Captain. My stepfather locked me in the closet when I didn't do as he demanded as quickly as he wanted. Sometimes he'd leave me there for the entire night."

Hippolates stared at Tangsten for quite some time. He had experienced a difficult childhood himself, although nothing like that. He couldn't imagine being locked in a closet. No space to move. No light. At least here they were waiting in a long and broad cavern with torches fixed to the wall, giving them a good bit of illumination.

"Did you love your stepfather?"

"No, Captain Hippolates."

"Did you ever gain your revenge on your stepfather?"

"I wouldn't call it revenge, Captain Hippolates. He liked to hit my mother when he was drunk. It reached a point that when I was too big for him to lock me in a closet, he tried to beat on me as well."

"You swung at him, Sergeant Tangsten?"

"He was a big man and he still had a few stone on me," Tangsten replied calmly. "I stabbed him. Right in the kidney. He didn't bother my mother or anyone else after that."

"You took matters into your own hands. Good for you, Tangsten. But there's a time and a place for that." Hippolates leaned forward then, resting his arms on his knees. "I hope that you won't be doing that today. I hope that you'll be following my orders. Initiative is a good thing. Just not today."

"You have nothing to fear in that regard, Captain Hippolates."

"That's good to hear," Hippolates confirmed with a nod. He had no desire to explore his Sergeant's psychological scars any further. "It's started?"

"The two guards who were supposed to be working their way through the village haven't reported," Sergeant Tangsten replied. "I'm assuming they're dead."

"If they are, it was their own fault," grumbled Hippolates.

Tangsten ignored the comment, never having gotten used to his commander's callousness. "When they missed the time to check in, I worked my way up to the barracks."

"No one saw you, I hope."

"Of course not, Captain."

"Good. What did you discover?"

"It looked like it was no more than a handful of Highlanders coming over the wall. Although I have no doubt that the rest of those brigands are with them. It was hard to tell, though, with the night giving way to the morning. I couldn't see a single soldier lining the battlements, although that could have been because the sun was rising just over the peaks."

Hippolates wasn't surprised by that news. Actually, he welcomed it. "Were they heading toward the mine or toward the barracks, Tangsten?"

"Toward the barracks."

Hippolates nodded in appreciation. "Smart. They want to give the rest of their fighters time to get over the wall before they're discovered."

"Should I warn the soldiers in the barracks?" Tangsten didn't like the idea of leaving almost a full company of unprepared soldiers at the mercy of these cutthroat Highlanders.

Hippolates spent a few seconds thinking about the question. "No, leave them be for now. We don't want to ruin the surprise."

"But, Captain, if those Highlanders ..."

"Leave them be, Tangsten," Hippolates repeated with greater heat. "We have three companies of soldiers here in the mine. If the information given to us is accurate, we should already enjoy an advantage of two to one. Perhaps even three to one. The soldiers in the barracks can join in the fun once they figure out what's going on. Assuming, of course, that the Highlanders don't kill them all in their sleep." That possibility didn't faze Hippolates in the least. He had a larger objective to achieve. And he would do so, no matter the cost. "I expect that they'll have little work left after we've had a go at these rebels."

"You think that we'll be able to manage the Lord of the Highlands and his fighters with little difficulty, Captain?"

Hippolates didn't appreciate the slight tinge of disbelief he detected in Tangsten's tone. "You don't believe that we will?"

"I don't know what to believe, Captain Hippolates," Tangsten replied in what he hoped his commander interpreted as a placating tone. "I've never come up against the Lord of the Highlands before. I've only heard stories about him. And those stories suggest that he is a daunting adversary."

Hippolates gave his Sergeant an understanding smile. "I've heard those stories as well, Tangsten. Just a young man, the Lord of the Highlands, or so they say, but already an unbeatable fighter. Often spoken of in the same breath as the gladiators of the Pit who used to stalk across the white sand like demons. The Volkun. The Crimson Devil."

Hippolates shrugged, as if to say that he had little reason to accept that interpretation. "Stalkers don't faze the Lord Kestrel. In fact, he hunts them for sport. And he likes to keep his skills sharp by fighting the Wraiths in the Murk. So much so, in fact, that he refuses to enter the brochs the Highlanders have constructed to protect against those monsters in the mist."

Hippolates gave Tangsten a friendly clap on his shoulder after he pushed himself to his feet. "Do you know what I think about those stories, Tangsten?"

"No, Captain."

"They're just stories, Sergeant. Nothing more than a load of crap that stinks just as bad. I promise you that. If half of what they say about this Lord of the Highlands is actually true then he's not entirely human."

"As you say, Captain." Tangsten had no desire to get into an argument with his commander, but he failed to keep that continuing hint of worry from creeping into his voice.

"I do say, Tangsten," Hippolates replied. "This Lord of the Highlands is no more than a figurehead. Just some unfortunate fool placed in this position because the rebels needed someone who could rally the Highlanders to their cause. Probably nothing more than an actor who doesn't really know how to use his sword."

"From what I've heard, Captain Hippolates, this Lord of the Highlands favors those double-bladed daggers that the Wraiths use."

"Be that as it may, Sergeant Tangsten," Hippolates replied, biting off each word, not appreciating his subordinate correcting him, "I have no doubt that he bleeds just like we do. Kill him and we kill the rebellion."

"Yes, Captain," Tangsten replied, making sure that he inserted more confidence into his voice. Although not because he agreed with Captain Hippolates' view of the Lord of the Highlands. Rather because he had no desire to be the target of Hippolates' wrath.

Captain Hippolates could say what he wanted. That didn't mean that Tangsten had to believe him.

He had heard quite a lot about Jakob Kestrel, much of it from his fellow soldiers, sometimes slavers, who had come up against if not him than his Highlanders. Based on their experiences, he tended to believe the stories that his Captain discounted so easily.

The Lord of the Highlands was said to be a formidable fighter, and young man or no, definitely not someone you crossed blades with willingly. And certainly not without a fist of your friends at your back.

He was also said to be an excellent leader with a cadre of devoted sergeants at his side. That he only fell into a trap if he wanted to fall into the trap.

That last worried him the most.

His Captain had to have heard the same, so why Hippolates believed that all would go as planned was beyond him.

Those thoughts darkened his mood, the fact that he was

still a mile underground not helping. Nevertheless, he did succeed in keeping his realistic perspective at bay. Because he did believe that if they killed this Lord Kestrel, the rebellion would die with him.

"Isn't it almost morning, Tangsten? You said the sun was beginning to brighten the sky?"

"It is," the Sergeant confirmed.

"Clever," Hippolates murmured.

"Attacking with the sun just coming up over the mountains," Tangsten nodded. "Blinding the guards on the wall. Making them easier kills."

"Exactly so, Tangsten. It's something that I would have done if I was in his boots."

This time, Tangsten succeeded in keeping his disbelief from his expression, although it took a great deal of effort. His voice as well, though the only way to do that was to keep his mouth shut.

"It won't do them any good, however." Hippolates strode toward the main tunnel that led up and out of the mine. "Come on, Tangsten. Rouse the companies on the way. It's time to kill the Lord of the Highlands."

"Done," Mikan whispered.

He and Jorie had just fixed the steel bars in place. The spiked end set deep into the dirt, the broader, flatter end fixed against the barracks' doors. There was no way that the men sleeping in the dormitory would be joining the fight for quite some time, the few windows too small to crawl through.

Saraa nodded in satisfaction. Her squad had performed better than she could have hoped for. Not because she doubted the skills of her fighters. She didn't. She had handpicked these Highlanders. But rather because she assumed that the alarm would be given before they made it all the way across the dirt field.

She had assumed that as soon as they stepped out from the cover provided by the small village that they would be in a race against time. That they would need to get the bars up against the doors at the very same time that the slavers were trying to force their way through.

She had feared for no good reason, however. She and her Highlanders hadn't been seen. They hadn't been heard.

All was as quiet as it had been before they scaled the wall.

Actually, thinking about it, their success really wasn't all that surprising. Not after all the preparation that they had undertaken to ensure that this incursion was managed as it needed to be.

With her first task complete, it was now time to move on to the next. This second task a bit more concerning, although Saraa had little choice. Not if she was to achieve her larger objective. And that's all that mattered to her now.

For just a second, she regretted the circumstances that put her in this position. Nevertheless, she needed to do this. She was the only one who really understood what was going on. What was truly at risk if she didn't do this.

"Did you see that?" whispered Grenna. The Highlander who had dispatched the two guards with such skill and alacrity crouched right next to her, their backs against the building so that they could survey the stockade and the entrance to the mine at the same time.

"What?" asked Saraa quietly, although she already knew the answer.

"Shadows in the entrance to the mine." Grenna nodded in that direction as the sun began to peak out from behind the mountains on the other side of the wall.

"What do you mean by shadows?" Saraa stood up, wanting to get a better look, although she didn't doubt what

Grenna told her. She assumed that it would only be a matter of time.

"Just inside the mine," Grenna gestured again, "along both sides."

It didn't take long for Saraa to pick out what Grenna had identified. Events were moving faster than she anticipated. But they were moving just as she knew they would, and there was nothing to do for it now.

She had a role to play, and she needed to play it.

Stepping away from the building, she pulled her sword free from the scabbard across her back.

"Highlanders," Saraa said, directing her words to the men and women who had braved the wall with her. "Stand and fight. We will hold this ground!"

The shadows that Grenna had identified were no longer shadows.

They were soldiers.

Swords drawn.

Axes in hand.

Sprinting across the dirt field right toward them.

"I KNEW this was too good to be true," grumbled Jakob, shaking his head in frustration.

"Saraa?"

"Yes, she's been discovered." He wasn't naïve enough to believe that his plan would work perfectly. He had assumed that something would go wrong and that they would need to adjust. Just as always was the case. Just not so soon. He had hoped to have his Highlanders into the mine before that happened so that he could make use of the tight space against the threat he feared the most. "Come on. We need to see if we can get Saraa and the others free."

Jakob and Lycia dropped down from the wall and sprinted through the village without making a sound, the other Highlanders following. With every step he took, Jakob felt more and more their raid shifting from opportunity to trap.

When he reached the edge of the village, he skidded to a stop, raising his hand above his shoulder so that the Highlanders stayed within the shadows of the ramshackle cottages.

The rising sun illuminated the open space that extended for one hundred yards all the way to the mine entrance. Saraa and her Highlanders were out on the dirt field, not too far away from the barracks.

He assumed that they had tried to keep the building to their backs to limit the direction from which the soldiers who were still rushing out of the mine could come at them. Unfortunately, the soldiers had been too much for them, surrounding Saraa and her fighters.

The Highlanders were holding their own, giving as good as they got. But Jakob knew that they wouldn't last for much longer.

The soldiers were too many.

The Highlanders too few.

It was just a matter of time before they were overwhelmed.

Then the break that Jakob had been dreading occurred.

Saraa overextended on her lunge, slipping in the dirt. She dropped to one knee. Before she could push herself back to her feet, one of the soldiers came at her from behind.

Rather than driving his dagger through the back of her neck, he placed one hand on her shoulder, pushing her back down. Then he reached around with his blade and placed the steel against her throat.

The Highlanders' defensive circle broken, the soldiers had little trouble pushing Mikan, Jorie, Grenna, and Sonia away from one another. Once that happened, the clash came to an end.

Not because the Highlanders weren't willing to continue their resistance. But rather because the soldiers had no cause to continue the combat. They appeared to be satisfied with bracketing off the Highlanders from one another.

Recognizing the uselessness of trying to break out of the small circles of steel that held them in place, especially with a blade at Saraa's throat, the Highlanders allowed the uneasy truce.

Jakob cursed softly. Hating what had happened to his Highlanders. Watching with dismay as soldiers continued to stream out of the mine.

He estimated that two full companies had formed ranks in front of the entrance with more soldiers still emerging from the dark.

He had been too confident in their success. He had believed that if he and his Highlanders were fast enough, they could turn this trap to their advantage.

But they hadn't been fast enough.

Instead the trap had been sprung on them.

Then again, as Jakob considered the situation from a few other angles, perhaps it wasn't that his Highlanders hadn't been fast enough. Perhaps it had been something else that had roused the soldiers from their hiding place before his Highlanders had gotten into position.

Somehow he and his fighters had been found out.

That was the only explanation that made sense.

Whoever was leading these soldiers had come here just for them. Just as Lycia had warned.

Yet there was more to it than that. He needed to think more about why he thought that. He needed to take into consideration all of the various angles even though he didn't want to, because he knew what his suspicions meant if he was correct.

"She's not going to be able to get away."

The fighting on the dirt field had stopped, the only movement now the last few soldiers rushing out of the mine and getting into position.

"We can't leave her." Jakob was about to step out from the shadows and walk onto the dirt field. Lycia's strong grip held him in place.

"Jakob!" Lycia said insistently. "It's too late for them. You can't do what you're thinking of doing. It's a no-win situation."

Jakob was about to argue against what Lycia was telling him. But, looking out on the dirt field once more, he heard only the truth in her words.

She was right. There was little that he could do that would save Saraa and her squad.

Swallowing that bitter herb, he was about to order the other Highlanders to pull back toward the wall when he heard a voice that he never thought he would ever hear again.

"Come out, come out, wherever you are, Lord Kestrel. It's time to play."

7

PLAYING THE ODDS

"We're trapped." Talia Carlomin stated the obvious, struggling to contain her vexation and worry. "We're exactly where she wants us to be."

The Carlomin Guard held the main gate, preventing the fifteen companies loyal to Hakea Roosarian from forcing their way into the compound. The chokepoint proving to be too much of a challenge for now.

The attackers reluctant to attempt to scale the wall. The archers standing ready atop the battlements, keeping Roosarian's soldiers near the alleys where they could take cover.

A stalemate.

But for how long?

That was one of Talia's many worries.

Her soldiers were outnumbered two to one. Three when the rest of the Fal Carrachian Guard arrived. Seeking to break out from their current plight would be an exercise in futility and serve little purpose other than they engaged in a battle that they couldn't win.

Talia closed her eyes for a few seconds and took several

deep breaths, needing to calm herself before her mounting frustration ran rampant within her.

She desperately wanted to rescue Davin. He had sacrificed himself for her.

And since then, not knowing if he was dead or alive.

Obsessing about what he did ... for her.

How could he have done that?

They were fighting together in the tunnels beneath the Rock.

Surviving together against the Stalkers.

They had a chance to escape.

Together.

But he made the decision for them both, concluding that she was more important than he was.

On the one hand, she appreciated grudgingly and was impressed by his courage and chivalry.

On the other hand, his choice rankled.

She didn't like it when someone made a decision for her, even when that decision might be the right one.

Worse, she couldn't ignore the truth.

Davin had traded his life for hers.

That conclusion threatened to crush her.

She hoped that he was still alive.

She was desperate for that to be the truth.

But she knew how much her hope was worth upon seeing the fist of Stalkers racing toward him right before he brought down the shaft between them, giving her the time that she needed to get off the Rock.

Because of his blasted courage, now she owed him a debt that she'd likely never be able to repay.

That frustration was the emotion that Talia chose to grasp, too afraid to allow the other feelings raging through her to take hold, not knowing how to manage them effectively, fearing that if she let them loose she would become a blubbering mess.

She needed to know for certain. She needed to find out if Davin was dead. And if he wasn't, she needed to save him if she could.

"We are," Sirena confirmed, not feeling the need to say anything else, Talia's mood matching her own.

"What from our allies on the Council?"

"They stand with us, of that have no doubt, Captain Carlomin."

"But they have a fraction of the soldiers that we do," Talia finished for her.

"Yes. Even if we sought to put the Roosarian soldiers in a vise, our allies attacking from the streets and alleys, we from the main gate, I still couldn't tell you what the final outcome would be. The surprise might tilt the clash in our favor, but ..."

"But there's no way to know for sure," concluded Talia. "And in such a clash, the odds of success always favor the larger force."

"Exactly. If we're to win this fight, we'll need to do more than rely on our allies. We'll need to give the Roosarian soldiers a reason to run."

"We will, Sirena, I promise you that," Talia replied cryptically. "When the time is right. Where are the Council members and their soldiers?"

"Where we asked them to be. They're hiding in the streets and alleys by the entrance to the Roosarian pier. Waiting for word from us. Again, though, they're not strong enough to do anything that would draw the notice of the soldiers standing against us here. Three companies of Roosarian's soldiers guard the pier and the ferry to the Rock. It's a stalemate there as well."

"I assume that they can be enough of a nuisance to distract three companies if we ask that of them?"

"Yes, I believe they can. No more than a nuisance, however. They can't take the pier themselves unless we do something to change the odds for them. And as I said, they can do nothing for us here. We stand against the companies set against us on our own."

"I'm well aware," grumbled Talia. "Have no fear of that."

It had taken her several hours to row across the harbor and back to the enclave that she and her mother had built. All the while she thought of what they could do to improve their chances against Hakea Roosarian and her Fal Carrachian Guard.

Several possibilities came to mind. A few better than others. Those few she wanted to ponder some more before proposing them to Sirena.

Once she finally reached the pier, however, other matters had taken precedence.

First and foremost was dealing with her mother. Isana had been there to greet her, watching her come across the water with the dawn, anxiety written across her face.

Fearing the worst, Isana was thrilled that her daughter was alive.

She was disappointed that Davin likely wasn't.

Isana liked Davin Noname. She thought that he was a good influence on her daughter. That he was someone who could help her in ways that no else could, if Talia allowed him to, understanding how her daughter's streak of stubbornness often got in the way of her making the right decision when it came to herself.

Despite her dismay, Isana fell back on her innate practicality.

What's done was done. They needed to move forward.

The gladiator would have understood that. He would have counseled it, in fact.

Isana advocated that whether or not Davin was still alive, Talia needed to forget him. She needed to concentrate on defeating Roosarian.

The needs of the many before the needs of the one. Her argument eerily similar to Davin's own.

To do that, they had to achieve a single though exceedingly difficult objective. They needed to figure out how to take the fight to the Governor. They had to go on the offensive despite being stuck on the defensive.

The longer they were cooped up in their enclave, the more time Roosarian had to solidify her position and get her soldiers and strategy in place.

The stalemate that the Carlomin soldiers earned upon pushing back the attack on the gate was more of an aid to Roosarian now than to them.

Because with each passing hour, as more Roosarian companies arrived from the Rock, the more likely the insurrection Talia had initiated – before time, her mother had noted quite frequently – would die on the vine.

As would they and everyone loyal to them.

Talia shook her head, vexed by the situation of her own making. Even more so angry with herself as she allowed Isana to get under her skin.

Her mother, who had left just moments before to check a report that an unknown vessel was sailing through the harbor to the east of the Rock and possibly toward their pier, was correct of course.

She hated when her mother was right.

Events had moved faster than either of them anticipated. Even more galling, they had ceded the momentum to Roosarian.

Talia needed to change the rules of the game before she lost the game.

But how to do that?

From her office window, with the sun just beginning to peek above the horizon, she could see across the harbor to the Rock. Launches sailed to and from Roosarian's unfinished citadel, bringing more companies of soldiers from their barracks to join the ones already stationed in front of the main gate.

Once Roosarian was satisfied that she had enough soldiers to make a play for their enclave, Talia assumed that the Governor would increase the pressure by sending those same launches full of soldiers against her docks.

Such a tactic only made sense. It would split Talia's forces and weaken their defense. Once Roosarian's soldiers gained a foothold on the docks, the Governor's victory would be assured. It would just be a matter of time. They would be caught in a vise.

Talia's soldiers were well trained, and she had no doubt that her sailors would put up a good fight as well, but just as in business, it all came down to a simple, guiding variable.

The numbers.

Roosarian held the advantage in numbers, the Fal Carrachian Guard larger by more than half compared to Talia's, even when she took into account the soldiers loyal to the other Council members.

Talia's allies would aid her. Of that she was certain.

They knew the truth of Roosarian and the pirates.

They had seen the evidence provided regarding the Stalkers.

They all believed that Roosarian needed to be removed from her seat of power.

It was the only way to ensure the future success of Fal Carrach. It was the only way to build a Territory that did not fall victim to the whims of a despot. Because that's what Roosarian was seeking to become.

But Talia could expect only so much from her allies on the Council. The merchants sought to control as many variables as they possibly could in their business dealings.

She understood that. It's why they were successful.

She understood as well that if the tides shifted, they would as well.

It was only natural.

They would move to protect their own interests. They would do what was required even if they didn't like what that was.

To ensure that the Council members remained strong in their convictions, Talia needed to demonstrate some success. Holding her ground, waiting for Roosarian to marshal her forces in preparation for a two-pronged attack, wasn't the demonstration that would bolster her allies' confidence.

When Isana had met with the Council members the same night the Stalkers were set loose on the Carlomin docks, she had argued that a good businessperson knew that there were times when taking a calculated risk was necessary.

She had argued vociferously that this was one of those times.

The other merchants had agreed with Isana. Wholeheartedly, in fact.

But taking a calculated risk came down to probabilities.

Probabilities were based on numbers.

And, at that moment, their nascent rebellion seeking its legs, the numbers were against them.

So how to turn the numbers in their favor?

Thinking about that rather than the perils she faced, Talia remembered a conversation that she had with her father before he passed. Abram had told her of his adventures as a scout in the Roo's Nest Guard before he met Talia's mother and took his life in a different direction.

Most of the time he was sent out on his own. He was always outnumbered.

And he not only survived, but also thrived. Because in those dangerous situations he didn't focus on what he couldn't do when the numbers favored his adversaries.

The numbers always favored his adversaries.

No, instead he focused on what he could do.

As he had liked to say, and as Talia believed, a little creativity mixed with a little risk could take you a long way toward achieving your objectives.

Talia was fairly confident that the Carlomin Guard could break free of the siege. But it would be a hard fight. A bloody fight. And making such an attempt would leave her with a spent force that would be taken from behind when the Roosarian longboats reached their docks.

That might even be Roosarian's goal. The Governor might want Talia to do just that, because then she could sweep in and be rid of her once and for all.

That possibility didn't appeal to Talia. Moreover, it didn't give her the flexibility to do what she really wanted to do.

Take on Roosarian directly.

Her mother was right. Talia couldn't deny it.

Davin likely was dead or soon would be.

Talia needed to focus on the larger picture.

Still, just because her mother was right didn't mean that Talia had to listen to her. At least not entirely.

It was all numbers, risk, probability. That was true.

She just needed to put all that in line in a way that allowed her to achieve all of her objectives.

The trick, as her father had liked to say, was finding the path that would allow her to do that.

And, unfortunately, based on her resources and the state of play with the sun now gleaming brightly in the east, the path that she could see didn't allow her to do all that she wanted to do.

She wanted to break the siege before it settled into place. She wanted to cross blades with Roosarian. She wanted to learn Davin's fate.

She couldn't do all that. She couldn't seek to invade the Rock and break out of her enclave at the same time.

So she really didn't have a choice.

That inescapable conclusion angered her, though she wouldn't ignore it.

If Talia was to do what she needed to do, she needed to forget Davin for the time being. And doing that felt like an arrow through her heart.

"Are you certain, Sirena? I heard what my mother said, but you know our soldiers best. You know what we can expect from them."

"I'm sorry, Captain Carlomin. Can we break out from the enclave and push back the Fal Carrachian Guard? Yes, I believe we can." She shrugged then as way of an apology. "Can we do that and attack the Rock as well with soldiers coming at our docks? No. I'm sorry, but we can't. We don't have the strength to do both."

"So you agree with my mother?"

"In this, yes. I agree with her. But I would ask that you remember one thing."

"It pains her just as it does you, as it does me, to leave Davin to his fate," Talia sighed in resignation.

"Correct, Captain Carlomin," Sirena nodded. "Our soldiers feel the same as we do. But they understand the reality of what we face. I have no doubt that with their desire to honor the gladiator, they will remind the Fal Carrachian Guard of the folly of challenging us."

"We need to do something for him, Sirena," Talia prodded. "Davin is important to what we're doing here." She was quiet for a time, her emotions roiling within her as she acknowledged the truth that she had known for quite some time but had not until that very second had the courage to see clearly, much less reveal. "He's important to me."

"I know, Captain Carlomin," Sirena replied sadly. She had

watched what was developing between Talia and the gladiator, and she had approved of it. Unfortunately, it seemed to be coming to an end before it really even had a chance to become something more. "I'm sorry. If there is anything that we could do for Davin, we would. He is one of us now."

"You might not be able to help Davin, but we can."

Talia and Sirena spun around, startled by the voice behind them. Gravelly. Hard.

Sirena's hand gripped the hilt of her sword, ready to pull her steel free. Her eyes widened as she took in their visitors.

The grey-haired, barrel-chested man who had spoken had arms the size of tree trunks. The woman in a multicolored robe standing next to him, her wild hair sticking out in all directions, radiated a sense of power that made Sirena want to shrink in on herself.

And if they weren't frightening enough, behind them stood two of the largest men she had ever set eyes on. So big, in fact, that she doubted either could have walked through the doorway without ducking and turning to the side.

Before Sirena could pull more than an inch of her sword free from its scabbard, not understanding how these three could have gotten on the Carlomin docks without her knowing, much less into the room without her hearing them, Talia stayed her hand with a light touch.

"You heard, Magus Rafia?" Talia asked, a hint of failure in her voice, feeling responsible for Davin's fate.

"We did," she confirmed with a nod.

"You're in quite a pickle," Declan said. "No real good choices."

"It wasn't meant to be this way. Roosarian moved before we were ready. The fault is mine."

"Spilt milk," Declan said with a shrug. "Is Davin still alive?"

"I don't know," Talia replied, the words giving her an almost tangible pain.

"He is." Rafia used the Talent to locate him within the citadel, although doing so proved to be quite a challenge. The essence of the Curse proliferated throughout the Rock, making it difficult for her to see all that she wanted to see. It was as if a shadow had fallen upon the citadel, that shadow slowly becoming more substantial as the tainted power gained a stronger hold. "Hakea Roosarian is with him now."

Hearing that sent a wave of relief through Talia. Anger as well.

It seemed that Roosarian had plans for Davin. That conclusion actually worried her more than the possibility that Davin was dead.

"You heard the challenge that we face?" asked Talia.

"We did," confirmed Declan. "As I said, not many good choices."

"Any suggestions?"

"A few, but it will require that you do something that I believe will be difficult for you," Rafia murmured.

"What would that be?" Talia didn't quite understand.

"Your trust, lass," Declan answered. "If this is going to work, then you need to trust us."

"If what is going to work?"

"The odds are against you, that's true," Rafia said, "but you're well positioned to shift those odds."

"What are you talking about?" Sirena interrupted, not understanding what was being discussed.

Talia nodded, already having figured out what Declan had in mind. "You're going to make a play for Davin so that I can make a play for Roosarian. Remove Roosarian and the city is ours."

"Exactly so," Declan nodded. "The Blood Company takes care of its own."

8

SHIFTING FORTUNES

Jakob stayed within the shadows of the small village, his eyes never leaving Saraa. She knelt just fifty yards away, the soldier holding a sharp blade to her throat.

There was no way that she could see where he was. Even so, it seemed like her eyes followed him.

Because of the tears trickling down her cheeks, he expected to see fear in her gaze. But there was no fear.

Instead the most dominant emotion appeared to be resignation. That this was her fate and she was slowly coming to grips with it.

That and a hint of something else.

What could it be?

Remorse?

Why remorse?

At having been captured and throwing their plan into disarray?

Or was there some other cause?

Something more regrettable?

Jakob couldn't tell. And there was no way to get the answer

unless he spoke to Saraa. Yet that seemed an impossibility based on their current dilemma.

The smart thing to do would be to leave Saraa and the other Highlanders to their fates. He understood that.

They would understand that if that's what he decided to do. No one would challenge him, question his decision, think badly of him, if he chose to cut their losses and retreat now.

He and his Highlanders had lost the opportunity that fate had given to them. And now, as a result, that same fate was demanding some hard choices.

If he continued with their original plan, he would only be taking the Highlanders at his back deeper into the trap.

That wasn't something that he was willing to do. But he wasn't willing to leave Saraa and her squad to the soldiers of Torstan Sharperson either.

It didn't take Jakob long to make his decision.

Lycia wasn't going to be happy with the risk he was about to take. But that was all right. He was used to her not being happy with him and the decisions he made. In fact, he didn't know what he would do if she didn't always look at him with a questioning eye.

Understanding that time was of the essence, Jakob used the Talent to connect with Duff, who was exactly where Jakob expected him to be.

"They don't know you're there?"

"They don't," Duff grumbled, the strain clear in his voice even as he spoke directly into Jakob's mind. *"Don't worry about that either. It's going to stay that way. They won't see us."*

"That's good to hear. Any problems?"

"Other than having to climb a mountain for several hundred yards without being discovered and then sidling along the precipice to reach a specific location using nothing but the most basic of supplies?" pondered Duff for a time, Jakob quite easily picking up on the sarcasm infusing his aggravation. *"No."*

"I thought you liked a challenge. In fact, the more of a challenge the better. I recall you telling me that many times."

"That's true, I did. Just not on this job. Easier the better with what I'm dealing with now." Jakob heard Duff curse. He assumed that his friend had come upon an obstacle as he worked his way up the stone that was giving him more trouble than he wanted. *"Are they in the side tunnels yet?"*

"They're on their way," Jakob confirmed. *"A quarter of an hour at most. I can probably buy us some more time if necessary."*

"That wouldn't hurt. This is a harder climb than I thought it would be."

"Maybe it's because you're beginning to feel your age."

"Funny, very funny," grumbled Duff, choosing not to offer the additional colorful curses that ran through his mind. Instead, he kept his focus on continuing his struggle up the mountainside.

The climb itself wasn't as bad as he was making it out to be. The primary challenge was having to do it without being seen by anyone below him.

It hadn't taken him and his Highlanders very long to scale the southern side of the peak and reach the height they required. What was slowing them now was having to work their way across and then down to a ledge that would leave them no more than forty yards above the two side tunnels and the main entrance to the mine.

Get there, and they could do what they needed to do. So long as they got there in time and without giving themselves away.

"Now tell me what happened," ordered Duff. *"You wouldn't reach out now unless there was a problem."*

Jakob explained quickly the wrinkle in their plan.

"They knew that we were coming just as we thought."

"Yes, they did," agreed Jakob.

"But it's worse than that. They knew exactly when we were coming. Probably how many as well."

"They did."

"You know what that means." Duff grunted from the effort of slowly sliding down toward the ledge that was only twenty yards below him now.

"I do. But we can't deal with that now. It will have to wait."

"Lad, you're more important to what we're doing in the Highlands than anyone else," Duff sighed. *"What would Saraa tell you to do?"*

"To leave her to her fate."

"She would," Duff agreed. *"And she'd be right to do so. She wouldn't want you there."*

"Yes, but Duff ..."

"What did Lycia tell you to do?"

"What do you think?"

Duff sensed the frustration in Jakob's voice. He understood it. But it wasn't relevant to the decision that needed to be made. *"She's thinking clearly. You're allowing your emotions to color your decisions."*

"I don't want to leave them, Duff."

"I know you don't. Neither do I. But sometimes we need to do what we don't want to do. That's the hard part of being a leader."

"I can salvage this, Duff."

"You should be going back over the wall so that we can fight another day."

"We can fight today," Jakob replied strongly. *"We can make this work for us."*

"You shouldn't be doing this," Duff said with more heat in his voice. Stubborn lad. Then again, who was he to challenge him? If he was faced with the same decision that Jakob was grappling with, he'd likely do the same as Jakob wanted to. Still, he needed to at least try to convince him otherwise. *"I'm just one of many. I need to do this. You don't. You need to be there for the High-*

landers. This isn't a risk that you should take. We can't afford to lose you."

"If I don't do this, we don't get Saraa and the others back."

"Didn't you listen to what I just said?"

"I did."

"But you don't agree with me?"

"I do agree with you."

"I take it that you're still going to do what you believe you need to do."

"I am."

Duff finally let go of the curses that had been playing through his mind. He should have expected as much from Jakob. Strong-willed. Determined. Unwilling to leave a comrade behind. He sounded just like someone he knew, so he really couldn't fault him for his decision or his obstinance.

"All right, all right," Duff finally acquiesced. *"Do what you need to do."*

"How much time do you need?"

"An extra ten minutes wouldn't hurt."

"I'll make sure you have it."

Jakob let go of the Talent, bringing his conversation with Duff to a close. That done, he shifted his focus to Lycia, her sour expression suggesting that she already knew what he had decided.

"I need you to trust me."

REMY STOOD ONLY a few feet to the side of the soldier with the knife at the woman's throat. He was leaning slightly toward his left, preferring to not put too much weight on his right knee.

The wound had healed. Or rather the wound had healed as best as could be expected. The pain a constant reminder of the debt owed. But at least he could walk. And, more important, he could still fight.

"Come out and play, Lord Kestrel," Remy called again, his gaze wandering over the small village that stood silent before him.

From what he could see from where he was standing, the Highlanders had done a very thorough job of sweeping the parapet clear of his soldiers. But the Highlanders had not yet gone back over the wall.

They were still here.

Waiting to see what was going to happen next.

And Remy had no doubt that the reason why he was here in this remote backwater was here with him.

"With what I know of you, oh great Lord of the Highlands, I didn't expect that you would hide away from me."

Silence still.

"You hate slavers. You've taken every chance you've had to reduce the number of soldiers serving in the Highland Guard." He motioned with his arm toward the men standing behind him. "As you can see, you've got slavers and soldiers both waiting for you. Why not come out and take your chances with us?"

Remy waited only a few more seconds before continuing.

"Knowing more of you than most, I never thought that you would take the way of the coward."

The Lord Kestrel remained in the shadows. No hint of movement. Not a sound.

Remy was disappointed. He didn't think he'd have to work so hard to pry loose the so-called hero of the Highlands.

"I never thought that you would scurry back over the wall like the vermin you are."

Remy scanned the huts to his front, looking for any sign of his quarry. Nothing.

"That you would leave your friends to die."

This time Remy allowed the silence to linger for more than a minute, believing that his last barb would be the final hook that pulled free his target from wherever he was hiding in the village.

At least he hoped that it would. He had absolutely no desire to pursue the Lord of the Highlands and his fighters in the peaks that towered beyond the stockade wall. Doing that would cede back to the Highlanders all the advantages that he had taken from them.

Freedom of movement. The chance to pick and choose when they attacked. If they attacked.

No, he didn't want to deal with that. It was a losing proposition and likely would ensure that the Lord of the Highlands continued to draw breath.

Better just to kill the rebel and all his followers now.

Simple. Clean. Fast.

Particularly since he knew just how slippery the young man could be.

"Reveal yourself now or I will kill your Highlanders," Remy threatened, his impatience becoming more acute. "Don't make them sacrifice themselves for you. That's the way of the coward. The way of one undeserving of their trust."

More silence greeted him. He was beginning to think that Captain Hippolates had made a mistake by hiding the Highland Guard in the mine. If Hippolates had accepted Remy's suggestion, soldiers in the huts could have already sprung the ambush, overwhelming the Highlanders and preventing them from retreating back over the wall.

But the Captain of the Highland Guard demanded that things be done his way, even if it wasn't the best way.

Remy shook his head ever so slightly. It was because of Hippolates' arrogance and willfulness that he was where he was now. Trying to lure a skittish colt back into the corral. No, that wasn't the best analogy, Remy decided. It was more like attempting to cage a rabid beast.

"I'll start with the woman!" Remy shouted. To emphasize his point, he limped over to the Highlander and yanked her head back by her hair.

He earned a gasp from his prisoner that sent a slight, pleasant charge of warmth through his body. He glanced at her quickly before sweeping his eyes back over the small village.

She was quite attractive beneath the grime and the angry scowl. Now he really hoped the boy showed himself. If he did, then Remy might be able to have a little fun with her first before he slit her throat.

"Now, you coward!" roared Remy. "Show yourself now or I make her bleed!"

"Don't do it, Jakob!" Saraa yelled.

That's as much as she was able to get out before the soldier pressing down on her shoulder moved that hand to her hair and pulled down even harder, exposing her throat and earning a strangled hiss as his blade cut into her skin and gained a few drops of blood.

Remy assumed that would do it. The Lord of the Highlands would make himself known at the first hint of harm to one of his followers.

Yet still nothing.

Remy was getting ready to draw more blood when he noticed the uneasiness that flowed through his men. He shifted his gaze to the direction his soldiers were looking.

A tall figure with the hilt of a sword sticking up over his shoulder walked out slowly from between the cottages.

He wasn't in a rush. It was almost as if he was trying to demonstrate that he was in charge of this drama rather than Remy.

Gutsy.

Foolish as well.

Remy would correct his misinterpretation swiftly.

And he would gain his revenge.

~

"This is not a good idea, Jakob."

"It might not be, you're right."

"Then why are you doing this."

"Because I need to, Lycia," Jakob replied, having reached out with the Talent to the gladiator to ensure that all was ready. *"What would you have done in my position?"*

He heard her sigh even as she was speaking to him in his mind. *"Fine. Fine. I probably would have done the same."*

"Probably?"

"All right. I would have done the same. There's no need to belabor this."

"There you go." Before she could try to convince him one more time to turn around and go back over the wall, he focused on what was supposed to happen next. *"Is everyone in position?"*

"They are," Lycia confirmed. She had seen to the distribution of the Highlanders herself, making sure that they remained hidden from the soldiers who had turned the dirt field into a parade ground.

"Good," Jakob replied. *"Be ready. One way or the other, this ends here."*

"What do you mean this ends here? What are you talking about?"

"I didn't tell you?"

"Tell me what?" demanded Lycia, not understanding what Jakob was talking about.

"I know this slaver."

"You know this slaver?" That took Lycia by surprise. *"How do you know this slaver?"*

"That's not important right now. What is important is that there's some bad blood between us. And I mean to spill his."

"THAT'S FAR ENOUGH."

Remy scrutinized the self-proclaimed Lord of the Highlands. He would never forget those eyes of his. Bright green. Flashing when he was angry, just as they were now.

He looked older now. Not because so much time had passed since he had last seen him. It really hadn't been that long. Six months? Maybe less.

But rather because the young man seemed to have changed so drastically since Remy had last confronted him.

When Remy had tried to kill him ... and failed.

That thought made Remy pause, even though several hundred soldiers stood at his back.

He stared a bit more closely at the young man who had given him his limp. The lines around his eyes. How he held himself. His hard expression, as if a smile was a burden for him. And that scar he had acquired on his cheek. It gave him an even grimmer countenance than the one that Remy recalled glimpsing right before the now Lord Kestrel had jumped off the plateau and into the Murk.

"You." Remy really should have had something more eloquent to say, but he was still mildly shocked by the appearance of this young man, never expecting that he would walk right into the trap.

Then again, he really shouldn't have been surprised. The lad had demonstrated an overdeveloped sense of loyalty even when he was a part of the chain gang and his thoughts should have only been of himself.

"Me," Jakob replied simply, apparently unconcerned by the

several companies of the Highland Guard facing off against him or the fact that a fist of his followers would be killed if Remy gave the word.

"I guess you're not a coward after all." Remy studied the young man a little while longer, nodding the entire time, although for what reason Jakob had not a clue. "Not that smart, however. If you were smart, you wouldn't give yourself up for that lot." He motioned to the Highlanders who were at the mercy of his soldiers' blades.

"We all have our faults."

"Remove the sword," Remy ordered after he was done with his examination. "Place it on the ground."

Jakob gave Remy a sardonic look, then did as he ordered.

"Well done," Remy said with a twist of his lips. "I'm glad that you're listening now, because you listened very poorly when I had you under the whip."

"Circumstances change," Jakob said quietly. "You have to change with them."

"That they do," Remy replied. "That you do."

"Sometimes faster than you might think possible."

That last comment made Remy lift his head. A slight tinge of worry began to work its way through him.

Was Remy seeing what he wanted to see? Not what he should see?

Remy shook his head imperceptibly. The lad's Highlanders were outnumbered. He himself was about to be taken. No matter what he might try, there was no way that the Kestrel could escape the snare that Remy had set for him. Those thoughts buoying him, Remy issued his next command.

"On your knees. Hands behind your head. Fingers laced together."

Jakob stared at Remy for a few seconds, eyes flashing, his expression changing. Becoming more measured. More challenging. Even so, he did as Remy instructed.

Once Jakob settled down onto the dirt, a squad of soldiers raced forward, circling around him, their swords drawn and pointed at him. Remy took his time as he limped over to stand in front of the young man who had caused all the trouble in the Highlands. Savoring his success ... and his chance for revenge.

Even so, a niggling concern was working its way through Remy.

He had hoped that taking his quarry would be this easy. Yet he had never thought that it would be.

More concerning, the young man didn't appear to be upset about his current circumstances or as fearful as Remy believed that he should be.

If Remy was in this same situation, he would be pissing his pants. Instead, the young man radiated the feeling that he was exactly where he wanted to be.

That bothered Remy, but there was little left for him to do except complete the scene. So best to get to it.

"What do you have to say now, Lord of the Highlands?" asked Remy, enjoying the opportunity to gloat over his prisoner.

"Not much," Jakob finally replied after allowing the silence to draw out. "I'll let my steel do my talking for me."

"Take your time, Bertie," Duff hissed, reaching out and fastening a large hand on his friend's arm at the exact moment that the Highlander's feet slipped off the rockface. The mistake sent a scrabble of loose stones clattering down to the ledge that was now only twenty yards below them. Thanks to Duff, Bertie didn't go with them. "If you rush, you fall."

"I know that now," Bertie replied quietly but in an edgy voice. If he had slipped, he probably would have died, and his wife never would have forgiven him for that. Not necessarily because he had left her, he knew, but because he would have left her on her own to care for all their children. So best to take Duff's advice. "Thanks."

"It was nothing," Duff grumbled. "Now climb down to that ledge as quick and careful as you can. We need to get there before Jakob does whatever it is that he's going to do."

The only reason that Duff had been there to catch Bertie was because he had stopped his own descent, turning his gaze toward the stockade and what was happening in front of the entrance to the mine. He hadn't liked what he had seen.

Jakob was on his knees, surrounded by a cadre of itchy soldiers.

Duff should have been more worried for his friend. But he wasn't.

He knew what Jakob could do. In fact, he was almost worried for the soldiers who stared at Jakob with such arrogance. Almost.

What he had told Bertie was the truth. If they were to have any chance of success, they needed to be on that ledge before Jakob escalated what was happening down below.

That thought in mind, Duff began his descent again.

He was glad that they had almost reached the end of this odyssey. They had used steel spikes driven into the stone and a system of ropes to climb up the mountainside and then clamber across the rockface until they were in a position where they could rappel down to the ledge.

After just a few more swings away from the precipice, his feet finally settled on the narrow overhang. All the other Highlanders had gotten there before him. All except for one.

Catching a flash of movement coming down by his side, Duff reached out, grabbing Tommie around her waist and pulling her in close. She landed on the ledge, but her foot had slipped out from beneath her.

In danger of falling to the ground forty yards below, Duff caught her just in time.

"We can't have that," Duff said with a smile, giving the archer a squeeze before placing her carefully onto the shelf.

"Thanks," Tommie said, not in a rush for Duff to let go.

"We don't want to give the bastards a clue that we're here," he clarified.

Tommie rolled her eyes. She was about to offer him a saucy response when instead she yelped quietly. Duff had seen his opportunity and pinched her side.

"I don't know if I should hit you or kiss you," she said with some fire in her voice. With her feet underneath her, she pushed him away and began to work her way swiftly but carefully along the ledge so that she could get into position.

"You can do both if you want," Duff confirmed, his smile broadening, "But it will have to wait. The fun is about to start."

Duff was impressed that Jakob had identified this ledge. If not for his use of the Talent, he wouldn't have seen it. Because it was invisible when looking directly at the mountain.

The elements had carved the rock in such a way so that there was an uneven stone wall at chest height that ran along the full length of the narrow ledge. That natural construction gave Duff and his Highlanders cover from the many eyes below.

The perfect hiding place, just as Jakob had said it would be. And, it gave them the chance to look down on the three tunnels that led into the mine.

Duff was pleased to see that the Highlanders who had braved the mountainside with him were all where they were supposed to be. All of them prepared. All of them more than willing to cross blades with Sharperson's soldiers.

"Tommie, you have the archers," he whispered to the woman who crouched down next to him.

She didn't respond, just nodding so that he knew that she

had heard him. She already had her bow in hand and an arrow on the string, just as all the other archers who were situated along the ledge did.

He nodded to himself, pleased. They were ready to go. And just in time.

Because when he looked down onto the field again, his worries threatened to get the better of him. If this didn't work, the entire rebellion would collapse.

He understood why Jakob had placed himself in such a dangerous position. He just wished that he hadn't.

Duff shook his head, seeking to clear away his negative thoughts. What's done was done. Jakob's decision had made the task that Duff and the Highlanders with him needed to complete that much more important. But that didn't mean they couldn't do it.

It was just another challenge to be met. And as Jakob had said, even though he grumbled more often than not, Duff did like a good challenge.

Although it was somewhat unsettling to know that if they didn't succeed, their Lord of the Highlands was going to get his throat cut.

Duff couldn't allow that. He had put too much effort into making Jakob into the Lord Kestrel.

Besides, the young man had grown on him.

"I EXPECTED MORE FROM YOU, BOY," Remy growled. "After all you did to escape us in the Murk and then what you did at that blasted tower, now you choose to give yourself up like this?" The soldier snorted out a bark of a laugh. "I expected more spirit from you. I must say, I'm very disappointed. You're making this too easy for me."

"Sometimes you have to do what's right, Remy. Not what's

smart. Although I doubt that you would understand that. You likely haven't done what's right the moment you set foot on these shores."

"In that, you're correct, my Lord Kestrel," the soldier replied mockingly. Remy gave him a slight bow that included a flourish of his arm, although he had to stop after barely bending, his knee protesting the motion with a sharp spike of pain. "I've done what's right by me as soon as I arrived in New Caledonia. And so far, it seems to be working out."

"Is it now?" mused Jakob.

"It is."

"Have you not thought about the likelihood of dying today? Of paying the price for what you've done to so many innocent people?"

Remy scoffed, allowing his gaze to wander about the field, taking in the several companies of soldiers standing behind him. The five hardened fighters surrounding his antagonist. All the while knowing that his commander would be making his way out of the mine with another company of soldiers in the next few minutes.

"Sorry, but it never crossed my mind."

"It should," Jakob offered.

"Why is that?" chuckled Remy, enjoying the macabre discussion more than he should. Likely because he had little to fear from the so-called Lord of the Highlands and soon-to-be dead man.

If he knew nothing else about the Kestrel, it was that he wouldn't put his own people at risk before himself. He didn't have the stomach for it.

Admirable. Also stupid. And the weakness Remy had preyed upon.

"Because you're not going to be alive for much longer."

"Is that so?"

"It is," Jakob confirmed with a nod.

"And I take it that you're going to be the one doing the killing," laughed Remy.

"That I am," Jakob replied, "and I'm going to enjoy it."

"Brave words from a young man about to lose his life."

"Perhaps," Jakob replied with a shrug. "Perhaps not."

Remy chuckled again. "I appreciate your attempt at bravado, boy, but it's time to move things along. As I said, you made the wrong decision by giving yourself up. We're not about mercy." Remy nodded toward the soldiers at his back again, then motioned to the ones surrounding Jakob. "We're about getting the job done. Once we kill you, we're going to kill all your friends. Then this rebellion of yours will come to an end, and we'll rule the Highlands just as we were before you decided to make things difficult for us."

"You really believe that, do you?"

"I do," Remy confirmed with a nod. "Keep in mind that I'm a realist. I see the world as it is, which is why I've done so well since coming across the Burnt Ocean. And I see how things stand currently. You can say what you want. You're going to die, the rebellion with you."

"This rebellion is about more than just me. It's about what's right."

"Since when does what's right matter?"

"It always matters," Jakob replied with a touch of heat.

"I doubt that very much," Remy countered. "Few rebellions are about what's right. They're about power. Who's going to have that power. Who's going to exercise that power. Because of that, the only thing that matters is who has the most swords. And as you can see, we do. You and your Highlanders are fighting a lost cause."

"Really?" mused Jakob, clearly nonplussed by the fact that his death approached so rapidly. "I guess we'll have to see about that."

Tired of the conversation, Remy gave the fist of soldiers

surrounding Jakob a nod and a quick motion of his hand, telling them to get on with the grisly task for which they had been selected.

Before any of the men could take a step toward him, Jakob was already up on his feet and moving. Spinning, he launched himself at the soldier behind him. In the same motion, he pulled the haladies from the sheaths hidden on his back.

Remy had demanded that he give up his sword. That requirement didn't bother Jakob in the least. Because he had used the Talent to mask the curved, double-bladed daggers that he preferred to use in close quarters fighting.

The soldier choked and gagged, a thin line of blood opening along his throat, Jakob slicing just under his chin with a lightning-fast slash. The man's eyes widened, slowly realizing what had happened. Before he could even think to bring his hands to his scarlet throat, the soldier dropped to his knees, then fell face forward into the dirt.

The other soldiers remained rooted in place. Stunned. Having a hard time comprehending what they were seeing. Not quite able to believe that the Lord Kestrel could move so quickly.

That hesitation cost two more soldiers dearly.

Jakob didn't stop to watch the first soldier die. He continued to move, gliding across the ground as he did when combating Wraiths in the Murk. With a quick stab, his steel punched through the chest of the soldier standing to his left.

The dying man sagged to the ground as soon as Jakob pulled his blade free, the steel slicing into his lungs, the soldier unable to draw a breath.

Jakob slashed behind him next, not bothering to look, sensing rather than seeing the movement.

The soldier thought to stab Jakob in the back while he was attacking his comrade. It didn't work out as he wanted.

Instead, the soldier missed when Jakob took a half step to

the side. His inability to halt his lunge put him right in the space where Jakob's haladie already was slashing.

The result was inevitable. The soldier continued to move forward, his throat cut after the light kiss of the blade. He collapsed onto the field, gurgling softly as he slowly bled to death.

Jakob turned back around then to face Remy. The last two soldiers of the five charged with killing him still hadn't moved. Their shock and fear holding them in place.

That was the only reason they were still alive.

Remy and all the other eyes on the parade ground stared at Jakob. Except for one pair.

The soldier holding the blade to Saraa's throat.

His eyes bulged. Astonished. Appalled. Angry.

His fingers tightened, intent on killing the woman under his blade.

Without even thinking, Jakob tossed the haladie in his left hand into the air. In a flash, a small dagger slipped down from his sleeve, settling in between his thumb and his forefinger.

With a quick flick, the steel was off toward its target. And just in time as the haladie that had been spinning in the air dropped back down into his hand.

Instead of killing Saraa, the soldier stood there, seemingly rooted in place, a steady stream of blood trickling down from his destroyed eye socket. His arms fell limply to his side, his dagger dropping to the ground and his body right behind it.

Saraa closed her eyes in thanks, never expecting to survive her capture.

"You made a big mistake, Remy," Jakob explained, glaring fiercely at the man responsible for the loss that he felt every day. "You killed my father. That was bad enough. But your even bigger mistake was that you didn't kill me when you had the chance."

Before Remy could reply, Jakob sprinted toward him.

The two soldiers blocking his way took a step back in fear before realizing what they were doing. Then they stepped forward, trying to recover, swords at the ready, having eyes only for the Lord Kestrel. Not even seeing the scores of Highlanders racing out from behind the cottages, screaming at the top of their lungs, desperate to bloody their blades.

9

NEVER SIMPLE

"Wedges on me!" Lycia ordered.

The instant Jakob killed the soldier holding Saraa hostage, Lycia charged out from the shadows. The Highlanders hiding with her followed right on her heels.

Thanks to Lycia, only the Highlanders demonstrated any coordination on what in just a few heartbeats became the battlefield, employing the strategy that Jakob had put in place before he walked out from among the houses with the goal of saving Saraa and her squad.

It was a simple strategy, one that Lycia knew was going to work as soon as she smashed into the soldiers who just seconds before had been standing at attention. Because Sharperson's men had no idea what to do since their commander was focused solely on escaping the Lord of the Highlands rather than countering the Highlanders' attack.

However, Lycia understood that her adversaries' disorganization wouldn't continue for much longer, so she wanted to take advantage of their weakness while she could.

Jakob had asked her to form the hundred Highlanders into

twenty fists. Each squad was to attack Sharperson's men in the shape of a wedge. Punching into the soldiers' ragged formation and then racing backward just as fast. Then punching forward in a different spot and moving back.

Then doing it again. And again. And again.

Constantly attacking.

Each attack occurring in a different location along the line.

Sowing confusion. Creating chaos.

The soldiers, previously in ranks, swiftly dissolved into a milling mass.

Their confused response only aided the Highlanders' efforts. The soldiers tried to defend themselves against the whiplike attacks, yet more often than not they only succeeded in getting into each other's way.

For the sixth time, Lycia and her squad jabbed forward. Her twin swords were no more than blurs as she cut through the leather armor and then deep into the flesh of the soldiers to her front who didn't know whether they should stand and fight or retreat.

A soldier to her right dropped to the ground, clutching at his thigh as she pulled her blade free with the teeth-jarring scrape of steel along bone. The soldier to her left sought to take advantage of what he saw as an opportunity, lunging with his sword for Lycia's exposed gut.

But the opening the soldier glimpsed disappeared before he completed the maneuver.

Lycia pivoted on her heel, allowing the soldier's blade to pass right by her and stab into the back of one of his comrades. At the same time the soldier realized his mistake, he fell to his knees, Lycia punching her steel through his throat.

Then, just as quickly as she had advanced, she and her Highlanders scampered back, relying on their instincts, preparing to advance once again into the disorganized scrum.

During that brief moment of separation, she tried to locate Jakob. But she couldn't see him. She could only assume that he was still trying to kill the one named Remy. The one who had killed his father.

She had heard the rage in his voice.

The pain.

She grieved for Jakob's loss.

She also wanted to save him.

Because right before she and her Highlanders rushed back at the soldiers, she observed several more squads advancing out of the mouth of the mine. Apparently not all of Sharperson's companies that had been concealed beneath the mountain had made their appearance before the start of the battle.

The level of difficulty the Highlanders were facing increased exponentially as more and more soldiers emerged from the darkness.

As she slashed at the soldier to her front, Lycia could only hope that Duff had gotten to where he needed to be. Otherwise, she and the Highlanders with her were going to be overwhelmed quickly.

"Ready, lads?"

"You're going first?" asked Martin.

He, Bertie, and Duff were perched on the edge of the narrow overhang, weapons strapped to their backs, each one holding onto a rope that they hoped was long enough so that they could slide and swing down the forty-yard drop without killing themselves.

"I am," Duff confirmed.

"Why you?" Martin demanded.

"Why not me?" Duff didn't understand his friend's question.

"It's always you who's the first to take risks," Martin explained. "You did it when Benyen's Mari was lost in the Murk."

"Because you both have families," Duff replied calmly, which had been the same response that he had given when he had snuck into the fog to find his goddaughter, coming across several Wraiths along the way. "I don't. If something happens, there's no one to cry over me."

"So what if you don't have a family?" Bertie scoffed. "You don't think that Tommie would cry if you slipped and fell?"

"I don't know," Duff replied. He and Tommie had grown closer, but he really hadn't given much thought to it. "I hadn't really considered that possibility."

"Maybe you should." Martin gave his friend an arced eyebrow.

"Do we really need to talk about this now?" demanded Duff, his focus on the battle below him.

"It's as good a time as any," said Bertie. "You need to stop being the one to take all the risks. Not just because of Tommie, but also because you're so important to Jakob and what we're trying to do."

"I'm a Highlander. Just because I have some additional responsibilities doesn't mean I'm going to stop being who I am."

Duff shrugged. He looked back over his shoulder, taking in the bedlam that Jakob had set off. It was almost time for them to begin their part in the clash.

"We're no different than you, Duff," Martin explained, "and we have responsibilities as well. You don't have to step up for us at times like this."

"I just thought that you would appreciate the gesture," Duff replied. He took another quick glance back over his shoulder. Lycia had led the Highlanders out from the village, and they were causing a great many problems among Sharperson's Guard. He was beginning to think that Jakob's harebrained scheme might actually work.

"We do," Bertie and Martin both confirmed at the same time.

"Well, if I've offended you, then you're both welcome to go before me," Duff offered. "Because if you're done busting my gut, we need to get moving."

Both Highlanders, one on each side of Duff, gave the other a long look. Then they nodded in unison, having reached their decision.

"We don't want to get in your way," Bertie said.

"Right," Martin confirmed. "You can go first. We'll be right behind you."

"Seriously? After all that?"

Both Bertie and Martin nodded again, giving him broad smiles.

"Of course you will," Duff grumbled, shaking his head in aggravation. "Just don't wait too long."

Before he had spoken his last word, Duff was gone, pushing himself off the ledge, rappelling down the mountainside. Right before he reached the top of the tunnel, he pushed off the stone hard with his feet, swinging away from the rock.

His timing was excellent.

A soldier pushed his way through the narrow tunnel, unprepared for the greeting he received.

Duff slammed into him from the side as he swung through the air. Feet pulled tight to his chest, he kicked out. When he connected with the soldier's gut and sternum, he sent him flying through the air.

The soldier landed with a resounding thud on the rough ground, the wind knocked out of him. Scarcely able to gasp for breath, before the man could even think to push himself up to his feet, Duff was there.

Dropping down from the rope, he pulled his hammer free from the harness across his back. When the soldier's uncovered head met the steel head of Duff's hammer, the hammer won.

Duff turned around quickly, hearing the curses being flung his way.

Several more soldiers had worked their way through the narrow side tunnel. Swords drawn, they were coming for him with blood in their eyes.

They should have learned from what had happened to their dead comrade. But they hadn't.

They had the advantage in numbers.

They were ready.

They thought that they had an easy kill.

Before the pair could take another step, however, Martin and Bertie came flying through the air. Each from a different direction, crashing into a soldier and sending him onto his back.

The Highlanders were just as efficient as Duff, killing their adversaries before they could get back to their feet.

That task complete, Martin and Bertie raced over to Duff, who stood in front of the entrance to the tunnel.

He was swinging his hammer wildly, although with little effectiveness. Less concerned about hitting stone or bone. More concerned about ensuring that the stream of soldiers who were trying to emerge out of the narrow passageway didn't see the light of day.

For the first time, Duff's overlarge hammer wasn't giving him the success that he had grown accustomed to. The weapon didn't work well in confined spaces.

The soldier trying to break out of the tunnel kept jabbing at him with his longsword, forcing him back several feet. If the man pushed Duff back just a few feet more, then the soldier would make it out of the mountain as would the long line of men behind him.

Duff swung one more time, seeking to knock the blade from the soldier's hand. No such luck.

The soldier pulled backward, allowing the steel head of the hammer to slam into the side of the mountain and knock away a good-sized chunk of stone.

While Duff struggled with his stuck hammer, the soldier lunged. Duff got his weapon free just in time, but he had no choice. He had to step back from the entrance.

Right before the soldier trotted out of the darkness, looking forward to his combat with the scarred Highlander, Bertie and Martin were there. They both preferred swords during a fight, but understanding what would be required of them, they had selected shortened spears that were as long as they were tall. Anything longer would have put their efforts to get down from the ledge at risk.

They stabbed at the same time, their spears puncturing the unsuspecting soldier's shoulder and belly.

The man dropped to the ground, moaning in agony, sword caught beneath him.

Bertie and Martin ignored the dying soldier, stabbing into the darkness with their spears with a rhythm known only to them.

The soldiers in the tunnel held their ground. They couldn't get at the Highlanders, their swords unable to compete with the spears stabbing toward them. And, worse for the soldiers, because of the narrowness of the tunnel, only one could face off against the Highlanders at a time.

A losing proposition for the soldiers to begin with, as that gave an unfair advantage to Bertie and Martin that they were more than happy to make use of.

When the second soldier in line collapsed to the ground, Bertie punching his steel into the man's groin and giving the spear a twist for good measure before pulling the bloody, gore-stained weapon free, it became even harder for the soldiers behind the two at the front to get much farther through the roughhewn corridor.

To attack Bertie and Martin, the soldiers first needed to drag the two dying men out of the way.

The Highlanders refused to make that an easy task for them. They stabbed at any sign of movement, wanting to keep their obstacle constructed of the dead in place.

The soldiers should have thought ahead. None of them had a crossbow. None of them had a spear. But they never believed that they would be discovered.

A deadlock, Duff realized.

He grinned broadly, more than pleased.

Martin and Bertie could hold this tunnel for as long as necessary so long as no one attacked them from behind.

Feeling more confident now, Duff glanced to the side. The three Highlanders assigned to the tunnel on the other side of the main opening to the mine were having just as much success as they were.

Excellent work all around.

If they could keep it up, and there was no reason they couldn't with the Highlanders coming down the ropes protecting the backs of Bertie, Martin, and the other men charged with bottling up the side tunnels, then the only threat to Jakob and his Highlanders could come from the main tunnel.

And there was the rub.

Because judging by the fight raging just a few dozen yards away, Jakob and his company were facing dire circumstances that only seemed to worsen as more squads of soldiers raced out of the mountain.

～

LYCIA STEPPED TO THE SIDE, unconcerned by the steel that cut past her by no more than the width of a knuckle. She needed her attacker close if she was going to do what she had in mind.

Off balance because of the power of his swing, the soldier was caught completely off guard when Lycia sliced across the small of his back with the sword in her right hand. Then, continuing with her spinning motion, she cut through the air with the sword in her left hand, slashing through the space behind the wounded soldier who already had collapsed to the ground.

Most of the time when she was with Jakob, she was confused. She didn't understand why. She just knew that there was some aspect to the green-eyed Highlander with the dry wit that kept her off balance. And not necessarily in a bad way.

But that wasn't her concern now. She wasn't confused when they fought together. When steel was drawn, there was a connection between them that she relished.

They knew what the other was going to do before they did it, and they adjusted accordingly. Just as they were doing now as they sought to eliminate the several hundred disorganized soldiers standing in front of the mine before those men realized that despite the ferocity of the Highlanders' assault, they still enjoyed a numerical superiority that could spell the end of the Highlanders.

After killing the two soldiers who blocked his path toward Remy, Jakob reluctantly delayed his hunt. Forced to fight his way through the milling mass of soldiers to reach the man responsible for his father's death, he fell in next to Lycia. Leaving the sword that he had acquired from the slaver where it lay, he used his double-bladed daggers with a bloody and deadly intent.

Slashing and cutting, Jakob took down one soldier with a slice across his knee that was so deep that it cracked the bone. Leaving the screaming man in the dirt, knowing that he wouldn't be getting back up, Jakob shifted his attention to the soldier who stepped into his path by mistake.

The man was terrified. Clearly, he had no desire to face off against him.

Good. Jakob was happy to see that. It simply made his job that much easier.

The frightened soldier didn't even bother to swing the sword he held in his hand. Instead, taking in Jakob's blazing green eyes, he stumbled backward, tripping over one of his dead comrades.

Shaking, tears streaking down his cheeks, the soldier tried to get up so that he could find some avenue for escape. He only succeeded in making it back to the seat of his pants.

Jakob punched one of his blades through the man's right eye. The soldier remained in place until he pulled the steel free, the dead man dropping to the ground with all of his many other comrades who had met a bloody end at the hands of the Highlanders.

For just a second, a small space opened up around him. Jakob looked to the right. Saraa was back in the thick of the fight, her rage plain for all to see. She had taken the sword from the soldier who had held the knife at her throat and was wielding it with an almost manic rage.

The man was dead when she pulled it free from the scabbard on his hip. Nevertheless, she stabbed him in the throat to prove a point before she joined the battle, her squad right behind her.

Some of the Highlander fists continued to employ the tactic that proved so effective at the start of the battle, one squad after another stabbing into the soldiers' ranks before stepping back and shifting the focus of their attack.

Unfortunately, that was happening less and less now. And not unexpectedly. As time passed the clash degenerated into more of a wild melee.

Jakob wanted to exercise more control over the fight, but that was going to be a challenge at best ... if not impossible altogether. He needed to pull back all the Highlanders and get them into a shield wall. However, the current tempo of the battle wasn't allowing for that.

At least with Duff holding the side tunnel, it would remain an even fight for a little while longer. The Highlanders' discipline, decisive action, and determination allowed them to not only hold their own against the soldiers, but also to push them back toward the mine, clogging the already tight space.

And, even more important to Jakob, of the large number of dead littering the ground, only a handful of Highlanders were among them.

A good start to the battle, but it was only the start. There was more to come with this drama. Much more.

Only some of the soldiers who had been hiding in the mine had come out onto the field when Saraa and her squad were captured. The rest of those soldiers were doing so now.

That meant that the Highlanders were even more heavily outnumbered, which only served to increase the risk that he and his comrades faced.

But that was all right. Jakob wanted to draw as many of the soldiers to the main entrance as possible. Because that's where he wanted to concentrate his attack.

And, with this latest company of soldiers emerging from the darkness, he could employ his hidden weapon, which he hoped would turn the tide of the battle.

"Tommie?" he asked, speaking with the archer through his use of the Talent.

"We're here," she replied.

"Good. Whenever you're ready."

"Oh, we're ready," Tommie replied, how she said it making Jakob think that she was salivating at the thought of what was going to happen next. *"We are definitely ready."*

Jakob cut his link to Tommie as soon as the arrows started streaking down from the ledge just above the entrance to the mine, the soldiers racing out into the light not knowing what hit them when they slammed face first into the dirt.

DUFF ALLOWED MARTIN and Bertie to do their work while he did his. Swinging his hammer in wide arcs, he prevented the soldiers who advanced out of the main tunnel from unstopping the side tunnel he had claimed as his own.

If that happened, the soldiers working their way along the base of the mountain stood a good chance of not only flanking, but also surrounding the Highlanders.

Duff couldn't permit that. If that happened, then the rebellion would die here, along with all of them.

Duff brought his hammer up to his chest, both hands on the handle, one toward the knob, the other closer to the head. And just in time.

The shriek of metal scraping across metal strangely soothed him.

He blocked the blade that would have split his head in two. The soldier who attempted the killing blow, bigger than any man Duff had ever laid eyes on, stared at him in confusion, never expecting Duff to move so fast or have the strength to prevent his sword from cutting into his scalp.

Even so, the soldier's eyes gleamed brightly, apparently pleased to finally have a challenge. Viewing his first failed attack as nothing more than a temporary setback, with both hands on the hilt of his sword, the soldier pushed down with all his strength.

Duff recognized the danger immediately. Muscles flexing, veins bulging, the Highlander attempted to keep the blade, which was inching closer and closer to his nose, from reaching its target.

If that steel touched his flesh, then the combat would be over for him.

Calling on the very last reserves of his strength to keep the blade in place for just a few heartbeats more, Duff did the only thing that he could. With a burst of unexpected speed and power, he brought his knee up with as much force as he could muster.

The gargantuan fighter groaned in agony when Duff's knee connected with his groin. His eyes going wide, nonetheless the soldier didn't move. The giant remained in place, refusing to allow the Highlander to escape him despite the waves of nausea rolling through him.

Duff grumbled in anger as his towering opponent continued to press down with his sword. Slowly, the steel cut closer and closer to the tip of Duff's nose. There seemed to be nothing that he could do to prevent his death.

The man stared wild-eyed at him, seemingly relishing the pain that Duff had inflicted upon him. Allowing it to fuel him.

Duff redoubled his efforts, calling on whatever reserve of hidden strength remained to him. But it was no use.

The giant was too big for him. Too strong.

He couldn't hold back the sword for much longer.

The soldier was tougher than Duff had thought.

So be it.

It was time to find out just how tough this man truly was.

Duff's first attempt hadn't staggered the soldier in any way, but remembering the mantra that his mother had ingrained within him, if at first you don't succeed, try, try again.

Duff employed the only tactic that he had left with a manic desperation. He drove his knee into the soldier's groin with a repetitiveness that was astounding both for its regularity and its force.

Finally, after the fourth blow, the giant began to waver. First, the man's eyes slowly lost focus, a thin stream of spittle running down his lips. Then, as the giant weakened, Duff finally able to push the blade away from him, the soldier released an agonized whimper that more resembled a squeak.

The soldier tried to keep his feet, knowing what would happen if he didn't. But he couldn't. Not with it feeling as if his crushed testicles now resided in his stomach.

The soldier began to slide to the side when Duff brought his knee up one more time, just to make sure, the giant no longer able to stand against the intense pressure and pain.

His steel scraping angrily across the haft of the hammer, Duff aided the giant in his descent, twisting away and allowing the hulking soldier to crumple to the ground.

The giant moaned unintelligibly, burying his face into the dirt as the strings of spittle coming from his mouth lengthened.

He knew he was dead. He knew what the Highlander was going to do next.

And Duff would have finished him just as the man expected, ready to do so, needing only to bring the head of his hammer to his shoulder. He didn't have the chance, however. He had a more important matter to address.

"Donal! Arry! Stay with Martin and Bertie. Protect their backs. You need to keep the tunnel bottled up."

Duff didn't wait for the Highlanders to reply. The men he left in place should be able to hold the side tunnel. But it wouldn't matter in the end if the Highlanders lost the larger fight.

With the company of soldiers now emerging from the main entrance to the mine, Duff recognized just how serious the situation had become. He couldn't allow these reinforcements to join the fight without an appropriate welcome. It was the only way to ensure that they were made to work for their victory.

"The rest of you with me," Duff called over his shoulder. "We fight our way to the Highland Lord!"

He didn't think they would get that far. The melee in front of him would be too much for them to reach the other side of the battlefield.

Still, it had seemed like the right thing to say at a time like that, in large part because he couldn't think of anything else. Besides, every one of the men and women with him would do anything they could to aid Jakob. He had done more for them already than any of them had thought possible.

They owed a debt to him. In their minds, one that could never be repaid. Even so, that didn't mean they wouldn't try.

Just as he feared, Duff and his small band of Highlanders only made it ten yards before they were engulfed in the maelstrom of fighters battling in front of the mine.

Nevertheless, their efforts served a critical purpose. They prevented the soldiers from breaking out of the shaft.

The Highlanders were able to form a thin ring of steel around the soldiers except for a few pockets of fighting beyond the larger fray, one of those being Jakob's combat.

Duff was satisfied. They had done better than he anticipated.

And now they had a simple goal in mind.

Keep the soldiers in place, even push them back into the darkness if they could. Just don't allow them to force their way into the light.

For the next several minutes, the battle raged. The soldiers loyal to Governor Sharperson struggling to get beyond the ragged shield wall. The Highlanders refusing to yield.

How much longer the stalemate would continue, Duff couldn't say.

He needed some other solution before the inevitable breach occurred.

But he needed to deal with more immediate threats first.

Two in fact.

A pair of soldiers who had just emerged from the mine were advancing toward him, intent on vengeance after he dispatched one of their comrades with a sickening smack to the man's head.

Normally, Duff wouldn't have been concerned. But these two knew what they were doing.

One of the men forced Duff to concentrate on him. That allowed the other one to stab at him from the side. Not in a rush. Waiting for one good opportunity to bury his sword between Duff's ribs.

This was not the kind of combat that Duff wanted to engage in.

Several times the soldier attacking from the side almost succeeded.

Duff only saved himself by pivoting out of the way an instant before the man's steel sliced into his flesh. But he couldn't keep doing this. Eventually, his luck would run out.

Duff understood that if he didn't shift the tenor of the fight in his favor, then he was a dead man.

This pair knew how to fight. They knew what they were doing. It was only a matter of time before they achieved their goal.

Those concerns driving him, Duff swung his hammer in a tight arc toward his left and the soldier who kept pestering him from that side.

The man danced backward, easily avoiding the blow. However, he wasn't Duff's primary target.

Duff checked his swing midway through, then shifted his weight swiftly, stepping toward the soldier to his front. Instead of swinging, he punched forward with the head of his hammer.

The soldier who had been working to keep Duff in the same position was taken by surprise, never expecting such a maneuver. Nevertheless, he was fast enough to get his head out of the way right before the jab cracked his skull, the hammer instead striking his left shoulder.

A heavy blow. The soldier's broken collarbone screamed at him.

Ignoring the pain of his injury, bringing his loosely hanging arm in tight to his body, the soldier sought to regain the initiative. He slashed for the Highlander's already scarred scalp, hoping to slice right across the old wound.

A smart and fast tactic. It wasn't enough, however.

Duff raised his hammer just in time. Although he blocked the blow, he cursed himself for failing to move fast enough.

He had wanted to knock the soldier to his front out of the fight with his punch. He hadn't, the soldier more resilient than he anticipated. All Duff had done was gain a few seconds, and he had wasted them.

Because the soldier with the damaged shoulder ignored his pain. Refusing to leave the fight, he forced Duff to remain engaged with him. And the man's grit gave the soldier's comrade the chance that he had been waiting for.

The second soldier, who dodged out of the way of Duff's feint, rushed toward him from the side, preparing to drive his steel through his back.

There was nothing that Duff could do to stop him. If he turned away the soldier he had wounded would take off his head.

All he could do was stand there and receive the blow. All he could hope for was that it didn't kill him outright and that at least he'd have a chance to kill one of these bastards before he died himself.

Yet instead of feeling the burn of the blade as it cut through his flesh, he heard a grunt of startlement right in his ear.

Not understanding what had occurred, he looked over his shoulder.

The soldier who had been about to kill him was lying on the ground, an arrow protruding from the back of his neck.

Quickly, not wanting to give the wounded soldier to his front the chance to strike at him, he looked up at the ledge. Then he smiled.

As he held the wounded soldier's blade in place against the haft of his hammer, Duff felt a surge of welcome adrenaline flow through him now that he had escaped death at least for a little while longer.

"Thank you," he mouthed, locking eyes with Tommie. The archer stood on the ledge, giving him a broad grin.

There was something else there as well that was quite obvious in her expression. Like she believed that he owed her now.

Duff would be the first to admit that he did.

Tommie nodded, then gave him a wave with her bow. She was back in the fight just a heartbeat later, another arrow already on her string as she looked for her next target.

Hearing the grunt to his front, he shifted his attention back to the injured soldier facing off against him.

The man was struggling now, unable to compete with Duff's greater strength. Duff pushing the soldier's blade away from him.

Duff smiled viciously. The soldier had just realized that he couldn't win this combat. Not without the help of his dead friend.

Too bad for him.

To seize the initiative, Duff used the same tactic as he had against the giant who towered above him. He brought his knee up in a swift motion.

Caught by surprise, the soldier grunted in shock and agony as his strength fled. Unable to draw any air into his lungs, he didn't have the breath to scream when Duff slammed his hammer into the side of his head.

Grunting in satisfaction, Duff stepped back then. He needed a second to get a feel for the battlefield.

It hadn't changed much since he was attacked except for the fact that there now was just a single, small pocket of fighting on the other side of the Highlander shield wall, the combatants so intent upon one another that they had little recognition of what was going on around them.

Jakob stood in the center of that small ring of fighters. Lycia was right next to him, holding back the soldiers seeking to come at him from the side and the rear.

He and Lycia were trying to break free from the noose. Although they weren't enjoying much success.

Duff corrected his initial assessment just a moment later.

Neither of them appeared to be all that concerned about their present circumstances. Rather, it seemed as if they wanted the soldiers to continue to attack them.

Because Jakob's goal wasn't to break free. It was to get past the few soldiers in his way so that he could kill the man who had taunted him.

Duff knew how that engagement was going to play out, even though the soldiers had yet to reach that same conclusion.

Believing that Jakob had matters well in hand, Duff shifted his focus to the larger battle.

The Highlanders continued to push into the mass of soldiers, more than anything else to prevent them from remembering that they still had the advantage in numbers.

He was pleased to see that what they were doing was working. Especially since every push forward by the Highlanders never failed to draw blood.

A good result.

How much longer they could keep it up ... well, that would all depend on when Jakob's combat ended.

The Highlanders had done an excellent job of preventing the soldiers from breaking out along the flanks and coming at them from the rear. However, if that was to continue, then they needed to adopt a new strategy that would allow them to counter the last company of soldiers joining the fight.

IF HE WAS FIGHTING by himself, Jakob might have been concerned by the fact that he was surrounded by a squad of soldiers.

But he wasn't.

Because he had Lycia at his side.

She understood why he was there, putting himself at risk in this way.

She understood why he was so intent on killing Remy.

And she was doing everything that she could to ensure that he had the chance to do what was necessary to accomplish his objective.

"You're going to make your men fight for you, Remy?" Jakob demanded.

He stepped back, avoiding a rushed slash from the soldier standing right to his front. Then he ducked and pivoted, knocking into Lycia's hip. Thankfully not hard enough to throw her off stride as she parried the sword slicing toward her neck.

"I have no reason to cross blades with you, boy," Remy replied with a bite of venom. "Not when my men will kill the Lord of the Highlands for me."

Remy brandished the sword in his hand, but he made no move to join the fracas. For that to happen, Jakob was going to have to force the issue and give him a reason to assume the associated risk.

"Still afraid of me, Remy?" He hoped that goading the man might work. "Worried that I'll cut into your one good leg as I did the one you can barely stand on now?"

"I've never been afraid of you," hissed Remy, his eyes burning with hate.

Even so, he made no move to push past the two soldiers fighting in front of him. He seemed quite content where he was. Safe from the steel that blurred in front of him.

Jakob pivoted, allowing a sword to slide right by his hip. Digging his back foot into the dirt, he kicked forward with his left leg. His boot smashed into the exposed soldier's knee, bending the joint backward at an awkward angle.

Hearing the satisfying crunch of breaking bone and tearing ligaments, Jakob continued to advance. The injured soldier sagged, the pain of his injury radiating through his entire body. So much so that when Jakob slashed across the man's throat with his bone-white steel, he barely felt it.

"You should be afraid of me, Remy." Jakob gave him a nasty grin. "Very afraid."

One soldier down. Just one more to go.

With Lycia keeping the other soldiers around them busy by demonstrating why she had earned the name the Crimson Devil, Jakob didn't have to worry about anyone trying to come at him from behind.

He would have liked to have watched Lycia as she battled the three soldiers who were still alive.

Two, he corrected. Jakob assumed that the strangled gurgle that he heard resulted from Lycia slashing across the throat of a soldier who had gotten too close to her.

"You don't scare me, boy!" Remy grumbled in anger and humiliation. "You never have." His words sounded hollow even in his own ears.

"That was the mistake you made, Remy," Jakob replied as he stalked toward the last soldier standing in front of him.

Clearly, the man was nervous as he slid backward slowly, raggedly weaving his sword in front of him. The soldier had watched too many of his comrades die not to be.

Right before the soldier bumped into Remy, the man rushed forward, swinging his sword in an incoherent pattern. He didn't target any particular part of Jakob's body. He just wanted to keep his steel between him and the young man who claimed to be the Lord of the Highlands.

Jakob allowed the desperate soldier to tire himself out. For every slash and slice, Jakob had an answer, always getting a dagger in the way. Or, more often than not, simply stepping out of the way.

"Kill him, Torrie!" Remy demanded. "Kill the usurper!"

That order gave Torrie an extra burst of energy. It didn't last long, and it didn't help him.

Torrie roared something incomprehensible, trying to lose himself in the combat. He only succeeded in making himself unwisely believe that blind fury could defeat calculated effort.

Torrie learned his lesson swiftly and with a devastating finality when he overextended himself on a lunge.

Instead of stepping out of the way as had been his practice, Jakob stepped to the side and then forward, one of his daggers held out to the front on a forty-five degree angle.

He didn't need to stab with the blade. In fact, he didn't even have to move his hand.

Torrie's momentum took him right onto the steel, the blade piercing his heart.

The dying soldier looked at Jakob for several seconds, not quite understanding what had happened, before sliding off the steel and falling to the dirt.

Jakob looked up then, locking eyes with his chief antagonist.

There was no one standing between him and Remy any longer.

Nevertheless, he hesitated for just a second. Not hearing the familiar ring of steel striking steel behind him, he worried about his partner.

"He's all yours," Lycia said quietly, her words in his ear. "Make it quick. We have other work to do."

Jakob didn't bother to turn around. Lycia had dispatched the soldiers at his back. Just as he expected that she would.

He simply gave her a nod, then strode toward the man responsible for his father's death.

"It looks like it's just you and me, Remy."

There was no malice in Jakob's tone.

Only certainty.

A certainty that the slaver was going to die.

10

A DANGEROUS GAME

Ursina listened with only half an ear to the conversation flowing around her. She wasn't very interested in Aislinn and Kendric reminiscing about their time in the Southern Marches.

In large part because she preferred to forget about her time in Caledonia. Better to think of the future rather than focus on the past.

That was why she was so intrigued by the Protector who sat by Aislinn's side.

Ursina studied him out of the corner of her eye, not wanting to draw his attention. Not yet.

She sensed the power within Aislinn and her Protector. Both were exceptionally strong in the Talent.

In the gladiator, however, resided another power. A stronger power. An energy that she could detect but could not touch. An energy that she didn't understand.

She didn't like that. Not knowing.

She desperately needed to know what that power hidden within him was. What it allowed him to do. What it might be able to do for her.

When she resided in Haven, she explored the different energies infused within the Realms. The Talent. The Curse. Spirit. The Light itself. So many others thought lost but likely just dormant. Yet Ursina recalled nothing that explained what this unique energy that surged through the Protector was.

It had an ancient feel to it. That's all that she could determine. And that failure on her part frustrated her more than she was willing to admit to herself.

She pulled her gaze back toward Kendric, who was telling some silly story about Aislinn when she was a child, when the Protector's eyes moved toward her.

She didn't want to reveal her interest. Not until she was ready to deal with him.

The Protector's gaze slipped right by her and across the dozens of daggers that her husband had put on display.

Her eyes narrowed for just a breath, a trace of worry wiggling its way through her. She really shouldn't have been surprised, yet for some unknowable reason the Protector's point of focus concerned her.

The Protector's eyes kept falling on the prize of her husband's collection. The gift that she had given to him.

She had thought it best to hide the artifact in plain sight. Perhaps that had been a mistake.

The weapon was fixed to the wall behind Kendric's desk, gleaming brightly as it reflected the fading light of the day that streamed through the window behind her guests.

She could understand why the Protector was so captured by the eye-catching artifact.

A single dagger made of three footlong dirks melded to a circular guard, a notch in the very center reserved for a jewel of unimaginable power.

A jewel lost decades before that she had failed to acquire when she had the chance.

Her failure still haunted her. Dagger already in her possession, by the time she found the vault, the jewel was gone. Someone had beaten her to it.

Thankfully, at the time, that had been enough for her Master. But he was growing restless, and that in turn was making her restless. Frightened as well, although she worked hard to keep that emotion she so hated under control.

If the provenance for the weapon was accurate, and Ursina had no reason to believe that it wasn't, the Giants of the Rime had forged the Blood Dagger. A weapon like many others crafted at that time. An amplifier for the Talent to be employed against the servants of the Curse.

Or so it was said.

As she had learned, history and myth mixed more easily with each passing year.

Ursina berated herself silently for allowing herself to become distracted, shifting her gaze back to her husband, pretending that she was interested in the story he was telling about his brother.

Aislinn Winborne seemed like a lovely young woman. Nevertheless, Ursina understood quite well that appearances could be deceiving.

She had little doubt that the heir to the Southern Marches had come to the Northern Territory for a reason other than just her stated desire to see New Caledonia for herself.

Aislinn Winborne was hiding something. Ursina just didn't know what yet.

Ursina had reminded her husband of that fact. Much to her irritation, he seemed to have forgotten what they had discussed so many times prior to his niece's arrival.

Kendric argued that the young woman was family. She deserved to be treated as such.

Ursina hadn't challenged him, not wanting to waste her breath. Kendric would come around to her perspective. She would make sure of that.

Niece she may be, but Ursina considered the young woman a threat until they discovered her true intentions.

One threat at a time, however.

For the moment, Aislinn Winborne would have to wait. Ursina needed to focus on the greater peril as she mulled what she had learned just hours before.

Her attempt to assassinate the Wraith who is not a Wraith had failed.

She knew no more than that. Her admittedly poor connection to the tool set to that task gone.

Perhaps in the end she would achieve her objective. The hunt continued and would continue until either all her hunters were dead or their quarry. So though it would be difficult for her, she would wait to see how the chase concluded.

Still, that shocking initial setback aggravated her. Primarily because she had never believed that such a thing could happen. Also because she never handled failure well since it was so rare for her.

Yet even more than that, learning that the Skath had been delayed in searching for the Wraith who is not a Wraith filled her with a sense of dread.

She and Kendric had fought the Wraiths since those monsters had first appeared with the Murk more than a year before. Ursina had concluded quickly that they stood little chance of holding Shadow's Reach when the Wraiths came in force.

And they would. It was only a matter of when.

Thus her decision to lead Kendric down a particular path. To seek to placate rather than fight.

It was the only option that she believed was open to them after their lack of success at killing one of the monsters in the mist.

Even so, the Wraith Hunter had confused her. She had

never met a creature like that before. There was a coldness within him that she couldn't quite understand.

So unconcerned about his own death. Concerned only about meeting the needs of the Wraith Lord.

Nor could she comprehend why the Wraith Hunter was so intent on finding the Wraith who is not a Wraith.

Having no other recourse, she had set several stratagems in motion to remove the one so nettlesome to the Wraiths, including her Master's Disciple.

Since then ... nothing.

More worrisome, she no longer had a sense of where the Skath was.

She did not know if her Master's Disciple had found the Wraith who is not a Wraith. And if the Skath had located the target, she did not know what had occurred.

She was still in the dark and feared that she might remain so. As her mother had said all too frequently, the maxim becoming a part of her own lexicon, Ursina didn't like not knowing what she didn't know.

Ursina needed to unmask this Wraith who is not a Wraith and serve him up on a platter to the Wraith Hunter.

It was the best, perhaps the only, chance that she and her husband had for maintaining their grip on the Northern Territory.

But how was she to do that now? She had few other choices for attending to this matter.

When the Wraith Hunter returned to the north with the Murk, Ursina concluded that there was no other way to achieve the objective set by that monster.

She realized that she needed help.

She had reached out to her true Master.

Her Master could give her whatever information she desired. Whatever power that she required. If he was willing to grant it to her.

She had asked her Master for both information and power. She had wanted to conduct the hunt herself. Certain that she was the only one who could bring it to a successful conclusion.

Her Master had been willing to provide the information. No more than that, unfortunately.

If she wanted the power that she believed would allow her to throw back the Wraiths when they next attacked Shadow's Reach, her Master required that she complete the original task, the more pressing assignment, that he had given her.

The task that was so critical to her Master's success.

That had burdened her for decades.

Do that, and her Master would gift her the power she required.

Her Master cared nothing for the Wraith who is not a Wraith. Her Master cared only that she locate the Bearer of the Blood Ruby. Once that jewel was found, joined with the dagger that she was staring at, the two artifacts combined into one would give her Master the chance for vengeance that he had craved since his banishment to the Spirit World.

Thanks to the information granted to her by her Master, she had found the scent of the Bearer of the Blood Ruby. She had learned as well something else that was quite surprising.

The Bearer of the Blood Ruby and the Wraith who is not a Wraith were one and the same. How that could be the case, why that would be the case, she did not know.

She did know that to challenge her Master in any way, to question the information provided by him, would mean her death.

Her Master was not known for his patience. Forgiveness anathema to him.

Ursina kept quiet, hating all the while the fact that the more she learned, the less she seemed to know. Another characteristic that she had acquired from her mother.

She had sent the Skath her Master gifted to her for this

mission after the Wraith who is not a Wraith who was also the Bearer of the Blood Ruby.

She would have preferred to go after her Master's prey herself, but he had forbidden it. He didn't trust her. He only trusted one of his Disciples for such a critical task.

That scathing insult had angered her, yet there was nothing that she could do other than accept her Master's decision.

Meeting the Skath to give the monster the Bearer's scent had chilled her to the bone. During the few minutes she had spoken with the creature, it felt as if she had walked into a crypt that had been sealed for thousands of years, the mustiness of the tomb covering every inch of her body in a thick layer of decay that still remained with her.

She had thought that after all that she had been forced to deal with in her life, all that she had done, some of it by choice, much of it forced upon her, that she couldn't feel such terror any longer.

She was wrong.

She had experienced a dread upon speaking with the Skath that she would never forget and that she never wanted to feel again.

The potency that creature exercised ...

So enticing ...

So terrifying.

What could have happened to her Master's Disciple?

One of the Dread Lords of the Spirit World, the Skath exercised a power that few could even comprehend. There was nothing that could stand against the creature.

She did not know if the Skath had located its target.

She did not know where the Skath had gone.

She did not know if the Skath would return.

She did know whether the trail that led to the Bearer remained in play.

From that was she to assume that the Bearer was dead and

that the Skath had returned to the Spirit World with its prize, ignoring her request to bring her the head of the Wraith who is not a Wraith?

Ursina growled softly. She didn't know. That was what was bothering her so much. Not knowing. If she didn't know what was going on, she couldn't do anything.

She felt helpless, and that was a feeling that grated on her.

Still, she didn't think the Skath would do that.

She assumed that if the Skath had claimed the Blood Ruby, the monster would have come for the Blood Dagger as well. Only with the two artifacts combined into a single weapon could her Master return to the Natural World from which he had been expelled.

A day that Ursina yearned for. Because she had no doubt that she would be rewarded for her service, having played a key part in her Master's release.

Until then, however, she had other matters to deal with.

To start, she needed to confirm her place in the coming world and that of her husband. Because she was not the only one vying for the favor of her Master.

She paused her musings for a moment.

She had thought the Skath an unstoppable force.

But could it be that the Bearer of the Blood Ruby had escaped? Perhaps even defeated the Skath?

That did not seem possible, yet if that monstrous creature had achieved its assigned task, would not her Master have summoned her by now?

To give her the power that he had promised her?

The power that she could use against the Wraiths to drive them from the Northern Territory and back into the Wyld once and for all.

Why hadn't the Skath come for the Blood Dagger?

That question annoyingly kept playing through her mind. Yet she had no good answer, and that aggravated her to no end.

Or rather the answer she had wasn't one that she liked. And that worried her even more.

It was for that reason that she was staring at the artifact that very second. The one that her Master had challenged her to obtain. To prove herself and her loyalty.

As soon as the Skath acquired the Blood Ruby, the monster would come here to retrieve the Blood Dagger and take both artifacts back to their Master.

That was the most logical course.

The necessary course, because then their Master would have what he had sought for so long.

Yet the Bearer was gone.

So was the Skath.

What had happened?

Ursina wanted to pound her fists against her armrests and release some of the tension rising within her, but she restrained herself.

So many questions and so few answers. That only served to stoke her anger.

She didn't like not knowing.

She never had.

Ursina wanted to know.

She needed to know.

Everything.

And here, now, she felt like she was walking blindly through the fog just as she had when she was a child.

Then, she had enjoyed the experience. The fists of grey surging down off the mountains to consume Haven. She using her skill in the Talent to find her way around the island despite the silencing gloom.

Now, she felt lost, and she hated that sensation.

Even worse, she felt weak, and that only added to her anger, pushing it toward a rage.

Their time was running out. She knew it. She could feel it.

She didn't know how much longer she and her husband would have before the Wraiths resumed their attacks on Shadow's Reach. The Wraith Hunter clearly wasn't the patient type.

Probably not very long at all if she didn't give the Wraith Hunter what he wanted.

She could still succeed. Of that she was certain.

She needed more time, however. There was so much more that she needed to do.

If she couldn't prevent the Wraiths from coming for the city, however, then none of that mattered.

And if her Master believed that she was going to fail, if he had begun to doubt her, then ...

Well, that was a possibility that she didn't want to contemplate. Because her Master wasn't known for keeping alive those of his servants he considered weak.

Realizing that remaining stuck in her own head with her worries and fears building up within her did nothing for her, Ursina forced herself to return to the conversation taking place around her.

"I still can't quite believe it." Kendric shook his head in wonder. "The Belerons had ruled for three hundred years. In fact, ruled well for much of that time, until the last generation, of course. And you took down the monarchy in a matter of days."

"We had a strong incentive to do so." Bryen shrugged as if it was really not worthy of discussion. "You know what they say. The strength of a chain is determined by ..."

"The strength of its weakest length," finished Kendric, who nodded in appreciation. "The son of Corinthus."

"Yes, Marden Beleron," murmured Aislinn. Saying the name left a bad taste in her mouth, bringing back memories she would have preferred to keep buried. Then she brightened. "You know, if not for the fact that Bryen was jealous, Marden would still be ruling Caledonia."

"How so?" asked Kendric.

"Marden Beleron was going to force me to marry him. Joining our two houses would have given him the stability that he required. Bryen didn't like that. Not at all. So despite the fact that I had given him his freedom, despite telling him that he needed to go and live his own life, he decided to come for me. It was all quite dashing and very romantic."

She gave her Protector a wink and a suggestive smile. Aislinn enjoyed teasing her love. And though he didn't reveal much, she could tell by how his eyes crinkled that she had succeeded in annoying him. Just as she intended.

"That's not all that went into my decision."

"But it was a large part of it, wasn't it?" Aislinn pushed. "You couldn't bear to be away from me."

Bryen sighed, realizing that he had no choice but to play Aislinn's game. "Yes, Aislinn is correct. I didn't like the thought of Marden Beleron forcing her hand in marriage. It wasn't right, and yes," he added upon Aislinn nudging him in the side with her elbow, "I fell in love with her. But that wasn't the only reason I returned to Tintagel."

"My niece is quite a catch," Kendric said, smiling, "and I'm certainly glad that you decided to aid her and my brother. But from what I heard, I won't give my niece the full victory she is seeking. You had some additional motivation."

"Yes, I wanted to free my friends," Bryen confirmed.

"How did you do it?" Ursina was more than just a little curious. The details coming from the other side of the Burnt Ocean of how he ignited the gladiator uprising that had served as the catalyst for the fall of the Beleron dynasty had been sparse at best.

Bryen studied Ursina for quite a long time, and not just because scenes of the bloody clashes that took place in the corridors of the Colosseum passed before his eyes.

No, it was because he understood that Ursina wasn't asking

for stories of the struggle against Marden Beleron and the soldiers of the Royal Guard. The blood and the guts.

She was interested in something else entirely. Ursina wanted to know more about the strategy that he had employed.

He wasn't surprised. In some ways the Lady of the Northern Territory reminded him of his grandfather, looking at the world in a slightly different way than everyone else.

Sirius was always digging beneath the surface of the obvious, Bryen coming to understand that was his way of learning more about you. Learning how to make use of you.

The same seemed to be the case with Ursina, which made sense based on her training.

Bryen hadn't engaged much in the conversation until just now. Instead, under the guise of examining the various daggers set about Kendric's study, he focused much of his attention on Aislinn's aunt.

Observing her. Reading her. Trying to make sense of her.

It was a skill that Declan had taught him while learning how to endure on the white sand, the Master of the Gladiators ingraining within him the need to understand his opponents to ensure his continued survival.

A necessary skill. Because that's how Bryen viewed Kendric's wife. As a potential adversary.

"I played off his ego."

Ursina stared right back at the young man who had risked his life for his friends. Who had chosen to return to the place where he had suffered for ten years to aid the woman he loved.

It was quite dashing, just as Aislinn had said. Heroic even.

Unfortunately, Ursina didn't believe in heroes.

She believed that people were driven by their baser desires. In fact, she believed that was the trick to gaining what she wanted in life.

Identifying what really drove an individual, and then using that against them.

She had yet to identify what it was that truly drove the Protector, but she would. Because she was getting the sense that she would have need of him if she was to achieve her larger objective.

A feeling, no more. Nevertheless, she had learned to listen to these intuitions when they came upon her.

Because his response to her question confirmed for her that he was much more than just a blunt weapon.

Obviously, he knew how to fight. He couldn't have survived in the Pit otherwise.

Yet there was more to him than just that.

The sense that was only growing stronger within her as she studied the Protector hinted that he did much the same as she did. Identified an individual's weaknesses, just as he had done with respect to Marden Beleron, and made use of them.

Even more intriguing for Ursina, though, was what the Protector was hiding from her.

A burst of urgency struck her, then faded just as quickly. She needed to learn more about that other power within him. The one that she didn't quite understand. The one that was linked to the Talent but distinct from it as well. The one that she wanted to turn toward her own purposes.

"The greatest weakness of a powerful man," Ursina finally replied, nodding to Bryen in appreciation.

"It tends to be, yes," Kendric agreed. "The cause for many a downfall."

"And something that my husband does not have to worry about," Ursina offered with a bright smile. "He understands the folly of allowing ego to reign. In fact, there are times when I believe that he is too modest."

Kendric smiled, appreciating his wife's compliment, then choosing to ignore it. "Yes, I have seen it firsthand. It's definitely a fault to be avoided at all costs."

"Are you referring to my father?" asked Aislinn with a sly look.

For just a heartbeat, Kendric didn't know how to respond, not anticipating his niece's question. Then he caught the smile that Aislinn gave him. She was teasing him. Just as she had done when she was younger.

"No, not my brother. He has many faults, but not that one. He understood the dangers of employing power for personal gain. That was something that our father made sure that we both understood." Kendric leaned back in his chair, clasping his hands over his full belly, a bemused smile creasing his features. "On that topic, he used a specific example multiple times to make his point."

"What example?" Aislinn was curious. Her father rarely spoke of his time growing up in the Southern Marches. He was always focused on what needed to be done rather than on what had been done. A perspective that proved frustrating for her. So she valued the chance now to listen to what her uncle had to say.

"We were still in our teens, your father and me. He was being groomed as the next Duke of the Southern Marches, I as his second. We got into an argument after a go in the practice ring."

"What about?"

"Honestly, I don't really recall. We argued a lot back then. Not because I wanted to take Kevan's place. Believe me, I didn't."

"Then what was it about?" prodded Aislinn. She believed her uncle. He hadn't demonstrated much interest in the affairs of the Southern Marches back then. In fact, he had spent most of his time finding ways to evade his responsibilities.

"He was always so serious when we were growing up." Kendric shrugged, giving Aislinn another bemused smile. "I wasn't. I was more interested in having fun."

"I remember that quite clearly," Aislinn said with a soft chuckle. "He didn't like that, did he?"

"He didn't," Kendric confirmed. "As we got older, as I began to learn that I couldn't always have my fun, and as Kevan learned that it was all right to have some fun from time to time, we began to understand one another better. Until then, however, we spent more time squabbling than anything else."

"And this example you mentioned?" Aislinn nudged.

"Ah, yes. The Blackgards. Your grandfather spent a lot of time talking about what happened to the rulers of Skaffa Falls."

"The family charged with guarding the Valley of the Dead?"

"Yes, the Blackgards accepted the task of watching for the return of the Ancient One. A responsibility that they still hold today."

"What was the issue that grandfather liked to talk about?"

"Rumblings at the time that one of the Blackgards, Dennys, who is the brother of the current Lord of Skaffa Falls – I think his name is Henry, though I can't remember for certain – wanted the seat of power for himself. Dennys had spent so much time in the Valley of the Dead that he had been seduced by the Ancient One, that creature of evil seeking to weaken his wardens from within by setting one Blackgard against the other."

"You never told me of this, Kendric," Ursina interrupted.

A strange look graced her incisive features. Bryen wasn't certain, but he thought that it might include a slight trace of fear, although it was difficult to tell because as soon as it was there it was gone.

"I never had cause to, my love. And it only came to me now because of our current conversation."

"So the Ancient One is real?" Aislinn gave Bryen a quick glance, not wanting her uncle or Ursina to catch her while Kendric absorbed a look of mild aggravation from his wife. Based on her Protector's expression, he was thinking much the same thing that she was. "All I've heard are stories of the terrible power that dreaded monster exercised."

"Stories they may be, but who can say? The Ancient One hasn't been seen or heard from for centuries upon centuries."

"Yet still the Blackgards maintain their watch," said Bryen. "They must truly value the responsibility they accepted. They would not do so without good cause."

"That they do, young man," Kendric confirmed, nodding to demonstrate that he agreed with the Protector's sentiment. "Regardless of whether the Ancient One is still a threat, from what I understand, several decades ago Dennys Blackgard was putting in place a plan to gain the support of the Sentinels -- the soldiers who guard against the servants of the Ancient One – and thereby claim Skaffa Falls for himself. His brother sniffed it out and put a stop to it before his younger brother could take action against him."

"Why did Dennys do this to his brother?" Ursina felt the need to play along, not wanting to give any hint that she might know more about the drama that occurred far to the north than Kendric did. Because Ursina did know more.

Quite a bit more, actually. In particular, the fact that Dennys Blackgard never had any interest in taking the ancestral seat of the Blackgards as his own. That there was little truth to the story. But she felt no desire to offer that knowledge, understanding how her doing so might lead to some very uncomfortable questions.

"Whether because he actually had been influenced by the Ancient One?" Kendric shrugged. "I don't know. My father didn't know either. But he saw in the story two valuable lessons."

"What were those?" prodded Aislinn.

"How difficult it can be when needing to decide between enacting a severe punishment versus granting mercy. Henry chose mercy for his brother, stripping Dennys of his title and his position as a Sentinel – a devastating thing to do since Sentinels are bonded to their responsibility through the use of the Talent – and doing the same to his two sons, whose names escape me. He banished them from Skaffa Falls, and no one has heard from them since."

"And the other lesson?" asked Ursina.

"That the quest for more power more often than not will come back to bite you in the ass."

Aislinn and Ursina laughed at Kendric's comment, taken in by his warm chuckle. Bryen offered a brief smile, more interested in watching how Ursina responded to what Kendric said.

He was certain that she was hiding something, and it was relevant to the story that Aislinn's uncle shared with them.

"Power is an interesting tool, is it not?" asked Ursina.

"How do you mean?" replied Aislinn, staring intently at her uncle's wife.

She wanted to like her. She wanted her uncle to be happy. Yet, there was some aspect to her personality that made it difficult for her to do that, and she had not yet identified what it was. That and the stories she had heard about her.

"It can cut both ways. Power can be used for good. To improve the lives of those who you are responsible for. But if you're not careful, as you use it, that power can corrupt you."

"Just as it did the Blackgards if the story is to be believed," Kendric nodded. "Just as it did Marden Beleron."

"Exactly so," agreed Aislinn. "Marden Beleron had no cause to be anywhere near the Caledonian throne. He had no concern for others. Only for himself."

"The Lady of the Northern Territory is talking about more than just power generally," Bryen said, his eyes fixed on those of the woman sitting across from him.

He wasn't one for skirting around the real topic that he knew that she wanted to discuss. That was a waste of time. Better to just get to it. Just as Declan had ingrained within him.

Ursina's lips slowly twisted into a smile. One that would have made most anyone else uncomfortable.

Not Bryen. He simply continued to stare at her. Waiting for her to head down the path that he knew that she wanted to take.

"I am," she confirmed, giving Bryen a brief nod of respect for figuring out her true intent. "I take it that you both know of my unique ability?"

Bryen and Aislinn nodded.

"I assumed as much. And I assume as well that you know that I can sense the same within you."

They both nodded again.

Right then, Ursina felt the almost uncontrollable urge to delve more deeply into the hidden power that she sensed within the Protector. She stopped herself, however.

Now wasn't the time. Better to begin on a different topic, and then perhaps angle toward what she really wanted to know.

"The Protector is correct," Ursina confirmed. "I am speaking of a specific power. I am speaking of the Curse."

Kendric nodded. "Yes, Ursina and I were curious, but we didn't want to give either of you any cause for concern." The Lord of the Northern Territory leaned in toward Aislinn and Bryen as if he were sharing a secret. "Because of the Wraiths, of course."

"And the Murk," added Aislinn. "You sensed the Curse within it."

"Ursina did," Kendric confirmed with a nod. "We are looking for ways to combat the Wraiths, concentrating on the taint they carry. We were hoping to speak with you about your knowledge of the Curse since it seems that you have a great deal more experience with that terrible power than we do. Perhaps some advice on how we might be able to combat it."

"More experience than we care to have, in fact," Aislinn

admitted, at the same time wondering at the truth of her uncle's statement. She found it hard to believe what he was saying, although it seemed that Kendric did, in fact, believe what he was saying, because she could tell that he wasn't lying. Or if he was, he didn't know that he was.

"The Ghoule Overlord was a practitioner of the Curse," Kendric said.

"Yes, the power that monster employed came from the Curse," Aislinn confirmed. "The power that he gifted to his Elders was the Curse."

"That power was in them?" Ursina desired to get a better sense of what she suspected. "Physically a part of them?" She needed to know because she had found very little at Haven that provided answers to her many urgent questions.

"Infused within them, yes," nodded Aislinn. "That's how the Ghoule Overlord exercised his power over the Elders. Over all the Ghoules in fact."

"So the story is true?" wondered Kendric.

"The story?"

"That the Ghoules of the Lost Land were once a people," said Ursina. "That they transformed when they turned to the Curse."

"I don't know that we can say that for certain," Aislinn shrugged, "but all signs point in that direction."

Aislinn studied Ursina, trying to understand her interest in this topic. And why that interest concerned her. There was a spark there in the back of Ursina's purplish eyes that disturbed Aislinn in a way that little had in quite some time.

"Why is this so important to you?" Bryen had seen the spark there as well. Rather than letting it lie, he decided to cut to the chase. He didn't have the patience to wait for Ursina to get at what she really wanted to know.

"The Wraiths of course," Ursina replied quickly, almost too quickly from Bryen's perspective. "I assume the monsters in the mist are much like the Ghoules that you so effectively defeated in the Winter Pass. That since they, too, are touched by the Curse, there might be some similarities that we can use in our efforts to stop the advance of the Wraiths and the Murk in which they come."

Bryen didn't say anything for several seconds. Ursina did well with her answer. Nevertheless, he knew that she wasn't revealing all the variables that went into her interest.

There was something more personal there. Something more innate and intimate. He couldn't quite determine what it was. Unless ...

He had been a fool. He should have assumed as much the instant he entered Shadow's Reach.

He couldn't use the Talent to confirm what he believed, because if he did Ursina would feel it. Instead, he remembered his experience with Tetric, the former advisor to Marden Beleron who had been taken by the Curse through the ministrations of the Ghoule Overlord, and the sign that few knew to look for.

He examined Ursina more closely, focusing but at the same time not focusing on her eyes. Those purple irises were quite unique and helped to hide for what he searched.

There. Just then. A flash that vanished as quickly as it appeared.

A spark of black in the very back. Barely there, though still visible to someone who knew what to look for.

He should have assumed as much. It certainly stood to reason, what with the tainted essence that permeated all of the city and that he now realized was centered on the Shadow Keep.

Bryen would need to be more careful with Ursina. Much more careful.

"You rebuilt the Weir," Kendric said, pulling Bryen from his dark thoughts. "That's quite an achievement and demonstrates a good deal of skill. Something that if I remember correctly required the strength of the Ten Magii originally, yet you achieved it on your own. How was that possible?"

"I had a great deal of assistance."

"From whom? The Order of the Magii?"

"In part," Bryen replied, not wanting to reveal all the help that he had received and from whom. "Aislinn, of course. Rafia Riverstone and Sirius Keldragan as well."

Bryen kept his expression neutral. He had seen how mention of Rafia and Sirius sent a shock through Ursina much as if she had been slapped across the face.

She did a good job of covering her unease by smoothing out the folds in her riding dress, but still it was there. Why she would have such a reaction, Bryen didn't know, but it was an interesting discovery indeed.

"That was quite an achievement," Ursina added quickly to cover her agitation. "I never had much cause to study the Weir. From what little I understand it's made of both the Talent and the Curse. Is it not?"

"It is," Aislinn replied.

She heard the lie in Ursina's words. She was sure that Bryen had as well. Ursina clearly knew quite a bit more about the Weir and the conflicting powers used to construct the barrier than she was revealing.

"How were you able to manipulate the Curse without becoming corrupted?" Ursina asked. Her tone offered a hint of innocence and mild curiosity, her expression something else entirely.

"Very carefully," Bryen replied, not feeling the need to expand on what he had done to ensure that he did not touch the Curse directly while he wove a new Weir with the assistance and guidance of the Ten Magii.

For just a second, Bryen thought that Ursina was going to

lose her temper. She wanted more from him. She wanted details.

Of that he had no doubt. And he didn't care. He said no more, wanting to gauge her reaction.

As the seconds slipped by, Ursina fought to maintain her composure, even though the unease and urge to act continued to build within her.

Yes, definitely more than just a gladiator.

More than just a Protector.

More than even a Magus.

That worried her like nothing had in quite some time. Not even the Wraiths.

But what Aislinn's love really was, Ursina wasn't quite sure, other than the fact that he seemed to relish being difficult.

She should have expected as much. No matter. She would get what she needed from him. Whether he wanted to provide it or not.

"This is all quite interesting, but how does this fit into what we're trying to determine with respect to combating the Wraiths?" Kendric was having some difficulty following the nuances of the discussion. There was a private dialogue taking place between Ursina and Aislinn's Protector, and he had no idea about what, because this other conversation wasn't taking place with words.

Bryen decided to share a little bit more with Ursina, if for no other reason than to see if he could provoke another similar response.

"During my lessons with Rafia," he began – there, again, that brief twist in Ursina's expression, a mixture of hate, disgust, and loss, "we reached the conclusion that the Curse exists in the world just as the Talent does. There is little difference between the two. Both are a form of power. Both may even come from the same source. But there is a break between the Talent and the Curse, because those who use the Talent use the natural magic of the world for others, to do good in a sense just as you said Ursina, while those who use the Curse do so for their own purposes. They put themselves before others. They seek power simply for the sake of seeking power. Because of that, all it takes to be infected by the Curse is a single touch. No more."

"You say that with a great deal of surety," challenged Ursina, not certain that she liked what she was hearing, because it was hitting much too close to home.

"I say it because I know it for the truth. There is the Curse and then there are those claimed by the Curse and used by the Curse. There is no control exercised by a Dark Magus, although she may believe that she is exercising control. Rather, she exercises her power solely based on the will of the Curse. Because once the Curse makes a claim upon her, she is no longer exercising free will. Whether cognizant of that fact or not, she is doing as the Curse wants her to do."

"A theory, no more," scoffed Ursina, feeling the need to challenge Bryen.

She didn't want to believe him. Even so, she found it difficult to disagree as she thought back to when she made the decision that had changed her life so drastically.

What it had felt like that first time when she had taken a step down that road that most other Magii avoided. That sense of almost indescribable power, the thrill and pleasure of that first touch, mixed with a pulse of fear upon realizing that she was no longer who she had once been and that she never would be again.

"Perhaps," Bryen admitted, although he sounded quite certain of himself. "Then again, perhaps not. I have not had the chance to speak with someone touched by the Curse to gain their perspective on the matter. Those I've come across who have turned to the Curse, the Ghoule Overlord and his Elders for example, usually weren't interested in talking with me. Usually they were interested only in killing me."

"Is there a single source?" Ursina asked, not wanting to take the next logical step down the path of the Protector's reasoning, doing so too uncomfortable for her.

She had been thinking about this question for quite some time. In fact, ever since she decided to follow the path that forced her to flee Caledonia with a target on her back.

She had believed that she was stronger than all the others who had chosen the road that she had taken. Better than all the others. More skilled. Smarter. She had discovered much to her regret that she was no different than any of them.

"Honestly, I'm not sure. Although it certainly stands to reason, doesn't it? A single source of the Curse distributed in various ways throughout the Realms. To the people of the Lost Land through the ministrations of the Ghoule Overlord. To the Wraiths thanks to the Dread. To other places in the world perhaps through similar or more insidious means."

Bryen stared directly into Ursina's eyes when saying that last, Aislinn's aunt trying and failing to hold his gaze. He realized that he had hit a sore point with her, which only served to confirm what he believed.

"It does," Ursina admitted finally, staring back at him now, refusing to demonstrate weakness.

That was the answer that she wanted from him, because if there was a single source, that could lead to a whole new avenue of opportunities.

Think of the power exercised by someone who could control the single source of the Curse, mused Ursina.

That stopped her dead in her tracks.

Could her Master be the source of the Curse in the Realms?

Such a thought certainly didn't sound beyond the realm of possibility. Banished to the Spirit World, her Master sought to exercise his power through various intermediaries, all of those attempts enjoying varying levels of success.

She needed to confirm if what she believed, what the Protector had suggested, was true.

To do that, she needed to talk more with the Protector. Privately.

She could tell that he was withholding a great deal more from her, and she meant to dig out every morsel of information that could be of use to her.

"I understand that you have some experience fighting against those touched by the Curse, but how is it that you know so much about this power?" Ursina sought to take a different tack to see where it led. "You couldn't have gained all this supposed knowledge that you have just by fighting the Ghoule Overlord and his Elders."

"The Curse attempted to make me its own," Bryen replied quietly and calmly. "I have experience not only in fighting those who have given themselves to the Curse, but also the Curse itself."

Bryen's meaning was not lost on Ursina, his simple statement taking her breath away.

"I'm sorry, young man," Kendric interrupted in a shocked tone. "What did you just say? I don't think that I heard you correctly."

"I said that the Curse tried to make me its own."

Kendric opened his mouth several times to reply, but the words never came as he struggled to comprehend what the Protector just told him.

"You speak as if the Curse is alive," Kendric finally spluttered.

"It is." Bryen leaned in toward Ursina then. "Wouldn't you agree, Magus?"

Ursina stared at Bryen with a hint of shock and fear marring her features. She wanted to challenge his belief, but she couldn't. Not after thinking about what he had just revealed.

Accepting his theory made certain things she had been learning and wondering about clearer. Certain pieces of the puzzle that didn't fit together before now finally finding their appropriate places.

Even though Ursina didn't want the Protector to be right, she knew that he was. She looked at him with a more discerning eye, finally beginning to understand how he had come by his knowledge. "You've been touched by the Curse."

"Not by choice."

There was a hint of accusation in his voice. Ursina chose to ignore it.

Her eyes widened when she began to understand what he had done. She knew that the Protector had killed the Ghoule Overlord. She was realizing now that he had done much more than that.

"You killed the Curse," she whispered.

The Protector didn't reply. He didn't have to. She could see it in his set expression.

She was beginning to understand now. The gift the Protector had just given her with his revelation.

She would use the Protector to achieve her objective of protecting Shadow's Reach from the Wraiths.

And, more importantly, she would use him to try to save her husband.

Aislinn and Bryen stood on the terrace that ran across the length of their apartment, which took up most of one side of the Shadow Keep.

They glimpsed the city wall off to the north.

Despite the distance, the massive braziers burning atop the

parapet were quite distinctive, lighting up the northernmost neighborhood of the growing town as if the sun was still shining down brightly despite the late hour of the night.

The large number of soldiers stationed there on the city wall as well as along the battlements of the Shadow Keep buttressed the cause and the need.

A city under siege.

That's what came to mind for Bryen. And perhaps that was the case. It certainly felt that way with so many soldiers of the Northern Guard standing ready against the coming of the dreaded Murk and the monsters lurking within.

Aislinn doubted that they had anything to worry about that evening. She had been checking to confirm the location of that tainted fog since earlier in the day, and it had yet to budge an inch. The Murk remained close to the southern border of the Wyld far to the north.

Strange based on what the Blademaster had told her. The Murk usually blanketed the city every few days now. However, the Wraiths last made an appearance upon the parapet more than a week ago, well before she and Bryen arrived in Shadow's Reach.

She was pleased by the city's good fortune, but she wanted to know the cause. Why the Wraiths had chosen now to halt their regular attacks along the wall.

She realized that musing about that likely wouldn't give her the answer.

Aislinn looked down to the ground a few hundred feet below them. "Remind you of anything?"

"It's very similar to your balcony in Battersea," replied Bryen, who rested his arms on the rail.

"It is," Aislinn said, joining him at the railing, giving him a nudge with her hip. "It brings back many memories."

"Good memories?" wondered Bryen.

He knew that she missed her home. It was only natural as

she had never been gone for so long from the Southern Marches. But he could tell as well that she didn't regret her decision to join him. Even though she had hated him with a passion when he burst into her room that night.

"Most of them, yes. Particularly the one involving you."

"Me?"

"The four assassins," Aislinn nudged again.

Bryen nodded. He would never forget that night. "The four assassins."

He hadn't thought about that encounter in quite a long time. He had been forced into serving as Aislinn's Protector, having just arrived in chains in Battersea that same day, when that attempt was made on her life.

He hadn't been happy about swapping one form of forced servitude for another. She hadn't been happy that her father had foisted him upon her.

They were both resentful at their fates, and the most obvious target for that resentment was the other.

Aislinn had taken her anger out on him before leaving him for the night, setting his clothes on fire with the Talent right before the assassins who had been hidden by the Curse had climbed to her balcony.

Bryen had been drawn to her bedchamber not long after that, feeling the inescapable urge to reach her side as quickly as he could, kicking in her doors to achieve that objective. The pull of the magical collar, the steel circlet now drained of its power but still around his neck as a reminder of that time and his continuing commitment to Aislinn, demanding that he go to her aid no matter the risk to himself.

The clash in her apartment had taken him back to his roots. Back to the white sand of the Pit.

It was the first time he felt comfortable in Battersea.

Killing the four assassins.

Well, three of the assassins. Aislinn had killed the last.

They had learned quite a lot about one another that night. And that had been the start for them.

They had found common ground shortly after that, both of them looking at the other differently as they got to know one another during the months that followed. From there, their relationship grew into something that neither of them anticipated, yet both were grateful for.

"Do you worry about that here?" he asked. "Ursina is playing nice, but only because your uncle requires it from her. She doesn't want us in Shadow's Reach, you in particular."

"Not yet," she replied, hearing the truth in her Protector's words, knowing as well that if he asked her that question again in the coming days that her response might be different. "I just can't get that memory out of my mind."

"I can understand why. It's not just because of the similarity in balconies."

Aislinn nodded. Bryen was right. She identified immediately the many structural similarities between the Shadow Keep and the Broken Citadel, her home in the Southern Marches.

"It's not quite right here," Aislinn agreed. "It's as if we're looking at the world around us through a veil. We're seeing what Ursina wants us to see rather than what we should see."

"Did you sense the extent of her power?" Bryen asked, pushing off the railing and facing Aislinn. He reached out, grasping her hand, squeezing her fingers.

They had come to the Territories because of the opportunity for a fresh start. But for both it seemed as if they had stumbled right into several challenges very similar to those that they had overcome in Caledonia.

"The Talent? Yes. It's hard to miss, isn't it?"

"It is indeed," Bryen confirmed.

"I didn't realize she was such a strong Magus. Not much weaker than either of us. On a par with Rafia."

"Not just that."

"What do you mean?"

"It's not just the Talent that I sense within her," Bryen said in a quiet, strong voice.

Aislinn realized what he was telling her, recalling what he could do because of his connection to the Seventh Stone. He didn't need to say it out loud. She could see it in Bryen's eyes.

The Curse.

Her aunt was a Dark Magus.

"Come to bed, Ursina," Kendric called as he lifted the sheets for her.

From what she could see as he lay there on their very comfortable mattress, clearly he had more than sleep on his mind.

"Soon, my love," Ursina replied, swaying seductively as she walked across the thick carpet to her husband, sitting down next to him so that the touch of her hip sent a welcome shudder through him. "There is still something that I must do."

She placed a hand on his arm, rubbing gently with her fingers.

Kendric smiled. He always relished her touch and the gentle heat that began to work its way through his body.

"Don't wait too long, Ursina," Kendric mumbled, leaning back against the pillows, his eyelids growing heavier. "It has been a long day. I don't know how much longer I can stay awake for you."

"I will be quick. Have no fear, my love." She continued to rub his arm, watching as Kendric drifted off into a deep slumber.

She loved her husband. He had done more for her than anyone else ever had. He had taken her in when no one else would. He had accepted her without asking all the questions that he had a right to ask that she couldn't answer. He had also given her the greatest gift she could have ever imagined.

For all of that, she would always be grateful.

Unfortunately, he was not the only one who had a claim upon her.

There were others. And those others were more demanding, more dangerous, than he was.

Kendric wanted to have his fun. She wouldn't deny him. Just not now. She had work to do.

Ursina continued to rub his arm for almost a minute more, until she was certain that he wouldn't wake until morning.

After giving Kendric a soft kiss on his cheek, she pushed herself up and walked to the balcony doors. She pulled them open to invite in the cool nighttime breeze.

Stepping up to the railing, Ursina searched with the Talent. She nodded to herself, pleased by what she discovered.

The Murk was still far to the north. It seemed that the Wraith Hunter was holding to their agreement. For now.

For how much longer, she couldn't say.

Setting that worry to the side, Ursina reached for the other power flowing within her. The tainted strands burst free from where they hid. With it came the link to the specific ability that her Master had granted her.

She shook her head in frustration, slamming a palm down against the rail.

She couldn't find the scent of the Bearer of the Blood Ruby. For the one who was also the Wraith who is not a Wraith. The one she needed to find for her Master and for herself.

Just days before the trail had been there. Clear as day. So much so that she could follow it in her sleep. But no more.

The trail that led directly to her target had faded away just like the Murk when that blasted fog drifted back to the north.

The link to the Skath was gone as well. The creature tasked with claiming her prey had vanished.

Ursina didn't understand her lack of success, and that worried her in a way that little else had in quite some time.

That fear gaining a foothold within her, she touched her belly. She wasn't showing yet. And she hadn't told Kendric. She would wait until she was a little farther along.

When she did, he would be excited. She was looking forward to that.

But she couldn't look too far ahead because she was worried as well.

Talking more with Aislinn and her Protector had put her on edge.

Another failure on her part, and that fact rankled.

Aislinn Winborne and her Protector should never have made it to Shadow's Reach. Yet they had. Despite her efforts to stop them.

She should have taken more precautions after their success against the Ghoule Overlord and his Legions.

Still, she had hoped.

Yet as her mother had liked to say, hoping doesn't make it real.

What was real was the threat that Aislinn Winborne and her Protector presented. The opportunity as well.

The questions that were circling through her mind as she looked out toward the lights lining the city wall were simple ones. Critical ones as well. Because how she chose to answer them could have severe repercussions for her and her husband.

Could she use the Protector as she believed she could?

Or did she need to remove him from the playing field?

She wasn't certain because she didn't understand the power surging within him that was distinct from the Talent.

Always confident in her abilities and her determination, she did believe that she could employ the Protector's hidden power to her advantage. She just needed to figure out some means to harness his unique energy.

Staring off into the darkness as she contemplated those heavy matters, her right hand slid down to her belly.

Regardless of what happened, she needed to protect her baby against whatever might come.

And she would.

No matter who it was.

No matter what it was.

Because finally she had a purpose that was greater than herself.

11

VENGEANCE GAINED

"Steady!" Tommie called. "Steady!"

She nocked another arrow. Then, in a fluid motion ingrained by constant practice, she pulled the heavy bow back until the string almost touched her cheek. More sensing rather than seeing, she released.

The arrow flew straight and true, puncturing the neck of a soldier who had been about to kill a Highlander who had tripped over the many dead littering the battlefield.

As the soldier collapsed in the dirt, the Highlander pushed himself up, jumping right back into the fight.

"Make every arrow count," she ordered as she pulled another three-foot-long, steel-tipped shaft from her quiver, nocking it to her string. "Once we're out, we're out."

The archers standing with Tommie on the ledge forty yards above the entrance to the mine didn't bother to respond.

They stayed on task.

Picking their targets carefully, they focused on helping any Highlanders down below who faced particularly difficult circumstances.

Tommie let fly again. The quarrel she released slammed

right into the chest of a soldier who had thought to come at Martin from behind.

A good strategy, but bad luck with Tommie watching out for her friend. Reaching for another arrow, her eyes scanned the melee.

Bertie was in good shape, having little trouble against a stick of a man whose sword seemed to be too heavy for him.

Not needing her assistance, Tommie searched for the scarred Highlander who had gotten under her skin in a good way during the last few months.

She shook her head in annoyance. She should have expected as much.

He just couldn't help himself. Always in the thick of the fight.

And from where she was standing on the ledge, she could do little to help him with the mass of bodies surging around him and preventing her from getting a clear shot.

She growled in aggravation, returning her focus to the clash taking place at one of the side entrances to the mine. The shrieks that she had come to hate because of what they represented had drawn her attention.

Stalkers.

Coming through the two smaller tunnels.

The soldiers who had failed to break through those narrow passages had made themselves scarce, replaced by the monsters haunting the Highlands.

"Concentrate on the two smaller tunnels!" Tommie ordered, nocking another arrow to her bow. At least for now the Highlanders fighting with spears at the side shafts were doing an excellent job of preventing the Stalkers from forcing their way past, the monsters' shrieks growing louder because of their failure to break out from beneath the mountain.

But it was only a matter of time before those beasts succeeded. And if they came through the main entrance in addition to the two smaller tunnels, then the Highlanders were in a heap of trouble.

"Kill the Stalkers first!"

The archers responded immediately. Shifting their aim. Looking for the first hint of those monsters stepping out into the light.

She had done all she could against this new threat. Based on experience she knew that it likely wouldn't be enough; however, there was someone else who could do more than she could.

Tommie scanned the battle for Jakob. Finally she saw him with the gladiator off to the side in a tight pocket of combat. They were surrounded, although that didn't seem to bother either of them.

In fact, observing how those two fought together, she doubted that fist of soldiers would be able to stand against them for very much longer.

Especially since Jakob was so intent on his task. Fighting his way through to the man who had held Saraa hostage.

"Jakob," Tommie called to him in her mind, seizing on the connection she still had thanks to his application of the Talent, knowing that there was no way that he would hear her shout over the din of the battle.

"Jakob!"

Still nothing. She was about to try again. Instead, she sighed with relief.

"What is it, Tommie?"

"Stalkers! The side passages!"

JAKOB SHOOK his head in anger, castigating himself because he hadn't been paying enough attention to the larger picture. He had focused on the more personal one right in front of him, and his doing that put at risk all that he and his Highlanders were seeking to accomplish.

"Worried, oh great Lord of the Highlands?" asked Remy, his voice dripping with contempt. "Realizing now that I'm going to kill you? That your sad, little rebellion will be coming to an end when my steel pierces your heart?"

Jakob didn't bother to reply.

They stood nose to nose.

Remy had demonstrated an unanticipated vigor during their combat. At least for a time.

The soldier realized that he had no choice but to fight Jakob when he lost all of his men, so he sought to seize control of the combat right from the start. He hoped that he could make a quick end to the boy by playing off his overconfidence.

Jakob had permitted Remy to believe that. With Remy's damaged knee, he doubted that the slaver could keep up his frenetic assault for long. Better just to let him tire himself out.

And he had been right. Remy was slowing down. He was flagging. Soon he would make a mistake that would cost him his life.

In fact, Jakob had glimpsed an opening that he had just been about to exploit when Tommie's urgent call slipped into his consciousness, delaying his attack.

He shouldn't have allowed himself to get distracted. He shouldn't have put what he wanted ahead of the needs of the people fighting for him.

That realization sobering him, Jakob shoved Remy backward with a hard push of his shoulder.

Caught by surprise, Remy stumbled, then fell on his ass in the dirt.

Remy's eyes widened in fear, believing that his adversary already would be standing above him, driving one of those cursed Wraith blades through his eye.

But he wasn't. The boy he had shackled not long after he

stepped ashore in Ballinasloe remained where he was. Standing stock still. His focus on the mine.

"Kill him, Jakob," Lycia said. "We need to get into the larger fight."

"I will," Jakob replied with a steady assurance. "I just need to do something first, because the larger fight is coming to us."

Sheathing his daggers in the scabbards on his back, Jakob reached for the Talent. A small ball of energy flashed into existence just above each of his palms. With a wiggle of his fingers they began to dance across his digits.

Remy gasped, not believing what he was seeing. Frozen in fear. Watching in terror. Thinking that the boy was going to kill him with just the flick of his wrist.

He didn't.

Instead, Jakob glanced quickly toward the main entrance to the tunnel as the last of the soldiers hiding beneath the earth ran out into the sunshine.

Next, he looked at the tunnels on each side of the main shaft that led into the depths of the mountain.

The Stalkers hadn't made it through those narrow crevices yet thanks to the heroic efforts of the Highlanders stationed there. They refused to retreat, poking into the darkness with their spears, earning blood and growls for their efforts, holding their ground, even as the Stalkers' attacks became more furious.

That wouldn't last forever, though. Eventually, a spear would miss, and then one of the monsters would sneak by. Once that happened, the entire rhythm of the battle would change, and not in favor of the Highlanders.

Jakob needed to prevent that from happening.

And he did.

With an overwhelming decisiveness.

A sphere made of blindingly bright energy shot from his

palm, streaking through the air with a hiss before smashing into the stone just inside the entrance to the side tunnel.

He had waited until the Highlanders stepped back, communicating to them with a separate stream of the Talent so that they weren't caught in the blast.

In an instant, the threat presented by the Stalkers seeking to emerge from that crevice ended. Tons of rock buried the monsters, a cloud of debris shooting out from the tunnel as the last of the massive stones came tumbling down.

Jakob then did the same thing to the crevice on the other side of the mine's main entrance.

In the blink of an eye, he had narrowed the battlefield to the Highlanders' advantage.

Satisfied with his work, Jakob fixed his gaze back on the man still sitting slack-jawed and openmouthed in the dirt.

"Enough of this, Remy. No more wasting my time."

"Duff, they'll be coming!"

Martin, Bertie, and the Highlanders who had been guarding the tunnel on one side ran over. They were grateful that Jakob had intervened. The Stalkers had been pressing them hard, and they acknowledged that keeping the beasts from exiting was an impossible task.

Yet even though the two passageways were no more, those monsters were still a threat. No doubt they were already working their way back through the mountain.

Duff assumed that it wouldn't be long before they made an appearance at the main entrance. And when they did, the dynamics of the Highlanders' current engagement with Sharperson's soldiers would change.

"How long do we have?"

"Minutes at most," Martin replied. "No more than that. They're crafty devils."

"When they emerge, those Stalkers will probably kill anything that gets in their way," muttered Duff, nodding his head as he considered what that could mean for the Highlanders. "They won't see much difference between us and the soldiers."

"Probably not," Bertie agreed, "which is fine with me so long as they go after the soldiers first."

"How do you want to play this?" Martin asked.

Duff thought about that for just a second, remembering the training that he had received from the Blademaster when Jurgen Klines had still been the Captain of the Royal Guard.

What would his former mentor do in a situation like this one?

He surveyed the battlefield swiftly, understanding that the longer he waited to make a decision, the less time he would have to prepare the Highlanders for the Stalkers.

Even with this last company of Sharperson's soldiers just now coming out of the mine and reinforcing those already in the fight, Duff believed that they could still win.

His Highlanders were not wavering in their efforts. In fact, not only had they seized the momentum, but they also were beating the soldiers back toward the shadows that danced around the entrance to the mine.

Yet even with that success, he was worried about the Stalkers. He didn't know how many of the monsters lurked within the mountain. Jakob hadn't been able to tell him because the taint of the Curse that revealed them also hid the beasts from a closer examination.

He hated the idea of potentially giving up the flanks. Of giving Sharperson's Guard the opportunity to press in on their sides and possibly even surround them.

He concluded that was the least of his concerns, however.

So long as his Highlanders held their position, they should be able to stand against anything that the soldiers or the Stalkers threw at them.

Besides, if it became necessary, he could use the village behind him as a defense. The soldiers would have a hard time coming at them if they retreated in among the dilapidated cottages. Particularly if the Stalkers viewed the soldiers as prey as well.

Several possible options.

None of them good.

Rather than take too much time mulling each one, he fell back on what the Blademaster had taught him.

Protect against the most immediate threat.

He didn't hesitate once he made his decision.

"Highlanders, form square!"

With a remarkable precision despite the battle raging across the dirt field, almost all of the Highlanders disengaged from their adversaries in less than a minute, although not without giving the soldiers a few parting shots before moving into the ordered formation.

The few stragglers who took longer to join the rest of their comrades did so once they killed their opponents or broke free from an intense combat.

Duff watched it all with a sense of pride, finding the ease with which the Highlanders accomplished the maneuver truly remarkable. All of his fighters were in position, exactly where they needed to be.

Even Tommie and the archers halted their deadly assault. They knew what was coming their way. They weren't going to waste any of their few remaining arrows on the targets below them. They were going to save them for the more dangerous threat.

The only fighting that was still going on was taking place off to the side near the soldiers' barracks.

Jakob.

Duff should have assumed as much.

Recognizing who he was fighting against, Duff certainly understood why.

And of course Lycia was right there with him.

He smiled. After watching for just a few breaths, it was clear that the gladiator was more than just a menace. She was downright terrifying.

That was one of the primary reasons he liked her.

And why he thought that she was a good partner for Jakob.

She was all controlled fury. He was all precision. A deadly pairing when those two mixed.

He would leave Jakob and Lycia to their work. He had larger concerns.

"Tighten ranks!" Duff ordered.

The Highlanders responded immediately, shifting closer to one another. Closing any gaps. Reducing the amount of space that they would need to defend when they were attacked.

Most of Sharperson's soldiers, stunned that the Highlanders had stepped back with such precision, simply watched. Impressed. Many even appeared to be grateful that the Highlanders chose to disengage.

Most of them had little desire to continue to fight against the men and women who had made the peaks towering above them their home. Because the battle hadn't played out as they thought it would.

The soldiers had believed that they would face only a century of Highlanders. Probably a few less than that from what Captain Hippolates told them. An easy fight even with capturing or killing the so-called Lord of the Highlands their primary objective. Because they were certain that the Highlanders didn't have the skill to stand against them.

None of what they thought proved true, their beliefs painfully false.

The soldiers discovered swiftly that the Highlanders were more than a match for them. Dangerous opponents. Motivated opponents. Vengeful opponents.

Men and women they had no desire to cross blades with again if they could avoid it, because as they looked across the space separating them from the Highlanders, they saw little else except for their friends and comrades lying dead or dying on the ground.

"Tighten those ranks, Highlanders!" Duff ordered again. There were really no spaces that needed to be closed. Even so, Duff felt the need to say something. He wanted to keep the Highlanders on their toes. Prepared for their next challenge. "Lucky for us, we have Stalkers coming our way. We're finally going to get a good fight."

That comment earned a round of laughter from the Highlanders.

"Hiding behind your men and women while playing at soldier, Westgard?" a strong voice called. "Why doesn't that surprise me? Always running rather than fighting. Always seeking the easy way out."

Duff turned his hard gaze toward the voice. Not quite believing his luck.

The nasal twang was unmistakable.

For just a heartbeat, he was transported back more than a decade. To a time when his world fell apart. When he had been forced to make some difficult decisions.

Decisions that he didn't want to make.

Decisions that still haunted him.

All because of the man attached to that voice.

Duff had been hoping for a chance like this as soon as he had learned who was leading Sharperson's Guard. But he never believed that he would get it.

The man who had set Duff on his path that led to the Territories rarely stepped to the fore. He rarely made himself a target. Unless he couldn't avoid it or there was something to be gained that he couldn't gain any other way.

Probably the latter now, Duff decided. Knowing exactly what that might be and not caring.

He had thought of this moment every day since he left the Royal Guard.

He had made a difficult decision back then. Now he was faced with another one. A harder one.

Stay and lead or go and fight.

He knew what he wanted to do.

He knew as well what he had to do.

No matter the cost, he was afraid to lose this opportunity. He might never get it again.

Besides, he trusted the Highlanders fighting beside him.

That thought guiding him, Duff moved to the first rank of the shield wall. Smiling coldly, he stepped between the Highlanders who parted for him then quickly closed ranks behind him.

Duff stopped when he was just a few yards away from the soldiers loyal to Governor Sharperson who were trying to imitate the Highlanders' discipline and failing miserably.

Hammer haft resting on his shoulder, one hand on his hip, the man who was the driving force of the rebellion in the Highlands stared with dead eyes at the man who was trying to suppress the rebellion.

Duff hated the man with an unmatched passion.

He should have killed the smirking bastard long ago when he had the chance.

His failure to do that, all because he made the right decision rather than the one he wanted to make, had bothered him ever since.

Nevertheless, his previous disheartening encounter with the soldier smirking at him had ingrained within him the need to protect those who couldn't protect themselves. To stand up when others were afraid to.

Because he understood the ultimate cost of not doing so.

He knew what could be lost.

"Afraid, Westgard? Is that it, Duff? Now that you have the chance that you've been dreaming about, you're too scared to take it?"

The man who was slightly taller than Duff stood a few yards in front of his soldiers. He wore twin swords across his back, although he preferred the battle axe on his hip.

His smile was more a frightening leer -- courtesy of Duff, in fact -- who had taken that same axe that now hung at the man's hip and smashed the steel knob into his mouth, ripping open his lip, which had never healed correctly, and knocking out several teeth. A reminder to both of the debts that each wanted to collect from the other.

Their commander's presence brought a ragged order to the soldiers standing at his back even as the murmuring among them continued, many of them looking around in shock. They didn't quite understand how one company of Highlanders could do so much damage.

The commander of Sharperson's Guard laughed then. He took another few steps forward. Then he pulled the axe from the leather strap on his belt, one hand gripping the handle as he tapped the head in a constant rhythm against his palm. Making it plain that he welcomed a duel.

Just as much as Duff wanted to kill him, the soldier wanted to kill Duff.

There was bad blood between them.

A lake of bad blood.

Particularly since they had spent so much time together in the Royal Guard.

The man with the twisted grin shook his head with a mix of amusement and slight disbelief. And to think that they had been friends when they both started their service to the Caledonian Crown.

Of course, the soldier's desire to kill Duff wasn't the only reason that he had chosen this course. He understood what Duff could do with that hammer of his. He was willing to take that risk, nonetheless.

Because he was playing the longer game, knowing what was to come if he could keep Duff and his Highlanders occupied for a little while longer.

If he eliminated his former Sergeant and friend, then he could salvage this battle and achieve his primary goal.

Kill the Highland Lord.

And if he couldn't kill Duff quickly, he could ensure that what was coming up through the tunnel behind him could.

Then he would let those monsters do the work for him.

Kill Duff.

Kill the Highland Lord.

Both options appealed to him. It was just a matter of how the next few minutes played out.

"I should have expected as much. Come on, Westgard. My men won't bother you. You've been wanting to kill me for years. This is your chance." The man's smile broadened, his wider leer giving him an almost murderous expression. "Let's see if you can."

Duff stared across at his enemy. Hesitating.

He was torn. He had a responsibility to his Highlanders. To Jakob.

Was shifting his focus to a personal vendetta the right thing to do? Knowing that this was only a pause in the battle? That the next round was going to be even more punishing than the first?

He glanced to the side quickly. Jakob was engaged in a vendetta of his own, the scramble of fighters off to the side the only fighting taking place at that moment.

For just a second, he considered going to Jakob's aid. But Duff didn't want to get in Jakob's way, trusting in the lad's skill, having seen it firsthand time and time again. Understanding that Jakob's combat against the man responsible for his father's death was something that he had to do on his own.

Just as Duff challenging the man who had knocked his whole world off kilter was something that he had to do. That it was the right thing to do. Wasn't it?

Martin and Bertie both looked at Duff at the same time. They knew the history between the two men and what was going through their friend's mind. They understood the internal struggle that he was dealing with. What Duff's decision to do what was right had cost him.

"Do what you need to do," Bertie said. He stood in the front rank of the Highlanders, just behind Duff.

"We'll hold them here," Martin confirmed. "Besides, you'll only be in the way."

Duff didn't look over his shoulder, although he nodded, then smiled. A vicious smile. A smile lacking in mercy. The smile of a man intent on bloody murder.

Swinging his hammer off his shoulder, gripping the haft with both hands, he strode toward the man who had taken his family from him. Who had thrown his life in disarray.

Who had set him on the path that had taken him to this very place at this very moment.

To a place and time when Duff finally could exact his revenge.

He would never gain the peace that he desired. He understood that was impossible.

But he could live with that, so long as he killed the arrogant bastard standing before him.

Eliasin Hippolates.

Captain of Sharperson's Guard.

Enforcer for the Governor of the Highlands.

And the man who murdered Duff's family.

"You're more than you seem, boy," Remy hissed. "I should have expected as much. It's the only way that you could have escaped me and survived in the Murk."

Remy was tired. Exhausted, in fact. And his injured knee was barking at him.

He was trapped, fighting against a young man with the power to rip him apart.

Even so, that didn't mean he was just going to roll over and die. His mind didn't function that way.

Instead, he continued to work through various scenarios that might give him the opportunity to, if not kill the Highland Lord, then at least escape.

Unfortunately, none of those scenarios except for one seemed to give him any hope of success.

If he was to have any chance at all of surviving this combat, he needed to make his adversary angry. He needed to force him into a mistake and hope that he got lucky in turn.

"And you're not, Remy. You're just a slaver at heart."

"Why don't you kill me now?" Remy prodded. "Take the path of the coward. Use your power. A power that you know I can't defend against. Forsake the blade so that you don't have to risk yourself." Remy chuckled then. "You know you can't stand against me with a blade. You know that if you do, I'll kill you like the coward that you are. Running. Leaving your father to die."

Jakob barely listened to what the slaver was saying, simply offering Remy a sad smile and then a shake of his head. Refusing to allow the slaver's taunts to affect him. "Do you really think that it's going to be that easy, Remy?"

"What do you mean?"

"You know exactly what I mean. You're grasping for answers to a problem that has only one solution."

"What solution would that be?" Remy asked, unable to stop himself even though he already suspected the answer.

"Your death, Remy." Jakob shook his head again, this time in disappointment. "You're hoping that you're going to get lucky. I promise you, that's not going to happen. Your luck has run out."

"The only way my luck runs out is if you take the coward's path and kill me with that power of yours," goaded Remy. "Do you have the guts to fight me like a man?"

Jakob stared at the man he held responsible for his father's death. He knew what the slaver was trying to do. He recognized his fear. His hope as well. The desperation that was playing through the back of his eyes.

Jakob had no intention of killing Remy with the Talent. He would give the slaver the hope that he so desperately required. Then he would rip it away from him.

"I'm not going to kill you with the Talent, Remy. Have no fear of that."

Remy smiled upon hearing that, relieved, believing that his wordsmithing had something to do with what he viewed as the first step in his victory. His expression changed quickly when he heard the rest of what Jakob had to say.

"My father died by the blade. You're going to die by the blade as well."

Remy's eyes widened. He had gotten what he wanted. A reprieve of sorts.

But he was beginning to realize that reprieve was going to be short-lived, the boy already striding toward him, his cursed double-bladed daggers spinning along his fingertips.

Remy pushed himself up as quickly as he could, staggering at first, his injured knee giving out when he didn't set himself correctly, his foot slipping.

When he looked back up after finally finding his feet, Remy took several steps backward as quickly as he could.

Too quickly, in fact, as he ended up on his ass again.

"Are we running or fighting, Remy?" Jakob's voice contained a heavy dose of disdain. "I thought you wanted to engage in a combat. But from what I can see, it seems that you've selected the role of coward."

Jakob halted his advance when he saw how Remy's face flushed red. The man was frightened. Desperate. Almost frantic. And now he was angry as well. Almost in a rage. His reason threatening to leave him.

Jakob had turned the tables on the slaver with a few simple words.

Jakob had succeeded where Remy had failed.

Jakob was calm, controlled, ready. Waiting. Giving Remy the chance to start the combat again.

Remy was spiraling down a drain, his emotions raw. Distracting. Urging him to rush into this fight even though he knew the likely outcome if he did.

"What will it be, coward?" prodded Jakob. "Shall we fight? Or will you be running away with your tail between your legs? Because if that's what you're going to do, I don't want to waste another second on you."

Remy's eyes almost bulged out of his sockets at Jakob's insult. Despite his rising fear, despite his reluctant and disheartening understanding that he couldn't stand toe to toe against this former slave, whatever reason Remy had left fled from him.

Remy lunged with his sword, seeking to plunge the steel into Jakob's belly. Then again. And one more time.

Attacking on a straight line.

Worried that if he moved too much to either side his bad knee would give out on him at the worst possible moment just as it had done seconds before.

He ignored the pain in his joint. How he moved awkwardly across the field. How he failed with each attack to draw blood, his opponent dancing away from him with a practiced ease that grated on his nerves more and more.

"Stand and fight, boy!" Remy roared, spittle flying from his mouth.

Jakob simply glared at him. Then he gave the slaver a mocking smile. "What's the matter, Remy? Don't like it when you lose control?"

Remy's face turned an even brighter shade of red. He had been searching for the key to unlock Jakob's weaknesses, believing that it was the only chance for him to survive this combat. But he hadn't been able to do it. And he hadn't considered that at the very same time Jakob was doing the exact same to him. Seeking to unlock Remy's weaknesses.

Not the slaver's damaged knee. That was obvious.

No, Jakob had been looking for a more fundamental failing. A characteristic more intrinsic to Remy.

And he had found it.

Jakob remembered how Remy had tried to lord it over them before his father died and he escaped into the Murk. He recalled how the slaver's men had responded to him and obeyed his orders. The conversation in the hollow with the deceased Dennis particularly telling.

Remy thrived on control. Over his surroundings. Over the people serving him.

When he didn't have control, he had very little.

With just a few words, Jakob had stripped away from him what little control Remy still had.

Without his control, there was very little to Remy other than rage and fear. And neither of those emotions was going to help him now.

"I am in control!" Remy shouted. "I am always in control!"

The slaver prepared to lunge for Jakob again, but he never

got the chance. Because Jakob already was moving toward him with a deadly grace, stalking across the field like an avenging spirit.

Realizing that he had been caught out, Remy stopped abruptly, slipping a bit in the dirt as his bad knee locked up again. Still, he succeeded in raising his sword, desperate to parry the slash that was just a hair away from connecting.

He did, the dagger in Jakob's right hand scraping across the steel rather than his gut.

Unfortunately for Remy, he didn't stop the dagger in Jakob's other hand.

Remy's eyes dipped down toward his chin. That was the best that he could do because he couldn't move his head. The bone-white steel driven through his throat, the sharp tip of the blade sticking out of the back of his neck, preventing it.

The slaver gasped and gurgled, all to useless effect. He raised his eyes, staring into the remorseless green orbs staring right back at him.

"My father is waiting for you in the Spirit World, Remy," Jakob whispered, his eyes flashing not with pleasure or satisfaction, but rather with remorse. Although that remorse was not for Remy. "This isn't over for you. It will never be over for you."

Jakob pulled his dagger free, Remy dropping like a stone right at his feet.

He stared at the man who had caused him so much pain. He didn't know why he said what he said. For some reason, it just seemed like the right thing to say.

He had no time to think about it, however. With this combat done, there was still a great deal more to do if the Highlanders were to have any chance of winning the larger battle.

"Did you get what you wanted?" Lycia stepped up next to him, looking down at the dying slaver.

She saw nothing other than a man who deserved to die. Jakob saw something more.

For several seconds, Jakob didn't reply, losing himself in the memories of him and his father that played through his mind.

"No," Jakob finally replied. "No, I didn't."

He couldn't bring his father back. Killing Remy didn't help him with that. And finally gaining his revenge didn't give him any comfort.

It was just a task that he needed to complete.

Now that it was done, it was done.

The hole caused by his father's death was still there. And it would always be there. Jakob understood that now.

Lycia read all that in the many emotions playing across Jakob's face. She understood, and she sympathized with him. "Good. Because if you did, I would be worried about you."

"Thank you," Jakob said softly.

Lycia nodded. "You're welcome. It's an honor to fight with you."

Jakob smiled warmly then, turning his sharp gaze toward her. Those flashing green eyes of his made her breath catch while they were locked onto her. "The honor is mine. But my thanks isn't for that."

"Then for what?" asked Lycia, confused.

"For reminding me of what's right. For making sure that I see what needs to be seen and not what I want to see."

Lycia could only stare at him, a jumble of emotions surging through her. None of them particularly useful to their current circumstances. Afraid of what she might say, she simply nodded.

Jakob nodded as well, then he turned his focus toward the tunnel's main entrance.

Sharperson's soldiers stood in ragged ranks, facing off against his Highlanders, who stared across the space hungrily, hoping for another chance at killing the men who had terrorized them and their families.

Between the two opposing forces, Duff was engaged in a

combat of his own. The Highlander battling with a controlled ferocity, his massive hammer swinging through the air with an incredible velocity. The soldier standing against him fighting with a sword in one hand and a battle axe in the other.

Jakob would have liked to have gone to his friend's aid. But he knew that it wasn't his place to do so. Just as Jakob had needed to challenge Remy, Duff needed to do this.

Besides, the greater peril was just then making its way onto the stage. He had sensed the evil drawing closer, racing out from deep beneath the mountain, during his duel with Remy. And now the first of those monsters was sprinting out into the light.

It was quite a surreal situation.

Tommie and the other archers on the ledge began to fire down at the Stalkers while those monsters attacked Sharperson's soldiers from behind.

Apparently the Stalkers felt the need to kill.

Who they killed was of little concern to them.

Whatever compulsion was upon them weaker than their bloodlust.

Jakob revised his perspective. His eyes locked onto the Stalker that had just emerged from the mine. The monster didn't cut into the soldiers who were now turning to face this new, unanticipated, unwanted threat.

Instead, the Stalker was sniffing the air, turning his head this way and that. Searching.

Searching for him, Jakob didn't doubt.

He wasn't surprised. As soon as the Stalker turned in his direction, their eyes met.

The Stalker raised its fang-filled maw to the sky, shrieking, the ear-splitting noise echoing off the surrounding mountains and drawing the attention of all the other monsters emerging into the light. The beasts that were already engaged with the soldiers ending their killing sprees.

Then, as one, the Stalkers sprinted toward Jakob.

He had guessed that this was why the Stalkers were hidden within the mine.

The monsters were charged with killing him.

And though he was more than happy to allow the Stalkers to eliminate Sharperson's soldiers, he didn't want his Highlanders to have to battle the beasts if that battle could be avoided.

He also believed that his Highlanders could defeat Sharperson's soldiers if he could draw the Stalkers away from the fight.

That left Jakob with only one option.

Not the best choice, true, but so be it.

"Jakob, what are you about to do?"

Lycia had watched him. Reading him. She believed that she knew what he was thinking.

"Something that I probably shouldn't."

"But you're going to do it anyway."

Jakob nodded. "I am. It needs to be done." He turned toward her then. "Get to Bertie and Martin. If this works, we can sweep Sharperson's Guard from the field. Make sure they're ready. They'll know what to do and when."

Lycia snorted. He thought that he could get rid of her so easily?

"They're ready," she replied, "and they know what they're doing. I'm going with you."

"But ..."

"No buts, Jakob," Lycia replied. "Stop wasting your breath. Let's get to it." She held a sword in each hand, ready for what he had in mind.

The easiest way to prevent the Stalkers from attacking his Highlanders was to collapse the main tunnel. But he couldn't do that now.

He wasn't concerned about Sharperson's soldiers standing close to the entrance. Rather, he feared what might happen to

Tommie and her archers. He'd likely doom them to a hideous death if he brought the main entrance down from where he was standing, and he wasn't willing to do that.

But he also wasn't willing to require his Highlanders to fight the Stalkers for him.

The monsters wanted him. And they could have him.

They'd just have to follow his lead now rather than the other way around.

"You're sure?"

"Let's get to it, Jakob," Lycia ordered, giving him a sharp nod. "Time's a wasting."

Jakob smiled then, bringing one of his daggers to his forehead and giving her a nod of respect, one fighter to another.

Then he turned, sprinting around the mass of soldiers and along the side of the mountain, Lycia right on his heels.

The Stalkers that were already outside the mine sought to adjust their angle of attack. But they were blocked from coming directly after their prey because Sharperson's soldiers stood in their way. Those same soldiers trying to kill the Stalkers.

Their efforts, although not always effective, gave Jakob and Lycia the chance to slip right by the beasts.

For just a second, Jakob wondered once again at the strange turn of events. How his enemies actually were aiding his efforts. He pushed that thought from his mind swiftly.

He had work to do.

Bloody work.

Seizing the Talent, he infused his daggers and Lycia's swords with natural magic as they raced into the gaping maw of the mountain.

12

SHADOWS IN THE NIGHT

Night had fallen in Ballinasloe, the darkness broken here and there by the torches set in large sconces that marked the major street intersections.

It was uncommonly quiet. Barely anyone in the streets. The carousing, drinking, and other activities synonymous with the waterfront neighborhoods never getting started that evening.

That wasn't really surprising considering what was occurring on the southern side of the harbor. Most people had decided to stay in their homes, avoiding the taverns and the brothels, not wanting to get involved, not wanting to be perceived as being involved.

Although not everyone.

A young woman wearing all black ran down the broad boulevard. She skidded around a corner, looking back over her shoulder.

"Stop, thief! You're only going to make this worse for yourself!"

A fist of soldiers chased her, several of them lagging, not used to doing anything more than strutting through the streets of Ballinasloe with a swagger that suggested that they owned the city, the residents always giving them a wide berth in the crowded marketplaces.

The young woman ignored the command, giving the Sergeant a rude gesture to demonstrate her disrespect, then running down the street for another hundred yards before turning right into an alley.

The Sergeant leading the patrol watched her cut down the darkened pathway, an evil smile playing across his face as he slowed his pace. His rabbit had just made a mistake, and it was going to cost her.

When he reached the entrance to the alley, the Sergeant had to wait before all of his soldiers caught up to him. He shook his head in disgust as two of his men bent down, putting their hands on their knees, gasping for breath. He feared that one of them was going to throw up his dinner. Truly embarrassing.

When this was all over, he would put all of his soldiers back into training. All of them having previously served in the Caledonian Royal Guard or one of the Duchy Guards, many had gone soft here in Fal Carrach.

Living the good life and owning the streets of the city. Forgetting the need to stay in shape. To stay sharp. Their pudgy frames and rounded bellies confirming it.

"Can we finish this now? You're allowing a girl to make you look like fools."

The four soldiers straightened at their Sergeant's insult. Then they nodded, though two still looked a bit green around the gills.

The squad walked down the alley slowly, making sure that their thief wasn't hiding in any of the doorways with the hope of slipping past them in the shadows. It wasn't long before they reached a small courtyard. The walls of the surrounding buildings, windowless, rose fifty or more feet into the air.

The young woman stood with her back to the far wall, glaring at the approaching soldiers with a simmering hatred.

The Sergeant stared right back at her, his lips curling up into a cruel smile. His men, several of whom were still winded and struggled not to show it, spread out around him so that the thief couldn't escape back the way she had come.

The Sergeant smiled then. His rabbit had trapped herself. How terribly sad. For her.

After all the aggravation she had given him, forcing him to chase her through the neighborhood, he decided then and there that he would allow his men to have a little fun with her first. Then they could decide whether to bring her to the Rock or just slit her throat and leave her in the gutter.

"You should have listened, rabbit," the Sergeant said with a broad grin. "Now it's only going to be a whole lot worse for you than it needs to be."

"I doubt that," the young woman called. She brandished a dagger in her hand.

The Sergeant studied her for a moment, giving his men time to step toward her, tightening the noose. Then he smirked and let out a bark of a laugh. "Why is that, rabbit? You going to stick me with that little blade of yours?"

Before the young woman could reply, a deep voice coming from a shadow that stepped out of the darkness behind him answered the Sergeant's question. "No, I'm going to do that."

The Sergeant failed to turn completely around to identify the shadow before the short sword slid through his back and between his ribs. He grunted in pain as the man holding the blade twisted the steel, although his attacker didn't pull the blade free. The shadow kept it there, holding the Sergeant in place.

A bolt of cold fire shot through the Sergeant, making him gasp, and then he couldn't feel anything at all below his waist. He couldn't even feel the rush of blood streaming down his legs, but he could see it.

He knew what that meant. He had seen the result of similar

work many times before. Yet there was nothing that he could do about it. He had lost all feeling in his lower extremities, and he was stuck like a pig.

Twisting his neck to the left, he finally caught a glimpse of his attacker. The Sergeant stared up at one of the largest men he had ever come across.

He recognized him. That sailor. The one who spent so much time with the gladiator.

Sven stared down at the Sergeant with a remorseless gaze. "You picked the wrong side." He then yanked his blade free, ignoring the Sergeant's painful gasp as he dropped to his knees, then fell face first onto the cobblestones.

Sven left him there, the Sergeant having just a few seconds of his life left. Lifting his gaze, Sven watched as his men slipped by him on silent feet. Before the rest of the soldiers knew what was happening, their focus still on the thief they had cornered, they were dead, ten soldiers of the Carlomin Guard doing the dirty work in an efficient, quiet, and clinical fashion.

The soldiers loyal to Hakea Roosarian had made an error. They had believed that all those fighting for the Carlomins were bottled up in their enclave.

They had just learned much too late that wasn't the case.

The Carlomins had made sure that no one could get onto their docks without their knowing. They also had made certain that there were ways to exit the enclave without anyone the wiser.

"Leave them," Sven ordered. "We'll let Roosarian wonder what happened to them." As his men stepped away from the dead soldiers, he turned to the young woman who had pushed herself off the wall and sheathed her dagger. "Shall we give it another go?"

The woman grinned. This was the second time that they had eliminated soldiers of the Fal Carrachian Guard in this manner. "Why not? Third time's the charm, right?"

Sven nodded. "Then let's get to it. We don't want to miss out on any of the fun."

The Huntress had sent into the city ten squads of soldiers under Sven's command. They had very specific tasks.

Their ultimate goal?

Chaos.

"Another round, Henley," Rufus said, placing a handful of coins on the counter. "For as many of the men as you can give another drink."

Henley didn't say a word as he wiped clean a mug. He just nodded. Then he motioned for the serving girls to make their way around the main dining room.

The golds that Rufus placed on the bar wouldn't cover the cost of half the soldiers drinking in his tavern that evening. That didn't matter to Henley. Every soldier would get a full mug of ale. And as many more as they wanted.

Better he lose some money tonight then have to deal with a throng of dead-eyed, angry soldiers nursing their wounds and bad memories.

The tavern owner understood why the soldiers needed their drink. Why they were so subdued. They had just gotten off duty for a few hours of rest after standing their post in front of the gate that opened into the Carlomin enclave.

Some of the men had been a part of the first attempt to break through the barrier. They hadn't succeeded.

From what Henley had heard, the Carlomin Guard had given Roosarian's soldiers quite a whipping, refusing to give ground, the bodies of their attackers piling up in front of them.

Henley couldn't say that bothered him all that much. He didn't have any real love for Roosarian. Her laws or her methods or her obvious desire to be more than just a Governor of Fal Carrach. But he did love his tavern, and he wanted to keep it in one piece.

Therefore, his willingness to help the soldiers drown their sorrows, because many of the men sitting on his benches looked to be reliving that humbling and deadly fight in their minds, several of them wearing bandages and slings. He didn't doubt that they were also mourning their lost comrades.

"Thank you, Henley," Rufus said, giving the tavern owner a nod.

Rufus had been close to the first rank during the initial clash in front of the gates. He hadn't enjoyed the experience.

In part because he believed that it was going to be an easy victory. He and his friends were the larger force.

However, the soldiers fighting for the Carlomins were highly skilled, more determined, and a great deal more disciplined. And it was that skill, determination, and discipline that had thrown back the Fal Carrachian Guard's opening assault, earning the impasse that extended into the evening.

A harsh lesson for him and all the other soldiers who took part in the battle.

Rufus was drinking because he knew what was coming next. Governor Roosarian couldn't allow the stalemate to continue for much longer. Not if she wanted to exercise power in Ballinasloe.

Therefore, he expected that the Fal Carrachian Guard would be attacking the Carlomin gate again, probably soon, and he didn't relish that prospect. Not in the least.

Having just fought the Carlomin soldiers, he had no doubt that any success earned during the next attack would come at a very high price.

The Fal Carrachian Guard would win. Rufus was sure of it.

Regardless of skill, determination, and discipline, he believed that the number of soldiers Roosarian could bring to bear would prove the difference in the end.

Even so, many of his comrades sitting with him now wouldn't be returning to this tavern after their next fight, their exit from this world permanent. That's why he wanted to drink. He didn't want to think about what the next scene of carnage would look like.

"You're all a bunch of lily-livered cowards!" screamed a shrill vice. Every eye in the tavern turned toward the back, staring at the slight somewhat disheveled man who had pushed his way through the door. "When the Huntress comes for you, you're all going to be pissing in your pants before you go to the other side! So enjoy the last few breaths you have!"

Then the man was gone, just as fast as he had appeared, back out the doorway.

Rufus usually was a level-headed fellow. That was why he was so well liked by his men. Soldiers didn't like Sergeants who put them in danger without good cause. They appreciated that Rufus tried to avoid that whenever he could.

But then, at that very moment, after having seen so many of his friends fall just hours before, never to rise again, he couldn't stop himself. Rufus couldn't control the rage that roared to life within him.

Rufus pushed himself up and off his stool, almost tripping on the bench behind him but keeping his feet as he raced after the little man who dared to challenge them. He didn't look over his shoulder. He didn't need to. He heard the scrape of the stools and benches across the floor as every soldier ran after him. All seeking to pound the little man into the cobblestones in front of the tavern.

Seconds after Rufus burst through the doorway and out onto the street, he skidded to a stop, as did the several score soldiers following him.

The little man was nowhere in sight. What Rufus did see chilled him to the bone.

Several dozen archers were aligned in a semicircle right in

front of the tavern. Their expressions were hard. Their bows were drawn, arrows nocked. Pointing right at him and his friends.

A strong voice from just behind the archers ruptured the silence draped over the street.

"Archers! Release!"

Rufus tried to make himself as small as possible, diving for the ground. He was too slow. The first arrow punched through his shoulder and out his back. The second pierced his thigh, shattering the bone. He collapsed to the cobblestones, screaming in anguish.

He tried to push himself back to his feet, understanding that his death was assured if he couldn't find a safe place to hide, but he couldn't escape the confusion that erupted around him.

Rufus was knocked back to the ground just an instant later. Seybold. One of his friends who had come across the Burnt Ocean with him fell on top of his legs, forcing him back down onto the cobblestones.

He cursed his bad luck, although Seybold's was worse. An arrow stuck out from his throat. His friend was gasping futilely for breath as he drowned in his own blood.

Despite the hindrance, Rufus' focus remained on escape. He didn't give a thought to attacking the line of archers. That was suicide. And he was certain that all the men with him who were still alive were thinking much the same.

The only safe place was the building behind him.

Yet when he finally was able to push Seybold off him and Rufus looked back toward the tavern, he realized that there was no escape.

Several of his friends who survived the initial onslaught pounded hopelessly on the main entrance to the tavern.

They were trapped.

Henley had bolted the door. Either he didn't want to be a part of this or he was a part of this, loyal to the Huntress.

It didn't really matter now, because Rufus knew what was coming next.

The end.

"Archers! Release!"

A TROOP of soldiers forty strong marched along one of the main boulevards of Ballinasloe. The street, wide enough for three teams of horses to trot abreast of one another, led away from the harbor, over the rolling hills, and to the north.

Climbing the last knoll, the city's northern gate came into view. If the soldiers continued on their way, marching out beneath the portcullis, they could take the road all the way to the Stone in the Highlands. It was the only causeway that linked the eastern Territories. Fal Carrach to the Highlands and then on to the Northern Territory and Shadow's Reach.

Not much thought had been given to building a road to the south, the Governor down that way not as interested in working with Hakea Roosarian on the proposed project. Cerula Makarin understood what a closer connection between Benewyn and Fal Carrach meant, and she had no desire to be placed under the thumb of Hakea Roosarian.

The soldiers understood Cerula Makarin's reluctance. They didn't want to be under Roosarian's thumb either.

For that reason, they weren't going any farther. Not with their target right in front of them.

"I can't stand this jacket," complained one of the men toward the back of the column. "It's too itchy, and it stinks. I don't think it's been washed for months."

"Quit your whining, Francis," replied Arin, the soldier marching along next to him.

Both kept in step with their comrades as the wall grew larger in front of them. The main gate was only fifty yards away now.

Thankfully, all was quiet that early morning. There were soldiers standing in front of the guardhouse and a few atop the wall, but they appeared to be disinterested or distracted.

Their usual numbers had been greatly reduced. With Governor Roosarian turning her Guard's focus toward removing the Carlomins, she had pulled as many soldiers toward that task as she could while still maintaining some semblance of a defense for the city.

"My jacket is wet," explained Arin. It wasn't visible in the darkness, but there was a very large bloodstain on the back. "So it could be worse for you. Now concentrate on what we need to do."

Francis nodded as the column came to a halt just beneath the open portcullis. The Sergeant at the front of the column approached the two soldiers who stepped out of the gatehouse doorway. Arin and Francis heard the quiet laughter that followed.

That's why Sergeant Willison had been selected for this task. He had an easy way about him and could make a friend out of anyone in seconds. Just as he was doing now.

However, Francis and Arin and the rest of the men with them weren't listening to the conversation. Instead they kept their gaze on Sergeant Willison, their hands hovering just above the hilts of their short swords.

The conversation between Sergeant Willison and the soldiers continued for a few seconds more, laughter echoing beneath the archway, when he placed his hand on the back of his head, rubbing gently at his bald scalp.

The soldiers behind the Sergeant moved swiftly, Francis and Arin with them, having waited breathlessly for that signal. They rushed past the Sergeant, who while bringing his hand down from his head had pulled the dagger free from the sheath he wore at the back of his neck. With two quick stabs, the soldiers conversing with him lay dying on the ground, desperately trying to stem with their hands the blood gushing out of the holes in their throats.

Francis and Arin sprinted into the gatehouse, climbing the steps, ignoring the handful of dead soldiers lying in pools of their own blood, their friends from the front rank already well ahead of them. They turned to the right as soon as they exited the tower and began running across the battlements toward the east.

Sergeant Willison had been quite clear. He wanted them in position within two minutes of reaching the top of the wall. Arin and Francis meant to do just that.

Every soldier in the troop was loyal to Talia Carlomin. She had given them work, a home, hope, opportunity, after they had lost their loved ones to the pirates marauding across the Sea of Mist.

Now they had their chance to pay back a portion of that debt and take their vengeance on Hakea Roosarian, the orchestrator of those attacks. The cause of their loved ones' murders.

As they ran across the top of the wall, with the majority of Roosarian soldiers ordered to the Carlomin section of the docks, Francis and Arin were confident that they would be able to gain control of the city wall and the other gates within the hour.

Roosarian had expected a conventional fight from the Huntress. Talia Carlomin wasn't going to give the Governor that.

Instead, the Huntress was going to do all in her power to disrupt and destroy. To punch at Roosarian's kidneys again and again, leaving her off balance and confused, before finally aiming a blow for her head.

It made sense to Arin and Francis. They had trained with the Crimson Giant.

The red-haired gladiator had a lot of sayings. One in particular played through their minds as they approached the next guardhouse.

"Don't fight fair. Fight to win."

They meant to do just that.

RAFIA STOOD at the bow of the sloop, her eyes searching for the pier that was just a little farther down the wharf, expecting it to be visible in the next few seconds.

The cutter slowly glided through the smooth water, only a few of its sails in use as it curled around the handful of vessels moored in the deeper water of the harbor. Declan stood behind her atop the helm, hands on the wheel, deftly maneuvering the cutter that had once been a part of the *Freedom* and had now become the vessel favored by the Blood Company.

"That's it?"

"That's it," confirmed Talia.

Rather than leading her small but able force in the fight soon to begin again, Talia had left Sirena in charge of the Carlomin Guard and the defense of the enclave she and her mother had carved out of Ballinasloe.

It had been a difficult decision for Talia. Initially, she had felt as if she were betraying the trust given to her by her sailors and soldiers. Leaving them to their fates while she abandoned them.

Declan had offered her a piece of advice that helped to confirm in her own mind the rightness of her decision.

"What's the point in cutting off the tail. The snake can still bite you."

Talia couldn't disagree with the gruff Sergeant of the Blood

Company's logic. In large part because it sounded like something her own father would have told her. Or Davin, the gladiator never reluctant to share with her what he was thinking.

Because Declan's advice rang true for her, Talia had taken on a separate mission. One that was both selfish, in that she felt that she was the only one who could do it, and essential.

She had decided that this was her best chance to go after Hakea Roosarian. Her adversary would be distracted. Focused on what was going on in the southern section of the harbor. Not concerned about her own safety so long as she remained at the Rock. Only concerned about the success of her troops in the city.

Besides, Talia trusted in Sirena's abilities and her judgment. The Captain of her Guard and the soldiers with her would more than hold their own against Roosarian's soldiers. Especially with her mother there to offer the attackers a few surprises.

Talia's objective was to ensure that their willingness to assume that responsibility wasn't in vain. To do that, she needed to cut off the head of the snake just as Declan hinted.

She needed to kill Hakea Roosarian.

If she succeeded, then Ballinasloe would be hers.

If she failed then all that she and her family had fought for would be burned to the ground.

So better not to think of that. Better to focus instead on what needed to be done. Not on what could go wrong.

Davin had told her that, among many other sayings that he had acquired from the man who had trained the gladiator and was at that very moment demonstrating the deft and gentle touch of a sailor who had spent his entire life on the ocean.

Talia shook her head more in bemusement than annoyance. Even though Davin wasn't there with her, he was still there with her.

"Then let's get started," Rafia said with malicious glee.

Reaching for the Talent, marble-sized balls of energy shot from her fingers, streaking through the air just above the surface of the water. Her focus was the Roosarian dock and the eight ships moored to it.

At the first touch of the white-hot energy, nothing happened. There were just a few initial sparks that appeared to fizzle out as the power burned through the hulls.

Rafia wasn't concerned. She had selected this particular tool because she wanted the energy to burrow deep into the vessels, ensuring their complete destruction.

Seconds later it seemed that she was going to get her wish, the first hint of flames appearing on each of the vessels as well as on the far end of the dock where the launches that traveled across to the Rock were moored. Those flames, stoked by the wind that Rafia sent in that direction with another burst of the Talent, rapidly became a conflagration hungry for anything in its path.

"That should do the trick," Declan called down from the helm, the gladiator nodding in satisfaction.

"That it should," Rafia agreed.

"Now let's go have some fun."

"You see them?"

"They're hard to miss," replied Sergeant Chesterton. He commanded several companies of soldiers positioned at the entrance to the Roosarian dock, which was the primary point for crossing the harbor to the Rock.

His focus wasn't on the pier that extended out over the water behind him. Rather he looked toward the city, observing dozens of figures scurrying through the alleys and streets that led out onto the main boulevard that ran along the harbor and right in front of their position.

The bulk of Roosarian's soldiers, three thousand in all, had crossed over under the command of Captain Vanion Oselnik. The Governor had charged him with eliminating Talia Carlomin and her family's presence in the Ballinasloe harbor.

Because the Governor was so desperate for a quick victory, Roosarian had left a skeleton force to guard the Rock. Only two companies in total. Along with the two companies under Chesterton's command that were responsible for defending the Roosarian dock and managing the launches that went back and forth to the citadel.

Chesterton didn't know if he should be worried by what he was seeing. Probably not. With Carlomin's soldiers bottled up, he had more than enough troops with him to hold his position.

The shadows in the alleys likely were just brigands or thieves hoping to get lucky while the Fal Carrachian Guard was committed to its more critical assignment. That didn't bother Chesterton. The ne'er-do-wells could enjoy their one night of freedom, because once the Governor crushed Carlomin, Chesterton had little doubt that his next assignment would be purging the city of any unsavory and disloyal elements.

"Sergeant."

"Not now." Chesterton stared hard at one of the larger streets that emptied out in front of the Roosarian dock.

The torches burning in the sconces set at the intersections gave him a good view for about fifty yards. Beyond that he couldn't tell with any certainty what was going on.

Yet he was sure that there were more shadows there than there had been just moments before. A lot more. It made him start to think that there were more than just a few thieves and cutthroats massing just beyond the glow of the flames.

"Sergeant."

"Not now, Eddin!" Chesterton was losing patience with his subordinate. Usually, he was calmer than this and less of a hindrance, understanding when he needed to keep his mouth shut while Chesterton tried to puzzle out their next move.

Chesterton squinted, attempting to pierce the darkness just beyond the light. Were those soldiers lined up in formation? Or were his eyes playing tricks on him because of the shadows and the gloom that consumed the boulevard?

It had to be the latter. All of the Carlomin soldiers were defending their enclave. There was no way that any of them would be anywhere else but there with the Fal Carrachian Guard preparing to attack again.

"Sergeant!"

"Now now, Eddin!" Chesterton shouted.

He turned on his heel quickly so that his second in command could see just how displeased he was. Chesterton also was about to offer Eddin a few choice curses as part of an upbraiding designed to strip the flesh from the soldier and leave him a simpering wreck.

Chesterton didn't say anything, however, the words drying up in the back of his throat. He simply stared in shock at the sight that greeted him.

The dock behind him was on fire. Most of his soldiers were running in that direction, hoping that they could put out the flames whipped up by the gusts of wind.

Foolhardy.

His men had no chance of doing that. The ships were doomed. They might be able to save some of the dock, but not all, the far end already ablaze.

Rather than try to put out the flames, his soldiers needed to cut the ropes holding the burning vessels to the dock and hope that they drifted away. Then they needed to destroy the pier a little farther down and open a gap over the water so the entire structure didn't burn down to the water.

When he heard the pounding coming toward him from the town, he realized that those thoughts were no longer of any use.

Chesterton turned slowly this time, reluctantly, pulling his sword from the scabbard on his hip. It was a lost cause. He understood that. But he preferred to go down putting up a fight, because he doubted that the soldiers marching toward him with such strict discipline would offer him any mercy.

Clever, he thought.

A game of misdirection.

Carlomin had pulled all eyes toward her enclave and now she was going to rabbit punch the Governor.

Very clever indeed.

Chesterton took a few steps forward, setting himself as the several columns of soldiers stepped onto the Roosarian dock and continued their rapid march toward him, apparently having decided that they would simply run right over him.

And why not?

Only Eddin and a few soldiers stood with him. The ones who had gone off to fight the blaze at his back would learn the error of their ways quickly enough.

"You're certain that they can't see us?"

"Quite certain," Rafia replied, knowing that Declan was asking only because they were in a tenuous position. "But they can hear us. So keep moving and keep quiet."

It was well past midnight, though the morning was still several hours off. The gladiators of the Blood Company were tight against the wall of the citadel or hidden among the large rocks that shot up out of the beach, none of them willing to leave themselves exposed.

Rafia wasn't concerned. She had used the Talent to mask their approach. The gloom of the night and the natural fog coming off the sea aided her efforts. The pounding of the surf on the shore muffling the sound of any movement.

Besides, even if she hadn't employed the natural magic at her command, she didn't think that they had much to fear from the skeleton guard manning the main gates to the Rock and the walls.

Their attention likely was focused on the two areas in Ballinasloe that couldn't help but draw their interest.

To the south, the sounds of a large number of soldiers moving through the streets drifted over the water, all of the lights in that section of the city concentrated around the main gate to the Carlomin dock.

The massive braziers being moved along the road that worked its way around the harbor suggested that Captain Oselnik wasn't going to wait for the dawn to try to root out those the Governor deemed rebels.

Knowing that because of the distance between the Carlomin compound and the Rock the soldiers manning the parapet could see very little in that direction other than the dim light of the braziers, she assumed that the soldiers instead were focused on the massive fire that was sweeping across the Roosarian dock on the other side of the harbor, consuming not only the pier but also all the ships moored to it.

Looking over her shoulder and seeing the destruction that she had wrought brought a small smile to her grim countenance. Her quick work had proven more effective than she anticipated.

It was absolute chaos on what was left of the Roosarian pier. Made even worse by the soldiers who rushed out of the darkness to ensure that the Governor's few companies stationed there could do nothing to stop the rampaging flames.

With all that was going on, Rafia believed that it was the perfect time to make a play for the Rock. The soldiers on the battlements were distracted. Probably even worried with the inferno consuming the dock.

Yet at the same time they would feel safe, the men

standing their posts a few hundred feet above her not believing that the main gate or the walls could be breached, having little to fear from an attacking force despite their depleted numbers.

And they were right in that respect. Rafia doubted that Talia's troops could accomplish either task. Taking the gate or scaling the walls. She doubted that even the Blood Company could succeed with either assault.

But the Blood Company wouldn't have to. Because the gladiators had another means for gaining access to the citadel thanks to the knowledge Talia had acquired just a few nights before during her ill-fated expedition with Davin.

"And the way is clear?"

"For now."

"What do you mean for now?" demanded Declan. "Stalkers?"

"That's my guess," Rafia replied. "We hold the advantage, though. They don't know we're here yet."

"But they will as soon as we start working our way beneath the citadel." Talia stood right next to the Magus at the entrance to the crevice that would take them into the Rock.

"They will." The Magus didn't see any sense in trying to sugarcoat the truth.

Talia nodded, having assumed as much. Still, she fought to contain her worry. For the success of her mission. Even more about Davin's fate.

Rafia understood. She had sensed the connection between Talia and Davin, a closeness forming between them as they worked together. And just like Declan and every gladiator on the beach with her, Rafia wanted to save the Crimson Giant from whatever Hakea Roosarian had planned for him.

That goal driving her, she extended her senses throughout the citadel. Although she couldn't pinpoint Davin's location because of the tainted power that enveloped the Rock, she could confirm that he was still alive. At least for a little while longer.

"Have no fear," Declan said, noting Talia's worry. "We'll take care of the Stalkers. You do what you need to do."

Talia nodded in thanks, using Declan's quiet confidence to strengthen her own.

"Blood Company," Declan said softly, not wanting to draw the eyes of any of the soldiers standing on the wall above them, "wedge formation. Eyes to the front. Eyes above. Just in case."

13

OLD FRIENDS

"I have been waiting for this, Makarin. For a very, very long time."

"Be careful what you wish for, Oselnik. You might not get what you want."

"I'm not worried, Makarin. You've been protected until now, hiding behind your boss. Behind your soldiers. But now you can't. Now I'm going to put you in your place." Oselnik put his hands on his hips, then spit a big glob of phlegm toward the entrance to the Carlomin enclave. "I'm going to enjoy this, Makarin. More than you could ever possibly imagine."

Sirena Makarin shook her head in disgust, giving Oselnik a sad smile as she looked down upon him from atop the wall that protected the Carlomin holdings in Ballinasloe.

She understood why Vanion Oselnik, Roosarian's peacock of a Captain, was relishing this moment. He believed that he was holding all the cards.

The numbers favored him. So did the fact that his enemy had nowhere to go. Because he knew that Talia Carlomin would not abandon what she had worked so hard to create here in Fal Carrach.

Oselnik perceived the soldiers loyal to Talia Carlomin as having taken a defensive posture, seeking to protect the enclave. It was the smart play. The only play. Since they had no other good choices.

In large part because of the overwhelming strength of the Fal Carrachian Guard. The long column of Roosarian soldiers extended across the entrance that opened into the small square centered on the Carlomin gate and then all the way back down the street for several hundred yards then up into the hills upon which the neighborhood was built, the last few ranks hidden in the gloom of the early morning.

That didn't surprise Sirena in the least. She had learned quickly that Oselnik was quite limited in how he perceived the world around him.

Oselnik saw what he wanted to see. He never considered what he couldn't see.

With that reminder, a calm confidence settled within Sirena despite the frightening sight of so many soldiers staring back at her.

"Say what you want," Sirena called down from atop the wall. Her soldiers lined the parapet with her, imperturbable, visibly unconcerned by the mass of men just thirty feet below them who in just minutes would be making another attempt to breach the gate. "Words have little meaning here. Only deeds matter. A lesson that you should have learned a long time ago."

Oselnik stood just a few feet in front of his first rank of soldiers. They held their shields and spears tightly, many of them fidgeting and shuffling their feet. The bravado of their commander had not washed on to them. Instead, they remembered or had heard about what had happened to their friends during the assault of just a few hours past.

Good, Sirena thought to herself. That would make things easier for her. Because the challenge the Roosarian soldiers faced during that first attack was nothing compared to what was going to come their way once this ridiculous conversation was complete.

Wanting to get to the end of her dialogue with Oselnik as quickly as possible, she gave him a wink and then a snort, her contempt for the man obvious to all who were watching. Then she smiled, pleased to see how easily she angered her rival, his fingers curling into tight fists and a flush of red creeping up his neck to his cheeks.

"One last chance, Makarin. Throw down your sword and pledge loyalty to Governor Roosarian. I'll go easy on you and your friends playing at soldiers if you do." The contempt in the Captain's voice set off a low murmur of anger among the Carlomin Guard. "You can empty and clean my piss pot. I might even allow you into my bed when I'm feeling particularly desperate for the attentions of a less-than-comely woman. That's got to be better than a sword between the ribs, don't you think?"

"In my opinion, the sword would be preferable," Sirena shouted back, "although not the one I have on good authority from several ladies of the night that has proven to be ... how should I say this ... a bit ... small ... and soft."

With that cutting comment she earned the laughter of the men and women standing on the battlements with her, Oselnik's red flush spreading more rapidly across his face.

Sirena's bemused smile grew wider. She could tell that it was getting harder for her rival. Her taunts were testing Oselnik's patience. Especially the last one, which had hit so close to home.

Sirena hoped to provoke the Captain of the Fal Carrachian Guard into an early attack. No such luck yet, however. He was sticking to his plan and using the conversation between them to give his sergeants some extra time to get the last of his troops in place.

Sirena was moderately impressed, although she didn't see

how adding a few more companies to the end of a column of several thousand soldiers was going to tilt the battle to come any more into Oselnik's favor than it already was.

Although she could understand his reasoning. Clearly Oselnik had no desire to fail a second time. Not with Roosarian watching so intently. Thus, the Captain's very simple strategy.

Break through the gate with overwhelming force and then swarm the compound beyond.

In most other circumstances, quite an effective strategy.

A bloody strategy as well.

The damage that the Carlomin Guard would inflict upon the attackers obviously was of little concern to their commander. The loss of life by his own troops nothing at all compared to his need to meet the demands of the Governor.

With the number of soldiers lined up behind Oselnik, Sirena couldn't deny that Roosarian's soldiers enjoyed a good chance of success.

Or they would have.

If Hari Hoohannen, Master Shipbuilder to Talia Carlomin, hadn't been working on a few innovations during his spare time all designed to aid the defenders and prove useful at a moment just like this one.

"Are you ready, Hari? I'm really getting tired of having to waste my breath speaking with this blowhard."

"That I can understand," Hari replied. The large man gripped a blacksmith's hammer in one hand, a shield in the other. Although if the next few minutes went as he hoped they would, he would have little need for either. "And yes, more than ready."

"Then there's really no point in ceding the initiative to the Fal Carrachian Guard, now is there?"

"No, there is not," the Master Shipbuilder agreed with a firm nod.

With a grim expression, he turned to his wife, Arellia. She

had worked with her husband to perfect their latest mechanism, and when she asked that she be put in charge of its use, Hari couldn't say no to her.

Arellia wanted to ensure that the weapon they had created worked as it should. He could understand. She was just as much of a perfectionist as he was, which was why they were such a good match for one another.

Of course, it wasn't really a brand-new contraption that Hari and Arellia had been working on. Rather it was an innovation on a weapon that had demonstrated its worth when hunting and then seizing pirate vessels.

Beginning with the design of the large ballistae fixed on the bows and helms of every Carlomin cutter, Arellia refined the apparatus by reducing its size by a third in order to give the weapon more maneuverability, now requiring only a two-person crew to operate. Perhaps most concerning, at least as the soldiers massing beneath the wall would soon discover, she had refined the weapon so that it could shoot three lances before the crew needed to reload.

"Do as you will, my love," Hari requested.

Arellia didn't bother to respond to her husband, instead intent on putting their latest creation into play. "Archers to the wall!"

The soldiers assigned to the task moved quickly to obey, pushing the already loaded ballistae that were as tall as they were along tracks fixed atop the parapet. Thanks to Hari's unique design, the soldiers could pivot each weapon in any direction by unlatching a lock with their foot, turning the ballista with the handles slotted into the side, and then relocking the weapon in place. All in just a matter of seconds.

But that unique aspect of the weapon's design wouldn't be called upon in the clash to come. Not with the plethora of targets waiting below in a very tight space. What Sirena had described as a killing ground.

Arellia smiled devilishly when she saw the look of shock and then horror that passed across Oselnik's face. She had never viewed herself as a violent person. Even so, she was going to take a unique pleasure in what she was about to do.

Because based on the evidence that Talia Carlomin had helped to uncover, she believed that Oselnik was the one responsible for burning her sister-in-law's forge. And, in her opinion, there was nothing sweeter than revenge.

"Archers, release!" she shouted. Her strong voice carried down the length of the wall in both directions, immediately followed by a cascade of swooshes.

The four-foot-long bolts streaked through the air, shooting down from atop the parapet with deadly effect, one right after another. What seemed like a never-ending assault to those unfortunate soldiers forced to stand against it, the steel lances screaming toward them with a frightening rapidity.

With the Fal Carrachian troops packed so tightly together, and the buildings lining the streets leading to the main gate making it all but impossible for them to escape the onslaught, there was no way that the Carlomin archers could miss.

The limitations of the battlefield, something that Vanion Oselnik had paid little attention to in drawing up his plan of attack, all but ensured the deaths of dozens upon dozens of soldiers who had no chance whatsoever to fight back.

The men operating the ballistae didn't take the time to survey the damage they inflicted. Instead, they stayed true to their training, making use of the automatic winding winch to load three more lances in less than ten seconds and then fire again, and then again, and then again, one soldier loading the ballista, the other firing, Arellia giving them the freedom to pick their own targets, of which there were too many to count.

Besides, the archers didn't need to see what was happening below them to know that the soldiers loyal to Governor Roosarian could not stand against them. The screams of terror and pain that rose to the top of the battlements and echoed off the wall and the surrounding buildings confirmed their success.

Any soldier struck by a lance was punched back off his feet, the force of the blow so powerful that a single spear could kill three soldiers at one time if the men were lined up one behind the other.

A gruesome, grisly death. A terrible weapon. Yet one that served a very distinct and necessary purpose.

It wasn't long before the first twenty ranks of Roosarian soldiers had ceased to exist, any survivors of the initial attack using the rows of their dead comrades as a shelter, because the shields they carried were of no use, a lance piercing the thin steel with ease. Only a wall of the dead several bodies deep could lessen the power of the blow.

From atop the wall, Sirena watched the slaughter impassively even as she began to feel slightly ill. It was nothing but chaos in front of the Carlomin gates.

And that chaos was spreading.

Ripples of fear rolled through the ranks of the Fal Carrachian Guard. The soldiers at the very back already were retreating, having no desire to join their unlucky comrades now lying dead or dying in the small square.

Pleased by the success of the ballistae, in large part because those weapons helped to keep her soldiers alive, as the archers continued their bloody work Sirena scanned the battlefield, doing her best to ignore the carnage that sickened her. She was searching for one person in particular.

The coward was inching his way along the edge of the street, just as often playing dead as he sought to escape the notice of the archers as he crawled over and around the bodies of the men he had commanded just seconds before.

Sirena growled in anger. She was done with Oselnik. It was time to deal with that bastard once and for all.

But first, she needed to employ one more tool. Then she could set her soldiers after him and gain the revenge that she craved.

"Hari, would you please light the way for us?"

Morning was still several hours away. The large braziers that Oselnik had made his soldiers push through the town from the Roosarian dock to illuminate the square for his attack had proven their utility.

Just not in the way that Roosarian's Captain had imagined.

The portable firepits aided Sirena's efforts by giving her archers the light they needed to find and kill their targets. But those braziers that continued to burn brightly didn't provide the breadth of visibility that she desired since she couldn't see much beyond the square.

"With pleasure," the Master Shipbuilder replied, exceedingly pleased at how effective the ballistae that he and Arellia perfected had proven to their efforts. And now it was time to determine if their other creation demonstrated a similar utility.

He motioned with his hammer to his sister, Harina, who stood just a few yards away from him and not too far from her sister-in-law, who offered instructions from time to time to the archers, helping those who might not be using their weapon as quickly and efficiently as she would have liked.

Harina didn't say a word. She simply nodded, turned, and then stepped to the back wall, looking down into the courtyard below.

Seven small catapults waited there. Each one operated by a crew of three. Right next to each catapult sat pedestals that were connected to trays that held ten ceramic balls all the size of a man's head.

The concept was quite simple and of Harina's own design. When the loader of the catapult picked up one of the ceramic balls from the pedestal, another ball rolled into place automatically. Ensuring a constant stream of materiel.

"Engineers, prepare to fire!"

The synchronization of motion that occurred upon Harina giving that command was frightening, the seven teams appearing to move as one as they winched back the arm of the catapult, locked it into place, and then loaded a ceramic ball.

Once all the teams were ready, she looked back across the battlements, meeting Sirena's eye. The Captain of the Carlomin Guard nodded. It was time.

Harina turned back to her engineers. "Release!"

A member of each team pressed on a foot lever, releasing the arm, the catapults sending seven balls flying through the air and over the wall.

In the dark of the night, the already terrified soldiers of the Fal Carrachian Guard couldn't see what was coming toward them through the air. They could only hear a strange whistle that was louder than the screams and shouts of the dying and those trying to escape the battlefield.

The soldiers didn't realize the extent of the threat until the ceramic balls struck the cobblestones, the outer shell cracking and releasing a liquid fire -- a mixture of pitch, tar, and another substance that Hari had been working on – that combined with the air exploded into flames.

Wood, flesh, and steel, it didn't matter. There was no way to remove the flammable mix. The intense, white-hot fire burned through anything, and it burned until it no longer had fuel.

The initial blazes that erupted in the square were bad enough. When the engineers adjusted their aim, firing their shells farther up the street and into the crowded ranks of the Fal Carrachian soldiers, another, more intense ripple of fear ran through the mass of troops still crammed into the street.

Once the soldiers realized that they couldn't beat out the flames, their attempts to do so only increasing the risk that they were set alight themselves, that ripple transformed into a wave of panic that only intensified as more and more of the horrifying spheres flew over the wall and smashed farther up the street, setting fire to the buildings, stalls, soldiers, anything unfortunate enough to feel the touch of that highly combustible sticky liquid.

In just minutes, several dozen blazes burned all along the causeway that only grew stronger as a stiff breeze picked exactly the wrong moment to gust in off the harbor.

As the fires spread and raged, soldiers burning alive, those touched by the flames sought to dive into the harbor. Yet they only made it a few steps before they collapsed over the bodies of their peers, taken down with a lance through the chest. The archers still engaged in their bloody work.

What was already pandemonium descended into a mass stampede, the Fal Carrachian soldiers forgetting their duty and caring for only one thing.

Escape.

A chance at survival. No matter how slim that chance might be.

They no longer thought of the riches they could enjoy upon claiming the wealth of the Carlomins. They cared only for themselves. They cared only about the possibility of somehow earning a few more minutes of life.

To do that, they needed to get away from the Carlomin gate and the fire raining down upon them.

Yet that was proving to be almost impossible. Their own friends and comrades, many of them dying around them, many of them already dead, blocked their way as the firepots and steel lances streaked through the air with a mechanical precision.

Then, with the Fal Carrachian Guard desperate to retreat but unable to do so, the last part of Talia Carlomin's strategy came into play.

A horrible, terrible slaughter. Yet one that was necessary.

Because the Carlomin Guard had no desire to fight against such overwhelming odds.

With Roosarian's soldiers reduced to nothing more than a desperate mob, Sirena nodded to the men managing the winches.

Slowly, the main gate opened. She left her position atop the wall to take her place in the center, rank upon rank of her soldiers lined up behind her.

They ignored the devastation, focusing on the last task that they needed to complete before they could declare victory.

"Soldiers of the Carlomin Guard!" she shouted, sword in hand, a determined light in her eyes, "we will claim this city for Talia Carlomin! Advance!"

14

DANGER FROM ABOVE

"Majdi, clear the ceiling!"

The gladiator usually held a scutum in the shield wall. However, he had taken on a different assignment as the Blood Company advanced through the tunnel.

Working their way down the roughly cut corridor upon entering through the crevice, the gladiators made good progress, facing little challenge from the monsters hunting them.

The Stalkers raced out of the darkness singly. Easy kills for the experienced fighters.

The shields prevented the monsters from forcing their way into the formation. The spears stabbed with a deadly precision, so much so that the swords in the back never had to demonstrate their skill.

Until the Stalkers changed how they played the game.

Some of the monsters, upon watching their ilk throw themselves uselessly against the wall of steel, adopted a smarter approach. They cut into the stone with their razor-sharp claws and scrambled up the walls of the corridor. Hanging from the ceiling, they waited in the darkness, exercising a patience that surprised Declan and Rafia, the monsters dropping down right into the middle of the wedge.

The first Stalker to perform the maneuver almost gutted Dorlan from behind, its daggerlike digits just about to rip through his back and into his belly.

Asaia halted the attack just in time with a quick flick of her wrist. The spike at the end of her whip punched right through the back of the Stalker's neck, the monster standing upright for a few heartbeats more before collapsing to the rough ground.

Since then, Declan had given Majdi and Jenus the task of taking care of any of the beasts that might have latched onto the ceiling above them.

Seeing the blood-red eyes glaring down at him, Majdi punched up with his spear, taking the Stalker in the throat before the monster could drop in among the gladiators.

Jenus stood a few feet behind him, his eyes never leaving the ceiling, scanning for those tell-tale gleams of red, prepared for the next attack.

The Blood Company's quick shift in tactics negated the threat the Stalkers presented. That and Rafia, the Magus always ready to use the Talent to help the gladiators clear the path of hazards.

That desire driving her, Rafia crafted a ball of light and sent the blazing sphere well ahead of them, eliminating the advantage the darkness gave the Stalkers.

As the last of the monsters seeking to prevent their advance died at the sharp end of a spear, the Blood Company reached the chamber where Talia and Davin had watched Hakea Roosarian and the cowled woman transform a human being into a creature that was less than human.

With all that had happened, it seemed like it had been years since Talia was last in this chamber that smelled like a slaughter pit, yet it had only been a few days.

Talia had hoped that Davin would be here. Locked away in one of the cells that lined the circular chamber.

No such luck.

Upon entering the space, the gladiators broke their formation, taking up positions at all the entrances, prepared for another batch of Stalkers to join the fight. Yet they were greeted instead by a strange quiet, what they interrupted as only a brief lull in the battle.

Rafia used the gift of time to walk around the hall. She stepped into the cells, sometimes standing there behind the bars for a minute or more, her eyes closed, often touching the stone wall or the steel door. The more she explored the chamber, the darker her face became, her fury made plain.

"This is where it happened?"

Talia nodded. "It was a terrible change to observe."

"I have no doubt of that," Rafia replied quietly. "The Curse is strong in this room. But there is more than just the Curse here."

"What do you mean by that?" Talia didn't understand. What else could there be but the Curse?

"The evil that permeates this room, these cells, there's an ancientness to it."

Rafia stepped up to the alcove cut out of the wall, a small box resting there, several empty vials still within it. She nodded.

Talia had sent a similar vial to her on the Isle of Mist, setting in motion the chain of events that had brought the Blood Company to Ballinasloe. These vials were empty, but the taint of the evil power they once contained was still incredibly strong.

It reminded her of a feeling that teased the edge of her consciousness. Yet she couldn't grasp the hint.

"I don't know what it is," she admitted reluctantly.

"You don't know what it is?" Talia found that shocking.

"I don't, because I have never come across this before. Still, if I had to guess ..."

"A guess works for me." Declan wasn't one who enjoyed confusion. He liked to know what he was fighting. Because then he could figure out how to kill it.

"If I had to guess, based on my lessons when I was first starting out as a Magus, we've come upon a menace that I had hoped had been banished from the Natural World never to return."

When she said it, Rafia gave Declan a meaningful look. In an instant, he understood to what she was referring.

His expression, already grim, became even grimmer. It seemed that even though he had left his family and the responsibility entrusted to him decades before, that responsibility was calling to him once again, this time hundreds of leagues from his birthplace.

"Banished from the Natural World?" Talia didn't understand the Magus' comment.

"I'll explain later," Rafia said, feeling the press of time and wanting to keep the Blood Company moving. "We have done good work here, but we are not done. The Stalkers are dead. At least those that I can identify."

"You can't tell where Davin might be or if there are other Stalkers still about?" asked Talia.

"No, I can't," Rafia admitted, chafing at having to reveal that truth. "Whoever created the Stalkers has used the Curse in a way that I don't understand and that I really don't want to understand. The Dark Magus has shielded the rest of the keep from me. I cannot find Davin. I cannot see any of the other threats that remain."

"Then we'll do as we need to," said Declan. "We'll do as we've trained to do."

"Fair enough," Talia said. "We still have the soldiers loyal to the Governor to deal with."

"We'll manage them," Declan said with a calm certainty. "You do what you need to do, Huntress."

Talia nodded, her expression one of steely determination. She had little doubt that wherever Roosarian was hiding within the citadel, Davin would be close by.

She would find him, and then she would cut off the head of the snake.

15

INTO THE DARKNESS

Jakob slashed to his left, his blazing steel slicing right through the wrist of the Stalker that was reaching for him.

The monster howled in anguish, blood spurting from its stump, its clawed hand lost in the melee taking place right in front of the mine.

Despite the severity of its wound, the Stalker continued to attack.

Desperate to fight its way past the soldiers.

Desperate to claim its prey.

The monster failed. The Stalker only took one more step before it shrieked again.

One of the soldiers saw an opportunity and took it, driving his sword right into the small of the Stalker's back.

The soldier didn't have a chance to celebrate his victory, the claw of another Stalker slashing right across his throat and ripping it out.

Rather than taking a bite from its grisly trophy, the Stalker jumped over the last few soldiers keeping it from its quarry.

The Stalker was about to lunge at Jakob's back, but the monster made a mistake. So intent on killing the one its Master wanted dead, the Stalker paid little attention to the confused maelstrom of combat of which it was a part.

It didn't see Lycia's gleaming sword plunge through its chest from the back, but it certainly felt it. Its heart pierced, the Stalker groaned and then dropped to the ground.

Lycia spent the next few seconds pulling her sword free – not the delay she wanted -- and then she was gone, driven forward by the howls that followed her, the Stalkers who had emerged into the light seeking to return to the darkness of the mine. Compelled to kill their prey.

Quite ironic, the gladiator thought. She was seeking to escape the Stalkers that were heavily engaged with Sharperson's soldiers, the only path for her to do that taking her toward the Stalkers yet to make their way out from beneath the mountain. All the while with enemies fighting all around her and Jakob.

"Lycia, you really don't need to be here," Jakob called over his shoulder as he raced into the mine.

"Leave it, Jakob. I'm here. I'm not going anywhere. Let's get to it."

Jakob grumbled under his breath, both impressed and irritated by her stubbornness, knowing that whether he liked it or not the gladiator was going to do what she wanted to do.

As he sprinted deeper into the gloom, Lycia on his heels, their way lit by their glowing blades, Jakob took some solace from the fact that they timed their run perfectly.

They entered the mine exactly when the last of the Stalkers exited. Or rather, the first batch of Stalkers exited.

Using the Talent, he saw that those monsters that had attempted to make their appearance through the side tunnels that he brought down were just minutes away from finishing their loop through the mountain and entering the main shaft in which he and Lycia stood.

"Jakob, they're coming after us," Lycia warned.

"Good, how far behind us?"

He didn't bother to look, trusting in Lycia's judgment. He wanted to get deeper into the mine first so that he didn't have to worry about Tommie and the archers.

"Thirty yards! They're beginning to pull free from the soldiers."

"Let me know when they're ten yards away."

Jakob assumed that it wouldn't take long for the Stalkers to catch up to them, so he wanted to get a little farther into the mine. With what he was about to do, he needed options.

And he wouldn't have those until he reached the lighter grey that he had seen just twenty yards down the passageway on the right.

There! He stopped when he reached the narrow tunnel that for the time being was empty of Stalkers.

"Ten yards!" Lycia shouted. She skidded to a stop, knocking into Jakob, almost taking him to the ground, her focus on the monsters pursuing them.

Jakob didn't hesitate. He didn't even bother to turn around completely, already catching the sign of movement to his front farther down the ramp that led out of the mine.

With barely a thought, from the tips of his shining blades Jakob shot several bolts of energy into the ceiling, concentrating on where the Stalkers were going to be, not where they currently were.

The effect was immediate and very final. The energy ripped apart the ceiling, massive stones crashing down onto the Stalkers and crushing the beasts.

A blinding and choking cloud of dust and debris billowed out from the destruction, the entire mountain rumbling, protesting how Jakob had scarred it.

Both Jakob and Lycia ducked down, crouching near the ground, turning their backs to the cloud that threatened to suffocate them. Needing to breathe, Jakob used the Talent to blow away the rocky grit.

When their section of the passageway was clear, they stood up again. Using the Talent, Jakob searched around them.

He nodded to himself, pleased. Almost all of the Stalkers who had stepped outside the mine had been caught in the rockfall as they raced back in. Only three escaped, and there was no way they were going to be able to get through the pile of rubble that blocked their way.

The soldiers on the other side should have no trouble killing those Stalkers. In fact, several squads of Sharperson's Guard already were in the midst of doing just that.

A good sign.

An even better sign was that the Stalkers hadn't made it as far as where the Highlanders were positioned. His friends stood ready to take on the soldiers as soon as Duff gave the command to advance. Those soldiers would learn quickly that a wrathful Highlander was a much more dangerous adversary than a Stalker.

Just as important, those Stalkers still in the mine couldn't get out.

Of course, neither could they.

A problem they needed to solve.

Jakob formed several small balls of the Talent and threw them into the air, lighting the shaft for fifty yards in both directions.

Lycia tried not to gasp at what she saw, but she couldn't help herself.

Eight Stalkers stood only a few dozen yards away from them, their blood-red eyes flashing in the light.

"They're here for you," murmured Lycia, not wanting to talk too loudly in the silence of the tunnel.

"That they are." Jakob grimaced. "That's why I came here.

That's why I didn't want you with me. I didn't want you to have to deal with this."

"Would you please get off it, Jakob." Lycia's annoyance bordered on anger. "I make my own decisions. I'm here to help you. A few Stalkers don't scare me."

"A few Stalkers?" asked Jakob, slightly amused.

"All right, more than a few," Lycia admitted. "But, as I said, I make my own decisions. I decided that I was going to fight with you, and that's what I'm going to do. You have no right to keep me from doing that."

"Fair enough. I'm sorry. It's just that ..."

"We don't need to talk about that now, Jakob," Lycia said, cutting him off. Not ready to deal with the topic. "Can we deal with these beasties first? They seem a bit anxious."

Jakob nodded, his gaze never having left the Stalkers standing in front of them. "You're right. The Stalkers first."

"I assume that you have a plan." She knew that Jakob took risks that others wouldn't, his rushing into the mine toward the Stalkers while dodging soldiers bent on killing him proof of that, but he always did so with a clear strategy in mind.

"Of course," Jakob replied. He watched as the Stalkers closest to them inched forward. They were preparing to attack.

"Would you care to fill me in?" Lycia asked, the tension in her voice increasing. She noticed the Stalkers' movement as well.

"Do you see the shaft to your right?"

The Stalker to his front, now no more than five yards away, bent its knees. The monster was about to launch itself at them.

"I do," Lycia replied, the balls of light above them offering her a glimpse down the narrow tunnel.

"Get into it! Now!"

Lycia was moving into the crevice before Jakob finished speaking.

Jakob didn't have the time to confirm that Lycia did as he

ordered. He was focused entirely on the Stalker that was flying through the air, claws reaching for his chest.

Jakob acted without thinking. He shot a blast of energy that slammed right into the Stalker's face, the monster shrieking in agony as its charred skin continued to burn.

Then, Jakob was off, following Lycia into the tunnel, although not without leaving a gift for the other Stalkers, firing several more streams of energy back through the tunnel, hoping that he struck at least one or two more of the beasts before he disappeared into the darkness.

16

SHIVER OF ANTICIPATION

A shiver of excitement raced up Hakea's spine. She had expected a great deal from the gladiator. Hoped for it, in fact. Because she didn't think that she'd be able to break him in just a few hours as had been the case with so many others.

Which was a good thing. Because she didn't want to break him quickly. She wanted to take her time. Enjoy it.

The Crimson Giant met her expectations, giving her all that she wanted and more.

He stood strong against her.

He challenged her.

She loved every minute of it.

She found the gladiator to be more than just intriguing. There was some aspect to the man who had once danced on the white sand that appealed to her in a visceral way. That brought her alive in a manner that no one else could.

Hakea understood that she should just kill him. That was the easiest thing to do. The smartest.

But she couldn't bring herself to do it. Not yet anyway. Not when she could have so much more fun with the gladiator.

She was too excited and frustrated both at the same time to

send him to the other side. Excited because she felt some strange almost unexplainable connection to the gladiator. Frustrated because she didn't understand why she felt the need to play with him first.

To tease him.

Taunt him.

Use him.

That's what she really wanted.

She wanted to use him. But he wouldn't allow it.

That's what excited her. Frustrated her. Made her want him in a way that she had never wanted anyone else before.

She couldn't shrug off the conflict within her. Even so, Hakea felt more energized than she had in quite some time. So much so that she couldn't wait to head back down to where the gladiator was being kept.

Hakea had absolutely no doubt that she could break him. She also had absolutely no doubt that it would take her quite a while longer to do that.

And she would relish every second until she reached that point when she realized that he was hers, heart and soul, body and spirit.

When that happened, when the gladiator gave himself to her, he would do whatever she wanted him to do to whomever she wanted him to do it.

Another shiver ran through her as she imagined what that moment would be like.

She couldn't wait. That sense of power that she craved and couldn't achieve in any other way was just out of reach.

Yet within her grasp.

And she would grasp it.

It would be that much sweeter knowing that she had broken the Crimson Giant. That she had turned one of the most feared gladiators in Caledonia to her own purposes.

That she had remade him.

She knew that she could do it.

Her first session with the gladiator had laid the groundwork. She was certain that he would crack when she began again in a few hours.

She stopped herself, offering a quiet curse beneath her breath. Her mounting vexation strangely giving her a greater clarity.

She was allowing what she wanted to believe to get in the way of the stark reality of dealing with the Crimson Giant.

To think otherwise ...

She was only kidding herself.

In truth, she was more frustrated than excited. In some ways she felt like a failure.

Nothing that she had done to the gladiator affected him in the least. He had revealed nothing to suggest that she was making any progress with him at all.

It was more than disappointing.

It was humiliating.

This was one of her unique abilities. She was a master at inflicting pain and gaining what she wanted. Yet the Crimson Giant made her feel like a novice again.

The gladiator didn't reveal his pain. He didn't reveal any emotion.

He simply stared at her with a hard-edged glare, offering her dread promises with his eyes that were more terrifying than anything she did to him or anything that she threatened to do to him.

Hakea refused to admit defeat, however.

That wasn't her way.

She would get what she wanted from him.

No matter how hard he fought, eventually she would take him for her own. She promised herself that.

But how to do that?

Needing to clear her head, she walked through the doors

and out onto the balcony that wound its way around the length of the Rock's central tower.

Her failure probably resulted from the fact that she was distracted. She couldn't focus her full attention on the Crimson Giant. Her thoughts were split between him and the threat presented by Talia Carlomin.

Hakea shook her head in annoyance, growling out a long line of curses just under her breath.

She should have heard of her rival's death by now. Yet not a single word.

She walked down the balcony and around the corner, staring to the south. She saw the fires burning, what she could only assume were her soldiers ravaging the Carlomin enclave. But she couldn't tell for certain, the distance too great to allow for a clear view.

Continuing farther along, Hakea stopped at the corner that gave her an excellent panorama of the city.

Her mouth opened in shock. She couldn't believe what she was seeing.

She had anticipated the battle to the south near the Carlomin docks. That was necessary for her to achieve her objective.

But the inferno consuming her dock and her ships?

She couldn't quite comprehend the devastation.

How was that even possible?

Hakea closed her mouth, her expression hardening as she cursed under her breath again.

That vixen Talia Carlomin had to be at the center of it all. That was the only explanation.

The arrogance of that woman!

To attack Hakea's holdings directly!

No matter.

Talia Carlomin was going to regret that decision, just as she was going to regret so much more once Hakea got her hands on her.

That blasted upstart was going to experience a very slow, very painful death.

She would squeal like a stuck pig before Hakea sent her to the other side.

For the next several minutes, she watched her dock and ships burn, realizing that she had few options for salvaging the situation.

She needed to take revenge. She needed to punish those responsible. The longer she waited, the weaker she would be perceived.

And she could not be perceived as weak.

But no good idea for reversing the tide came to her. Her soldiers were being cut down on the dock as if they were no more than a few stalks of wheat. Her ships, now just a fleet of flaming hulks, drifted aimlessly through the harbor. They would be beneath the water by morning.

She had two companies of soldiers with her. She could send them into the fight.

Yet just as soon as she thought about taking that course of action she realized that she had no means to get them across the harbor. All of the launches except for the one tied off at the dock at the base of the Rock were burning with the last of her frigates and her pier.

Hakea screamed in rage.

Feeling impotent.

Helpless.

She needed to do something.

Anything.

She needed to talk to Sergeant Chesterton. But the man wasn't known for his creativity. So she doubted that she could dig a worthwhile idea out of him that she hadn't already thought of herself.

With just one available launch, for all intents and purposes she and her two companies of soldiers were stuck on the Rock.

Which upon further thought might be exactly what Talia Carlomin wanted.

To keep her out of the fight.

Hakea nodded sagely. Clever indeed on the part of her adversary.

Isolating her.

Preventing her from exercising command in her city.

However, not clever enough.

Her favorite tools for eliminating her rivals still could get across the harbor. They had little fear of the great whites patrolling the cove.

Pleased that she had found an answer to the challenge, she walked back into her apartment, heading for the door. She would task the Stalkers hidden in the depths of the Rock with clearing what was left of her dock. Then she would send them to the Carlomin enclave to clean up whatever mess remained there.

Simple.

Effective.

All she needed to do was assign those monsters to their tasks.

Hakea reached for the doorknob, then pulled her hand back quickly.

It was too quiet. There was always a squad of soldiers guarding her door, and they were always chattering about some useless topic.

Yet now, she heard nothing at all.

The silence sent a bolt of warning through her.

The doorknob began to turn very slowly. So slowly that it was barely even noticeable.

Hakea stepped back onto the balcony on silent feet.

Pulling free the dagger she wore on her hip, she slid into the shadows, throwing the torches on each side of the doorway over the balustrade, extinguishing the light around her.

And just in time, a shadowy figure pushing the door open, a dagger in hand.

TALIA STOOD with one foot in front of the other, dagger in her right hand. With her left she pushed open the door that led into Hakea Roosarian's private quarters.

Slowly.

Very slowly.

Not wanting to give away to her target that she was there for her.

Behind her were three dead soldiers.

Talia slipped out of the shadows like a Wraith in the Murk, killing the first man with a neat slash across his throat before the other two soldiers were even aware that they were under attack. She stabbed the second soldier through the throat before the third even moved.

The last soldier's mistake was his decision to try to pull his sword free and engage her rather than stepping back and putting some space between them.

He wasn't as fast as Talia. He couldn't get more than an inch of his steel out of his scabbard before she stabbed him in the heart.

She didn't pull her bloody blade free until she eased him to the floor.

She waited in the foyer then for several minutes, wanting to make sure that she wouldn't be disturbed. It wasn't long before she doubted that she would have much else to worry about with respect to the soldiers guarding the Rock. They would be occupied soon enough with the Blood Company if they weren't already.

Closing the door behind her without making a sound, Talia took a few seconds to acclimate herself to the large space.

Crystal chandeliers hung from the ceiling. Gold scrollwork ran through the granite mantles and fireplaces. Intricately crafted furniture sat atop hand-woven carpets of vibrant colors. Murals were painted onto the walls, all of them of important moments in Caledonian history, and if there wasn't a mural there was a tapestry that served the same purpose.

Talia snorted quietly, shaking her head in disbelief. She should have assumed as much from Hakea Roosarian.

Truly ostentatious.

An almost unimaginable wealth just in this room.

And testimony to the woman's greed and real desire.

Walking a few steps past the foyer, Talia began to understand. The first few rooms were for show. To set the tone for anyone invited by Hakea into her chambers. Because through the doorway at the far end, Talia spied several large tables covered in papers and maps.

Roosarian's workspace. Probably where she was plotting her next conquest once she gained absolute control of Fal Carrach and Ballinasloe.

Her eyes were drawn to the drapes in the back that ruffled at the touch of the wind, the door that led out onto the balcony open. She would leave that space for last.

Talia believed that Roosarian was hiding somewhere within this warren of rooms. But where?

One foot in front of the other, dagger held at the ready, Talia began her search. She started in the outer rooms before moving deeper into the apartment, wanting to ensure that she couldn't be taken from behind and that her quarry couldn't slip by her.

Therefore, she took her time.

Not wanting to rush.

Not wanting to miss anything.

Not wanting to give herself away.

After working her way through the entire apartment, certain that her prey was still there, just not yet revealed, Talia stopped in Roosarian's office. For almost a minute, she stood there. Waiting. Listening. A cool breeze billowing through the open balcony doors.

Still no sign of her, and Talia was certain that Roosarian wasn't hiding somewhere in the apartment behind her. Talia had been incredibly thorough with her search.

That left only one other possibility.

Talia edged out onto the balcony.

Taking her time.

Allowing her eyes to adjust to the darkness.

She focused on her task. She didn't even notice the two battles playing out in the harbor, one a quarter mile away from the other, both already having turned in her favor.

She sensed that Hakea Roosarian was close.

Very close.

Yet where could she be?

Farther along the balcony?

Her heart skipped a beat when she realized that she didn't need to look any further, the air shifting just to her left.

Talia ducked to the right and rolled back into Roosarian's office, a foot-long dagger slamming into the wall and chipping out a piece of stone right where she had been standing just a moment before.

If the blade had struck true, it would have taken her right through the ear.

Talia was back up in a flash, stabbing with her dagger toward the shadow that detached itself from the wall.

"I WILL TAKE your head for this!" shrieked Roosarian as she chased after her nemesis.

The Governor of Fal Carrach allowed her rage to drive her. She slashed with her dagger in an indecipherable pattern, not caring where she cut into Talia Carlomin, only caring that she did so.

Yet despite her burst of frenetic energy, she failed to draw blood.

Talia ignored the stream of curses that followed her, staying true to her objective, moving more with Roosarian then moving away from her. She placed her own dagger where it needed to be to parry a strike, and when that wasn't required she simply glided out of the way.

Another lesson that she had picked up from Tennyson, the old sailor who had taught her how to use a dagger.

Why use your steel when you didn't have to?

That was one of Tennyson's favorite questions, and it had stuck with Talia.

Better to use your wits, your agility, in a knife fight.

Use your steel when it was time to kill.

When defending against a dagger, it was usually better to get out of the way.

That knowledge guiding her, Talia led Roosarian around the room, allowing her adversary to burn her energy. Every so often, she knocked over a chair or flipped over a table as she danced through the apartment, hoping to catch her adversary in a mistake.

Unfortunately for Talia, Roosarian, her rage flashing brightly, deftly avoided the obstructions and continued her frenetic assault.

Roosarian cut and slashed, her movements refusing to reveal a pattern that Talia could discern. Instead, she had no choice but to step back, to the side, lunge with her dagger just to keep Roosarian honest, then slide away and put more space between them, ducking and rolling whenever Roosarian got too close, always back on her feet before her adversary could press her and get in tight.

Talia had no doubt that Tennyson would have been proud of her. She rarely needed to use her dagger. And when she did she never failed to catch Roosarian's steel with her own.

All the while, Roosarian screamed at her, spittle flying, her eyes wild. Spite and hate erupted from her mouth. An unintelligible stream of invectives.

Talia disregarded it all.

Both were in a rage. But Roosarian's anger was hot while Talia's was cold.

Talia remained true to her purpose.

She wanted to kill Roosarian. The urge to do that almost too much for her.

Because of all that the woman had tried to do to her and her mother and their business.

Because of all that this hateful woman had done to so many others so that she could increase her own power and wealth.

Because of her culpability in her father's murder.

But no matter how much she wanted to kill her, she was there for another reason as well.

Then Talia saw her chance.

She feinted to her right, pretending to stumble. Roosarian, eyes widening at the unexpected opportunity, rushed forward. At the last second, Talia kicked a chair sliding across the floor.

Her tactic worked, the legs of the chair striking Roosarian in the hip and sending her sprawling to the carpet.

Talia was on her opponent in a heartbeat.

Rather than attacking raggedly as Roosarian had done, Talia stayed true to herself. Always under control. Every movement measured. Every decision precise. All of her focus on achieving a single objective.

Talia slashed once to the left, then brought her dagger back around as if she was going to attack the same way from the other side.

Roosarian went for the play, smiling, believing that she had anticipated Talia's next move, preparing not only to counter, but also to attack.

Roosarian paid for her poor assumption.

Talia sold the feint, then stepped forward and shouldered Roosarian hard in the gut, knocking the wind from her and slamming her against the bookcase that ran along the wall at her back.

When Roosarian tried to push off the bookcase, she couldn't.

Talia held her blade to the Governor's throat.

With a swipe of her other hand, hitting Roosarian's just so and earning a gasp for her efforts – another lesson Tennyson taught her -- Talia knocked loose Roosarian's dagger, the Governor's fingers numb.

Talia had won.

She had Roosarian right where she wanted her.

She could kill her with just the flick of her wrist.

She experienced a slight burst of accomplishment, but she kept herself under control. She needed something from the Governor first. Then she could give in to her bloody urges.

"Where is Davin?" Talia demanded, keeping her steel against Roosarian's throat.

"The gladiator?" Hakea asked, the look of disbelief that crept onto her visage quickly changing into one of understanding. She smiled knowingly then. "You care about your gladiator? How romantic and quaint."

Roosarian tried to laugh. She couldn't. The blade at her throat prevented it.

"Where is Davin?" Talia asked again, biting off the words, her eyes flashing with a cold fire.

"You care so much for him? The man's a killer. No more than that."

"He is what he is," Talia replied sharply. "Now where is he?"

"He's a killer. Mark my words." Roosarian gave Talia an appraising glance, viewing the conclusion of the combat between them as an opportunity to negotiate. "Let me go, and I will leave you and your mother alone. We will come to an arrangement, you and me. I will govern the Territory so that we will both profit. Partners. That's what you want, isn't it?"

"You have no idea what I want."

"Don't play the child with me. You want the same thing as I do. More wealth. More power. More control. I saw it in how you fight. You crave control. Just like me, that's what you need the most. Control. Over everything and everyone."

"I am nothing like you," hissed Talia. "Now tell me where Davin is before I slit your throat."

Roosarian snorted. "You are more like me than you are willing to admit. Now tell me what you really want. You could have almost anything you like if we were working together."

"Where is Davin?"

Roosarian didn't reply for several seconds, struck by how focused her nemesis was on the gladiator. Her expression became more calculating, Roosarian having just discovered Talia Carlomin's weak point. With that, she saw a chance to use that failing against her.

"Dead," she spat.

Roosarian knew that she had read Talia correctly when, for just a second, her adversary's expression changed. That cold fire becoming white hot.

Recognizing that, Roosarian decided to take her chance.

While she had been talking with Talia, first trying to negotiate with her, then attempting to provoke her, with her right hand behind her and out of sight, Roosarian had been working her fingers across the spines of the books at her back. She found the one that she had been looking for just a heartbeat before.

Pushing on the book with a finger, a small, hidden door right behind Roosarian slid open. With Talia pressing her against the bookcase, Roosarian allowed her momentum to take her. She fell away from Talia's dagger and tumbled through.

Before Talia could draw another breath, shocked at how Roosarian had escaped her blade, the hidden door slid back into place just as swiftly as it had opened.

Talia's eyes flashed with anger as she stood there feeling the fool.

Roosarian had played her, and Talia had allowed it.

She didn't know which burned in her gut worse.

Talia reached down and pressed in on the book that had opened the door.

Nothing happened.

She tried again, pushing harder.

Still nothing.

She began pushing on several other books.

None of them moved or released the hidden catch. Nothing that she did worked.

Roosarian had escaped, and somehow she had prevented Talia from coming after her.

Talia let out a stream of curses that would have made Tennyson proud. She had failed to kill the woman who needed to die even though she had her under her blade.

Worse, she was no closer to rescuing Davin.

17

MEMORIES AND SPIRITS

"I thought this would be a much more challenging combat," cackled Hippolates. "I guess I was wrong. I guess I remember you a bit differently than you are now."

Hippolates feinted a stab with his sword, just to see what Duff would do. The Highlander didn't even bother to move. He simply continued to circle around Hippolates, looking for an opening.

Hippolates wasn't surprised. They had spent hundreds of hours in the practice ring together. He couldn't even recall how many clashes they fought in side by side.

They knew each other better than they knew themselves.

And Hippolates was going to use that to get past his former Sergeant's defenses.

"Time has not been kind, my friend," Hippolates continued. "Not kind at all. And I'm afraid that scar ringing your head is the least of it."

Hippolates dodged out of the way of Duff's hammer with a seeming ease, the steel singing through the air where his head had been just a second before.

"Because of the way we left things, I assumed that you were

so consumed by your desire for revenge that you wouldn't allow anything or anyone to stop you from coming after me."

Hippolates slashed with his sword through the space separating them. He didn't think he would cause a great deal of blood to flow, if any at all. He just wanted to see how Duff would react.

And Duff responded exactly as Hippolates thought that he would.

Rather than stepping back, Duff knocked the steel to the side with the haft of his hammer. At the same time, he hissed softly in pain as the tip of the blade scored his forearm.

Barely a wound at all. No more than a thin line that leaked a few drops of red that stained the cuff of Duff's shirt. Even so, that slight wound broadened Hippolates' grin, his cackle increasing in pitch.

"Obviously I was wrong," Hippolates smirked. He feinted another slash, Duff stepping back this time. Hippolates also stepped back, putting more space between them. "You're getting slower, Sergeant Westgard. You're getting old. You're not the fighter I remember you to be. You're too lost in the past, not seeing what's right in front of you."

Duff ignored Hippolates. Or at least he tried to. Because it was becoming more difficult to do with his former friend's incessant chatter and familiarity.

Even so, he refused to allow Hippolates to control the pace of the combat. With that in mind, he began to circle around his adversary at a faster clip.

Hippolates quickly mimicked him, spinning in a smaller circle.

Duff didn't think Hippolates' smirk could get any wider. He seemed to view this combat as a game.

And maybe it was to him. Maybe Hippolates decided that he already knew how this duel was going to end. That he had little to fear from Duff.

Therefore, he was going to have a little fun before he put Duff out of his misery. Milk the moment for as long as he could.

Hippolates could think what he wanted. Duff wasn't going to make it easy for him, even though he was having a hard time concentrating, and he didn't understand why.

Duff remembered how Eliasin liked to chatter when they used to train together on the practice ground in Tintagel. The man's mouth ran continuously, spouting nothing useful. Similar to the annoying constancy of a mosquito buzzing around his ear.

The Blademaster had tried to get Hippolates to fight without saying a word. Nothing he did worked.

Hippolates had a need to talk. He couldn't help himself. And it seemed to make him a better fighter.

The Blademaster had moved on to more important challenges, simply offering the suggestion to Hippolates that eventually the diarrhea that spewed from between his lips would be the death of him.

Hippolates had laughed at that and then forgotten the warning. Because he believed that his constant chatter gave him a key advantage during his combats. It threw off his adversaries, distracting them, just as he was trying to do now to Duff.

For the most part, that was true. Hippolates had talked himself to several victories over individuals he had no right to defeat. His unending jabbering teasing an adversary with greater skill in arms into a fatal mistake.

A tried-and-true approach and one that Hippolates would never relinquish. His incessant prattle made it easier for him to identify and then take advantage of the openings that his opponents inevitably offered him.

Always.

Hippolates just needed to figure out the right thing to say in order to get under his adversary's skin.

To throw off the other combatant.

To cause that one heartbeat of hesitation in which he could strike.

For most, Hippolates found that questioning their ability, their manhood, their womanhood, other similar insults, tended to do the trick. It really wasn't that difficult. He just needed to play off of their egos.

For others, he needed to dig a little deeper. Some had the capacity to ignore him for a time.

But only for a time.

Based on how the combat was going so far, Hippolates believed that he was enjoying a good bit of success against Duff.

Although it was taking longer than it would with most others, he had his former Sergeant exactly where he wanted him.

Because Hippolates had found the chink in Duff's armor long ago.

Now he just needed to cut deeper.

"So how are Alison and the children?" Hippolates asked with a vicious leer.

Hippolates smiled mirthlessly when he saw the dark flash in the back of Duff's eyes. He had definitely struck a chord. Now, to ensure his victory, he simply needed to play it.

Simple.

Easy.

Fun.

"Oh, my apologies, Sergeant Westgard. I had forgotten. Truly, I am so, so sorry."

Catching how Duff's eyes tightened and his breathing shortened, Hippolates lunged a half step, sword to his front.

Duff dodged backward to avoid the steel, though not with the grace the Highlander usually demonstrated.

Hippolates' eyes narrowed, seeing what he wanted to see. Duff was moving even slower than he had been at the start of their combat.

He smirked, pleased with himself. Hippolates had found the right thread, just as he knew that he would. Now he just needed to pull on it until Duff unraveled.

"Terrible. Just terrible about what happened to Alison and …" Hippolates shook his head sadly, an expression of contrition passing across his face. But only briefly, his smile returning in a flash. "Forgive me, I can't remember their names. Your three beautiful children. Their names all started with the same letter of the alphabet, but it's been too long since they died that I just can't seem to recall."

Seeing Duff lower the head of his hammer just a tiny bit as Hippolates' words struck home, he lunged again.

He thought he had the Highlander.

Right in the gut.

But no.

Growling in irritation, he watched with a hint of admiration as Duff pivoted to evade the strike and then got his hammer back into position to block Hippolates' backhanded slash that was aimed for his throat.

It seemed that Hippolates had a little more work to do to weaken Duff's determination and will. He needed the former Sergeant pining for what he had lost. Focusing solely on what he had lost. Then he would be an easy kill.

Stepping back a few feet, Hippolates circled around Duff once more. Despite his failed attack, the Captain knew that the end of the combat was fast approaching. That just a few more nudges would do the trick.

"Perhaps you could help me, Sergeant Westgard?" Hippolates asked with a false sense of innocence. "Do you recall the names of your children? The children who died because you put your duty before them? Your children who died because you weren't there to protect them?"

Hippolates constant stream of hateful comments was like a physical blow, one right after the other, just as he hoped that they would be. However, they didn't affect Duff in the way that Hippolates anticipated.

The taunts added to the ball of grief, remorse, and guilt that had stayed with Duff for more than a decade. They reminded him of all that he had lost.

They also set a fire burning in the pit of his belly. A fire seeking vengeance.

Yes, Duff was slower in this combat, just as Hippolates believed that he was.

But it wasn't because of his age as Hippolates had first insinuated. And it wasn't because of the terrible tragedy that Hippolates was trying to turn to his advantage.

No, Hippolates' words had little meaning for Duff. He knew how to push them to the side. After testing his skills against Hippolates for so long, he had learned how to ignore the barbs and jabs.

They evoked painful memories, yes. But they also guided him down a path that he had avoided traveling for quite some time.

A path that he enjoyed being on, because in addition to remembering what he perceived as his own failings with respect to his family, he recalled the joy and fun that he experienced before the terrible day that ripped his family from him.

He wasn't having such a hard time concentrating because of what Hippolates was saying.

He was having a hard time concentrating because Duff believed that his thinking of his family brought their spirits to him.

Because he could see his wife and his children.

Plain as day.

Just a few feet away.

Just behind Hippolates.

Standing at the edge of the space that he and Hippolates had carved out for this combat.

Wherever he turned, wherever he looked, the ghosts of his family danced around him.

Smiled at him. Laughed at him. Loved him.

Alison. His wife.

He could see her smile even now as she watched him, her spirit drifting so that she was always in his line of sight.

She had always been there for him. Always. Through the good and bad.

When he made mistakes. When he lost friends. When he raged against the fools who made decisions that almost cost him his life and had cost the lives of men and women he led.

When he just needed to be. When he needed to breathe. When he needed to reclaim his humanity after a particularly difficult mission.

Never questioning. Always caring. Always supporting him. Listening. Understanding.

Alison was looking at him now. The hint of a smile curling her lip.

That's what had caught his eye when he saw her for the first time in the market so long ago. That smile of hers.

Gently mocking with a promise of something more.

His breath caught when he saw them standing right next to her.

Bennie, Berra, and Bryn.

His triplets.

They were smiling too, following him with their eyes. Making him remember all the time he spent with them. Wandering through the woods. Swimming in the stream that ran behind their cottage. Teaching them to hunt. Reading books with them. Playing games.

Caught by their gazes, he was unable to break free. He didn't want to break free. He wanted to be with them. He had wanted to be with them for so long.

Duff smiled at his children and stopped moving around Hippolates. He lowered his hammer.

Staring behind Hippolates.

Not seeing the soldiers standing in their ragged formation.

Seeing only his wife and his children.

It was like they had never been taken from him.

How he had loved his children. How he still did.

They had wrapped him around their fingers. They could get him to do anything that they wanted.

And he never minded, knowing exactly what they were doing every single time.

Yet when they really needed him, he wasn't there.

When Hippolates had come looking for him with his squad of miscreants, Duff had been out on an assignment.

He hadn't been there when his family needed him the most.

He hadn't been there when Hippolates and his thugs murdered his wife and his children.

Tears formed in his eyes, unable to look away from Alison, Bennie, Berra, and Bryn.

What he would give to go back to that day. To be there for them.

He probably would have died.

So what?

He could have done something if he had been there to fight for them. He might have been able to save them.

Duff twisted to the left at the very last second, Hippolates' sharp blade slicing across his side. Because of his instinctive movement, the steel cut across his leather armor rather than slice into his flesh.

"Slow, indeed," Hippolates laughed. "When you were younger, I never would have touched your armor. Just as I said, time has not been kind to you, my friend." The Captain shook his head in disappointment. "No wonder you failed to protect your family. No wonder they died because just as you always did, you put your duty before them. You failed to remember that your family should always come first."

Hippolates' words struck the chord that he wanted. But they didn't affect Duff in the way that he desired.

Duff pulled his gaze away from the spirits of his family, reluctantly, realizing he had no choice, staring hard at Hippolates. At the man responsible for the murder of his wife and children.

At the man who was trying to use his family to kill him.

His former friend was enjoying himself.

His words just as sharp as a blade, and he more than willing to twist them in the wound.

Picking at him.

Needling him.

Trying to use Duff's memories against him.

It had worked for Hippolates many times in the past against so many others. But here, now, Hippolates had made a mistake.

Duff had been slower than he normally would be because he was thinking of his family. Because he was watching his family.

That was true.

But seeing his wife, seeing his family, gave him a gift as well that he had never thought possible.

Their smiles burned away the despair that had burdened him ever since that fateful day.

He felt lighter now. Freer.

And now those memories of his wife and his children stirred another emotion within him.

A stronger emotion.

Resolve.

A darker feeling as well.

The desire for revenge.

But Hippolates didn't see that. He only saw what he wanted to see.

Judging that the time was right, Hippolates again lunged with his sword.

Duff knocked away the steel.

"Still lucky, I see," Hippolates murmured. "Be careful, Sergeant Westgard. As we both know, luck eventually runs out, and I'm sure that yours probably already has."

Hippolates lunged again, aiming for Duff's heart.

And then again, this time targeting Duff's groin.

One more time. Just missing Duff's belly.

"A pity, really, don't you think?" Hippolates said almost to himself as he sought to push Duff over the edge. Slightly confused. Becoming concerned at his lack of success.

He thought that he had Duff right where he wanted him, but the Sergeant responded to his attacks with a remarkable grace that was lacking at the beginning of the combat. He decided to press harder.

"Right before your wife and children were taken from you, they didn't beg to see you. They just begged to die. The pain was too much for them."

Hippolates shrugged then, shaking his head slightly, his voice infused with a false sadness. "Do you think that they could ever forgive you? You forsook them, did you not, Duff? Duty before all else. Always duty before all else. Duty even before family. And look where it got you? Fighting here in the Highlands rather than living in that lovely cottage you had just outside Tintagel. Sad. So ... so ... so sad."

Believing that he had stuck the needle in as far as he needed to, Hippolates lunged once more with his sword. Hippolates pivoted when the steel slid past Duff's side, anticipating that the Sergeant would get out of the way in time, thinking that this was the moment. Thinking that the combat was about to come to an end as he brought his axe down with his other hand, driving the sharp steel toward Duff's hip.

Hippolates' attack scarcely registered with Duff, his eyes fixed on the spirits of his wife and his children.

Duff reacted based on instinct, muscle memory, rather than thought.

Every strike that Hippolates attempted, Duff parried. No matter what Hippolates tried, Duff held his ground. His hammer sang through the air around him, ensuring whether sword or axe, the steel of Hippolates' blades never came close to grazing his skin.

Yet he didn't hear any of it. He didn't see any of it.

All he saw were his wife and his children.

And he so desperately wanted to hear their voices.

Hippolates was astounded by Duff's performance, not understanding how he could defend himself when his eyes were staring off into space. In fact, he was so amazed that he began to wonder if he had made a terrible mistake. Because by all rights, Duff should already be dead. Several times over, in fact.

Even more unsettling for Hippolates, Duff was smiling. Why, he didn't have a clue.

It was as if his former Sergeant was there but not entirely there.

Seeing but not seeing.

Hearing but not hearing.

His actions driven by some other force that had taken control of his body.

Hippolates didn't understand what was happening. Yet having no other recourse, he continued his attack, seeking some way past Duff's hammer.

Duff's eyes remained locked with those of his family. He felt as if he were watching the combat that he was participating in from afar.

In some ways, his duel with Hippolates reminded him of his time in the training circle with the Blademaster.

He had always enjoyed the challenge of matching steel with Jurgen Klines. He never succeeded in defeating his mentor. He never came close, in fact. But that had never bothered him. It had never stopped him from trying.

During those combats, instinct was just as important as skill. More important, in fact.

The Blademaster had hammered that concept into him.

And right then, as he faced off against Hippolates, not really seeing him, only seeing his family who stood less than ten feet away, he allowed his instincts to guide his actions and his decisions.

He couldn't take his eyes off his wife and children. He didn't want to.

He was thinking of what Bennie, Berra, and Bryn could have made of themselves. What they would have looked like if they had the chance to grow older.

How much more beautiful Alison would have become as she aged.

She likely would have wondered whether she had made the right choice as Duff got older. He had not been a good-looking man to begin with. The scar across his scalp certainly didn't help.

Duff smiled more broadly then. He had avoided this road for so long, and he shouldn't have.

For the first time in a very long time, he felt at peace.

Perhaps it was time. Perhaps he had served his purpose. Perhaps he had done what was required of him in this life.

Maybe it wouldn't matter now if he joined his family.

Yet as those thoughts crossed his mind, he frowned as Alison and his children shook their heads.

Did they know what he was considering?

They nodded at him.

His children's smiles transformed then. Their expressions becoming unbreakable. More demanding.

Duff didn't understand why at first.

Needing an answer, Duff focused on his wife's ghost.

Alison was smiling. That same smile he never got enough of.

But then that smile slowly disappeared. Her expression hardened just as his children's had. Becoming more resolute.

Then she nodded. She seemed to believe that he knew what he needed to do.

Finally, he understood.

He knew now what was required of him.

The sharp sound of steel striking steel ringing right by his ear pulled Duff's gaze away from his family.

He looked to his left.

Hippolates had slashed at his neck. Without even thinking, without even realizing what he was doing, Duff had moved his hammer to block the blow.

Hippolates' sword chipped a piece of wood from the handle, the steel locked in place now, caught in the haft.

The Captain of the Highland Guard pressed down with his blade. He was trying to push the hammer closer to Duff. Trying to keep Duff focused on the most obvious point of attack.

At the last second, Duff twisted to the side even as he kept his hammer in place with just one hand on the haft.

Hippolates' axe slid into the space where Duff's belly had been just a heartbeat before.

A clever move, Duff acknowledged. Not clever enough, however.

Because when Hippolates tried to pull his axe back for another slash, he couldn't.

Duff's right hand latched onto Hippolates' wrist, gripping tightly, his fingers crushing the bones and earning a gasp of pain from his former friend.

Hippolates couldn't break free from Duff's iron grip. Even

more remarkable, Hippolates couldn't bring his sword any closer to Duff's neck.

Duff's unnervingly calm eyes stared into his. Hippolates struggled and strained, desperate to break free, desperate to bring a weapon to bear.

But he couldn't.

Duff was too strong.

As the muscles in Hippolates' arms began to quiver, as his face slowly turned red, a large vein on his forehead pulsing more vigorously as he fought to get away from Duff, he didn't understand where Duff's strength was coming from.

It was like Hippolates was battling a boulder. He couldn't move a hair. Duff wouldn't allow it.

Hippolates' eyes widened then as he began to understand that perhaps he had misjudged his old friend. Perhaps he had made a mistake. Perhaps he had committed a fatal error.

"You know what your problem is, Eliasin?"

Although Duff asked the question in a quiet, frighteningly calm voice, all the Highlanders and the soldiers standing on the dirt field heard him. Silence falling in front of the mine once the last of the Stalkers had been killed.

Hippolates didn't have the strength to reply, sweat pouring down his forehead as he failed time and again to break free from his former Sergeant. He realized in that moment that he was losing this fight.

"You talk too much."

Giving Hippolates a knowing smile that sent a shiver of fear down the Captain's spine, Duff tipped his right shoulder.

Unable to break Duff's hold on him, when Duff pulled down on his wrist Hippolates fell forward.

As a result of the swift and wrenching movement, Hippolates' sword came free from the haft of the hammer. He flailed his arm as he tried to keep his balance, desperate to prevent Duff from dragging him toward the ground with him.

But Hippolates couldn't stop himself. He had ceded the initiative, and he realized when a shot of ice struck his heart that he would never be able to regain it.

Duff used the momentum that he created to bring his hammer down in a devastating, one-handed blow that crushed the back of Hippolates' head.

There was a sickening crunch and a small explosion of blood, bone, and brain when steel met skull. Then nothing but silence as Hippolates dropped dead in the dirt.

Duff stared down at Eliasin Hippolates, former Captain of the Highland Guard.

He took a deep breath, seeking to steady his nerves. He couldn't remember the last time that he had felt edgy after a combat.

Maybe it was because he had been waiting for this moment for quite a long time.

He had earned his vengeance. Never believing that he would.

Yet he didn't feel any differently now that Hippolates was dead.

Instead, he just felt hollow, memories of spending time with his family playing through his mind.

Duff looked up then.

Alison and the children stood there. Together.

In unison, they gave him a nod. Signifying a job well done.

When they smiled, Duff smiled.

His smile vanished as his family slowly faded away.

He wanted to go to them.

To be with them.

But he couldn't.

Not yet.

He had seen it in Alison's eyes before she disappeared.

It wasn't his time yet.

There was still more that he needed to do.

He would be with his family again when he went to the Spirit World.

When it was his time to cross to the other side.

Duff began to cry then, the tears at the edges of his eyes finally breaking free.

He thought that his revenge would taste sweet.

Instead, it tasted bitter.

Because his family was gone and there was nothing that he could do about it.

That thought saddened him.

Now of all times.

When after more than a decade, he finally gained his vengeance.

For him.

For his family.

And now that he achieved it, he felt nothing but an overwhelming sorrow. The sense of loss that he had struggled to contain for so long finally consuming him.

Rather than fight it, he gave in to it. He didn't want to hold it back any longer.

He needed to acknowledge what had been taken from him. What his family had meant to him.

Because he needed to move on now.

He needed to find a new purpose.

When his tears finally slowed and he turned to face what remained of Sharperson's Guard, he realized that he must have been quite a sight. Streaks of tears running through the blood and grime that covered his face. Part of Hippolates' brain and shards of his skull sticking to the head of his hammer.

The soldiers who obeyed the man he had just killed stared back at him with a variety of different expressions, the most common being trepidation. A good number appeared to be in shock at having seen so many of their friends slaughtered by the Stalkers before they eliminated the monsters themselves.

Of course, the Highlanders standing at his back who dispatched many of their comrades as well probably had something to do with the ripples of unease that were working their way through the ragged, bloodied ranks.

"You experienced for yourselves what happens when you fight against the men and women sworn to the Highland Lord," Duff said in a strong voice that carried through the small valley and echoed off the surrounding mountains. "If you choose to fight, you die. Simple as that."

To stress that point, an arrow streaked down from behind the soldiers, burying itself in the ground between Duff and the men who were loyal to Torstan Sharperson.

Many of the soldiers looked up the mountainside. The sense of discomfort among them blossomed upon seeing the several dozen archers standing above them, arrows on their strings.

What was most concerning was that their expressions weren't hard. They were anxious. They were looking for a reason to shoot.

It wasn't very difficult to assess the predicament that the soldiers faced. There was little to prevent the archers from striking them down before they took more than a few steps toward the Highlanders who had shifted their formation from a square to a wedge. Clearly anxious to advance. Looking for any excuse to attack.

"What will it be? Fight and die or surrender and maybe live?"

After Duff's prodding, there was nothing but silence and some nervous shifting and shuffling among the soldiers.

"Tommie!" Duff called.

Another arrow streaked through the air, slamming into the dirt just an inch from the boot of the soldier who stood only a few yards away from Duff.

The man had been gripping his sword nervously, apparently struggling to reach a decision. When the second arrow appeared right next to his foot, the soldier's eyes revealed his alarm. Finally understanding the nature of his circumstances, he dropped his sword.

There was only one decision to make after all. And that one soldier's action set his comrades in motion. It wasn't long before all the soldiers who served Torstan Sharperson dropped their swords, shields, and daggers.

Duff nodded with approval, glad that the battle had come to an end.

"Saraa!"

The Highlander rushed forward. She had been standing in the first row of the wedge, sword in hand, ready to continue the fight. Almost desperate to do so, as if she was seeking to make up for her mistake of getting caught.

"Are you all right?"

Saraa nodded. Except for the small trickle of dried blood from when she was under the soldier's dagger, she survived the larger fight unscathed.

Duff saw her concern for Jakob in her eyes. So better to give her something to do rather than allow that emotion to perhaps set her on a course that she would regret.

"Have someone take these men over to the barracks. Treat them as they did the miners."

"Chain them or flog them?"

Duff gave Saraa a long look, concerned, because she was being serious. Her eyes shone brightly at the thought of inflicting some punishment on these soldiers just to see how they would react to the same torture that they enacted upon the men and women forced to work in the mine.

Wanting to head off any potential misunderstanding, he clarified. "Chain them. No flogging. Also, set up an aid station at the edge of the village. We came through the battle in good shape, but I want those who need care to be seen to immediately."

"And the soldiers who require care?"

Duff looked at Saraa for an even longer period of time, his concern for her growing. It wasn't so much what she said as how she said it.

She asked a legitimate question, but there was no emotion in her voice. Not a single trace of empathy, which was unlike her.

"The Highlanders first. Then any soldiers where giving them care won't be a waste of our time and resources. Clear?"

Saraa nodded and ran off, understanding exactly what Duff meant. There was no point in trying to help those soldiers who couldn't be saved. Better just to send them to the other side so that the living could keep on living and the dying could die.

Duff watched Saraa go, sensing that there was something else going on with the Highlander in addition to the trauma she had just experienced. Something more worrisome.

But he didn't have time to think on that now, so he turned his focus to a more pressing question.

What was he supposed to do to help Jakob?

He knew that Jakob could manage himself against the Stalkers. If he could kill Wraiths in the Murk, if he could bring down the entrance to the mountain, then he could kill the Stalkers sent here to kill him.

Still, Duff didn't want to leave him on his own. Jakob was important to the Highlanders. He was the symbol of their rebellion. He was the reason for their success, giving them the ability to battle the Wraiths in the Murk.

And blast it, Jakob was important to him as well, even if Duff didn't like to admit that. Even though he had tried not to get too close to anyone after he lost his family, it hadn't worked with a few people. Jakob being one of them.

He needed to help Jakob if he could.

Surveying the damage to the mountain that Jakob had wrought with the Talent, he realized that going after him from this direction was no longer an option. He wasn't too concerned, however. Knowing Jakob and what else he could do with the power at his command, Duff had no doubt that he would find another way out of the mountain.

So where might he try to do that?

Since arriving in the Highlands more than five years before, he had learned that these imposing peaks were riddled with tunnels and crevices. Many of them were dead ends. Many of them weren't.

There were always multiple means of ingress and egress in every spire. You just needed to be patient and know what to look for in order to find them.

As he mulled that challenge, Martin and Bertie ran up, having just emerged from the barracks where Saraa and her squad had barricaded almost a full company of soldiers.

The soldiers who had been trapped inside stood up against the side of the mountain, their faces revealing their shock at what had happened to them. Their distaste as well now that they wore the manacles that they had used so many times before on their slaves.

How quickly their fortunes had turned.

"Duff, you need to take a look at this."

"In a minute. I want to check the side tunnels first."

There was nothing for it. He needed to go after Jakob. The lad could manage Stalkers. But how many at one time he didn't know.

He needed to free the miners as well. Jakob had told him that he had located those forced to work in this dreadful place. The slavers had deposited them in a cavern not too far away from the main entrance.

"We already did. There's no chance of using them. Jakob was incredibly thorough."

"When is he not," Duff grumbled.

Still, he couldn't fault the lad. Jakob had taken a major risk, but it had paid off.

The Stalkers who had made it out into the light had all gone after Jakob as soon as they caught scent of him. Most of the monsters were killed when Jakob brought the main tunnel down. Sharperson's soldiers eliminated those remaining because they had no other choice.

If they didn't, the Stalkers would have killed them.

Duff hadn't paid much attention to that fight. He had been engaged in his combat with Hippolates.

The Highlanders had observed. Dispassionately. Waiting to see who would prove the victor. Ready to join the fight themselves when it was all over. Not really caring who their next opponent would be.

The soldiers had won, although the Stalkers had ripped savagely through several squads before meeting their own bloody ends.

When the soldiers finally turned back toward the Highlanders with that threat removed, they realized that the Stalkers were nothing compared to the men and women standing against them now.

Because several of the soldiers, still caught up in a battle rage, made the mistake of charging at the Highlanders' square. Those few foolish men had died in seconds. Cut down with a frightening efficiency by the less-than-impressed Highlanders.

Upon seeing that, Sharperson's soldiers remained in place, waiting to see what was going to happen next. Understanding that the battle was over, yet not ready to acknowledge it until after Duff killed their Captain. Finally accepting that their fates were now in the hands of the men and women they had terrorized for the last few years.

Duff followed Bertie and Martin into the barracks. The main room was exactly as Duff expected it would be. He had lived in a barracks much like this one before he was promoted to Sergeant in the Royal Guard and then been given a small room of his own.

"What's so special about this barracks?"

Martin grinned at him. "Come on. We'll show you."

Bertie and Martin led Duff through a small door and into a large storeroom that was filled with weapons and other supplies. What couldn't be missed were the several barrels full of manacles and chains.

Duff knew exactly what he wanted to do with those.

When he pulled his gaze away, he realized that Bertie and Martin were grinning at him, both of them with a hand on a barrel filled with scrap metal.

"So why are we here?"

"Do you remember when we were at Donel's village and we went after those children?"

"Hard to forget."

Donel and his Highlanders had hunted down the Stalker that was skirting the edge of their village, and they had found more than one set of tracks.

Those Highlanders living closer to the village had thought that Matten and his family were safe because that other monster had been moving in the opposite direction. But the Stalker had doubled back, hunting for easy prey.

Matten and his wife had died to give their children the time they needed to escape. Duff and his squad had located the path the children had taken because Jakob had found the tunnel hidden beneath the floor.

Martin and Bertie waited patiently as that memory played through Duff's mind. When he smiled, having figured it out, the two Highlanders nodded. Grasping the heavy barrel, they dragged it across the floor and out of the way.

A trap door. Although not as well hidden.

"How did you find it?" Duff was impressed.

"We saw the scuff marks in the floor. We decided to take a look for ourselves."

Martin reached down, grabbed the rope set in the boards, and pulled the hatch up.

A deep darkness greeted them.

Bertie was ready, throwing down a burning torch.

It fell more than ten feet before hitting the ground.

Duff stuck his head through the opening, pleased to see the ladder.

Taking the second torch Bertie gave him, Duff threw it farther down the tunnel.

"Well done," Duff said when he pulled his head out of the opening.

This is what they needed. The tunnel led into the mine. He was sure of it.

The question was how far and to where, and there was only one way to obtain the answers to those questions.

"We're going after Jakob?" asked Bertie.

"No, Jakob is on his own for now," Duff replied, a hint of reluctance in his voice. He didn't like his decision, but he knew that it was the only decision that he could make. "We need to free any of the miners who are still in there."

"And once we get the miners?" asked Martin.

Duff ignored him. "If this tunnel runs straight, it might take us right to where the miners are being held. It might give us some other options as well."

"That's all well and good, but what about Jakob?" pressed Bertie.

"The Lord of the Highlands, as we have just seen, is capable of bringing down a mountain all on his own," lectured Duff. "Therefore, I have little concern about his safety no matter how many of those cursed Stalkers are in this mountain with him." He hoped that Bertie and Martin believed him.

"He's also got the Crimson Devil with him," Martin offered. "Bad luck for the monsters."

"That he does," Duff confirmed, "and that young woman is a menace. Just as destructive as he is in her own way."

"So we're going to leave them on their own?" asked Bertie, clearly not liking that choice.

"Of course not." Duff reached for another torch and stepped down onto the ladder. "We're going to take this tunnel into the mountain and see if we can find him. Get Tommie and some of her archers. I want them with us." Bertie ran off to do that. Duff gave his next order to Martin. "And get Saraa. She can go after the people enslaved here while we go after the Lord Kestrel."

18

TEST OF METTLE

Bryen had left the Shadow Keep early that morning, a light fog adding a thin layer of dew to his clothes. Not the Murk, thankfully. Just a wispy mist drifting down from the mountains.

Even so, he sensed the unease in the people walking the streets with him. Especially the soldiers, their nervousness hinting that they understood they had earned a reprieve and slipped the hangman's noose, but only for a time.

Knowing what he planned to do, Aislinn had wanted to go. And, in fact, he would have liked to have had her with him. Her assistance would have sped up the work.

But she couldn't say no to her uncle. Kendric wanted to show his niece all that he had accomplished in making the Northern Territory and Shadow's Reach what it was today.

A long tour, he assumed, Bryen not expecting to see Aislinn again until early that evening.

Still, her absence wasn't going to dissuade him from the task that he had set for himself. After their conversation with Ursina that more resembled a confrontation, he and Aislinn had spoken about what they had to do next.

Follow their instincts and find the source of the Curse in the city.

And who better to do that than the one man who knew how to find and manipulate the Curse without being corrupted by its tainted power?

The sense of evil cloaking the city was almost imperceptible when he began his hunt. Barely there. Poking at the fringes of his awareness. Stronger in some places. Weaker in others. Continually moving. Continually shifting. Yet always leaving behind a tantalizingly faint residue of corruption and decay.

Depending on where he was, the scent of the Curse, strong for a few seconds, weakened only a few heartbeats later. Meandering through the city without rhyme or reason. At least as far as he could tell.

And so it went. Bryen tracking the scent as best as he could, all the while feeling as if he were caught in a game, playing hide and seek with a malevolent power.

It was much like trying to catch the wind. There one moment, gone the next, always slipping through his fingers.

For Bryen, it was an incredibly frustrating experience. It was as if the Curse knew what he was trying to do and it relished teasing him, the corrupted power drawing closer then slipping just out of reach time after time.

He had expected that his hunt would be much like this, what he was dealing with now a familiar feeling for him. He had experienced the same sense of futility in Caledonia when learning to deal with the Curse and then again during the Blood Company's escape from the Jagged Islands, those remote skerries rich in the Curse thanks to the presence of the Kraken.

In both previous instances, he had succeeded. He had found a way past the taint's attempts to escape him. To play with his senses. To manipulate him and lead him down the wrong path.

Yet here he was struggling.

He should have been able to do this.

To lock on to the Curse.

To follow the trail to the very end.

But he couldn't.

The source of the Curse was shielded. He was sure of it, the barrier allowing that corrosive power to hide in the shadows.

Rather than continue his exercise in frustration, Bryen decided that he needed to take a different approach. Instead of hunting for the Curse, he would simply wander through the city and see where the Seventh Stone took him.

The ancient artifact that had joined with him was designed to store and amplify power, whether the Talent or the Curse. Because of that, it was drawn to power, clean or corrupt, seeking it out, no matter how faint.

Giving free rein to the Seventh Stone, Bryen began again, walking through the city with no apparent goal in mind. Wandering through various neighborhoods. Not rushing, taking his time in the many marketplaces that took over the city squares once the sun was higher in the sky. Even examining a few rings in the jeweler's district that he thought might appeal to Aislinn.

Every so often he allowed a strand of energy from the Seventh Stone to reach out to the taint that teased his senses. Never trying to catch it. Never trying to follow. Simply confirming that it was still there. Touching it briefly and then breaking the contact just as quickly.

The first few times the Curse jumped away from him. Wary.

As he continued with his muted effort, the Curse began to linger around him longer. Not jumping back. No longer concerned by what he was doing.

It wasn't long before Bryen could reach out to the Curse with the Seventh Stone and follow its trail through the city for several minutes. Then, before the Curse fled from him as he knew it would if he maintained the contact for too long, Bryen released his hold.

Never in a rush. Taking his time. Believing that his patience would bear fruit in the end. Understanding that he was playing the long game as he meandered through the city when, not surprisingly, he came finally to a smithy that backed up against the southern wall, a large arch revealing the small courtyard beyond.

He walked into the shop with a smile, having been here before with Aislinn. There was a rhythm to the work taking place just through the door that led to the back of the shop that appealed to him. Helped to center him.

They were familiar sounds, having heard them every day while growing up in the shadow of the Colosseum.

From all the activity and the dozens of packages waiting for their customers set on the shelves affixed to the wall behind the counter, clearly it was a very prosperous forge. He peeked through the large doorway, watching the men and women stride briskly by the entrance, intent on the projects assigned to them. Every so often a flash of fire shot up into the air when an apprentice stoked the bellows to keep the heat at exactly the temperature the smith required.

"He's not here."

Bryen turned, having heard someone approaching and knowing that she wasn't a threat.

Juliette. The woman who owned the foundry and from what the Blademaster had told him, the best blacksmith in the Territory.

"I actually wasn't looking for the Blademaster."

"Really. Then what pulled you in my direction?"

Bryen found her word choice interesting. "It's just where my wandering took me." He nodded toward the many weapons hanging from the wall as well as the other tools that had been put on display to demonstrate the quality of her work. "I couldn't help but admire your skill."

"That's very kind of you."

"I'm only speaking the truth. Where did you ply your trade before making the journey across the Burnt Ocean?"

"Tintagel."

Bryen thought about that. "Did you by chance know a smith named Kollea?"

Juliette's eyes crinkled. "Of course I did." Then she understood, hope in her eyes. "Kollea survived the Pit?"

"She did," Bryen confirmed with a smile and a nod.

"I'm glad to hear it." Juliette sighed with relief. "After what happened to her, the injustice, I feared the worst."

"Kollea is just as good at shaping steel as she is using it."

"That doesn't surprise me in the least." Juliette stepped around the bench and leaned her arms across the counter. She took a moment to study the young man standing before her.

The word intimidating didn't do him justice. And it wasn't just because of the sword hilts visible above each shoulder. The sense of power that radiated from him was almost paralyzing.

"Kollea and I were two of just a handful of women who owned forges in the Caledonian capital. We formed something of a partnership. When she was taken to the Pit ..."

Juliette pushed herself up from the counter, pressing her hands onto the polished wood. "Kollea being condemned to the Colosseum was the final nudge that sent me here. She was treated poorly. She was another example of how the rich and powerful could get away with whatever they wanted under the Belerons, and, if you tried to stand up for yourself, they would crush you without a second thought."

"I doubt anyone could crush Kollea now."

"I'm even happier to hear that. You saved her?"

Her question really wasn't a question. Bryen studied Juliette for several long seconds. He was beginning to realize that she knew more about him than he thought she did.

"She saved herself. I just gave her the means to do so."

"It's a relief to know that Kollea got her fresh start. She deserved it." Juliette slapped her hands gently on the wood in pleasure. "That's why I'm here in Shadow's Reach as well. After what happened to Kollea, the city turning sour under Marden Beleron, I needed to start fresh someplace else."

"As did I," Bryen admitted.

"I can understand that, Volkun. Your reputation is one that I can only assume is difficult to escape."

"You told her?" he asked the Blademaster.

Jurgen Klines had walked in behind him, believing that the Protector didn't know that he was there. Learning much to his chagrin that he had failed to take him by surprise.

"No, I didn't, Protector." He stepped around Bryen and then next to the blacksmith. "Juliette is as sharp as her daggers."

"My apologies, then. I forget at times that I'm not as invisible as I would like to be."

"I saw you in the Pit," Juliette explained. "I went looking for Kollea shortly after she was forced onto the white sand. They made her fight a man who must have been twice as big as she was. It was a pleasure to see that he didn't last long against her."

"Kollea is a very efficient fighter. Many of her opponents misjudged her, and she was happy to take advantage of that error. They paid the price as a result."

"I'm glad they did. And I'm even more glad to hear that Kollea is alive and well. Is she with you?"

"She's in New Caledonia, but not with me in Shadow's Reach."

Juliette nodded, deciding that it wouldn't be right to pry. The Protector didn't seem the type who would appreciate too many questions. "Kollea was impressive. As were many of the other gladiators I watched fight that day. But you, Volkun, when

I saw you glide across the white sand ... it was like watching a master at work. I couldn't take my eyes away from you."

Bryen shrugged, immediately feeling uncomfortable, trying to deflect her praise. "It was training and luck. No more than that."

"Maybe," she said. Clearly she didn't believe him. "May I?" She motioned to the swords on his back.

Bryen stared at Juliette for just a breath, measuring her. Then he reached over each shoulder, pulling his swords free from their scabbards. He brought the blades together at the hilt to form the Spear of the Magii, the double-bladed weapon gleaming brightly in the light that streamed through the window and flashing every time the flames of the forge flared.

"When the darkness surrounds, the light will prevail," Juliette read, the inscription running along the length of the steel. "Do you know what that means?"

"It's a reminder," offered the Blademaster. "A lesson as well. Probably also a hope."

"A reminder?" wondered Juliette. "How so?"

"Weapons such as the Spear of the Magii were crafted for a very specific reason. To be used against monsters created by the Curse or those using the Curse."

"Forbidding and frightening," chuckled Juliette as she ran her hands along the length of steel, never having seen such skilled workmanship before, and she had spent more than three decades working the bellows.

"Indeed, and as the Protector has demonstrated, quite effective when employed by someone with the requisite skills."

Bryen smiled at that. "The Blademaster is correct. A Magus gave me this weapon, believing that it would help me with a task that he said only I could accomplish."

"And what task was that?"

"It proved to be several tasks actually, all connected. Kill the

Ghoule Overlord, rebuild the Weir, and prevent the Ghoule Legions from invading Caledonia."

"And you did that," Juliette murmured, offering the Protector a nod of respect. News of those victories had traveled swiftly across the Burnt Ocean.

"With a great deal of help from many others, the Blademaster included."

"The Protector is being modest. If not for him, I and many others would not be here today. Caledonia would no longer exist."

"You're giving me too much credit, Blademaster. I didn't ..."

"You know what they say when people aren't willing to accept the credit they deserve?"

"No, what?" asked the Blademaster, his eyes scrunching up with amusement. Juliette had a way of putting someone in their place, and he sensed that this was one of those times.

"That they're too insecure to acknowledge the truth about themselves."

"A harsh assessment," suggested the Blademaster.

"But true, wouldn't you say?"

The Blademaster opened his mouth to protest, then thought better of it upon catching the gleam in Juliette's eyes.

Bryen watched the entire exchange, knowing that more was being said in that one look than an hour of dialogue could.

He shouldn't be, but Bryen was enjoying the Blademaster's momentary discomfort. And he was glad that the blacksmith didn't turn the full force of her gaze upon him, because it reminded him of one of Rafia's stares.

"Remarkable," she said while examining the weapon, marveling at the craftsmanship that went into forging such a beautiful weapon.

She knew that she was a good blacksmith. No, she was an excellent blacksmith. She could say that without a drop of conceit. Yet this artistry was beyond her.

What she would give to see the Giants of the Rime at work in their mythical forges. She spun the spear in the air a few times, stepping away from Bryen and Jurgen to ensure that neither had to worry about the razor-sharp blades on each end.

"I never thought to see an artifact crafted by the Giants of the Rime. Truly impressive." She handed it back carefully, nodding in thanks for the opportunity the Protector gave her. "My work certainly pales in comparison."

"You're being too hard on yourself," Bryen protested. "I was wondering if I might see that piece." He pointed to a thick bracelet that would cover most of a woman's forearm.

"A good eye. For your lady love?"

"Yes, I thought I might get her something to mark our time here in Shadow's Reach. Besides, with all that's going on, she might have a use for it."

That comment brought a crinkle to the Blademaster's eyes. He would need to speak more with the Protector about his concerns.

Juliette reached behind her, handing the intricately designed bracelet to Bryen, who flipped it through his fingers. Light but strong. Useful in defending against a dagger's blade, though not a heavier weapon like a sword.

He smiled upon seeing the barely visible indentations. Brushing his fingers across them, a thin, sharp blade came free with an almost silent snick.

"Ingenious. Incredibly well crafted."

"Thank you. It's my own design."

"I get the feeling that I'm missing something."

"You are." Juliette reached over and pushed gently on another almost imperceptible indentation on the inside of the bracelet. An even small dagger came free. No more than two inches in length it was meant to be held between two fingers. Nevertheless, just as deadly as the other in the hand of someone who knew how to use the miniature dirk.

"Now that's clever. I'll definitely take it. How much?"

"It's yours."

"I couldn't accept, Juliette."

"I get the feeling that you did quite a lot for Kollea when I couldn't. Think of it as a gift. My way of saying thank you."

"You're too kind."

"Besides, when people see my work on the Lady Winborne's forearm, it will lead to another revenue stream for me. Every well-off woman in the city will want one."

"Even more clever than the bracelet," Bryen chuckled.

Juliette nodded in thanks for the compliment.

"Is Aislinn all right?" asked Klines, no longer able to hide his concern.

"Yes, she is. She's with her uncle. He's showing her the city and all that he's done."

Klines nodded. "Then why are you here and not with her?"

"I got the sense that her uncle wanted some time alone with her. And I have no doubt that Aislinn can use that time to gain what she wants."

"Information."

"Exactly so. She hopes to dig out some nuggets that she couldn't with Kendric's wife by his side."

"And specifically what are you digging for?" Klines asked.

Bryen smiled. He never could put anything past the Blademaster. "I'm interested in learning more about his wife."

Juliette nodded at that. "Smart move."

"Why would you say that?"

Juliette leaned on the counter once more. "You've spoken with her?"

"A few times, yes."

"What's your take having done that?"

Bryen wasn't sure what he should reveal to the blacksmith. He looked to the Blademaster, who gave him a brief nod to ease his concerns. The Blademaster trusted her. Bryen could as well.

"That she's hiding something. Many things, actually."

"What else?" prodded Juliette.

Bryen smiled again. He could see why the Blademaster was so taken with the blacksmith. Direct and to the point. Not wanting to waste time. "That she's the one who's making the decisions in the Territory. Kendric rules in name; however, she's the one exercising the power held by the Governor."

"Perceptive. And right on the money."

"What can you tell me about her?"

"Much of what I know about her is common knowledge in the streets. I'll save the tastier morsels for the end. You know when she arrived here?"

"Five years ago," replied Bryen.

"Correct, and as soon as she arrived everything about the city changed. Within a day of her setting foot within the walls of Shadow's Reach she was on Kendric Winborne's arm."

"He said as much. He looks back on that day as the best of his life."

"Maybe it was. Maybe it wasn't. It's too early to tell. It's just surprising that he was smitten at first sight, since he very much enjoyed playing the field while in Caledonia and here in the Territory."

"You mean that you weren't smitten with me the first time I walked into your shop?"

"Far from it, Jurgen. Sorry, but looking at you, I thought that you were going to waste my time because you didn't have the skills required for the work."

"I don't know whether I should be offended."

"Your choice," Juliette replied with a suggestive gleam in her eye. "I'm just saying that based on our experience, all doesn't seem quite right with respect to the relationship between the Governor and his Lady."

"It is possible," Jurgen argued.

"It is possible," Juliette agreed with a nod. "Unlikely, however. The world doesn't usually work that way."

"It could work that way."

"It could," Juliette admitted. "Although, again, unlikely."

"You're going to drag this out, aren't you?"

"It's my story to tell, Jurgen." She gave him a hard look and then a smile and wink to let him know that she was just having a little fun with him. "Besides, you're the one slowing me down with all your questions." Bryen smiled at that, never having seen anyone treat the Blademaster in this way. Never having anticipated that the Blademaster would allow it. "As soon as she wrapped her arm around Kendric's, things began to change here in Shadow's Reach."

"How so?"

"Kendric Winborne always had a grand vision for what he wanted Shadow's Reach to become, and I certainly don't fault him for it. Yet he struggled to make his vision into a reality. He's a man of big ideas. He knows what he wants. But when it comes time to make those plans real ..."

"He loses his way."

"That's right, Protector. And it's not uncommon. Kendric Winborne views himself as a visionary. He needed an engineer who could take him from the intangible to the tangible."

"And that's what Ursina did."

"Correct. Within days of her taking up residence in the Shadow Keep, construction began on projects that had been languishing for several years. The growth of the city during the past five years has resulted primarily because of the leadership and management skills demonstrated by Ursina Winborne. We would not be where we are today without her."

"You don't seem entirely pleased to be acknowledging that fact."

"I'm not. You've spoken with her a few times now."

"I have."

"I've spoken with her once. Just once. When I did, I sensed as well that she was hiding something. That the person I saw was not the person she truly was. She is shielding her true self with a veil."

"That's a good way to put it," murmured Bryen.

"I experienced a strange sensation as well when I was speaking with her. Did you sense it?"

Bryen looked at Juliette with keener eyes. The Blademaster was right. As sharp as her blades indeed. He glanced at the Blademaster. He nodded again. "I did."

"Not only that she wasn't quite what she seemed. I sensed a power there that sent a spike of fear down my spine." Juliette shook her head not only at the bad memory, but also because she was having such a difficult time describing what she felt. "It was as if she could crush me like a bug with barely any effort."

"That's an excellent way to put it," Bryen confirmed with a nod.

"Thank you. I thought it might be. She came in here once looking to acquire a few daggers for her husband. With just a single glance from her, my blood turned to ice, and I couldn't get warm again for the rest of the day." She shivered at the memory. "I've spoken with many of the craftspeople working on the Shadow Keep. I do work with them and for them. They've experienced much the same as I have. They're afraid of her, just as I am."

"Why would they be afraid of her? Because they get the same feeling as you do?"

"In part, yes. Also because some strange things have been occurring in the past year as they've struggled to strengthen the foundation of the Shadow Keep."

"Strange things? Like what?"

"Stonemasons and other laborers working in the tunnels and basements of the citadel disappearing. Accidents can happen on work sites. Tunnels collapsing. Buttresses failing.

They're inevitable when you are forced to work too quickly, as has been the case with my friends. But these occurrences are too many and too frequent to be just accidents."

"How many workers have disappeared?"

"In the last year alone ... forty-three."

"Forty-three?" demanded the Blademaster. "Why didn't you tell me that?"

"You didn't ask?"

"I didn't ask?"

"Stop getting all huffy, Jurgen. You're learning about this now, so don't get your knickers in a knot. We never had cause to discuss this before."

"My knickers in a knot?"

For the first time, Bryen saw anger break through the Blademaster's usually stolid countenance, a hint of red appearing on his cheeks. "You're enjoying this, aren't you?"

Juliette gave him a broad grin. "Aren't you?" She turned toward Bryen. "Jurgen is always so serious. It's important to play with him from time to time to ensure that he doesn't get too full of himself."

"Too full of myself?" challenged the Blademaster. "I'll have you know ..." He stopped himself, realizing that he was playing her game just as she wanted him to. He let out a long breath, releasing his anger, though not without some difficulty. "You're a challenging woman, Juliette."

"And yet you're still here."

"I'm still here," the Blademaster admitted.

"And I'm glad that you are. Now back to the story?"

"Please."

"Forty-three lost. Very few talk about it. At least openly. Because they fear the Lady of the Northern Territory."

"How do you know that they weren't all lost in accidents?"

"The demons in the darkness."

"The demons? What do you mean by demons?"

"It began more than a year ago, coinciding with when workers began to disappear. There was talk of growls and shrieks in the corridors beneath the citadel. Those claims became more common when the miners broke through the stone into natural tunnels beneath the keep that no one knew existed. That was bad enough. Worse was the sight of blood-red eyes peering back at them in the darkness."

"Stalkers," murmured the Blademaster. It only stood to reason, helping to confirm his own theory as he had seen those monsters emerge from the crevices that burrowed through the plateau upon which Shadow's Reach was built.

"Stalkers," Juliette confirmed. "That's why the work has slowed. Few are willing to brave the tunnels anymore. Although it's the strangest thing."

"What is?"

"Those monsters have been sighted many times in the corridors beneath the fortress, yet none have attacked the unfortunate workers who have come across them."

"Really? That's true?" The Blademaster found it hard to believe.

"It is," Juliette confirmed with a sharp nod.

"Why is that the case? From what I understand, Stalkers are predators. They live to kill."

"They live to serve," Bryen corrected. "They hunt and kill their selected prey. It's usually not an indiscriminate act unless their hunger proves stronger than the compulsion placed upon them."

The Blademaster nodded in understanding. "So if they're not charged with hunting and killing the workers beneath the keep ..."

"They leave them be unless the hunger is too much for them."

The Blademaster looked hard at Bryen. "You're suggesting a level of control that could only be achieved by ..."

"Yes, that's what I'm suggesting," Bryen replied before the Blademaster could complete his thought. He trusted Juliette. But only because he trusted the Blademaster. He was not yet ready to share with her everything that he suspected.

"It is surprising, isn't it." Juliette noted the wordless private conversation that was taking place between the Volkun and Jurgen and chose not to force her way into it. If there was more that she needed to know, Jurgen would tell her later. "Forty-three workers gone. Assumed dead. Yet no bodies found."

"No bodies?" asked the Blademaster. "How is that possible? I assumed ..."

"Assuming can be dangerous," Juliette interrupted. "Forty-three workers gone. Not a single body. And not enough accidents to explain their loss."

The Blademaster chose not to ask why Juliette never shared this critical information with him. He knew what her reply would be. He had never asked her, so why would she tell him?

A frustrating woman indeed. Yet still he couldn't believe his luck in finding her.

"Do you think these workers ..." began Klines.

"Are being used by Ursina?" finished Bryen. "Yes, I do."

"Used?" asked Juliette. "How could she use them if they're dead?"

"Stalkers are not natural creatures," Bryen explained. "Those workers might not actually be dead."

"Not natural," repeated Juliette. Her eyes widened as she began to comprehend what the Volkun was implying. "She made them."

"I believe she did, yes."

"But why?"

"That's one of the questions that I'm trying to answer."

"But if she made them, then that means ..."

"I would keep that thought to yourself, Juliette," Bryen

urged. "Nothing good would come of it if you shared that with anyone else."

After a few seconds passed, she nodded. "You're right about that."

"Then how do you explain the attacks beyond Shadow's Reach?"

Bryen shrugged. "A guess only."

"I'll take a guess."

"Her control over her creations is only so good. It's stronger the closer the beasts are to her. It becomes weaker as they gain more distance from her. They still will obey the compulsion she sets within them, but as the distance between them increases, the Stalkers will gain more of an ability to give in to their baser urges. They will not be able to control themselves."

"Unfortunately, that makes a bit too much sense," admitted Klines. "It would explain why the people living beyond the city are so afraid of the Stalkers. Several have had run-ins with the monsters, and it usually didn't end well for them."

"Although that fear has proven a boon to our business."

"It has," Klines admitted. "Sadly so."

"I'm assuming that the Stalkers are using the tunnels scattered throughout the tor to emerge unseen beyond Shadow's Reach?"

"I've seen it with my own eyes. I killed one of the monsters myself, actually."

"You did what?" demanded Juliette, her shock and anger plain. Not at what he had done, but rather that he had kept it to himself. "Why didn't you tell me?"

"You didn't ask," Klines replied innocently.

"You insufferable old goat."

"I've been called much worse."

"I'll keep trying then," promised Juliette.

"I'm assuming that concerns about these Stalkers have been raised with the Governor?" asked Bryen.

"They have. Several times, in fact."

"What has he done?"

"Nothing. Kendric Winborne says the people living beyond the city have nothing to fear."

"They accepted that? They've seen these Stalkers in the flesh, have they not?"

"They have, but what are they to do? If the Governor doesn't believe you, or doesn't want to believe you, then you have no choice but to protect yourself. They can't force him to do something that he doesn't want to do."

Bryen nodded in agreement. Juliette was correct. There was little that those living beyond the walls could do other than to do their best to make do. "They might not be able to do much, but perhaps I can."

The Blademaster's gaze narrowed. "What are you planning, Protector?"

"I haven't decided yet. I'll need to speak with Aislinn first. But I was thinking that another conversation with Ursina Winborne might be in order."

"You would take such a risk? Believing what she can do? The power she can exercise?"

"It's better than cutting at the edge. Best just to get right to the point."

"Another of Declan's sayings," grumbled the Blademaster. "One of these days, one of Declan's many maxims is going to get you into trouble."

"Some of them already have," Bryen admitted with a grin.

"Before you go, one other thing."

"I'm being followed."

"You knew?" the Blademaster said, somewhat surprised. Then he shook his head. "Of course you knew."

"Something I learned from my grandfather," he explained.

"So you know that Benin and some of my men are watching your watchers."

"I do. They can leave them be. It's just Ursina wanting to know where I am and what I'm doing. Before she makes a play for me, she wants to have one more conversation."

"How can you be so certain of that?"

"Because I have something that she wants. Something that she can only obtain from me."

THE CONVERSATION with the Blademaster and Juliette continued to trouble Bryen as he made his way slowly back through the streets of Shadow's Reach, still searching for the source of the taint. Allowing the Seventh Stone to guide his hunt.

His excursion was coming to an end where it started. Not surprising in the least as he strode through the main square that surrounded the Shadow Keep, the citadel beckoning to him as the Seventh Stone pulled him toward it. The malaise of evil teasing him. Almost as if it was a game between them.

Bryen knew exactly where he needed to go now. The conversation with the Blademaster and Juliette confirming what the Seventh Stone was revealing to him.

He had to find some way to get into the corridors beneath the citadel. But to do that, he needed to get past Ursina Winborne. The Lady of the Northern Territory watching him approach, waiting for him in the shadows of the archway.

URSINA STEPPED out into the center of the road that led beyond the walls of the citadel, smiling pleasantly, hands clasped in front of her as Bryen walked toward her from across the square.

She knew that she needed to handle the conversation to come with the utmost delicacy. Aislinn Winborne was a threat because of who she was and her position with respect to her husband. After all, she was the heir to the Southern Marches. She could claim the Northern Territory as her own if she chose.

The Protector was a different animal entirely. More dangerous, perhaps. Though still just a tool to be used.

Admittedly a clever one. Not just a blunt object. But a tool, nonetheless.

The trick would be figuring out how to get from him what she wanted. Because she doubted that he would acquiesce to her demands without a fight.

Her goals were simple, although not necessarily easily achieved. She needed to learn more about the power hidden within him. The power that she believed that she could use against the Wraiths and the Murk.

With that desire dominating her thoughts, Ursina also needed to determine how she could employ that power herself. Without having to rely on the Protector.

Because, as always, for her it was all about control.

And, for her to attain the control that she so craved, so required, knowledge and understanding were essential.

To that end, Ursina had spent much of the morning in her library hidden behind her private office.

The shelves were filled with books that she had brought with her from Caledonia, most of them stolen from Haven. They were worth a fortune to someone who knew how to dig out their secrets. All of them on topics that most Magii refused to study, avoiding them like they would a black dragon or a bloodsnake, afraid to take a single step upon the path that reading just one brief passage from any of those texts would lead them.

Ursina had hoped that with her research she might learn the best way to handle the Protector and appropriate the power he controlled.

But no such luck.

Thus, her desire to get the Protector alone.

"There is something about you, young man, that I find quite perplexing."

Bryen didn't respond. Instead, he stopped right in front of her, seemingly at his ease as he leaned against the spear that he held in one hand. He didn't feel the need to help Ursina in any way. He knew exactly what she wanted from him, and she would have to work for it.

"And I can't put my finger on it."

"That's why you want to speak with me. Because that bothers you. Not knowing what you don't know."

For just a breath, Ursina stared at him with a hint of surprise visible in the twist of her lips, his words throwing her off balance. She recovered quickly.

It was a common enough phrase. What unsettled her was simply the fact that her mother liked to use it quite often, and she had no desire to think of her mother. Doing so allowed memories to rise up within her that were better left buried.

"It does," Ursina confirmed. "I've heard of you, Volkun. Of your exploits on the white sand."

She stopped then, giving him the opening that she thought he would take so that he could brag about his many victories in the Colosseum.

Yet he didn't say a word, the silence dragging out between them.

"You don't want to share your experiences in the Pit? All those combats that made you a living legend? That legend only growing in the aftermath of your overthrow of Marden Beleron and then your defeat of the Ghoule Overlord and his Legions? I must say, I'm surprised that you're being so reticent about all that. Most anyone else would be turning such remarkable success into fame and fortune."

"I have little interest in either fame or fortune," Bryen

replied simply. "Besides, what's done is done. There's little to add to what's already been said."

"I wasn't expecting modesty. Aislinn truly is fortunate to have found you," Ursina said, forcing out a gentle laugh through gritted teeth.

"Aislinn might not agree with you," Bryen replied with a lift of his eyebrows and a small smile.

"Why do you still wear the Protector's Collar?" Ursina motioned toward the silver encircling his neck. "I would think that you would want to remove that token if the magic it once contained no longer has a hold on you."

Bryen studied Ursina with a jaundiced eye. He didn't miss how she knew that the power once contained within the collar was gone. Just another small indication that strengthened his belief about Kendric's wife.

Not wanting to beat around the bush, he decided to challenge her. He wanted to see how she would react.

"I take it that you knew Sirius."

Ursina's eyes bore into him. Her fingers tightened into fists. Her nostrils flared. From anger or fear, he didn't know. Perhaps both. Still, his play worked. Just one more sign confirming what he already believed.

"I do," Ursina finally admitted, having no good reason to lie and assuming that the Protector would sniff it out if she tried. "Wait. What do you mean by knew?"

Bryen stared into Ursina's eyes for several seconds, trapped by those orbs of deep purple, only pulling free when he caught that intermittent flash of black at the very back. He shifted his focus to her expression. As understanding dawned within her regarding Sirius, instead of sadness Ursina seemed more relieved than anything else.

That was curious. Then again, perhaps not. Perhaps it made perfect sense.

"Sirius died saving my life," Bryen explained, a strain of

sorrow trailing in his voice, "fighting the Ghoule Overlord so that I could do what I needed to do with respect to the Weir."

Ursina nodded, doing the best that she could to demonstrate some type of remorse. She gave up quickly, knowing that her effort to do so would only come across as false. Instead, she offered an expression that she hoped would be taken as regret. "I'm sorry to hear that. He was a good instructor."

"I thought so as well." Bryen could have said more. Instead, he held back. He could tell that Ursina wanted to ask a question. He didn't want to get in the way of that.

"And what of Rafia?"

Bryen waited again before responding. Based on Ursina's strained tone – she had tried to conceal it, only succeeding in part -- clearly there was some deeper emotion there. A connection. Something more personal between her and Rafia. He just wasn't sure what it was.

"Well," Bryen replied with a nod, "the last time I saw her."

Ursina appeared to be relieved and concerned both at the same time. That was peculiar indeed.

Bryen realized that he could continue to play Ursina's game and gain some useful information, but he didn't have the patience to dance around whatever it was that she really wanted from him. Once again taking Declan's advice that it was better to go straight to the heart of the matter, he pushed her.

"Just ask what you want," Bryen prodded gently. "There's no point in continuing to work your way around the edges."

Ursina's eyes hardened then. She wasn't certain whether she should be insulted. She wasn't used to such directness or the fact that she didn't unsettle him the way that she did so many others, and she didn't know what to make of that.

"You are a dilemma to me, Protector."

"And why is that?"

"You know that I'm a Magus."

"I do."

"So you know I can tell that you are a Magus as well."

"We went through all this last night," Bryen replied. "I am a Magus, though not by choice."

His last comment stopped her for a moment. What did he mean by that? Rather than pursue the trail that he had lain for her, possibly in an attempt to divert her, she decided to let it go. She decided to be direct as well.

"You are not just a Magus. There is another power within you. It seems familiar to me, but then again it's not. I want to know what that power is."

Bryen nodded, his gaze sharpening to the edge of a blade. Finally, they had reached the real issue between them. "I take it that you're used to getting what you want."

"I am," Ursina replied with an absolute confidence, the flash of her violet eyes confirming it.

"Then consider the disappointment you're about to experience a lesson in humility."

Ursina's face scrunched up into a frown, her cheeks coloring as her anger began to simmer within her. This conversation was not going as she thought it would. This gladiator was more than just a challenge. He was also a threat.

"Walk with me, Bryen. Allow me to show you what we're doing here at the Shadow Keep."

Bryen nodded that he would do as she asked. He then took up a position by her side as she led him beneath the archway.

For the next several minutes as they strolled around the inner grounds of the citadel, dodging the cranes, scaffolding, and piles of supplies, along with the workers scrambling about, Ursina explained what she and her husband were doing and how it benefited the city and the Territory.

He chose not to raise the issue Juliette had revealed to him just a few hours before. The hidden cost of all that based on what was happening beneath the Shadow Keep.

"It's quite impressive," Bryen murmured, "the progress that you and your husband have made."

"Yes, it is," Ursina agreed, "but progress often requires sacrifice."

Her comment almost made him miss a step. Bryen caught himself just in time. He felt as if he had drifted into a conversation with Sirius, what was not being said just as important as what was being said.

"But you know that, don't you?" Ursina nudged.

"Meaning?"

"Your reputation precedes you, Volkun. You killed the King of Caledonia. You killed the Ghoule Overlord."

"Your point, Lady Winborne?" Bryen asked, tired that the same topics were coming up once again. Topics that he would prefer to leave in the past. "Other than the fact that I'm very good at killing what needs to be killed."

Rather than being frightened by what the Protector said, what was really a veiled warning, Ursina instead appeared to be pleased by it. As if she had just learned something essential about him. Although what it could be, Bryen had not a clue.

"A trail of blood seems to follow you, Protector. I would hate for that trail to follow you here."

"I only kill what needs to be killed, Lady Winborne," Bryen replied quietly, recognizing the threat in her words and not caring. After all that he had faced since his time in the Pit, one Magus who had strayed from the path wasn't going to frighten him. "Such as these Stalkers that are plaguing the Territories. And, if I can find the source, whoever might be responsible for them."

Ursina didn't respond immediately, but he couldn't help but notice her squint, a flash of anger behind her eyes. He was pleased to have hit the mark, even more so that she was struggling not to give anything more away.

"That's a matter of little concern here in Shadow's Reach."

"Really? How so?"

"Those monsters have not crossed the Northern Steppes. And if they try, then my husband and I will deal with them."

"You're certain of that? The stories I've heard suggest that some of those beasts are a concern for the outlying farmers."

"Rumors, nothing more. If evidence is provided, then my husband and I will deal with it. However, I doubt that any evidence will be found that could turn fiction into fact."

"That's good to know, Lady Winborne," Bryen replied, not missing her play on words. What she was saying by not saying anything at all. "As you described it, I was hoping to avoid continuing along my trail of blood here in your city."

With his expression and tone, Ursina didn't miss the real meaning hidden within his words. But rather than pursue what he was implying, she chose to take another path.

"So tell me, young man. What are your intentions?"

"With respect to?"

"With respect to my niece."

Bryen tried not to laugh, finding her supposed concern amusing. "My intentions are my own. You can certainly talk with your niece if you're curious. We have spoken a great deal about what we plan to do while in New Caledonia."

A flash of fear shot through Ursina. "And what is it, young man, that you plan to do here in New Caledonia?"

Bryen gave her a mysterious smile. "I'm already doing what it is that I need to do."

"What would that be?" Ursina bit out the words, hating the fact that she was allowing him to bait her but unable to help herself.

"Why, starting a new life, of course," Bryen replied amiably.

"That's not really an answer."

"It is an answer. You just don't like the answer."

"You're being evasive," her frustration finally becoming visible.

"I'm being honest."

"Are you always this difficult?"

"Some have said so."

Bryen was being tedious. He wouldn't bother to deny it. But he was doing it for a reason, and not just to get a rise out of Ursina.

He did it because he had learned something important about the Magus.

She valued control. At all times. Over everything. Even so, if he pushed her, if he could figure out how to get under her skin, she still struggled to control herself.

From the expression that she was giving him now, he believed that he had achieved his objective. And it hadn't even taken very much effort to nudge her over the edge.

He felt the first faint touch then. She was done talking. She wanted to test him.

Good, because he wanted to test her as well. Reaching for the Talent, he blocked her attempt to probe the power within him, cutting off the thin strand she sent his way just as if he was cutting off a piece of thread with scissors.

His swift and decisive action caught her by surprise. She had never anticipated that he would sense what she was doing. That he was more than just raw in his ability because he had so little time to train as a Magus.

She sent out another strand of energy. And again. Then one more. Then several more. Desperate to learn more about the power within him.

With each failure, her initial surprise and aggravation became a mounting frustration. Goaded by the insolent smile he gave her, the Protector unconcerned and unaffected by what she was doing.

The combat taking place between them, which was invisible to the naked eye, continued for several minutes more.

Ursina and Bryen facing off against one another. No more than a few feet apart.

Bryen calm, composed, as if he were back on the white sand. Ursina anything but, her control flagging as her rage at her many failures threatened to consume her.

Losing patience, she gave in to the whisper in the back of her mind. She allowed the Curse to reach out, the insidious thread of corruption snaking out from her palm.

Ursina jumped back in shock, the Curse slamming right into the Protector's shield. But he did more than just that.

Rather than allowing the thread of black to dance across the barrier he crafted of the Talent, with a few flicks of his fingers the shield shifted its shape, circling around the thread of tainted energy. Surrounding it. Encasing it.

Ursina watched it all, unable to prevent it, not quite believing what she was seeing.

How could he do such a thing? It simply wasn't possible.

What the Protector did next stole her breath away. He took the ball of glowing white energy into his palm, the thread of black in the center flashing frantically, seeking some way to escape, unable to do so. Then, staring into her eyes, he slowly closed his fingers into a fist.

In a flash, the ball of energy blinked out. And with it, the tainted thread that she had sent his way.

Ursina didn't know what to say. She didn't know what to do. And she struggled to control the trace of fear that took up residence in the back of her brain.

His voice brought her back. "Thank you."

"For what?" Ursina asked. Confused. Even more, concerned.

"For confirming what I suspected."

Bryen stepped back from her then, putting some space between them.

Ursina thought that she had been trying to obtain what she

wanted from him, but all the while the gladiator had been doing the same to her. Worse, he had succeeded while she had failed.

That discovery ate at her like nothing else had since she left Caledonia.

His eyes caught hers again. His emotionless gaze sent a shiver of fear through her.

"I spent a long time on the white sand, Lady Winborne," Bryen explained in a voice that was colder than a mountain stream. "Ten years. I learned a great deal while I was there. May I give you a piece of advice?"

He didn't wait to see whether she would allow it.

"Don't start a fight you can't win."

19

THE RIGHT PATH

Talia worked her way down the passageway. Slowly. Wary. Fearing what might be lurking in the darkness.

It was dry. Musty. A cold breeze whispered through the gloomy corridor that every so often threatened to extinguish the small torch that she had taken from the balcony.

She held the flickering brand in one hand, her dagger in the other.

She refused to allow Roosarian to escape.

If there was one secret passageway built within the walls of the Rock, there had to be others.

Her assumption in that respect had proven correct. She had discovered another hidden entrance in Roosarian's bedroom just behind the headboard on the right.

It had taken Talia several minutes to find the masterfully crafted seam in the stone wall. She wouldn't have located it if she didn't know what she was looking for.

The next step had taken her five minutes.

Finding the release lever in the floor just to the side of the bed. Within easy reach. Roosarian could roll off the mattress, push in on the indentation with a toe, and sneak behind the wall in just a few heartbeats.

Clever.

Much to her chagrin, Talia realized upon entering the tunnel that she was not going in the same direction as Roosarian had during her escape.

Still, she had little choice, having no other way to find her fleeing quarry, and, more importantly, Davin.

Talia had seen nothing on the way to Roosarian's apartment that hinted at where Davin could be. With few other good choices, she realized that there was no reason not to continue down the hidden corridor.

So that's what she did, yet to come upon any junctions.

Only darkness and a few muffled sounds from the other side of the thick stone walls that suggested that the Blood Company was engaging the soldiers assigned to defend the Rock.

Taking some comfort from that discovery, Talia continued through the tunnel for several more minutes. Although she could see very little and had no idea as to where she actually was, she got the sense that the passageway was looping around the citadel and gradually taking her lower.

Every few seconds she stopped.

Listening.

Unable to see anything in the darkness beyond the dim glow provided by her torch, she wanted to make sure that nothing waited for her up ahead. Either Roosarian or one of her creatures.

Halting once more, this time she stayed in place longer than she had before.

The hair on the back of her neck tingled. She sensed that she might not be alone in the passageway, a heavy presence draping itself around her.

She waited more than a minute. Counting off the seconds. Desperate to identify the source of her unease.

But nothing.

Having no choice, she continued forward.

After several more minutes of walking, stopping, listening, then walking again, following the same regimen over and over, the hint of danger growing with every step she took, Talia finally came up against her first obstacle.

A solid steel door.

Examining the barrier with her torch, she realized that there was no lock on it. At least not on her side.

Reaching for the handle, she hesitated.

This didn't feel right to her, the warning in the back of her brain almost screaming at her. Nevertheless, she had nowhere else to go but back the way she had come, and she didn't want to do that. That would mean she had wasted a great deal of time and effort.

Holding the torch out in front of her, she reached for the door handle again.

Thankfully, the steel opened on silent hinges.

Talia waited a few seconds. Listening. Not hearing a sound.

She reached past the doorway with her torch.

She saw nothing but darkness.

No sound. No movement.

Under other circumstances similar to these, Talia would have been pleased. Not now, however.

The air was wrong. Not the smell. That hadn't changed. The corridor still reminded her of walking through a crypt.

A few heartbeats later, her eyes widened, realizing what had made her so distinctly uncomfortable.

Just as she feared, she wasn't alone.

There was a heavy presence in the corridor with her.

Looking up, she caught a flash of blood red well above her head.

Talia stumbled back a few steps, almost falling, having to reach back with her free hand to keep her feet.

A Stalker had been waiting for her on the other side of the door, and now that monster, which faded so seamlessly into the darkness, lunged for her.

Talia scrambled backward much like a crab, seeking some room to maneuver. The torch singed her flesh as she did so. Yet the pain didn't register. Her attention solely on those blood-red eyes that streaked toward her.

Swiping blindly with her dagger, she got lucky.

Her steel sliced all the way to the knuckle across the dagger-like fingers that reached for her.

The Stalker hissed, rearing back in pain.

Talia gained only a brief respite, the Stalker, ignoring its injury, stabbing for her again and again. Releasing its rage at the wound it received through its incessant attack.

She couldn't see the monster.

She could sense the creature.

Relying on that instinct, she defended herself as best as she could, the Stalker's jabs only visible when the beast's claws lunged into the small circle of light that surrounded her.

She would have found it all amusing if it wasn't so terrifying that keeping her alive was a single, slowly dying torch.

Without that the Stalker already would be feasting upon her.

Yet Talia knew as well that the torch would offer her scant protection in just seconds, the last of the flames licking at the base, her scramble to escape the monster's initial attack removing several very necessary inches from her crude lantern.

She needed to adopt a new tactic.

Swiftly.

Talia hated taking a risk if she didn't have time to consider all the variables. But with the pressure that the Stalker was applying, she didn't have the time to do that now.

The Stalker lunged for her again.

Rather than dodging out of the way as she had been doing, she swiped with her dagger, missing the back of its claw by the width of a hair.

Nevertheless, the Stalker reluctantly took a step back, seeking to avoid the steel, remembering its previous wound, which had left its other claw a bloody mess.

And this time, rather than stepping back, Talia lunged again, stabbing with her torch.

Her aim was true, thrusting the dying brand right into the Stalker's face.

The monster shrieked in pain, its claws reaching for the remains of the lantern, desperate to remove the burning embers from its smoldering flesh.

Her attacker distracted, Talia didn't hesitate. The likelihood of killing the Stalker in complete darkness with just a dagger was poor. If she wanted to live, she needed to run.

Her fear driving her forward, Talia sprinted down the pitch-black tunnel. She kept one hand out in front of her, afraid of running into the door that she knew was just a few dozen yards ahead of her.

Glancing back over her shoulder, she glimpsed the dim glow of several pieces of the still smoldering torch growing smaller as she raced away.

Ten yards farther on, she looked again.

A bolt of terror shot through her.

The embers from the torch were getting larger now.

The wounded Stalker was coming after her. Those embers burning into the Stalker's flesh not slowing the beast.

Talia skidded to a stop, her hand slamming against the steel door that she had opened.

She stepped through the doorway and looked back the way that she had come.

The shriek of rage that echoed down the corridor made her

cringe. Those blood-red eyes, framed by the last few burning cinders, were less than ten yards away from her and drawing closer with a terrible speed.

Talia slammed the door shut, and just in time.

The Stalker didn't try to stop, crunching into the steel at full speed.

The frame of the door rattled. With her hand still pressed against it she felt the deep indentation that the monster made in the barrier.

Then there was a welcome, comforting silence.

Until the Stalker shrieked again, ramming its entire body against the damaged door once more.

Talia jumped back from the weakening frame.

She couldn't see in the darkness, but she could tell what was happening. The steel was bending with each strike, the jambs along the stone wall cracking and coming loose.

Having few good options, Talia did the only thing that made sense.

She ran.

As fast as she could.

Pushing herself forward. Desperate to escape.

Less concerned about running into something and more concerned about the Stalker that in a matter of seconds would be taking up the chase again.

She was a hundred yards farther down the tunnel when she heard the noise that she had been dreading. The screech of metal being ripped from the stone frame.

She didn't need to look back over her shoulder to know that the Stalker was closing the distance between them.

As the seconds passed, her feet pounding along the stone floor, she felt the Stalker gaining on her.

Drawing closer with every step of its clawed feet.

She could almost feel its razor-sharp claws digging into her back, a shiver running down her spine, when she saw a thin gleam of light just up ahead.

Another door!

Knowing the consequences of slowing down, she hit the door hard with her shoulder.

Blast it!

It didn't budge.

A terrifying shriek echoed behind her.

The Stalker was closer than she thought.

Refusing to look back the way she had come, she fumbled for the door handle, her fear and aching shoulder making her clumsy.

After several frantic efforts, finally she found the latch, pulled the door open, and dove through, slamming it behind her as she did so.

She didn't know where she was.

Only that she was beneath the Rock.

And she could see thanks to the scattered torches burning in sconces fixed along the wall.

After sliding across the floor on her back, she turned, knowing exactly what was going to happen.

This time, the enraged Stalker needed only one try to break through the steel.

The monster burst out of the passageway, the door flying off its hinges, the creature never halting its progress as it charged at Talia.

Realizing that she didn't stand a chance, still she held her dagger out in front of her, hoping that she might get lucky, that she might stab the monster in the eye or the throat, although also accepting as well the hard truth that her luck likely had run out.

The Stalker was going to kill her.

She was going to fail.

She wasn't going to get to Davin in time.

That thought chilling her to the bone, her vision narrowed to the single claw reaching for her.

Talia gasped in shock a split-second later.

The scene freezing in front of her.

The monster was held in place just above her, three spears reaching right over her head, two punching into the Stalker's chest, the third through the monster's throat.

She looked back over her shoulder. Declan stood there along with two gladiators whose names she couldn't remember.

She scrambled backward and worked her way through their legs, finally pushing herself back to her feet when the light left the Stalker's eyes, the monster dropping lifeless to the ground.

Declan turned then, pulling his spear free from the Stalker's throat.

"No luck?"

Talia shook her head, trying to regain her breath after the last few harrowing minutes.

"We didn't find Davin either. Rafia tells me there's only one more place for us to look."

20

THROUGH THE MOUNTAIN

"So your goal was to get all the Stalkers to come after us?"

Lycia ran right behind Jakob as they sprinted down the tunnel. Their only light came from the Talent infusing their weapons.

The shrieks from the monsters racing through the shaft behind them gave them both an added burst of speed. Even so, they could feel the Stalkers gaining on them. Their hunters' clawed feet digging into the rock and dirt of the passageway, their hunger driving them forward.

"It was."

"You've done an excellent job of doing that."

"Thank you," Jakob replied, ignoring the sarcasm coloring Lycia's comment.

"Do you always have to do what you set your mind to so well? It's all right to fail every once in a while."

Jakob snorted softly. "I promise that I'll keep that in mind for the future."

"Please do," Lycia grumbled. "Next time, maybe bring down the entrance to the mine with a few more of the beasts on the outside. Then we wouldn't have so many of these Stalkers after us now."

"I hope there isn't a next time," Jakob murmured. If there was, then events wouldn't be progressing in the Highlands as he wanted them to. The Highlanders' circumstances already were difficult enough as matters currently stood.

"Me too," conceded Lycia. Her tone suggested that she was smiling. "Besides, usually when a man takes a woman into a dark place like this, it's for a reason other than trying to escape monsters hungry to feast upon them. This really wasn't what I had in mind when you asked me to come with you."

At first, Jakob was going to tell Lycia that he hadn't asked her to come with him. In fact, he hadn't wanted her to come with him. He had told her that several times, but she had ignored him and insisted on staying at his shoulder.

When he wrapped his mind around all that Lycia really was telling him, he kept silent.

His first few ideas for replying sounded witty in his own mind, but he feared how Lycia might take those comments. Perhaps a bit too direct, touching on topics that were better left unsaid when the status of their relationship ...

Well, not their relationship. Their friendship ...

Was it a friendship?

A partnership perhaps?

And if a partnership, was it more than a partnership?

Could it be a relationship?

Jakob stopped his mind from continuing to spin uselessly around a topic that he didn't fully understand and that he had no desire to explore. There were more pressing matters to be dealt with.

And he had no doubt that Lycia was simply trying to get a rise out of him. It was something that she enjoyed and at which she was uniquely skilled, that she reveled in when she succeeded, even in the most arduous of times.

To get his mind off of the seed that Lycia had planted in his brain, he shifted his attention to the unfinished shaft, spending just as much time focusing on the walls and the ceiling as he did where he was placing his feet.

This tunnel lacked the basic protections against collapse. Some of the buttresses were in place. Many of them weren't.

Clearly, the slavers cared little for the safety of the miners.

That wasn't unexpected.

It was also a variable that he could use to their advantage as they sought to make their escape.

Jakob stopped abruptly, skidding through the dirt and loose rock, before turning to face the direction from which they had come.

His action caught Lycia by surprise. She didn't have the time to halt her progress.

Instead of risking a fall, she ran right into him with a good bit of force.

He didn't move an inch, his arms wrapping around her to ensure they both remained on their feet.

In a flash, they were face to face. Chest to chest. Their lips just a hair away from touching.

For a few heartbeats, neither of them said a word. Neither of them moved.

Then, Jakob, finally realizing the position that they were in, dropped his arms to the side, releasing his hold on her.

But he didn't step back, and neither did she.

"Now's not the time for this," Lycia said softly, her eyes gleaming with amusement ... and perhaps something else as well.

"I'm well aware," Jakob replied, ignoring what that emotion hidden in the back of Lycia's eyes could mean. Pulling his gaze away from hers with some difficulty, he stared into the darkness behind them. Looking for the tell-tale sign of their pursuers.

He leaned over her shoulder with one hand, his other hand gripping her hip and holding her in place.

Before Lycia could whisper something inappropriate in his ear -- and he knew that she really wanted to, because he did as well -- he shot from his palm several bursts of white-hot energy that streaked back down the tunnel, illuminating the passageway as they passed.

He counted three pairs of blood-red eyes.

The two Stalkers who were closest to them, both creatures no more the twenty yards away, died the instant the Talent ripped through their chests.

The third Stalker, a good distance behind the first two, and observing what happened to its brethren, dodged out of the way by scrambling up the wall, putting its clawed hands and feet to good use.

Jakob was ready for just that play.

His third burst of energy wasn't aimed toward that Stalker. Rather, Jakob targeted the wooden supports on the wall that the Stalker scrambled up.

When the Talent struck, the energy destroyed the buttresses and blasted a massive hole in the wall, burying the Stalker in several tons of dirt, broken timber, and shattered stone.

Even if Jakob didn't kill that monster, there was no way that the Stalker was going to be able to free itself. Not anytime soon anyway.

Three of their pursuers removed from the chase. But still twenty or more to go based on his latest search around them with the Talent.

"I just wanted you to get by me," Jakob explained as he surveyed the damage that he had caused. "That's what I was trying to do when you ran into me. Let you pass."

Jakob was pleased with the result of his work. Any other

Stalkers coming down this tunnel would need to backtrack and find another way to come after them.

He had bought them a little time. Although likely not very much.

From the other side of the pile of debris he heard the shrieks and howls of the Stalkers that escaped his attack.

"Really?" questioned Lycia. "Because it seemed to me like you really wanted me to run into you."

"Why would I want that?" countered Jakob with a raised eyebrow, inserting a confidence in his voice that he wasn't feeling.

He realized instantly that he had done the right thing. Because Lycia hadn't expected him to do that. And he could see in the dim light provided by their blazing blades that he had caught her off guard.

Good. It was only fair since she did the same to him on a far-too-frequent basis.

"There's an easier way to do that, you know. To get me to run by you. You just needed to tell me what you wanted me to do."

"There is, you're right," Jakob admitted, giving Lycia a sly grin.

His comment caught her by surprise for the second time in just the last few seconds, her smart reply that was right on the tip of her tongue staying there.

"We need to get going," Jakob said, his hand still on her hip until he curled around her. "I'll be right behind you."

He enjoyed teasing Lycia, because he rarely got the chance to do it. But he had a larger concern.

Jakob wanted to make certain that the Stalkers couldn't come at them from this direction. A worry because he had identified several gaps in the pile of rubble near the ceiling. One or two of the industrious monsters could force their way through if they put their minds to it.

To ensure that didn't happen, Jakob shot two more streaks of energy from his palm. The result was immediate. Several more tons of stone and dirt fell, sealing the passageway completely.

After the rocks settled into place, Jakob listened for a few seconds.

He still heard the Stalkers on the other side of the barrier. Their shrieks were a mixture of anger at missing their target as well as pain.

That brought a vicious smile to Jakob's usually composed features.

He might have taken a few more of the monsters out of the hunt, and that pleased him to no end.

Even so, he and Lycia remained the prey. If they were going to escape their pursuers, they needed to be smart and quick.

The Stalkers wouldn't stop coming after them until either they were dead or he and Lycia were dead.

The first didn't bother him.

The second did.

Jakob had no doubt that the Stalkers would find them again. It was just a matter of when, not if, with the many tunnels that honeycombed through the mountain.

Which meant that he and Lycia needed to make good use of the little bit of time that they had earned.

Because if the Stalkers were tracking them as he believed they were, then he and Lycia were caught between a rock and a hard place. He would have laughed at his pun if their circumstances weren't so dire.

He needed to use the Talent if they were to have any chance at all of escaping the Stalkers. But it was his use of the Talent that gave the Stalkers a stronger taste of where their prey was.

"We need to move faster. We've only earned a partial victory here."

When he turned back around, Lycia already had begun

running down the tunnel. Jakob caught up quickly, settling in right at her heels.

She smiled when she sensed him right behind her. She could still feel the warmth of his hand on her hip, and it hadn't been an unpleasant sensation.

"Can you give us some more light? The glowing blades help, but only so much."

Lycia was right. If they wanted to pick up their pace, they needed a better sense of what was in front of them.

There were no lanterns hanging from the wall in this tunnel. There was nothing but a pitch black except for the small dome of light that extended for a few feet around them.

Jakob solved the problem in a flash. Literally.

Crafting a ball of energy on the palm of his hand, he flicked it above them, the sphere stopping just below the ceiling, staying with them as they ran down the corridor, their route illuminated for more than a dozen yards all around them.

"Well done," Lycia murmured over her shoulder.

Jakob nodded, not bothering to reply.

Both caught up in their own thoughts, for the next few minutes they ran straight through the mountain.

They didn't hear the shrieks of the Stalkers or the scratches of their claws in the dirt and rock. Still, they knew that their hunters were close.

Closer than they had anticipated, in fact.

As they came upon the first junction since Jakob had brought the ceiling down behind them, right before they stepped into the intersection, Jakob pulled back on Lycia's arm.

She sensed it just as he did, but he had been faster than she was.

From the tunnel on the left a Stalker lunged out of the darkness, daggerlike claws reaching for Jakob.

Since the monster was on her side, Lycia took up the combat. She stabbed lightning fast with the dagger she held in her hand, having sheathed one of her blades because of the tight quarters of the corridor. The blazing steel cut deeply into the monster's side, burning through flesh and muscle.

With the sword in her other hand, she prevented the Stalker's claw from slashing across her face.

She didn't bother to swing her steel. She didn't need to. Instead, she held her sword in place, allowing the beast to sever its own razor-sharp digits when they struck her glowing blade.

The badly wounded Stalker tottered back, unsteady on its feet because of the nasty gash in its side and the terrible damage to its claw.

Lycia didn't give the Stalker the chance to recover, shifting to the attack immediately. She stabbed again with her dagger and then one more time. Just to be certain.

The first time into the Stalker's gut. The second time between two of the monster's lower ribs.

When the Stalker's uninjured claw came weakly toward her, she stabbed a third time. This time she took advantage of how the Stalker exposed itself to slide her dagger right through the monster's armpit after she ducked its ragged attack.

The Stalker was dead. Lycia was certain of it.

The monster just didn't know it yet. Not even when it dropped to its knees, its bloody claw reaching weakly for Lycia even as it bled to death from its multiple wounds.

Trusting that Lycia could manage the threat to his left, Jakob focused on the Stalker that hid in the darkness to his right.

As he prepared to engage the monster, he realized that they had lost whatever time he and Lycia gained from his blocking the tunnel at their backs. The Stalkers had found another path within the mountain that allowed them to maintain their pursuit faster than he would have liked. Then again, with the number of passages that cut through the mountain, it was a wonder that the peak hadn't yet collapsed in upon itself.

Jakob fixed on the blood-red eyes of the Stalker that was no more than a few yards away, the beast racing toward him with a hint of excitement and desperation in its eyes. How many of the Stalkers were following this one he couldn't say with any certainty yet.

But first things first.

Having no desire to fight so many of the beasts at one time, glimpsing several pairs of blood-red eyes not too far behind this Stalker, Jakob decided on the easiest course of action that he believed would give him the best chance of success.

Using the Talent, he ripped away the wooden buttresses that came together where the two tunnels met.

The effect was instantaneous and very final.

A deep rumble echoed through the corridors accompanied by a cloud of dust and debris as the ceiling to Jakob's right gave way, crashing down on the Stalker before the monster could leap into the junction of the two corridors.

Despite the tons of stone that filled the tunnel, Jakob shot several more bolts of energy into the ceiling.

He needed to make sure. He couldn't afford to allow any of the Stalkers to come at them from more than one direction at a time. If that happened, then they were dead, their attempted escape from the Stalkers already on precarious ground.

The mountain protested for several seconds more, the ground shaking, the rock tumbling down onto the pile, Jakob heightening the crescendo by sending blast after blast of power into the shattering ceiling.

When he was done and the dust finally settled, Jakob didn't know how many of the Stalkers he had taken from the hunt.

He was certain that those beasts that had sought to come at him from that direction would not be making their way through the pile of rubble blocking the path.

Jakob turned to his left then. Lycia stood there, dagger and sword covered with the blood of the Stalker that lay dying on the ground on the other side of the junction.

"Very thorough of you," Lycia said as she examined the damage, giving him a nod of approval.

"I do what I ..."

"I know," Lycia said, cutting him off. "You do what you can."

Jakob didn't know if Lycia was amused or irritated with him. And, at that moment, he didn't care. So he chose to ignore her comment.

Using the Talent, he searched down the tunnel to his right and then the tunnel that they had been following that led deeper beneath the mountain.

Other than the Stalker that lay dying at their feet, there were no Stalkers to be found.

For now.

About a quarter mile away he sensed several of the beasts turn into the tunnel on their right side from another corridor. It wouldn't be long before they reached the junction where they stood.

The tunnel that he and Lycia had been following was clear in the direction that they had been going.

How much longer that would be the case ...

Even so, it was an easy choice to make.

They had earned a little breathing room again. But only a little.

Jakob placed his hand on the small of Lycia's back and guided her down the tunnel they had been using. Taking the hint, she sprinted ahead of him, putting a few feet of separation between them.

"Is there a reason you always end up behind me?" Lycia asked, not wasting much time before calling back behind her.

In times like this, when death was just around the corner, she always preferred a little light humor. It helped to keep her loose, distracting her from the seriousness of their circum-stances.

"A play on words at a time like this," Jakob replied. He wasn't really paying attention to what Lycia was saying. Instead, he extended his senses down the many tunnels working their way beneath the peak, seeking to gauge where the next attack might come from because several of those tunnels connected to the corridor that they were using just a little farther ahead of them. "Impressive."

"I do my best."

"I've noticed," Jakob replied. The closest Stalkers were still a good distance away. With any luck, they could put even more distance between them if they didn't run into any other difficul-ties, the tunnel they were using continuing beneath the moun-tain straight as an arrow for another few miles. "And to answer your question, I can't think of a better place to be."

Lycia almost stumbled upon hearing Jakob's response.

She didn't know what to do with what Jakob just told her. She was at a loss for words, at least temporarily, and that was a rare occurrence.

His comment not only made her smile. It also made her blush. And it sent her mind down a path that was better left untrodden. At least for now.

Thankfully, Jakob couldn't see her reaction from where he was. Not wanting to give him a chance to make her even more uncomfortable, she decided that she needed to shift to a safer topic.

"Well done with the light," Lycia offered.

"Thanks. It's something I learned on my own just recently. I tweaked a skill that Aloysius taught me." He offered more of an explanation than he usually would, realizing that he might have gone too far with his previous comment and wanting to ease any tension it might have caused between them.

"You're more useful than you look," Lycia said.

Aloysius was his first instructor in the Talent, that training cut short. She knew as well that Rafia was training him as she could, from a distance, but that there was little time for any real instruction. Not with Rafia focused on the Stalkers around the Isle of Mist and Jakob attempting to free the Highlands from the grip of Torstan Sharperson.

"Thanks," Jakob replied. He almost lost his feet when he tripped over a rock that protruded out from the side of the tunnel, catching himself just in time.

He didn't know how to take Lycia's last comment. As a compliment or as an insult. Her tone suggested that it could be both.

For the next quarter hour, they ran down the tunnel without saying a word to one another. Every few minutes they stopped to listen for any movement. Any sign that the Stalkers were coming closer. When nothing but silence met their ears, they continued on their way.

It was more good practice than anything else, a skill that had become ingrained within Jakob while battling Wraiths in the Murk. Using the Talent to search around them continuously, refusing to be caught unprepared, Jakob had a good idea as to the location of almost every Stalker in the mountain.

The Stalkers were coming closer, but the monsters chasing them had yet to make up any ground. In large part because there was no tunnel that connected directly to the shaft that Jakob and Lycia were using.

Their hunters had no choice but to wind their way around, racing to close the gap by curling toward them, the greater distance that the monsters had to cover aiding Jakob and Aislinn's attempted escape.

Still, they were far from safe.

There was a large junction about a mile ahead of them. They needed to be past that point before the Stalkers got there. If they failed to do that, they would be trapped.

"Do you know where we're going?" Lycia asked finally, the silence preying upon her. "As I might have told you before, I really don't care for running. I prefer fighting instead."

"I remember, believe me," Jakob snorted. "Even against a few dozen Stalkers?"

Lycia considered Jakob's question for a few seconds. "True, that might be a few too many. Although if we could find a good place to defend ourselves, I'm sure that we could put on a good show."

"That's what I was thinking as well."

"Have you located somewhere within this miserable mountain where we could do that?"

"I haven't figured that out yet," Jakob admitted reluctantly.

He was so focused on tracking the Stalkers that he had paid less attention to how the mountain's internal terrain might aid them.

"You're less useful than I thought," Lycia said, having quickly changed her opinion of him. "If we survive this you might want to think a bit more about planning ahead."

"I'll keep that in mind," Jakob promised through gritted teeth. "I'll see what I can find up ahead of us. In the meantime, come on. We need to keep moving."

21

HUNT FOR SAFETY

"How do they know where we are?" Lycia asked. "This is becoming much too frequent for my tastes."

She and Jakob had fended off three attacks in the last hour. Despite moving silently, barely disturbing the gloom, still the Stalkers kept finding them, rushing out of the pitch black with a deadly intent.

"They're tracking me."

"What do you mean they're tracking you?" demanded Lycia.

"Whoever created these Stalkers gave them the ability to find me because I can use the Talent."

"You mean like a magical scent?" Lycia tried to put it into words that made it easier for her to understand. "You have a magical scent?"

"Put simply, yes. That's how Rafia explained it to me."

"A magical scent? Really?" She wasn't in a position to question Jakob since she had no skill in the Talent. Even so, it would have been nice to know that before they raced into the mountain with the Stalkers right on their heels.

She had assumed that once they gained the monsters' attention, they could then lose them in the dark of the many tunnels that burrowed through the stone. A misplaced hope, apparently.

"That's what she said. And you know Rafia. Better not to ask too many questions when she's in a certain mood. Better just to take her at her word."

Lycia nodded. She wasn't in a position to dispute that either. The Magus had quite a temper at times.

"How did the Stalkers acquire your magical scent?"

"That's a good question. I didn't get to ask Rafia. Something came up and she needed to end the conversation sooner than either of us wanted."

He and Rafia spoke regularly through the use of the Talent, Rafia spending much of that time instructing Jakob in the use of his natural magic. But with all that was going on in the Highlands and around the Isle of Mist, where Rafia and Declan were dealing with the much more regular incursions by the Stalkers, they were not connecting as frequently or for as long as they would have preferred.

"And every time you have to use the Talent against the Stalkers, you're actually leading the Stalkers right to us?"

"Correct."

"So what you're saying is that you're a lodestone for these monsters and that I'd probably be safer on my own."

"Probably, yes."

"You know, you really should have told me ..."

Jakob cut her off abruptly, his voice urgent. "From above. Over your right shoulder."

He had almost missed the two Stalkers shadowing them. The tunnel they were jogging through had broadened in height and width.

A ledge lost in the darkness tracked the path not too far above them, and it gave the Stalkers an excellent point of attack.

Responding instinctively, Lycia skidded to a stop and

turned, sword held up and to her front. Because of the darkness she could see little more than two pairs of blood-red eyes staring down at her.

Before the Stalkers could attack, a flash of white shot past her shoulder. When the power that Jakob released hit the ledge upon which the Stalkers were preparing to launch themselves, the tunnel shook as if an earthquake had struck, rocks breaking free from the ceiling, a cloud of dust and grit forming around them.

His prescience proved quite effective and timely.

Instead of soaring through the air and punching their claws and fangs into their prey, the Stalkers tumbled unceremoniously from their perches.

One of the beasts hit the rough ground headfirst. The Stalker didn't break its neck, an unfortunate piece of bad luck in Lycia's opinion.

Nevertheless, the fall dazed the Stalker, and she was quick to take full advantage. Taking a single step to the side, she drove her blazing steel through the monster's neck.

The other Stalker landed with more grace among the rubble, although the monster didn't escape injury. Hissing in pain, the Stalker struggled to right itself as one knee buckled, one of its clawed feet piercing a jagged rock.

Nevertheless, the injury didn't prevent the Stalker from lunging for Jakob, daggerlike claws slicing toward his chest.

The injury did prevent the Stalker from attacking with its customary speed.

Jakob was grateful for that weakness. Pivoting, he allowed the Stalker to slide by him. With a single swipe of the dagger in his hand, he sliced across the Stalker's throat.

When the Stalker finally halted its stumbling progress and turned back around, not quite sure how it missed, the monster reached for its neck. Only then did the Stalker realize that what had started as no more than a trickle of blood from the slash across its flesh was much worse than that.

Jakob had severed the beast's artery, the blood pulsing free in time with the monster's rapid heartbeat.

Gurgling more than growling in anger, the Stalker tried to launch itself at Jakob. Instead, the monster stumbled and then fell to its knees, its strength fading as the last of its blood flowed from the horrible gash.

"Any more Stalkers that we need to worry about?" Lycia stepped up next to Jakob.

Extending his senses around them, it only took Jakob a second to reply. He grimaced at what he discovered.

They were still at least a quarter mile from the next junction, a score of Stalkers racing to beat them there from both the east and the west. And there were more of the monsters just now beginning to emerge onto the ledge above them, only a hundred yards back in the tunnel.

"We need to move. Now." Jakob gave Lycia a gentle nudge in her back to get her going.

They were in a difficult position to begin with. Their circumstances would worsen dramatically if the Stalkers succeeded in getting at them from above.

With his use of the Talent, he saw that the ledge hidden from view and running above them stopped about fifty yards farther down the tunnel.

Good. At least they had that going for them.

The narrowness of the shaft only would allow one Stalker to attack them at a time. But not now. Not until they got back within the tight confines of the corridor just up ahead.

"They're above us," Lycia warned.

"I know."

"Can't you bring the ceiling down?" asked Lycia.

"Not yet," Jakob replied, his voice tight. "This section of the mountain is pockmarked with cracks and faults. That's why it's so open here. I'd probably bring the ceiling down on us as well."

"That doesn't appeal to me."

"Nor me."

"Then what do we do?"

"Run faster," Jakob urged.

Lycia didn't need to be told twice. Her concern for the monsters tracking them from above quickened her pace. Jakob stayed right with her, his hand still on her lower back when they reached the narrower section of the corridor, the high ceiling replaced by one that felt like it was pressing down upon them.

Lycia was about to tell Jakob that he could stop nudging her along when he dug his feet into the ground and spun back around, several small spheres of white-hot energy shooting from the fingers that had been guiding her down the tunnel.

Lycia turned as well, blazing blade in hand.

And just in time, a Stalker leaping out of the darkness, claws outstretched, seeking to rip open her chest, not realizing that it was a half-second too slow.

The Stalker disappeared under a pile of dirt and rock as the ceiling in the broader expanse of the tunnel collapsed in a deafening roar.

Jakob and Lycia ducked away as a cloud of crushed stone and detritus blasted toward them. When they turned back around, both covered in a thin layer of grit, they smiled.

The rockfall blocked the entrance to the tunnel they were in. And neither heard the shrieks of any Stalkers from the other side.

Perhaps they had all been caught in the rockfall, Lycia mused. She could always hope. But she wouldn't hold her breath.

A success, though limited.

Though they had escaped this latest attack, they still had a long way to go before they reached a place of safety.

"The ones behind us, if there are any still alive, can't get to us."

"That's right," confirmed Jakob.

"But there are still Stalkers trying to get ahead of us."

"There are," Jakob replied, although he was talking to himself at that point because Lycia was already running down the tunnel.

Jakob sprinted to catch up, once again taking a position just a few feet behind Lycia and to the side so that he wouldn't get in her way when she had cause to use her sword. And she would have cause. He was certain that it would just be a matter of when.

"You saved us but you told all the other Stalkers exactly where we are because you used the Talent."

"I did," Jakob admitted. There had been nothing for it. If he hadn't used the Talent, they wouldn't have made it out of the larger chamber.

"Then I hope you have something in mind, because I'm really getting tired of this."

"I do, have no fear of that."

Lycia snorted in response, pumping her legs a little faster. "Based on the tone in your voice, I'm worried. Very worried."

Jakob and Lycia sprinted down the tunnel, the ball of light just above their heads, staying with them, giving them just enough illumination to see by.

The junction was just ahead. Fifty yards. No more. Drawing closer with every step they took.

They needed to get through the crossroads before the Stalkers reached them. If they didn't, they were dead.

It was as simple as that.

And it was a tight race.

The screeches that confirmed the Stalkers were racing toward them from the tunnels just up ahead that ran to the east and west kept them from flagging. Even so, they worried that their extra effort might not be enough.

The Stalkers were close.

Much too close.

"We're not going to make it!"

"We will," Jakob said between breaths. "Trust me."

"You're asking a lot," Lycia grumbled. She ran with a sword in one hand, a dagger in her other. She fully expected that she would need to put her weapons to use before they reached the junction.

"I know." Jakob hoped that he wasn't wrong. He'd been tracking the Stalkers with the Talent. He believed that he and Lycia were ahead of their pursuers by just enough to make it through the junction before the Stalkers got to them. He would find out in just seconds. "Have I been wrong before?"

"No," she admitted reluctantly, "but there's a first time for everything."

Jakob didn't have time to take issue with her lack of belief.

Lycia sprinted through the intersection. As she did so, she glanced to her left. Her eyes widened for just a heartbeat as she glimpsed the Stalkers sprinting toward her from the west.

She was through the junction so swiftly that she didn't have time to look to the other side and determine how close the Stalkers coming from the opposite direction were.

Jakob, running on Lycia's heels, did look in that direction. And a good thing that he did.

Lycia had been right to be concerned. He was cutting it close. Perhaps too close.

A fist of Stalkers sprinted toward him from the east. And as fate would have it, they were only steps away from entering the junction.

Not wanting to get into a drawn-out combat, knowing what would happen if he did, Jakob sought instead to create a brief moment of chaos.

He slashed with the dagger in his left hand. His strike was perfectly timed, his blazing steel slicing right through the wrist of the monster that was a few steps ahead of the others and reaching for him, its claw just inches away from his shoulder.

The wounded Stalker, fully expecting to grasp its prey, staggered because of its injury. Thrown off balance, the monster's feet went out from under it, taking the entire fist to the ground.

For the next several seconds, the Stalkers struggled to regain their clawed feet, their primary obstacle for completing that task their own brethren.

A brief clash broke out among the beasts.

All of the Stalkers frantic to continue the hunt, it didn't bother them in the least that doing that meant fighting their own brethren to extricate themselves from the pile of bodies that formed in the middle of the intersection.

Jakob didn't even look over his shoulder to judge his success as he dashed after Lycia. His eyes were locked onto the gladiator's back and pumping legs.

He was happy to have earned a few extra seconds that lengthened the slim lead they had. Much too quickly, however, the Stalkers' shrieks were no longer directed at one another, but rather toward him and Lycia.

Using the Talent, he quickly determined what they were up against. Based on the number of Stalkers and their proximity, the odds clearly were not in their favor.

"They're right behind us!" Lycia called over her shoulder. "Just keep going!"

Thanks to his use of the Talent, Jakob knew that the tunnel was coming to an end and, worse, it led into a large chamber.

He needed to slow down their hunters if he could. Because if he didn't, the Stalkers would have little difficulty flanking him and Lycia once they broke free from the passageway. Their hunters might even succeed in getting ahead of them, and the thought of being surrounded by a score of angry, rabid monsters didn't appeal to him.

To avoid that peril, as soon as Jakob exited the corridor, he turned back around, skidding to a stop on the rough stone and gravel. Raising one hand, a dagger in his other just in case he wasn't fast enough, he shot several bolts of energy back down the corridor.

He didn't strike the monsters intent on killing him. Because that wasn't his objective.

Instead, as he had done before, ignoring the Stalkers that were racing through the darkness only yards away from him, shrieks of hunger threatening to break his concentration, he targeted the roof.

The moment the Talent struck, a cloud of dross and crushed rock erupted from the tunnel. Massive chunks of stone and tons of dirt crashed down, filling the passageway.

Jakob didn't have the time to be as thorough as he wanted to be. Still, he was satisfied with what he accomplished, blocking most of the corridor and forcing the Stalkers not caught in the deadly rockfall to dig their way through the rubble.

That would keep their hunters busy for a time, giving him and Lycia the opportunity to increase their lead.

"What the ..."

Lycia stopped abruptly just a few feet in front of Jakob upon entering the chamber, not even bothering to look behind her to see what kind of destruction Jakob had wrought.

She didn't feel the need to. She knew how thorough he was when he put his mind to a task such as that.

Instead, as the ball of light shot more than a hundred feet into the air and stopped just below the ceiling, for a few heartbeats Lycia forgot the monsters hunting them. She was astounded by what rose before her.

The settlers who first began making their way across the Burnt Ocean just a decade before were not the first people to set foot on this distant shore.

"Come on," Jakob urged. As he ran by her he threw several more spheres of light to their front so that they could see where they were going.

Now it was her turn to catch up as Jakob headed toward the latest challenge.

A huge staircase that rose several hundred feet to their front. At the very top a wide archway wreathed in shadow beckoned.

Jakob was impressed and curious. Even more he was anxious to evade their pursuers. He ran up the worn steps two at a time. Lycia right on his heels.

Both kept their heads down and their legs pumping as they pushed their way toward the top.

They were more than halfway up when Lycia sensed a threatening presence right at her back, a shiver of fear running down her spine.

She was about to turn, sword in hand, refusing to be cut down from behind, when several bursts of energy shot right over her shoulder.

The bolts slammed into the Stalker's chest, knocking the monster into the air and off the steps. The charred carcass landed on the gravel at the base of the staircase with a loud thump. Unfortunately, Jakob's demonstration of power didn't prevent the dead Stalker's brethren from continuing the hunt.

Another of the more motivated monsters had dug through the pile of stone and dirt faster than Jakob thought possible. Because of its frenetic industriousness, the Stalker also cleared the way for its brethren waiting impatiently behind it.

Having lost their lead, Jakob began walking backwards up the steps, sending blast after blast of energy down toward the monsters sprinting across the cavern floor. Several dozen Stalkers emerging from the tunnel and racing toward them, the first of the beasts digging its claws into the crumbling stone steps.

Jakob dispatched that monster with a lance of light that burned right through the creature's chest. He then took several more of the Stalkers out of the fight with well-placed strikes. But there were too many of the monsters. He couldn't prevent all of them from ascending the staircase.

It didn't help his efforts that the Stalkers didn't care about his success. They were oblivious to the danger he presented, more than willing to assume the risk of attacking him directly even if it meant dying badly for their boldness.

Because they had no choice.

They couldn't make their own decisions.

They could only obey the compulsion that had been put upon them.

The demand that they kill the one known as the Lord of the Highlands who stood just above them as swiftly as possible no matter the cost to themselves.

Jakob reached the top of the towering staircase still shooting bolt after bolt of energy toward the monsters swarming below him, struggling more and more to hold back the rush. Lycia catching her breath right next to him, he realized that there were too many Stalkers for him to keep up the fight.

Even with the Talent, Jakob couldn't handle them all.

The Stalkers were too fast. Too determined. Too willing to sacrifice themselves if that meant that just one of their brethren could get to him.

"Through the archway!"

Surveying with just a single glance the danger coming

toward them on the steps, for once Lycia chose not to argue. Without a word, she raced through the stone gateway.

Jakob shot several more bolts of energy down toward the Stalkers that were scaling the steps with the intensity of predators knowing that their prey was almost within their grasp. Then he turned and ran after her, the spheres of light following him.

As soon as he was several dozen yards past the archway, Jakob used the Talent to bring down a large section of the entrance, several massive blocks of stone smashing into the polished tile of the floor. The rubble would slow the monsters down, but it wouldn't be enough to stop them entirely.

In fact, several of the Stalkers already were scrambling up the large pile of rock, a claw appearing in the small gap at the top. And then another, followed by one more, the sounds of scraping and digging echoing in the chamber. It wouldn't take the monsters long to burrow through thanks to their razor-sharp claws.

He could stand and fight. He could control this space better than he could the top of the steps. But he decided against that strategy almost immediately, understanding that it was a losing proposition. Reluctantly, he turned on his heel and trotted deeper into the darkness.

"Let's go."

"You know where you're going?"

Lycia had no choice but to follow. The Stalker at the top of the rock pile was stuck. Although not for much longer. Once the monster forced its shoulders through the gap, it would be right back after them.

"Sort of."

"Sort of?"

Before Lycia could ask Jakob what he had in mind, she stopped short. She had to. Otherwise she would have run right into his back.

Looking over his shoulder she saw that there were nine tunnels to their front from which to choose.

"What are you looking ..."

Lycia never got the chance to finish asking her question, Jakob bolting toward the tunnel on the far left.

She ducked as soon as she was in the passageway. The tunnel was a lot tighter than the one they had taken to reach this point, the ceiling pushing down on them from above.

Thankfully the balls of light stayed with them, drifting just to their front.

A good thing too, because not only did the roughly cut corridor require them to stoop to make their way through to avoid slamming their heads against the small, very sharp stalactites that hung down from the ceiling, but it also twisted and turned, often at severe angles.

Lycia stumbled as soon as she ducked to avoid one of the tapering columns. Catching herself before she fell, she searched for what had caught her foot.

She couldn't tell for certain because of the shadows dancing around her, but it looked like it was what was left of a metal track, a few bits and pieces of steel running along the ground, the top of the spike that had almost sent her tumbling sticking out of a piece of broken metal.

Keeping her gaze moving from the stalactites to the floor of the tunnel and back again to avoid any more mishaps, she sought to close the ten-yard gap that had opened between her and Jakob.

"Jakob, where are we ..."

Lycia slid to a stop, though not fast enough as she slammed into his back this time.

She was about to offer him a few choice curses for his lack of warning, but those words got stuck in her throat. She couldn't believe the sight that greeted her.

Jakob didn't say a word. He simply began pushing an old,

rickety, metal cart that was set on the tracks that led off into the darkness.

"Give me a hand," he said. "We don't have much time."

Lycia jumped into action, a shriek that echoed down the corridor speeding up her efforts. The first of the Stalkers to make it through the collapsed archway had entered the tunnel behind them.

Placing her hands on the rim of the transport, she pushed as hard as she could. With Jakob beside her, it wasn't long before they got the cart up to a good speed.

"Are you certain of the tracks to the front?" she yelled at him, the screech of the metal wheels protesting on the steel tracks making her ears hurt.

"No," Jakob replied, although that didn't stop him from continuing down the tunnel. They weren't just walking now. They had built up some momentum. "But I'm hopeful."

"You can't be serious. Hope doesn't …"

"I know," interrupted Jakob. Lycia used that saying quite a lot. He was familiar with it. His father had offered it to him as well more times than he could remember. "Hoping doesn't make it real."

"Then why …"

"We don't have much choice," Jakob cut in again. "There's only one direction that we can go."

Several more shrieks blasted down the passageway. The first Stalker was no longer alone in the chase. Several of its brethren had joined in.

"They're already through the archway. We need to go faster. We can't fight them here and expect any chance of victory."

"I know."

"Jakob, this is a really bad …"

"I know," he replied again. They were sprinting now, the cart rattling along the tracks, sparks shooting out from one of the wheels. He hoped the cause wasn't a mechanical issue, but rather just a stone that had gotten lodged in front of the wheel. Because if the latter wasn't the case, what he planned to do ensured nothing other than abject failure and a painful death for both of them. "Again, we have little choice. Get in."

Lycia was about to protest. However, when she glimpsed what was right in front of them and growing larger with every step they took, she pulled herself over the side of the rusty cart as quickly as she could.

Jakob ran with the cart for a few more feet. Then, with one final push, he pulled himself over the rim and into the transom, landing heavily on Lycia.

"Not very graceful," Lycia grumbled as she worked to extricate herself from beneath him, his right hand in a place that it shouldn't be. "It's almost as if you planned on doing that."

"Sorry. We hit a bump right when I jumped in."

"That's the best excuse you could offer?"

"Hold on!" Jakob ordered.

"What are you ..."

Before she could say anything else, Jakob reached for her, pulling her in close to him, gripping the rim of the cart tightly with one hand.

And just in time.

Because as soon as he took hold of Lycia, the track dropped into the darkness. The cart and them with it.

22

A HISTORY LESSON

Bryen strode through the Shadow Keep, demonstrating a confidence that he didn't feel.

He had taken a risk.

A big risk.

Declan had taught him that in any combat, you needed to make your opponent see what you wanted them to see. Not what they wanted to see. He had done that with Ursina.

Yet, as he entered his rooms, first making sure with the Talent that he was alone, he wondered whether he had made a mistake.

Should he have revealed so much to her? Let her know that he knew what she truly was?

He was playing a game, that was true, but he worried that by challenging the Dark Magus it was no longer his game. Rather, he feared that he may have ceded the next move to her.

Too late now he realized. He had sought to provoke her, and he was certain that he had succeeded. It was her play now, and he doubted that she would wait long to act.

Thinking of what he might need to do next, Bryen walked out onto the balcony that gave him an excellent view of the city wall a half-mile distant. Beyond the mountains, the rolling hills ran for hundreds of leagues to the north where they met the Wyld.

Still not a hint of the Murk. Nothing more than a cloudy day and a strong, cold breeze sweeping across the plateau.

Strange.

Allowing his mind to drift, he began to consider the anomaly that had been tickling the back of his brain. The Wraiths had not appeared for more than a week, the city and its residents enjoying an uncommon respite.

Bryen didn't place a lot of faith in coincidence. He believed that things happened for a reason.

So what was the reason that the Wraiths had left the city alone for such a long period of time?

His wandering thoughts returned him to his conversation with the Blademaster and Juliette. They had given him a rough sketch of what was going on in Shadow's Reach. Based on that and his confrontation with Ursina, he began to color the canvas along the edges.

A good start.

Nevertheless, he still felt as if he wasn't seeing the entire painting.

Too much was still missing, and there was a theme running through all that was happening here that he couldn't yet identify.

What it could be, he didn't know. Although he could sense whatever it was playing at the very fringes of his perception.

There, then not.

Dancing away from him as he failed to grasp it, time after time.

Frustrating to say the least.

If he was going to figure this out, he needed help. Closing his eyes, Bryen reached out to the Seventh Stone, the magic of the artifact awakening within him.

When he opened his eyes, two misty figures stood next to him on the balcony.

Viktor Keldragan, responsible for stealing the Seventh Stone from the Ghoule Overlord, was one of the most powerful Magii who had ever lived.

Bryen resembled his uncle quite closely except for a few key differences. The Magus lacked the three-clawed scar and thin black burn that marred Bryen's cheek and neck. And his hair was brown rather than the white with a few flecks of brown that Bryen had earned courtesy of his time in the Pit.

Standing next to Viktor was Mikayla Benewyn, a striking woman with long auburn hair. Another of the Ten Magii who had aided Bryen in building anew the Weir.

Their spirits were linked to the Seventh Stone for all eternity because of the sacrifice required of them when they crafted the initial barrier that prevented the Ghoule Overlord from invading Caledonia. A magical barrier that had lasted for more than a thousand years, until Bryen was forced to destroy that Weir and craft a new one.

"Trouble follows you, nephew," Viktor said quietly, giving him a small smile.

"That does seem to be the case," Bryen replied, unable to dispute Viktor's claim. "And here I was thinking that coming to New Caledonia would allow me to leave all that behind me."

"Some are called to serve. Time after time. Because they demonstrate that they can deal with perils threatening to destroy the world that others cannot."

"True," Viktor agreed with an amused expression, "but do you really need to be so dramatic, Mikayla?"

"I'm just speaking the truth, Viktor. You don't need to get testy about it."

"I'm not getting testy," Viktor protested, a hint of testiness seeping into his voice. "I agree with you. Much has been required of Bryen, and it appears that much more still may be demanded of him."

"Yes, it does seem that way," Bryen admitted.

"Each of us has our own fate, Bryen," said Mikayla. "Of that, I know you're quite aware. Better to accept it. Better to acknowledge it. Because there is no way to escape it."

"And it seems that Bryen's fate is to serve as a bulwark against those who have turned to the Curse and seek to spread that evil power throughout the Natural World."

"Too true, Viktor," Mikayla agreed.

"You observed it all?" Bryen asked.

"How could we not?" Viktor shrugged. "We see the world through your eyes when we choose to, and when we sensed what hid within the Dark Magus, we couldn't help ourselves."

Bryen nodded, expecting as much. "There's a piece to all this that I don't understand."

"What do you mean?" asked Mikayla.

"I suspected that Ursina had been touched by the Curse, and she proved it when I irritated her."

"That you did," Viktor confirmed, having watched with both admiration and pride as Bryen squashed with remarkable ease the exploratory thread of black that Ursina sent toward his nephew.

"I should have done more than just show her up. By all rights, I should have killed Ursina. She's on a path from which she can't turn away and over time she will become an even stronger vessel for the Curse."

"But you didn't," prompted Mikayla.

"I didn't," Bryen replied, still not understanding his decision in that regard.

"Why didn't you?" asked Viktor. "Sirius would have. Rafia as well."

Viktor really hadn't been surprised by Bryen's decision, but his nephew needed to figure this out for himself. The Magus smiled then.

He realized that he was adopting the same strategy for teaching as he had done with his brother. The difference being that Sirius had chafed quite frequently because of Viktor's approach and Bryen never did.

Bryen thought about Viktor's question, allowing the tense encounter with Ursina to play back through his mind. There was some aspect to their engagement that had held him back. That had stopped him from giving in to his initial, visceral reaction upon learning that the Curse coursed through the Magus.

But what was it?

His thoughts kept drifting back to that small thread of tainted evil that Ursina had shot toward him, the Magus believing that she could take him by surprise.

Why that scene? What about it was so important? Why did he think that this was the key to shedding light on the mystery that was teasing him?

He hadn't been surprised that Ursina employed the Curse, recognizing her mounting frustration as he blocked her efforts with the Talent. Glad that he could push her over the edge and offer the confirmation he desired.

No, there was something else to it. Not just that she revealed that she had turned to the Curse.

When he had manipulated that fragment of the Curse with the Seventh Stone, studying the tainted magic before he destroyed it, there had been some aspect to that corrosive energy that had made him hesitate.

What was it?

He was much more accustomed to the Curse and its properties not only because of his experience combating those who could manipulate the Curse, but also because of his managing that tainted power himself, the inevitable result of his joining with the Seventh Stone. So he was more than just familiar with it.

He lifted his head, his eyes brightening. That was it.

He was not entirely familiar with the power that Ursina had been employing. It felt the same but also different to him. That's what had prevented him from killing her.

"Because I was curious."

"How so?" prodded Mikayla.

"Because the Curse within Ursina is different than what I've come up against before."

"Can you explain?" Viktor requested.

"It's hard to describe ..." Bryen needed a few seconds to think about it. "The power that Ursina wields ... this might sound strange, but it feels older. More ... I don't know. There's an undercurrent running through the Curse gifted to her that suggests that it's not entirely of the Natural World. That it comes from somewhere else. I know that's not much of an explanation, but that's the best that I can do."

"And her power just might," Viktor confirmed with a nod, pleased that his nephew had been able to decipher the puzzle placed before him.

"It might? What do you mean?"

"Just as you can, we can feel it as well," Mikayla replied. "One of the benefits of being tied to the Seventh Stone."

"It's fairly faint," Viktor said, "but it's there. A contaminated spirit that has wormed its way within the Curse that is permeating the citadel and expanded out into the city."

"You described it in a way that makes sense, Bryen," Mikayla nodded. "There is an undercurrent within the Curse that offers a taste of an evil that has not touched the Natural World for thousands of years. At least not in such strength as it is now."

"Have you heard of the Ancient One?" Viktor asked. The spirit of the dead Magus was warming to the topic. Before he lost his life helping to craft the first Weir, he had enjoyed teaching and mentoring new Magii. Since becoming tied to the Seventh Stone, he had little cause to do so ... until the artifact merged with Bryen.

"Sirius mentioned the Ancient One once or twice, but no more than that."

"That's unfortunate," Viktor replied. "Learning about the Ancient One is critical to learning about the Curse. In particular, if we're correct, how that evil taint passes between the Spirit World and the Natural World."

Viktor held up his hands to halt the protest that he knew was coming from Bryen. "I know, you didn't have as much time as you needed to learn from my brother as would have been good for both of you. Nevertheless, we can make up for that gap in your knowledge now."

"What do you know of the Ancient One, Bryen?" Mikayla asked. She, too, had enjoyed her time instructing those learning to use the Talent before she had needed to take on a much larger responsibility, rising to become the Master of the Magii.

"As I said, not much. More from Declan than Sirius, actually. Yet both were adamant that the Ancient One was real and not a myth. The ruler of the Spirit World and the leader of the Army of the Dead. The Ancient One ripped the Veil, seeking to merge the Natural World with the Spirit World, but he failed. The Sentinels stopped him, imprisoning him in the Spirit World and continuing their watch to this day, seeking to ensure that he can't touch again the Natural World as he did in the past."

"The Sentinels do, in fact, continue to guard against the coming of the Ancient One. But they can't stop him from touching the Natural World even though he is still locked away behind the Veil." Viktor held up his hands again, this time as a way of apology. "But we are getting ahead of ourselves. We'll get to all that later."

"Did either Declan or Sirius tell you that we believe the Ancient One is a Blackgard. One of the first Magii, in fact."

Mikayla's revelation immediately caught Bryen's attention. "No, they didn't. His name?"

"Marcus Blackgard."

"Blackgard?" That name was quite familiar to Bryen's ears. The next time he saw Declan, they would need to have a conversation. "You're sure of that?"

"Yes, a Blackgard. Except for one member, a family where honor comes before all else," Mikayla said with a hint of admiration in her tone.

"Keep in mind that when the Blackgards first came to rule in Skaffa Falls, the Ancient One had yet to come into existence. At that time, the Span built across the Eight Isles didn't lead to the Valley of the Dead, but rather to a beautiful, secluded island surrounded by mountains that rose up at water's edge and an ancient wall at the very base of those mountains on the inland side. Why that wall was there, or who built it, no one could explain. Although it proved essential to the Sentinels' success against the Army of the Dead as the Magii used that wall to fix the defense they crafted with the Talent that prevented the servants of the Ancient One from escaping to the continent. A construction similar to the Weir, in fact."

"Strange although not surprising how curiosity led to the darkness that almost consumed the Realms," mused Viktor.

"Indeed," Mikayla agreed. "The Order of the Magii believes that it was because of Marcus Blackgard's curiosity that the Curse came to be."

"Is that even possible?" Bryen wondered. The Curse was so pervasive in the Realms, a rival to the Talent, that he found it hard to accept that the evil taint could have come into existence because of a single man.

"No, probably not," Viktor concluded. "Although there might be some semblance of the truth linked to it."

Mikayla picked up the story from there. "We don't know all that happened. All we can assume is that just as other Magii have turned to the Curse either because of greed or the lust for power or the arrogance of believing that they can resist the temptation of that evil, the same happened to Marcus."

Mikayla shrugged her shoulders. "Whether or not he was the first to take that route, who can say? He was seduced by knowledge that was best left unexplored. And he thought that he was stronger, smarter, more capable than any other Magus, failing to or unwilling to comprehend that the Curse is an insidious power that always identifies your weaknesses and takes advantage of them. A truth you know better than most."

"To continue his studies in private, Marcus built a small citadel on the island that is now called the Outpost and will be used as a last defense by the Sentinels stationed there if the need ever arises. There he enjoyed his solitude and began his experiments," continued Mikayla. "You have to give him credit. His goal was certainly admirable."

"What was his goal?" Bryen asked.

"He became obsessed with finding a way to destroy the Curse," Mikayla explained. "So you can understand why I find it hard to give credence to the theory that Marcus was the first Dark Magus. In the end, instead of destroying the Curse, the Curse destroyed him. Turning him. Tainting him. Slowly. Over a period of years. Until he was all but unrecognizable in body and mind."

Mikayla shook her head sadly. "By the end of that terrible process, he became something else. Something less than human. Rather than seeking to destroy the Curse, he instead sought to destroy the Talent so that the Curse could run rampant in the Realms. To do that, he ripped the Veil separating the Natural World from the Spirit World."

"He did that knowing what was waiting for him?" wondered Bryen.

"He did," Mikayla confirmed. "Again, arrogance. He believed that there was nothing in the Natural World that could prevent him from achieving his goal. And that almost proved to be the case once he subjugated the creatures of the Spirit World. Once he had those monsters under his thrall, working in conjunction with the beasts that he created with his experiments, there was no one to stand in his way."

"Except for his family," interrupted Viktor, feeling the need to contribute to the story in some small way.

"Except for his family," Mikayla confirmed. "The other Blackgards were the only ones prepared to challenge him. If not for them, Marcus might have succeeded. He might have destroyed the Talent and conquered the Natural World."

"A difficult position for the other Blackgards to be in," Bryen murmured.

"It was," Mikayla agreed, "particularly since the Ancient One's monsters outnumbered them at the start of what became known as the War Against the Spirits. The Blackgards were able to hold back the creatures subservient to the Ancient One, although they were not strong enough to defeat the invaders. Instead, it became a war of attrition, fought over decades, the other kingdoms in the Realms recognizing the danger and sending soldiers to fight alongside those pledged to stop the Army of the Dead."

"Was it the Ancient One's army that led to the change in name for the island?" asked Bryen.

"In part, yes," Mikalya replied. "What had been a bucolic isle transformed before the very eyes of the Blackgards and their Sentinels."

"In obvious ways as well as ways less so," interrupted Viktor.

"The fields and forests became battlefields, the ground

ripped apart with the Talent and the Curse, a light mist that never dissipated drifting down from the mountains encircling the island and settling within the vale, the sun struggling to break through, some suggesting that the mist was the magical residue of the battles between the practitioners of the Talent and those of the Curse. Because of the huge number of men and women who lost their lives fighting against the creatures from the Spirit World, renaming the island the Valley of the Dead certainly seemed appropriate."

"It wasn't just the constant fighting that made the Valley of the Dead what it is today," clarified Viktor. "The very presence of the creatures of the Spirit World coming through the Rip in the Veil and setting foot on the island changed the land and may actually be the cause of the mist that now resides upon it, the evil within those monsters affecting the Natural World in a profound way. That and the fact that because the Rip in the Veil can't be closed, the Spirit World is leaking through and contaminating the Natural World. Thankfully, the Ancient One does not have the power to expand the size of the Rip and step through himself because of what the Magii did to ensure that he couldn't."

"At least not yet," Mikayla murmured quietly, "but that's a story for another day."

"Nevertheless, his servants still can make their way through," continued Viktor, ignoring Mikayla's comment, "and unfortunately despite their best efforts the Sentinels stationed there cannot stop them all."

"I certainly wouldn't take them to task for that." Bryen understood that only so much could be expected when faced with such a threat. "With respect to the essence of the Spirit World seeping into the Natural World, why has it not spread beyond the island?"

"I believe we have gotten a little ahead of ourselves, so let me step back for a moment," requested Viktor. "The Rip in the

Veil does more than allow the servants of the Ancient One to enter the Natural World. It also allows the Spirit World to touch the Natural World. The only reason the decaying essence of the Spirit World hasn't spread beyond the island is because of what the Order of the Magii did when the Ancient One was first imprisoned there. It's similar to what we did to construct the Weir, although distinct at the same time. Those Magii were able to contain the essence of the Spirit World within the stone wall that circles the island, fixing their natural magic to that construction. An impregnable barrier, or so they believed at the time."

"Then how can some of the servants of the Ancient One walk in the Realms?"

"Because no solution is ever perfect," Mikayla replied. "The magic of the Magii remains strong. It continues to hold back the Ancient One. But with respect to some of his servants getting off the island ..."

"You don't know, do you?"

"We don't," Viktor admitted reluctantly, "and the Order was never able to figure out how. It's not like Marcus Blackgard was going to share his secrets with me."

"Testy, testy," murmured Mikayla. She turned her focus to Bryen. "As you can see, this is a challenge that has plagued your uncle for quite some time. He was looking for the answer to the question you asked when he was pulled into the fight against the Ghoule Overlord, so he never had the chance to obtain the answer that he wanted."

"Mikayla has the right of it," Viktor grumbled. "What the Magii working with the Sentinels did to prevent the corrosive essence of the Spirit World from drifting free to contaminate all of the Realms is truly a marvel. But it's not perfect. And somehow the Ancient One found a flaw that he continues to exploit."

"As you've learned thanks to your many battles with the

Curse," Mikayla continued, knowing that he understood she was speaking about not his combats against the Ghoule Overlord or his Elders, but rather his having to fight the Curse when it was within him and seeking to turn him to its purposes, "just a single touch is all that it takes for the taint to take hold. The same holds true for the Ancient One. The power he exercises is frightening and enticing, both at the same time. We would like to learn more about it, but the risk is too great."

"What do the Sentinels do to protect against the power of the Ancient One?"

"The Curse is quite strong as you know, and that essence of the Spirit World that is escaping through the Rip in the Veil is almost unstoppable. Therefore, to ensure that they could move safely to certain locations and perform the tasks required of them despite the foul spirit that has permeated the island, they carved out paths throughout the Valley of the Dead that are protected with the Talent."

"Keep to the path," Viktor murmured. "A favorite saying of the Sentinels. It has gained many meanings over the years as the challenge of defending against the Ancient One and his creatures has become more difficult. Nevertheless, the original meaning that serves as the foundation for the maxim remains accurate and very literal. Keep to the path when making your way through the Valley of the Dead or risk joining the Ancient One's army."

"How many Sentinels are there?" Bryen asked.

"Since their victory over the Ancient One, the Blackgards maintain a fighting force of one thousand, give or take a few depending on retirement or the loss of life during the performance of their duty."

"Yes, it's important to note that once a Sentinel always a Sentinel," explained Mikayla. "It is not a responsibility that is assumed lightly. The Sentinels are a corps of warriors bonded to each other and to their task with the Talent, giving them some limited immunity from the Curse."

"Limited immunity?"

"Think of it as sand running through an hourglass," suggested Viktor. "Those who are not Sentinels become corrupted the second the Curse touches them. For the Sentinels, the process takes longer. Four or five hours, sometimes more, for the Curse to achieve its objective. That delay allows the Sentinels to hunt and fight the monsters of the Spirit World that slip through the Rip in the Veil. Then, if they leave the Valley fast enough, they experience no ill effects from the corrosive miasma haunting that island. There's a healing process as well that the Magii assigned to the Sentinels will employ when there is need."

"How did the war come to an end?" Bryen asked. "You said it lasted for decades."

"It did," Mikayla confirmed. "Marcus Blackgard called for a truce, because he believed that he finally had what he required to break free from the island. He met with his brother, Henry, who was the leader of the Blackgard family and the Sentinels."

"It must have been quite a confrontation," suggested Viktor.

"I can only imagine," Mikayla replied. "It is said that the ravages of war have a huge impact on a person. Henry had aged since he had last seen his brother; however, Marcus was unrecognizable. He wore dark robes that appeared to be made of mist. It was as if he had become a part of the Spirit World himself, having been touched by the Curse and the spirits of the dead for too long, molded into something else. He had lost his hair. Oozing splotches marred his deathly grey skin. His teeth had turned black to match his eyes. He had become a monster himself."

"Why did Marcus want to speak with his brother?"

"Marcus kidnapped Henry's wife and two children, hoping to use them against him. Marcus ordered Henry to surrender. If

Henry allowed his Army of the Dead to cross the Span and reach the mainland, Marcus promised to return his family safely. If he didn't, he promised Henry that he would murder his wife and children."

"A difficult position to be in," said Bryen, unable to imagine the pressure Henry Blackgard must have felt, torn between his love for his family and his duty to the Sentinels. The entire world, in fact.

"Indeed," Mikayla agreed with a sad nod. "Incredibly difficult. Henry was torn. For a time, Henry convinced himself that he could do it. He was going to give in to his brother's demands. He loved his family. He couldn't consign them to their fate."

"But in the end he couldn't do it," Viktor interjected.

"Henry sacrificed his family to ensure that his brother, Marcus Blackgard, could not escape the Valley of the Dead. He allowed his brother to believe that he was going to acquiesce to his demands, then sprang a trap that allowed the Sentinels and their allies to push the Ancient One and his Army of the Dead back into the Spirit World through the Rip in the Veil. All at a great cost in life, including Henry's wife and his two children."

"And for his service?" prompted Viktor.

"Henry believed that he should be condemned for even considering giving in to his brother's demands. Instead, he was lauded for his courage and honor. He was also given an even heavier responsibility. Because he had not betrayed his brothers and sisters in arms, the Blackgard family became the ancestral leaders of the Sentinels and remain the Lords of Skaffa Falls to this day. Their primary responsibility continues to be protecting against the coming of the Ancient One."

"Exactly so," said Viktor. "Because the Rip in the Veil remains, the responsibility accepted by the Blackgards and the Sentinels is just as important as ever, although there are many in the Realms who have forgotten them and the Ancient One."

Bryen was quiet for a time, nodding to himself, going over

all that Viktor and Mikayla had just revealed to him. It was a lot to take in. Still, he didn't feel as if the story was complete. "What is it that you haven't told me yet?"

"You're much too perceptive."

"It runs in the family, uncle."

Viktor was pleased by Bryen's comment, breaking out into a broad grin. "I won't dispute that."

"I might," challenged Mikayla.

"Even though the Ancient One remains imprisoned in the Spirit World," began Viktor, ignoring Mikayla's barb, "we believe that he can still manipulate events in the Natural World. He can't enter our world. Not yet. But as Mikayla explained, he can send some of his servants through the Rip in the Veil and in that and other ways he can corrupt those who are willing to trade their souls and their free will for the power and privilege that he can gift them."

"Can you prove that?" Bryen wasn't going to argue with them. He was just curious.

"We don't have a great deal of hard evidence," mused Viktor. "But there are enough pieces here and there that confirm it for us. As you've discovered, Ursina Winborne is a prime example."

"Why do you believe that's a possibility?" Bryen asked, even though he wasn't really disputing his uncle's logic.

"You've touched the Curse," Mikayla began.

"As I was taught to do so, yes, and also against my wishes," Bryen cut in. "But you knew that already."

Mikayla nodded. "Then returning to the beginning of our conversation, the Curse that we have sensed here in the Shadow Keep differs from the Curse that the Ghoule Overlord employed. Your description of it is right on target. Older. Ancient."

"As if we are standing in a crypt," suggested Bryen.

"Or as if we're standing in the Spirit World," Viktor offered.

"The history lesson has been useful," Bryen said, "but what am I to do with it? Ursina is a Dark Magus. I'm sure of it. She might even be a servant of the Ancient One if what we've discussed is accurate. Still, that does not change what needs to be done here."

"No, it does not," Mikayla agreed. "Although it does add another level of complexity."

"Any advice then?"

"Be wary," Viktor said. "If Mikayla and I are correct about the Ancient One, what Ursina is playing with is more dangerous than she knows. I have no doubt that you can defeat her if it comes to it. Aislinn can as well. When you two work together, you are virtually unbeatable. Just don't assume that Ursina is the only hazard here. There might be an even greater threat waiting for you if you don't keep your eyes open."

"That's not all, Protector," Mikayla added. "You and Aislinn both are a threat to her. She has touched the Curse. If she serves the Ancient One, she will have no choice. She must kill you, because she knows that you have the strength to kill her. The question that you must mull is do you allow her to make the first move or do you?"

23

TWISTS AND TURNS

The cart careened down the steep slope, picking up speed with every rotation of its sparking wheels, struggling to stay on the narrow steel tracks, threatening to bounce off at any second.

At the very bottom of the incline, the rickety transport, rust having eaten its way through the sides in several places, curled sharply to the left then almost immediately back to the right.

And so it went for the next few minutes, the rattling cart curling from side to side at stomach-churning angles, seemingly with a mind of its own, never slowing, picking up even more speed on the straightaways, protesting with a never-ending scream that sounded like the dead of the Spirit World seeking to break free, its ancient and corroded mechanics pushed to the limit.

Their strong grips on the rim of the hutch, Jakob and Lycia held on to each other just as tenaciously, knocked into the side of the cart on every curve with a bruising power, the forces trying to pull them out of the transport almost too much for them.

Time after time, they worried that on a hairpin curve the

hutch would leave the track entirely. But they had little control over that.

They had little control over anything. All they could do was hold on for dear life and hope that they weren't thrown from the cart.

"Do you know where we are?" Lycia banged into Jakob, almost torn free from his grasp, when the cart heeled sharply to the left.

"Roughly," Jakob replied, trying to maintain his position in the hutch, and more often than not failing. The demand of keeping his place straining every muscle, he felt as if he were no more than a slab of meat getting pounded again and again with a butcher's tenderizer.

He continued to search for the Stalkers with the Talent. A difficult task since his first concern was surviving their potentially lethal ride through the mountains.

Still, he determined that a handful of the monsters chose to try their luck on the tracks themselves, loping and climbing after them. Of those, a few experienced the pitfalls of following in the wake of a hurtling cart across already weakened tracks that were more than happy to finally give way after so many years of disuse.

Unfortunately, not enough of their hunters selected that path, so two or three of the Stalkers dying for their efforts scarcely improved their odds of escape. Because a score of the monsters continued to pursue them.

Most of the Stalkers decided to avoid the tracks that twisted and turned through the cavern and come at them from a different direction, working their way through the tunnels in the pockmarked mountain in search of new routes that would allow them to get ahead of their quarry.

"Do you have any idea what's coming our way?" demanded Lycia, slightly exasperated.

"Vaguely."

She would have been even more exasperated by Jakob's response if not for her slamming against the side of the cart, Jakob crashing into her, as they raced along a particularly tight curve, both of them pulling themselves to the other side of the hutch as swiftly as possible, fearing that if they didn't their transport would take them off the rails.

"You can't do better than that?"

Jakob did just a second later. During the very brief straight-away that followed the incredibly sharp turn, he took the risk of freeing one hand from the lip of the cart.

With a flick of his wrist, he sent the sphere of light that had followed along with them on their harrowing journey farther out to their front. That action breaking the hold of the suffo-cating darkness that surrounded them, they gained a much better view of where they were and the deadly challenge they faced.

"Down!"

Jakob issued his warning just in time. Both he and Lycia ducked right before they lost their heads to a long, narrow stalactite that reached down from the ceiling and blocked the very center of the track.

They were lucky that the slender growth of minerals wasn't very thick. If it had been, the sliver of stone would have stopped them cold, their escape ending right there along with their lives.

Rather than halting their progress, the tip snapped off when the cart struck it. Even so, the blow almost knocked the cart from the tracks, sending a shiver through the decaying steel that made them both worry that their conveyance was going to fall apart around them.

Somehow the cart stayed in one piece, only losing a large chunk of rusted steel where the tip of the stalactite hit. Lycia and Jakob quickly shifting their weight to the other side, bringing the wheels back down to the track before they took another hard turn to the left, which was followed by an even steeper drop of several hundred feet that left their stomachs in their throats.

After their collision with the stalactite, and tired of only seeing a few dozen yards to their front, Jakob shot a dozen more spheres of light all around them, wanting a better view of the perils ahead.

What he and Lycia saw took their breaths away.

The cavern was larger than the city of Ballinasloe. Stalagmites extended up from the floor as if they were seeking to touch the stalactites that reached down from the ceiling. Many of the natural formations were hundreds of feet tall and at the base twice the size of the brochs that were so important to surviving in the Highlands.

Through, around, and over these gargantuan flowstones steel tracks looped, curled, dropped, rose, and ran for what appeared to be miles in all directions. The disorienting latticework was supported by steel towers, too many bridges to count, and long cables, all hammered into the walls and the dozens upon dozens of stalagmites and stalactites that extended into the distance, clarity lost at the edge of the light provided by the glowing spheres.

A truly dizzying display.

"This is incredible," Lycia whispered.

"It is," Jakob agreed.

Neither really could grasp what they were seeing. They were barely able to take it all in. Yet even as they struggled to comprehend what they had discovered within a Highland peak, one question dominated their thoughts.

Who constructed this remarkable web?

And not just the tracks twisting and turning around the cavern in what seemed to be a haphazard pattern, but also the large pieces of rusted machinery that lay dormant atop the largest of the stalagmites whose summits had been scraped flat.

"What are those?" Jakob mumbled to himself. His eyes were drawn to a massive crane as they shot through the very center of a stalagmite on their first straight track of any length since they had climbed into the cart. He looked back at the massive construction, dozens of ropes and huge buckets with metal teeth at the bottom hanging idly.

"I don't know."

"Do you have any idea who could have done all this?"

"Not a clue," Lycia replied. "Although I'd really like to find out."

"As would I."

Before they could continue their musings, Jakob reached with one hand and pulled Lycia against him, crushing her against his chest.

Lycia was about to ask what he was doing when he shifted his weight to the other side of the cart, taking her with him.

She understood when she heard the snap of steel just behind them.

Jakob was doing his best to balance their weight across the cart so that they'd stay on the rails at least for a little while longer.

The tracks were old. Brittle in many places.

Nothing had rolled across the narrow metal tracks in centuries.

Because of that, on the really sharp turns that sought to expel them from their carriage, like the two that they had just experienced, their stomachs trying to escape through their mouths, they were at risk of their conveyance being thrown from the track.

Not a prospect that Lycia favored. And from what she could see when she peeked above the rim of the hutch after pushing herself free from Jakob's warm and much-too-inviting grip, it was only going to get worse.

"Here I was thinking that you just wanted to get close to me," Lycia offered with a smile.

Her humor earned a bark of laughter from Jakob, who just a heartbeat later pulled Lycia in close to him again, taking them both to the right side of the cart when the wheels on that side left the track completely, their conveyance struggling on a hairpin turn, those same wheels slamming back down just a second later and allowing them to both breathe again.

For the next few minutes, they could focus on nothing else other than shifting their weight across the cart, the spheres of light giving them warning of what was coming their way, slipping off the tracks becoming their dominant concern the farther they progressed through the cavern.

Several times their hearts dropped into their stomachs after particularly severe turns, the track behind them cracking or falling away entirely, and a few times the steel rails began to break apart before they crossed over them, the only thing saving them the speed of their passage, the hutch making it across before the disintegrating rails fell away into the darkness far below.

Lycia was quite pleased that they were well ahead of the Stalkers thanks to Jakob's quick thinking, but now she really wanted to get off this ride, and as quickly as possible. The green tinge to Jakob's face suggested that he was interested in doing the same.

Just seconds later they realized that they were about to get their chance. However, they had little hope for an easy landing.

About a hundred yards farther along, the track, which now sloped down precipitously toward the cavern floor -- curling around one stalactite while burrowing through three stalagmites -- was about to come to an end. A barrier of wood and steel awaited them at the very edge of the darkness.

"Do you see a brake?" asked Lycia, her concern creeping

into her voice. She was searching for any solution that would help to prevent their imminent crash.

"There is no brake."

"How can you be sure?" challenged Lycia. "There has to be a brake."

"There was a brake," Jakob clarified. He held up the long piece of metal that had snapped off some time ago, rust visible at the very end.

The brake.

"Get ready," Jakob warned.

"For what?"

Lycia's eyes were drawn to the base of the track. They had passed through the three stalagmites. Now it was just open track that sloped down at a vertiginous angle and stopped abruptly at a bumper block.

"To jump."

"To jump," Lycia repeated, not quite comprehending what Jakob had in mind. "Are you completely out of your ..."

"Now!"

Jakob bent at the knees and launched himself into the air a split second before the cart crashed into the buffer. His strong grip around Lycia's waist pulled her with him.

When the cart slammed into the barricade, it heeled over, the back wheels coming up and off the track. That gave Jakob and Lycia the height and momentum that they needed to clear the barrier.

As the cart flipped up and over the bumper block, for just a few seconds Jakob and Lycia were flying through the air. Then Lycia gasped, the shock of the cold water she splashed into knocking the air from her lungs. When she finally pushed her head back above the surface, she coughed up a few cups of the subterranean lake before drawing breath again.

"A fun ride." Jakob was treading water next to her. "Although not something that I want to do again."

"Neither do I," Lycia replied.

The spheres of light hovering above them revealed where they landed. Lycia was grateful that it hadn't been on the rocky cavern floor, but rather a huge reservoir of water, the far side just visible in the dusk. Maybe a few hundred yards distant. Certainly a manageable swim for them both even with their weapons sheathed across their backs.

After spinning around slowly while treading water to take stock of what they faced, Jakob and Lycia looked at one another, still a bit shocked that they had survived.

The bumper block was a mangled mess and their hutch lay upside down on the shore, its wheels shorn clean off and a long rip down the side exhibiting just how fragile their conveyance had been.

They were lucky to have made it this far.

They smiled, both realizing it at the same time. Then laughed. Not quite believing that they landed in the only safe spot in the entire cavern rather than ending up broken and battered next to one of the flowstones.

Their good humor was short-lived. Their faces fell, silence descending in an instant.

"Did you feel that?"

"I did," Lycia murmured softly.

"What was it?"

"I don't know." Lycia scanned around them, not seeing anything other than the dark, glassy surface of the small lake. "What could survive in here without any ..."

In a flash, Jakob disappeared, pulled beneath the surface without having the chance to utter a word.

"Jakob!" Lycia screamed.

It happened so fast that Lycia could do nothing to help him even though she was treading water only a few feet away.

Desperation driving her, Lycia twisted around in the water, looking for any sign of movement. The spheres of light continued to float above her, illuminating the reservoir and a good portion of the cavern.

Jakob was still alive. She knew that for sure. So long as the light remained, so long as he maintained his connection to the Talent, he had not yet crossed over to the other side.

But she didn't know where he was in the reservoir. The light didn't penetrate the pitch-black water for more than a few feet.

She ducked her head underwater, looking for any sign of Jakob, counting the seconds in her head since his disappearance.

Lycia needed to find him. Quickly.

She couldn't expect him to last for more than a few minutes beneath the surface.

Catching a hint of movement out of the corner of her eye, she hoped that Jakob had fought his way up from the depths.

Her heart rose in her throat. It wasn't him. It was probably whatever had taken him.

She ignored the handful of wakes that cut through the placid water. She didn't know what creature had pulled Jakob below. She did know that there was more than one in the water with her, and they were growing bolder.

When one of the animals swam by only a few feet away, she glimpsed slithering through the water a long, sinuous body that was several feet thick.

A water snake of some type?

Declan had taught her a great many things growing up within the shadow of the Colosseum, but nothing regarding a serpent that might live in a small lake beneath a mountain.

Lycia thought about stabbing the creature with her sword since it was so close. Even if she didn't kill it, she might be able to persuade it to leave her alone.

She decided against it, however, assuming that her effort might lead to a combat that she stood little chance of winning while she treaded water. In large part because she was certain that more of these water snakes swam below her.

Better to keep her focus on finding Jakob.

Save him and they could both make their escape.

She dipped her head beneath the dark water again.

Where was he?

Time was running out.

Pulling her face out of the metallic-tasting water, she shook her head in frustration. She could do nothing to help Jakob from where she was.

Identifying several large bodies slithering toward her, drawing ever closer as they circled her much like a shark before it attacked, she needed to decide quickly.

Try one last time to find Jakob, who somehow was still alive because the Talent was still being used, or prepare to defend herself.

It proved to be an easy decision for her. She would worry about the creatures swimming around her if she couldn't find Jakob.

Taking a big gulp of air, she dove down, kicking with her feet.

Ten feet.

She moved her jaw to release the pressure in her ears.

Twenty feet.

She hovered there. Spinning around slowly. Glimpsing vaguely a few long, dim shapes not too far away from her.

But not Jakob.

She kicked again, and then once more.

Thirty feet down now.

He had to be here.

He wouldn't go easily.

And she had to get to him soon.

He had been below the surface for far too long now without taking a breath.

Spinning around in the water, she struggled to pierce the gloom. Using what little light the spheres floating above the reservoir provided, she saw no more than shadows at this depth.

Where could he be?

He had to be here!

Jakob was still alive.

He would fight.

She just needed to find him.

Lycia slowly spun around again, waving her arms to keep herself in place, a long dagger from the sheath on her thigh in her hand.

There!

Her eyes widened when she saw what had taken Jakob, her discovery filling her with an almost uncontrollable wrath as she kicked over to him.

She had been wrong about what was in the water with them. It wasn't a snake. At least she didn't think it was.

The creature looked more like an eel. Forty feet long. A hard, scaly hide. A girth of at least two feet, maybe more. The spikes running from the animal's brow and down its back making her think of the Bakunawa that hunted them across the Burnt Ocean, just on a smaller scale, her perspective solidified by the gaping maw filled with sharp teeth the length of a small dagger.

The beast was wrapped around Jakob, who was resisting. But one of his arms was crushed to his side, trapped by the thick, muscular coils. And with the other, he was using his dagger to fend off the eel's constant, lightning-fast jabs.

Seeking to bite down onto Jakob's head, so far the eel only had succeeded in bloodying its razor-sharp beak.

But Lycia knew that wouldn't last forever. Because it was clear that Jakob's strength was fading, the stream of bubbles from his mouth becoming more inconsistent, his motions slower as unconsciousness threatened to take him.

Ignoring the handful of eels swimming toward them, their sinuous bodies gliding through the water and giving their monstrous frames a unique grace, Lycia kicked hard and fast, propelling herself through the water.

The massive, dragonlike eel pulling back for another strike, her timing was perfect. At the same time that the eel jabbed one more time at Jakob, Lycia stabbed with her dagger from behind.

She wasn't trying to pierce the animal's rough hide. Rather, she placed her dagger out in front of Jakob, leaving it there, making sure that her aim was good.

The eel caught her movement too late, unable to halt its progress. The animal's momentum did the rest, the eel impaling itself on her blade. The sharp steel knocked out several long teeth before punching through the beast's upper jaw and, because the eel was moving forward at such a great speed, right into its brain.

The light left the creature's eyes in an instant, the eel's head drooping away as a screen of blood formed in the water. Perhaps most important, the coils that had been crushing the life from Jakob loosened.

Spinning back around, dagger in hand, Lycia kept her eyes on the eels that were swimming toward her. Two took up a position around them, circling slowly, seemingly intent on waiting her and Jakob out.

The other animals dove deeper, following their dead brethren, several taking a bite before the corpse was even cold once Jakob had unwrapped himself.

As the dead eel dropped deeper into the depths, now a meal for its ilk, Jakob recognized the more immediate danger. Desperate for air, he had only a few seconds left before he drowned.

Spots dancing at the edge of his vision, his lungs threatening to explode, he used the Talent to form a ball of bright white energy just above his palm.

The gloom of the water disappeared.

It was then that Lycia realized she had miscounted. There were more than just a few eels swimming around them. There were at least ten. She couldn't tell for certain because as soon as the light flared, the eels scattered, escaping back into the gloom of the deeper water.

Clearly, these animals were well adapted to their surroundings, preferring the darkness and fearful of the light.

Free of the eels for the time being, Lycia placed a hand under Jakob's shoulder and began kicking for the surface, helping him get his head back above the surface.

He spent the next several seconds gasping for air.

"Thank you," Jakob finally managed to whisper, his throat raw.

"It was nothing."

"It was everything."

Lycia nodded, not knowing what else to say. She had never been comfortable with praise.

Unwilling to look him in the eyes, she realized that when Jakob reached the surface, he allowed the ball of light in his hand to blink out.

The water was black again, the only light coming from the spheres above them. The result was immediate. The eels began circling again, their wakes drawing ever closer.

"They don't like the light," Lycia said when she spun back around, catching Jakob's eyes. "Quickly, before ..."

Jakob responded before she could finish her request. He dropped several balls of fiery light down into the water around them. As soon as the darkness below them brightened, the eels vanished.

"Are the Stalkers still coming after us?"

Jakob took a moment before replying. As soon as he had begun his combat with the eel, he had pulled back his senses, less concerned about the Stalkers' locations than the creature intent on making a meal of him.

"They are. There are a few that are still following the tracks. With all the twists and turns I don't know how long it will take them to reach the shore, but we still have a little time. The Stalkers not on the rails are seeking some way to get to us through the tunnels slicing through the mountain."

"So we really only have one choice."

"Correct."

Without another word, Lycia sheathed her dagger and began swimming through the reservoir toward the far shore.

Jakob fell in beside her, the balls of light that he had crafted moving with them beneath the surface to ensure that the eels left them alone.

When they dragged themselves out of the water after a swim that felt much longer than the twenty minutes it took them to reach the beach opposite where they had left the unsafe confines of their hutch, they sat back against a massive stalagmite that was at least fifty feet around at the base. Shoulder to shoulder, they breathed deeply, needing a few minutes to recover.

For a few heartbeats, there was nothing other than a welcome silence. But the additional time that they craved wasn't to be had.

The screech of a Stalker blasted through the huge cavern, echoing off the walls.

"They're on the shore?" Lycia pushed herself back to her feet, every muscle in her body protesting. She offered her free hand to Jakob, imagining what he must feel like if she felt this bad, pulling him up from where he sat against the flowstone.

Rather than send more spheres of light streaking up toward the ceiling with the hope of catching a glimpse of what came their way, and not wanting to make the Stalkers' hunt for them any easier, as the light that permitted them to see the Stalkers also allowed the Stalkers to see them, Jakob took the safer course.

He extended his senses, mapping out a picture of the cavern in his mind and pinpointing the location of every Stalker involved in the chase. He then used a tiny thread of the Talent to connect to Lycia so that she could see what he was seeing.

"On the beach, yes," Jakob confirmed with a nod. "Those monsters will have to go for a swim if they want to continue the hunt."

"That doesn't bother me in the least," Lycia said with a nod. She assumed that once those monsters entered the dark water of the reservoir, the eels would take an interest in them.

It would be a worthy combat, she believed.

Monster vs. monstrous eel.

And she had a clear favorite. With any luck, the eels would reduce the number of Stalkers hunting them.

"Nor me," replied Jakob, "but it's not the Stalkers about to take a dip that worry me."

"The ones above us," nodded Lycia, slightly shocked by the large number of passageways running through the walls that enclosed the underground lake.

Thanks to Jakob's use of the Talent, she also saw the many crevices about fifty feet above them, dark splotches on the crag. Thankfully, there were no ledges. All of those tunnels came out over the water.

Nevertheless, not an insurmountable obstacle for the Stalkers. Not with their razor-sharp claws.

If they didn't want to get their feet wet, they would have little difficulty climbing down the rough stone walls.

"They're not going to stop, are they?" Lycia already knew the answer to her question.

"No. What was that saying you told me? The rule for when

you were fighting on the white sand? Declan's primary warning I think it was?"

"Kill or be killed?"

"That's the one. The Stalkers either kill us or we kill them."

"Not very uplifting," grouched Lycia.

"No, but simple," Jakob said, giving her an unexpected smile. "And more often than not simple is good."

Jakob placed his hand on the small of Lycia's back, turning her toward what she quickly realized was another tunnel set in the wall just past the massive stalagmite that dominated the small beach.

"Let's go," Jakob urged. "We need to move. Let's see if we can get a little farther ahead of them before it's time to focus on the killing."

24

MAKING A BREAK

With all the challenges that he faced in that moment, strangely it was the scratch, scratch, scratch that bothered him the most.

Leather straps around his wrists and his ankles held Davin in place on a long stone table. The slab was centered in a smaller room that was connected to the long corridor beneath the Rock that led to the chamber where Davin and Talia had watched the cowled woman turn human beings into Stalkers.

Captain Oselnik stood above him, walking slowly around the table. He had his dagger out, trailing the steel tip across the stone tabletop.

Oselnik likely thought that by doing that he could frighten Davin. Get him to think of all the terrible things that Roosarian's captain and the soldiers just past the entrance to the chamber could do to him.

Davin was less than impressed. Oselnik's antics didn't bother him in the least. He had dealt so many times before with his opponents trying to scare him that little fazed him.

Adversaries on the white sand.

Ghoules.

Elders.

Kraken.

What was a pompous, puffed-up blowhard who liked to play at soldier?

If the Captain of the Fal Carrachian Guard believed that he could frighten him after all that he had experienced in his short lifetime, then the man was more of a fool than he appeared to be. Although Davin certainly would have welcomed the opportunity to take the man's dagger and slide it right into his gut, the steel scraping against the stone setting his teeth on edge and irritating him in a way that little else had in quite some time.

He did his best to ignore the Captain, but Davin couldn't ignore what else in the room drew his focus. What sent a faint shiver of fear through him when he pulled his gaze away from his would-be torturer and shifted his attention to the cells on either side of him.

To the blood-red eyes that stared back at him.

Hungry eyes.

Yet strangely impassive at the same time.

According to Oselnik, who couldn't stop himself from talking, feeling the need to share with Davin whatever crossed his mind, Roosarian had created the Stalkers in the cells on each side of him just hours before in this very room, not yet having given them their assignments.

The Captain hadn't needed to tell him what Roosarian had in mind for them. Davin already knew. She would send the monsters against the Carlomin holdings on the southern side of the harbor.

And he didn't need to ask the loquacious captain why the Stalkers were focused so intently upon him. Davin already knew that as well.

His blood.

His body was scored in a dozen different places. Most of the wounds had scabbed over, although not all. There was one spot in particular. On his arm. A slow, steady trickle that ran down to his forefinger and then dripped onto the floor.

That's what the Stalkers stared at so intently.

His blood.

They could see it.

They could smell it.

They craved his blood.

Davin caught them sniffing every few seconds, some of them licking their fangs after doing so.

They were hungry.

If not for the steel bars separating them, regardless of the compulsion Roosarian may have placed on them, these monsters would have given in to their baser instincts and Davin would be nothing more than dead meat. Although that still remained a good possibility.

His captor's unending stream of words drew him back from where he had been looking and what he had been thinking.

"I could kill you now and there is nothing that you could do to stop me."

Davin didn't bother to reply, his eyes drifting back to the Stalkers that stared with such intensity at him. Oselnik spoke the truth. There was no point in trying to deny it.

Besides, the Captain was speaking more for himself than for Davin. He clearly was on edge. Thus his nervous walk around the table upon which Davin was strapped down.

Davin could understand why. Oselnik's plan hadn't worked out as he wanted.

Oselnik had been on the dock leading the soldiers charged with taking the Carlomin compound. When what he thought would be an easy conquest began to sour, Oselnik realized that the inconceivable was occurring.

He was losing. His soldiers couldn't stand against the infernal weapons being brought to bear against them.

It didn't help that many of the men who made up the Fal Carrachian Guard were sellswords. Many had served in various Guards prior to coming to New Caledonia, but their ties to Fal Carrach and the Governor were tenuous at best. They would cut bait and run as soon as they concluded they stood little chance. Realizing that, Oselnik left them to their fate, thinking of what he needed to do to keep himself alive.

As he had done so many times before, he would twist the narrative to ensure that his role in what had swiftly become a disaster would be viewed in a more positive light.

His soldiers didn't have the courage to stand and fight. They were cowards.

Oselnik couldn't keep them there. He couldn't stand against the Carlomin soldiers on his own. Not with those terrible weapons the Carlomin woman unleashed upon them. Not with all of his soldiers fleeing.

Unable to keep his soldiers in the fight, he recognized reluctantly that he had no choice. He had to retreat. He had to bring order to a desperate situation. He had to demonstrate his abilities as a leader.

Better to regroup. Better to develop a new strategy to take on the woman the Governor so desperately wanted to kill.

It was necessary to their success. He had seen the worst that Talia Carlomin could offer. Once they countered that, they could finish her.

Oselnik had convinced himself of the story he kept repeating under his breath. And if he could convince himself, he believed that he could convince the Governor as well.

Yes, he definitely had made the right decision to leave his soldiers to their fate. He could use the burning Roosarian pier to his advantage as well.

He had seen the flames, feeling the need to investigate. He was concerned about the Governor. He needed to make sure that she was all right.

With his soldiers unable to stand against the Carlomins and their lethal, never before seen weapons, Oselnik had no choice but to return to the Rock when the fire consumed the pier.

A more than plausible tale, Oselnik decided.

To prove his utility to Hakea Roosarian and remain in her good graces, he hoped to pick up the pieces from here.

But as he walked around the table and more closely examined his new strategy, Oselnik began to grasp that there might not be any pieces for him to pick up. Not if the destruction of the Fal Carrachian Guard was so complete that few of his men remained to stand against the Carlomins.

"But I won't," Oselnik said magnanimously. "I'll use you instead. The Huntress will want you back. She'll want you alive. I'm sure that we can come to a deal."

For a few seconds, there was silence except for Oselnik's dagger scratching across the stone table.

Then, unable to contain himself, Davin laughed.

The Captain was a coward at heart. Davin had known that a minute into his first encounter with him.

Now Oselnik confirmed that he was a fool as well.

"Talia Carlomin doesn't care about me. I'm just a gladiator. She cares about getting her revenge."

Oselnik stopped walking around Davin, standing in front of him now, his back to one of the cells that held several Stalkers. His positioning blocked one of the beasts from staring at Davin, which earned the Captain a growl of anger.

Oselnik ignored the Stalker, unconcerned, confident in the strength of the steel and Roosarian's hold over the monster.

"I think she does. You've been at her side since you arrived in Ballinasloe."

"I was forced upon her," Davin chuckled. "She didn't have a choice." Davin shook his head in amusement, the only part of his body that he could. "I'm sure she's glad to be rid of me, and you're a fool for thinking otherwise."

"I find that hard to believe."

"Believe what you want," Davin murmured, having grown tired of the conversation. "It's the truth. You can offer me to her if you want, but she won't do a deal with you. She knows what she has. What's within her grasp. She's not going to give that up for anyone or anything."

"Really? And what does she have?"

"Victory," Davin snorted, the effort sending a few spikes of pain through his body.

"She has won nothing yet," Oselnik replied with as much heat as he could muster, which, because of his concern for himself, was very little.

"She has won, and you know it. That's why you haven't killed me yet. That's why you're hesitating instead of doing what you need to do."

"You talk too much, gladiator."

"I speak the truth, coward, and you know it. You just don't want to hear it."

Oselnik came in tight to him then, his face red with rage. He pushed the tip of his dagger into the gash on Davin's arm, the blood flowing more freely now.

Davin ignored this new source of pain as best as he could. This was nothing compared to some of what he had to deal with on the white sand. Or at least he tried to convince himself of that, just as Declan had taught him.

Doing so by focusing on the growl from the Stalker that was standing just behind Oselnik, only the steel cage separating them. The monster had stepped out of the gloom and was right up against the bars.

Davin smiled even as Oselnik pressed the point of his

dagger deeper into the wound. He knew what he needed to do if he was to have any chance of getting himself out of this mess.

Risky. More than just dangerous. Likely suicidal.

But when had that ever stopped him before?

"Keep talking and you'll experience the most painful death that you could possibly imagine, gladiator. Instead of the Crimson Giant you'll simply be known as the Crimson Pulp."

"Really? I can imagine something quite painful and gruesome, yet I doubt you have the capacity to do that to me."

Oselnik twisted the tip of the dagger in Davin's arm, hoping to earn a squeal for his effort. "I'm sure I can accommodate you."

Rather than screaming in pain as Oselnik wanted him to, Davin forced out a laugh instead. "You came back here to the safety of the Rock because you failed to take the Carlomin enclave. How very sad. You can't even accomplish the most straightforward of assignments."

Oselnik stared hard at Davin with an overpowering hate, then pulled his dagger free. With his other hand, he hit Davin hard across the jaw, needing some way to release his boiling anger.

Davin kept laughing, unable to stop himself, even as blood and spittle flew from his mouth.

Enraged, Oselnik punched Davin hard in the gut, then the arms, then the chest. Anywhere he could. Davin unable to stop him.

Davin stopped laughing as new waves of pain shot through him. But he didn't cry out. He refused to cry out. Instead, angering Oselnik all the more, he gritted his teeth and kept his mouth shut. Using the pain to enhance his clarity.

Oselnik hit him a few more times, reopening several wounds that had scabbed over, new rivulets of blood trickling down and dripping onto the stone floor.

The Stalker's low growl became more than just a growl as a result.

"I failed at nothing!" Oselnik shouted, hitting his prisoner wherever he could with a manic fury. "We'll still take the compound."

"No you won't. It's too late. You missed your chance." Davin chuckled softly again, ignoring the more intense waves of pain that rushed through him, black spots growing larger before his eyes. "You have proven your incompetence, Oselnik. You're no match for the Huntress. No one can best her. And because of that she's going to take Ballinasloe and Fal Carrach. When she does, you're dead. Sirena Makarin will come looking for you. And when she finds you, she'll strip the meat from your bones."

Oselnik couldn't move. He couldn't think. His rage knew no bounds as his face purpled and his knuckles turned white. He was about to strike the gladiator again when a harsh voice from the other side of the doorway stopped him.

"Leave him be, Captain Oselnik. He's only speaking the truth, isn't he?"

Hakea Roosarian stormed into the chamber in a cold fury. All that she had built was collapsing around her. She didn't know where it had all gone wrong, and she didn't know what to do to stop it.

Talia Carlomin had turned the tables on her, and Roosarian had no idea how to turn them back in her favor.

Even so, she had promised herself that she would right her floundering ship and gain her vengeance as soon as she escaped the woman's blade and slipped into the secret passageway.

To do that she would start with the gladiator. She would hurt him, and that would hurt Talia Carlomin as if Hakea slid a knife through her heart. She was sure of it.

A pity, really. She and the gladiator could have had such fun together.

"Governor Roosarian, I cannot allow him to speak such lies. I cannot ..."

"Enough, Captain Oselnik. I've already sent some Stalkers to hunt on the Carlomin docks because of your lack of success. You had three times as many soldiers as she did. Yet you still failed to break through the gate. Is that not correct?"

Oselnik searched for some other excuse that he could offer. The keen glint in the Governor's eyes suggested that it would be better not to provide one now. "That is correct, Governor Roosarian. But there was little that I could do. The soldiers did not have the skill or the courage necessary for what was required of them."

"Are you not responsible for their training Captain Oselnik?"

"Yes, but Governor Roosarian, I can assure you that I did everything that I could ..."

"To spend as much time as possible in the brothels lining the waterfront," Roosarian interrupted, her tone sharp, commanding, revealing that she had no desire to listen to any more of her Captain's poor attempts to dissemble.

"Governor Roosarian," Oselnik tried one more time. "I assure you that ..."

"Enough, Captain." Roosarian's patience, never good to begin with, had come to an end the minute she had been chased from her apartment by the woman she wanted dead. "Davin Noname is telling the truth, isn't he? You're here because you failed there."

"Yes, Governor Roosarian," Oselnik grumbled quietly, barely able to get the words out, yet knowing as well that he couldn't lie. Not with the look that the Governor was giving him.

"I would be disappointed if I was surprised," Roosarian admitted, "but I'm not, because I knew what I was getting when I accepted you into my service. I knew that you would fail to meet my expectations, I just never knew how badly that would prove to be the case."

"I'm sorry, Governor Roosarian," Oselnik mumbled, trying to save his position and possibly his life. "Truly. I admit to making some mistakes. But I promise that in the future ..."

"Step over there, Oselnik. If I have need of you, I'll let you know."

Oselnik reluctantly moved back toward where Roosarian pointed, closer to the cage holding the Stalker that was fixated on Davin ... and his blood that continued to color the tile red.

Roosarian stepped up next to Davin then. She shook her head sadly as she took in the beating that he had suffered. The many wounds that would have caused most other men to scream in agony yet to the gladiator appeared to be nothing more than the bites of a fly. Then she smiled and tsked.

"To think that you could have been on the top floor of the Rock with me if only you had made a smarter decision."

"Live and learn," Davin replied quietly. He tried to keep the spark of humor for which he was known both in his voice and his eyes. From the expression that Roosarian gave him as she looked at him upside down, he didn't think he had succeeded, his pain getting in the way.

"It seems that you won't be doing either, Davin Noname. Living or learning. And I had such high hopes for you."

Davin thought of several witty rejoinders, yet he didn't have the strength to offer a single one. He was tired. He was in pain, almost every part of his body pulsing with a scorching agony. He didn't have the patience or energy for her gloating.

He was done. He wanted to move on to the next stage in this encounter. The final act.

The question was, would it be him or Roosarian who got the chance to set the scene.

"Just do what you're going to do and be done with it. If it's time for me to go to the other side, then so be it."

"A last wish that I'm happy to fulfill. Have no fear of that." She reached down, stroking his cheek gently. "And then you'll fulfill mine."

"And what wish would that be?" Davin asked, regretting the question as soon as it left his mouth.

With the pain of his injuries it was taking him longer than he would have liked to piece together what Roosarian had in mind. His eyes widened when it came to him, remembering her original threat, feeling fear for the first time in a very long time.

"You're going to kill Talia Carlomin for me," Roosarian purred. She leaned over him, their lips no more than a few inches apart.

At the same time, she pulled out a vial of the black liquid that Talia had taken with her when she escaped the Rock. The heinous substance that turned a human being into a monster.

Roosarian leaned back again. She pulled the stopper free. Reaching down, she grasped Davin's cheeks with her free hand, pressing them together and forcing his lips apart.

He tried to fight what she was doing to him, but he couldn't. Barely able to even move his head. The leather straps were too strong. Roosarian's grip too unyielding.

He resolved then and there that it was better to die horribly then become something horrible.

Unbeknownst to Roosarian, who stared at him with a manic glee, Davin did the only thing that came to mind. The only thing that might save him. The thing that could and likely would kill him. But better a real death than the fate Roosarian had in mind for him.

With what little give he had in the strap holding his left wrist, he flicked a few droplets of blood toward the steel cage.

They fell short.

His eyes widened in alarm.

Roosarian, grinning down at him with a savage expression, tilted the vial toward him. He thought that he could actually see that first black droplet, that only black droplet that would be needed to turn him into a Stalker, at the very edge of the glass, about to fall through the air and right down his throat.

He flicked his wrist as vigorously as he could. One time. A second time. A third. Watching out of the corner of his eye, unable to take his gaze away from that drop of black, as his blood splattered across the steel bars.

"What the ..." Oselnik began to exclaim, a few drops of blood marking his shoulder and his cheek.

Davin didn't think it was going to work. He had hoped that it would, but he knew after his years of instruction with Declan what hope was truly worth.

Roosarian was going to get her wish. She was going to turn him into a Stalker. She was going to task him with killing the woman who had claimed a piece of his heart.

That drop of black, almost free from the vial, hung there, less than a heartbeat away from dropping into his mouth. Who he was, both body and spirit, was going to be stolen from him.

He couldn't believe that this was how it was going to end. He had thought that once he escaped the Pit nothing could kill him.

He had been a fool to even consider that notion.

He was about to become a walking nightmare.

And he could do nothing to stop it.

The instant before the drop fell from the vial and trickled between his lips, Davin heard an improbable sound that was music to his ears.

The screech of metal being ripped free followed by the sickening squelch of a claw sliding into flesh.

Taken by surprise, Roosarian pulled back the vial before the drop fell into Davin's mouth and relaxed her grip on his cheeks, she and Davin both looking toward Oselnik at the same time.

A bloody claw extended through the Captain's gut, the

soldier standing there, looking down in shock at the terrible wound.

Then the claw was gone, Oselnik dropping to the ground, not long for the living.

The Stalker so obsessed with Davin's blood stood there. So desperate for a drink, the monster had ripped the steel door free from its hinges.

"What do you think you're doing?" demanded Roosarian, her voice commanding, yet tinged with fear as well. Clearly, she had never anticipated that a Stalker might disobey her. "Return to your cage. This instant."

The Stalker stared at Roosarian, offering her a deeper growl.

Roosarian had not yet realized what was going on, but Davin had. The compulsion she had placed on the Stalker couldn't compete with the monster's desire for blood. It's desire to feast.

Davin concluded then that he was going to die. That strapped down to the slab he was no more than an offering. Still, better to die at the claws of a Stalker than become a Stalker himself.

Startled when the Stalker stepped toward her, Roosarian dropped the vial, the glass shattering when it struck the stone floor, the Governor of Fal Carrach having no choice but to dodge out of the way when the Stalker sliced for her gut.

She escaped by a hair. Scrambling away. Screaming in rage.

Davin, who was so certain of his coming death, couldn't believe his luck. The Stalker missed the Governor but cut right through the strap holding his left hand.

Even better, he had a few seconds to try to save himself. The Stalker wasn't interested in him. At least not yet. The monster only had eyes for Roosarian, chasing the Governor around the table upon which he lay.

With his one free hand, Davin reached over and undid the

strap holding his right wrist. As soon as he was done, he dropped back down onto his back, avoiding another swipe by the Stalker as the monster swung and missed once again, Roosarian ducking beneath the stone slab on the other side.

Roosarian went for the door, but the Stalker was too fast, forcing her back toward the far side of the chamber and the cage that held three other monsters, all of them watching what was happening with an insatiable hunger, their blood-red eyes shining brightly.

Left on his own again and not knowing for how long, Davin worked as quickly as he could, lifting himself back to a sitting position, undoing the strap wrapped around his left ankle.

Hearing a metallic screech, he looked to his right side.

The Stalker swiped at Roosarian again, missing, instead slicing across the lock that held the cell door in place.

For just a second, Davin's heart stopped. He feared the Stalkers could free themselves because of the damage to the lock. But apparently not. The door still holding.

He immediately went back to work on the last strap, his nerves almost getting the better of him. He breathed a short-lived sigh of relief when, after several fumbling attempts, finally he freed himself.

And just in time.

He rolled off the stone slab, falling to the floor, the Stalker's claw, aimed for the Governor and missing again, chipping out several splinters of stone where his leg had been just moments before.

He peeked over the top of the slab.

The Stalker that had tasted his blood was standing there. Focused on him now.

Roosarian was gone. She had slipped through the open doorway and escaped when she had the chance.

Now it was just him and a very hungry Stalker.

The monster didn't wait, lunging for him across the table.

Davin dodged out of the way, escaping by a whisker, his many injuries slowing him down.

The Stalker tried once more.

Davin ducked. Again evading the razor-sharp claw, although just barely.

The Stalker swiped for him again and again and again, Davin always keeping the table between him and his attacker. Stumbling around it as best as he could, trying to bring his legs back to life.

His clumsy efforts would have been funny if not for the fact that Davin was going to die if he didn't figure out some way to win this game.

But then the Stalker wised up to what Davin was doing.

The monster jumped up onto the slab and stared down at Davin.

There was nowhere for him to go now.

Rather than cowering in fear, the gladiator looked right back at the monster, giving him a broad grin. Then he drove the thin metal spade that he had found in the mason's toolbox beneath the slab right through the top of the Stalker's clawed foot.

The monster shrieked in pain, swiping for Davin.

He dodged out of the way, then slashed with the spade, slicing across the back of the Stalker's leg.

Davin heard a snap, thinking that he might have gotten lucky. That he might have cut the Achilles' tendon.

When the Stalker stumbled upon trying to put weight on its injured leg and then fell off the slab entirely, he knew that he had.

Best to make the most of his luck.

For just a heartbeat, Davin entertained the thought of leaping over the stone and driving the spade through the Stalker's eye.

The protesting shriek of rusty steel stopped him.

He looked over his shoulder.

The door of the other cage, the one that the floundering Stalker had sliced with its claw, swung open.

Three Stalkers stood there, each one staring at him. Although none had yet exited the cage.

Realizing that this was the best that he could hope to accomplish against the wounded Stalker, Davin stepped back slowly from the stone slab. Keeping his focus on the Stalkers, he staggered and almost fell.

He glanced down briefly.

He had almost fallen over Oselnik's body.

When he looked up again, he saw that one of the Stalkers had exited the cage so quietly that he hadn't even heard the monster.

Davin took another step back.

The Stalker watched him. More than just curious. Then the monster took a step toward him.

Out of the frying pan and into the fire.

Davin hated it when one of Declan's sayings popped unbidden into his mind.

He took another step back toward the door.

The Stalker mimicked him again, drawing closer.

Out of the corner of his eye, Davin watched as a second Stalker exited the cell just behind the first, the third about to do so.

Giving in to the urge to get as far away from these monsters as he could, Davin turned and ran through the entrance in a lurching gait, slamming the door closed behind him and throwing the bolt at the very same instant that he heard the crunch of a Stalker slamming against the steel.

Davin didn't waste any time, keeping the bloody spade in his hand as he tottered more than trotted down the passageway, seeking some way to exit the Rock.

The Stalker had almost knocked the steel door from its

hinges with just that one blow. Another, which he knew would be coming soon, would knock it clear off.

And he had no desire to be anywhere near when that happened.

Fighting one Stalker was bad enough.

Three at one time in his current condition was insane.

25

BATTLE ON THE WEB

"Are we ever going to get out of here?"

"It is a bit aggravating, isn't it?" Jakob agreed.

"My brother is aggravating," Lycia clarified. "This is infuriating."

Leaving the beach, they had worked their way around the forest of stalagmites, then sprinted through the tunnel at the far end.

They were grateful that the Stalkers hadn't caught up to them. But it was a fleeting relief, because they still weren't free of the mountain.

The corridor led them to another massive grotto, the spheres of light staying with them.

The underground hollow appeared to be just as large as the one that they had just exited. There was no pool of water to swim across with eels biting at their heels. Definitely a good thing. Still, they were uneasy. Both assuming that there was another lethal obstacle that they'd need to overcome.

From where they were standing atop the ledge, they just weren't sure what it was yet.

Once again, massive stalagmites and stalactites greeted them. However, instead of metal rails and carts as was the case in the last chamber, they gazed out upon an intricate network of ropes, ladders, platforms, and wooden beams.

Built across the top of the chamber, the flowstones once again used to anchor and support the construction, a web of walkways unfolded above the floor of the cavern.

"I'm assuming whoever built the tracks in the other chamber constructed this as well," murmured Lycia.

"I would assume so," nodded Jakob.

"The tracks were corroding. Flaking away. I don't know that I'd trust rope and wood if it's been here for hundreds of years."

"A valid concern," Jakob agreed.

Just like Lycia, he wasn't anxious to test his luck.

Their entry point was only a few feet in front of them. A frayed rope ladder that he hoped could bear their weight. He had his doubts. If the steel tracks had deteriorated so badly over time, he was certain that this latticework of rope and wood wasn't in much better condition.

"Maybe we should take our chances on the cavern floor," suggested Lycia. "We'd be able to go faster. With the ropes wearing thin and the wood likely rotten, we'd be pushing our luck."

Lycia was right. They could go faster if they made their way across the floor of the grotto. And speed was the key, because the Stalkers were gaining on them.

Right next to the ladder that would take them up into the web was another ladder that gave them access to the ground.

Although he couldn't see them because the spheres of light penetrated the darkness only so far, he knew from his use of the Talent that there were several more tunnels that led into this chamber. Some at the same level that he and Lycia were on. Others that opened onto the cavern floor.

Several Stalkers already were in those tunnels. It would only be a few minutes more before those monsters joined them in the cavern.

If they were ever to make it out from beneath this mountain, they needed to get moving. Now.

Still, Jakob hesitated. It didn't feel right. Trekking across the hollow seemed too easy.

Why go to the trouble of putting in place such an intricate web several hundred feet above the cavern floor if there wasn't a good reason to do so?

"You ready?" asked Lycia.

She only took a few steps toward the ladder that would give them access to the bottom before Jakob reached out and grasped Lycia's arm, holding her in place.

"Wait a second."

The back of his neck was prickling. That was never a good sign. And it wasn't because of the Stalkers hunting them.

Directing a few of the glowing orbs closer to the ground, he stared at the rough terrain below them. Because of the stalagmites, there was just as much shadow as light.

"What's the matter?" Lycia sensed his unease.

"I'm not sure," he replied softly.

At the edge of the gloom, near the base of the stalagmite closest to them, he thought that he glimpsed a faint hint of movement.

It could have been nothing. No more than a trick of the dim light.

Then again, it could be something much more worrisome.

Leaning on the side of caution, Jakob shot a handful of spheres from his palm, the light drifting down and burning away the shadows.

"I'm glad you stopped me," whispered Lycia.

"So am I."

"You know what those are?"

"Cave dragons," Jakob replied, nodding. He should have expected as much. Nothing in life was ever easy. And certainly not here within the mountain.

As a part of Jakob's education, his father had taught him about some of the more dangerous animals in the Realms. It was the soldier in him, Jakob understood. Dougal wanted him to be prepared for anything.

Dougal also taught him how to fight any animal in the Realms that could kill him.

Of course, just because Jakob had that knowledge didn't mean that he had any desire to challenge the beast that he was staring at.

And with good reason. Because Dougal had been very clear.

Don't fight a cave dragon if he could avoid it.

"Are they like black dragons?"

"Black dragons?" asked Jakob. "You've come up against those behemoths?"

"In the Trench, yes. Nasty. Bad-tempered. Fast."

Jakob was impressed. Anyone who didn't have a cracked mind avoided the Trench at all costs. To enter that forbidding place willingly demonstrated a courage – and the potential lack of good sense -- that few could match. He'd have to ask Lycia about that experience if he ever got the chance.

"Black dragons are similar to the cave dragons that haunt caverns like this one. Nasty. Bad-tempered. Just a smaller version."

The beasts, which weren't very large compared to some of the other species of dragon -- twelve to fifteen feet from nose to tail -- still were formidable adversaries. Just like their larger brethren, they were incredibly fast. Relentless once they picked up the scent. Vicious as well, snouts filled with needle-sharp teeth.

"Wonderful."

"Even better, one bite from a cave dragon and you're dead."

Lycia thought about that. "Poison?"

Jakob nodded.

Perhaps a cave dragon's only weakness was that it was land bound, never having developed wings because of its habitat. However, it had developed a different characteristic that gave it a distinctly virulent advantage.

Because game was scarce in mountain hollows, all it took for a cave dragon to catch its prey was one bite. Just a scratch would be enough, in fact. A fast-working toxin was transmitted through its saliva. Once that poison got into the prey's bloodstream, it was only a matter of minutes before the quarry died.

"So there's no chance of making our way across the cavern floor?"

Jakob didn't reply immediately. Thinking.

He had maintained the link between them that he had crafted with the Talent so that Lycia could see what he saw when he extended his senses. She knew just as well as he did how close the Stalkers were and how quickly those monsters would be joining them.

Just then another cave dragon stepped into the light. And then one more. Three in all having burrowed out a nest in the stalagmite that Jakob and Lycia would have no choice but to pass if they climbed down the ladder as part of their escape from the mountain.

Sending a few more spheres of light in among the flow-stones, Jakob caught glimpses of movement deeper within the grotto.

Jakob had no idea how many cave dragons lived in this cavern or whether they made use of the tunnels in the base of the walls to hunt, and he didn't care.

Three of the beasts were more than enough for him to make his decision.

He would follow his father's advice. Don't fight a cave dragon if he could avoid it.

Though they may not like it, he and Lycia had another choice.

"No chance," Jakob confirmed. He nodded toward the ladder that would take them up to a wooden walkway just above them. "Did you want to go first?"

"You'd like that, wouldn't you?" countered Lycia.

"I was just trying to be polite," Jakob replied, refusing to allow Lycia's comment to fluster him.

"Well, then, if that's the only reason," Lycia said with a wink, "I'll go ahead."

She pushed past him, climbing up the ladder as quickly as she could, ignoring how the fraying ropes swayed dangerously when she put her weight on each rung, several splintering and cracking ominously.

Jakob shook his head in amusement, keeping a careful eye, ready to help Lycia if the rope ladder gave way under her. Thankfully, it didn't. And once she reached the platform that was thirty feet above them, he followed, a small smile curling his lips.

Only a woman who had fought black dragons in the Trench would tease him knowing that the Stalkers were springing their trap while cave dragons watched from below, hoping that they would make a mistake.

Lycia was waiting for him on the elevated walkway, which swayed slightly from side to side because of their weight and movement. Despite its battered and worn appearance, the deck held strong. A welcome discovery.

"Can we trust what we'll be walking across?" asked Lycia.

"I wouldn't."

"Not very helpful."

Jakob shrugged. "You already knew the answer."

"Then what would you suggest?" Lycia asked in a reasonable tone.

"Go as fast and as carefully as we can."

Lycia stared at Jakob for just a second, lifting an eyebrow. "Fast and careful? Those two tend to be on opposite ends of the spectrum."

"I agree."

"Then how are we ..."

Jakob stepped in close to Lycia then, giving her a confident grin. "Are you always so difficult?"

"Only when I'm about to die," she replied, the small smile tugging at her lips widening.

"Then you must be under the threat of dying quite a lot," murmured Jakob.

Lycia couldn't disagree with his logic, giving him a nod, choosing to ignore the faint taste of his sarcasm.

"Come on," Jakob said. He started walking across the rope and wood bridge that began to sway as soon as he set foot upon it, his sights set on the dark tunnel in the wall several hundred yards distant. He didn't bother to look down, having no doubt that the cave dragons below were tracking them, anxious for a misstep and a fall.

There was a way out from beneath the mountain. It was just a question now of whether they would get there before the Stalkers got them.

"Why are you going first this time?"

"So you can look at my rear for a while. It's only fair."

Lycia snorted out a laugh. "And this is what you do when your life is at risk? Make jokes?"

"Better humor than being difficult," Jakob replied, giving her a shake of his bum as he walked farther along the airborne trail.

Jakob's action earned a louder snort of laughter from Lycia. "You would get along quite well with my brother."

"Can't wait to meet him."

"You might regret saying that," Lycia countered.

Knowing where he wanted to go, having used the Talent to

map his way through the maze of ladders, walkways, bridges, and beams, Jakob picked up the pace, Lycia staying right behind him.

Remarkably, despite the age of the wood and rope, other than for a few rotten boards that gave way beneath their feet on the hanging bridges, there were no other miscues or obstacles that slowed them down.

The web was sound and solid. Remarkable for a construction centuries old. Thanks to that competent craftsmanship, they might just stand a chance.

In less than a quarter of an hour, Jakob and Lycia made it almost all the way across the latticework hanging above the cavern floor. The cave dragons followed their progress intently, but without a slip, the beasts could do nothing more than stare hungrily at their escaping prey.

Sensing the end of their odyssey, Jakob and Lycia moved even faster when they reached the last bridge, this one constructed of wood that was fixed to the top of two of the taller stalagmites. The crevice that would allow them to exit the mountain was just a few hundred yards in front of them.

They both smiled as they sensed the end of the chase, catching a welcome glimpse of sunlight peaking from between the jagged rock, the long-sought exit calling to them.

Their relief lasted for less than a heartbeat, the shriek of a Stalker stopping them in their tracks.

Looking back over their shoulders, the monster stood at the far end of the cavern. Not yet having attempted the crossing. But they had little doubt that the Stalker and the rest of its brethren would have little trouble traversing the obstacles to their front.

"Can we make it?" They were so close to the exit. Nevertheless, Lycia was worried. She knew just how fast a Stalker could be.

"There's only one way to find out," replied Jakob.

Lycia nodded, giving Jakob a determined look. Then she was gone, sprinting down the walkway toward the natural light.

Jakob was about to follow Lycia, but he hesitated, then stayed where he was when he saw seven ... eight ... no, nine Stalkers join the monster that had reached the cavern first.

He could follow Lycia. He could try to bring down the exit just as he had collapsed the entrance to the mine, his action of many hours before beginning their race through the mountain.

However, he knew the truth. The Stalkers would find more of the passageways that pockmarked the mountain and catch up to them somewhere else in the snow-capped peaks.

Whether within the mountain or without, the monsters would continue to hunt him. They would never stop. They couldn't stop. Not with the compulsion placed upon them.

It was as he and Lycia had discussed.

Kill or be killed.

Jakob should have run after Lycia. That was the most sensible thing to do.

But as his father had liked to say, there was little reward without the risk.

Jakob sensed an opportunity, and he wanted to make the most of it.

So he held his ground.

The Stalkers staring at him across the expanse of hanging walkways and bridges growled with pleasure, even offering a few soft screeches, excited that their prey no longer ran from them.

Then the Stalker who had been the first to face off against Jakob lifted its fanged maw to the ceiling. Screeching in triumph. Ordering its brethren forward.

In a blur, the Stalkers began working their way toward him, climbing ladders, sprinting across bridges and walkways, sliding down cords, weaving their way through the maze of wood and rope, intent on being the first to drive their claws into the quarry who had evaded them for so long.

"Jakob!" called Lycia.

Bathed in sunlight, she had reached the crevice that led out of the mountain. She had assumed that Jakob was right behind her.

A mistake on her part.

Apparently he felt the need to play the hero. Another quality that reminded Lycia of her brother, Bryen as well. Always willing to take a risk if it saved someone else from having to take that same risk.

More than aggravating. Infuriating as well.

"Jakob!" she called again. "Move your ass!"

Jakob ignored her. He needed to wait just a few seconds more if what he wanted to try had any chance of working.

All of the Stalkers were navigating the latticework now, their movements near the cavern ceiling having caught the attention of the cave dragons. Those animals moved silently around the stalagmites, their eyes never leaving the new prey that had entered their den.

Jakob just needed all of the monsters to reach a certain spot on the web. A point of no return.

The question was, how much longer could he wait?

The two Stalkers in the lead had advanced across the web at a breathtaking clip. They were now only two hundred yards away from him, that distance fading with every clawed foot that crunched into the wood. Yet the last Stalker at the back of the pack was only a few walkways beyond the ladder that provided access to the web.

If Jakob didn't get them all, then he'd only be delaying the inevitable rather than putting an end to this hunt.

He needed that last Stalker to pick up the pace. But how to give the monster a nudge?

The two Stalkers in the lead were only a hundred yards away now and closing fast.

In response, Jakob began to step backward slowly along the walkway.

All of the Stalkers were where he wanted them to be. Except for the last one.

Only seventy-five yards now, the pair of Stalkers closest to him advancing with greater speed, driven forward by their hunger to kill.

Jakob had to entice the last Stalker farther out onto the web. His only thought for doing that was to enrage the monster. But he needed to do it at a distance of several hundred yards. Only one option came to mind.

Jakob crafted a sphere of energy just as Aloysius had taught him in the shadow of the Shattered Peaks.

Fifty yards.

He could hear the Stalkers' clawed feet digging into the wooden bridge as they raced toward him.

With a flick of his wrist, the compressed ball of white-hot power shot across the cavern.

Jakob didn't hit the Stalker, who at the very last second leapt forward to evade the attack. But he didn't need to. Instead, Jakob struck the rope bridge the monster had been standing on.

The effect was instantaneous.

The bridge burst into flames, the ancient, brittle rope burning to ash in seconds.

The Stalker reached for a rope just to its front, desperate to get off the collapsing walkway and escape its fate.

Too little too late. The distance too great, the Stalker missed the rope, dropping through the air to smash heavily against a stalagmite, then sliding and tumbling down the last hundred feet to come to rest in a battered mess.

Somehow, the monster survived the fall without incurring a serious injury.

The Stalker had no chance to congratulate itself, however, because the cause of its death stood right in front of it.

Two very hungry dragons.

The Stalker was fast, although not as fast as the cave dragons.

The animals lunged at the same time. One grasping a leg, the other an arm, the Stalker shrieking in fear and pain as the cave dragons engaged in a tug of war.

"Jakob!" Lycia yelled again. Her tone was more than insistent this time. Almost despairing in fact.

At her call, Jakob pulled his eyes away from the struggle between the cave dragons, focusing once again on the monsters racing toward him.

Only twenty-five yards away.

"Jakob!" Lycia shouted, her voice now carrying a tinge of fear and a great deal of anger.

Jakob ignored her, waiting for the exact right moment.

He acted when the closest Stalker was no more than ten yards away. He wanted to ensure that none of his hunters escaped what he had planned.

And none of them did.

Calling on the Talent, Jakob sent a stream of energy blasting through the chest of the Stalker that had been preparing to launch itself at him.

When that monster crumpled to the wooden walkway, Jakob didn't bother to target the other Stalkers. He concentrated instead on the web keeping the monsters safe from what lurked below, using the power at his command to destroy the latticework, burning rope and wood crashing down to the cavern floor, the Stalkers mixed in with the wreckage.

Just a second before nine Stalkers were racing toward him, already savoring their victory and thinking of how his flesh would taste. The next they disappeared, along with almost all of the latticework that had hung above the cavern for he didn't know how long.

None of the Stalkers escaped his attack.

Jakob stood at the very edge of the walkway, the last few boards charred to a crisp, surveying the detritus.

Several of the Stalkers weren't moving, either stunned or dead from the fall of a few hundred feet. A few were back on their feet, somehow surviving the perilous drop. Injured. Unsteady. Yet still focused on him.

Although not for much longer.

The cave dragons were ravenous. They began with the easy prey. Digging through the wreckage, making quick work of the unmoving Stalkers. Then hunting the surviving Stalkers with a frightening silence, seeking to gain that single bite that would release the toxin in their saliva into their prey's bloodstream.

Jakob turned away, having no need to watch what was happening below him.

He didn't feel any regret or remorse. He just wanted to get moving. He wanted to get out from beneath the mountain.

When he looked up, Lycia stood right in front of him, shaking her head.

With her mercurial expression, he didn't know if she was amused or annoyed.

"Show off much?" the gladiator finally said.

Jakob didn't know how to reply at first. Then he shrugged. "My father always said, don't fight fair. Fight to win."

"Did he now?"

"He did."

"I've heard much the same myself. More than I cared to, in fact."

"Is that right?"

"It is," Lycia confirmed with a nod.

Jakob could tell that Lycia wasn't done with him. He

expected a lecture or a remonstration. And he wasn't in the mood for either. To prevent that from happening, or at least to delay it, he motioned for Lycia to lead the way out through the crevice.

"Shall we?"

"You're a pain in my ass," grumbled Lycia.

Yes, definitely annoyed.

"I do what I can," Jakob replied.

26

THE POOL OF INK

The space carved out of the granite had an arresting design. It appeared as if a gargantuan claw had reached into the mountain and ripped free a handful of rock, leaving the hollow behind.

Ursina had discovered the chamber during the construction of the Shadow Keep, the workers assigned to setting the citadel's foundation breaking through the stone wall by mistake and revealing the cavern. A green moss growing along the walls and on the ceiling offered a bright luminescence, requiring her to use only a few torches to light the large expanse, the flickers of flame sending streaks of green and red playing through what she had claimed as her private workspace. So private that only her husband knew of it, although he preferred not to come down here unless absolutely necessary.

Even the miners who had found it had no recollection. She had made sure of that.

Needing time to think after her confrontation with the Protector, Ursina went to the one place in the Shadow Keep that offered her any solitude. Her mind wandering for the past hour. Trying and failing time after time to break through the muddle of her thoughts.

She castigated herself for having managed the conversation so poorly.

More worrisome, how could he have found her out so easily?

She had become incredibly skilled at hiding her unique abilities. Even her fellow members of the Order of the Magii had failed to identify them until she made a foolish mistake.

A mistake that her mother noticed.

Obviously, the Protector was more dangerous than she anticipated. Nevertheless, she still believed that he was necessary to her achieving her goal of protecting Shadow's Reach from the Wraiths.

Especially now that the Wraith who is not a Wraith was in the wind. If she didn't provide the Wraith Hunter with what he required, then their temporary truce would fade away just as the Wraiths faded into the Murk.

Ursina realized there was no way around it.

She couldn't wait for the Wraith who is not a Wraith to be taken. She needed to employ a different approach to protect her fortunes here in the Northern Territory.

Otherwise, all that she had worked for would be cut from her like a Wraith's dagger across her throat.

Ursina needed to claim the Protector as her own so that she could harness his power. It was her only chance to prevent the Wraiths from conquering Shadow's Reach and slaughtering its inhabitants.

Doing that would require that she kill Aislinn. A price that she was willing to pay.

Her niece by marriage had no meaning in the larger scheme of things. Besides, she was no more than a potential impediment.

Ursina would make certain her husband believed Aislinn's

tragic death was nothing more than an accident or a poor decision on the young woman's part.

That was a challenge for later, however.

She needed to concentrate on the first and most critical step.

How to claim the Protector and his power?

Ursina sensed the energy within the young man the moment that she met him. Although she rarely felt any concern when dealing with someone skilled in the Talent because of her own strength in natural magic, he was different.

There was a power within the Protector that she didn't understand that went beyond that of the Talent.

And after her encounter with the Protector, she reluctantly admitted to herself that she had little chance of defeating him if it came to a combat between them.

That knowledge still stuck in her craw. Souring her. Yet she was too much of a realist to allow that unpleasant reality to impede her larger designs.

Ursina shook her head in resignation. She needed to do something that she didn't want to do.

But before she did, she wanted to see if she could obtain more information that would be useful to the conversation that was to come next. She needed to learn more about the Protector.

And there was only one way to do that.

Closing her eyes for just a moment, Ursina took a deep breath, seeking to settle her nerves. Once she felt calmer, she called on the Curse concealed within her, relishing the sense of invincibility that always flowed within her blood when she touched the power granted to her by her Master.

Not having the time to savor the feeling as she so liked to do, she sent a stream of the tainted power into the pool of black that lay perfectly still within the massive cauldron that had been chiseled out of the wall a thousand or more years before.

The inky liquid stirred at her touch, the water rippling, then bubbling and swirling, taking on a life of its own.

Thinking of the Protector brought his image to mind. For several minutes, nothing happened other than the inky mixture raging with greater violence.

Then, when the churning liquid threatened to escape the rim of the cauldron, images began to form, emerging out of the agitated pool of black and hovering in the air right in front of Ursina's eyes. One after the other, a kaleidoscope of remembrances all focused on the Protector.

Ursina had learned from her Master that there was a collective memory to the Curse that stretched all the way back to its birth. With her skill, she had the strength and ability to tap into it.

However, she didn't have the power to travel back very far in time. She could pull free only the last few years. Still, she believed that limited view would suffice for her purposes.

The images gained greater clarity as the roiling black became more volatile, showing her the Protector through the eyes of those touched by the Curse who had interacted with or faced off against him.

The first was Tetric, the former Advisor to the Belerons. She had known the Dark Magus.

Ursina had worked with him for a time with the goal of weakening the Belerons to help prepare the way for the coming of the Ghoule Legions, those servants of the Curse waiting just beyond the Weir in the Winter Pass. She didn't keep to that task for very long, though, her responsibilities taking her away from the Caledonian capital until she was forced to flee from the Kingdom.

Ursina watched and listened to the several confrontations between the two. She learned a great deal, including the fact that Tetric had come to fear the Protector. With good reason it seemed.

The number of images multiplied, coming faster, as she continued to send a stream of the Curse into the boiling ink.

Ursina viewed the Protector through the eyes of Ghoule Elders and the Ghoule Overlord. And then finally her own.

She began to realize that she was right to worry about what he could do, because through these memories she was beginning to understand the extent of his power.

Yet she could not see all that she wanted to see. Several images that she believed were essential to her understanding the true nature of the Protector and the power he wielded were blocked by a cloud of misty white that she could not pierce no matter what she tried to do.

That had never happened before.

It didn't make sense.

After several failed attempts at destroying the mist, Ursina realized reluctantly that she had learned all that she was going to learn. Particularly after she watched the Protector in the Sanctuary, fighting the Golem, rebuilding the Weir, and then thwarting the Ghoule Overlord.

She also observed through the eyes of the monster that sought to conquer Caledonia an event that caught her off-guard, glimpsing the mortal wound that the beast had inflicted upon Sirius, the Magus forcing the Ghoule Overlord to fight him before he could go after the Protector.

Ursina thought that she would feel more emotion when Sirius slumped to the ground, his blood staining the translucent stone that formed the top of the spire. Yet she didn't. She barely felt anything at all.

The only real emotion that she experienced then was anger. At herself. She should have paid more attention to the legend of the Ten Magii, the Seven Stones, and the Weir while she resided in Haven.

But she hadn't. That was her mother's area of study, and she had no interest in working in any area that was of interest to her mother.

Back then, Ursina had wanted nothing more than to get away from her mother. And she had achieved her objective, although not in the way that she hoped that she would.

Ursina cursed herself for a fool. She should have done this earlier. Even though she couldn't learn all that she wanted to learn, she could have used the information that she was obtaining now to her advantage.

When she first met the Protector, she had sensed the power that he controlled. More of the Talent than she had sensed in anyone else before.

What she found even more interesting, however, was that there had been a faint trace of the Curse as well. More like a residue.

Why that would be the case she couldn't say with any certainty.

That finding bothered her immensely, although not as much as the fact that she had discerned another distinct power within the Protector. A power that she thought she should be able to identify but couldn't.

That power teased her, understanding of what it might be at the very edge of her comprehension. And she no closer to solving the puzzle despite the tainted potency running through her veins.

Having learned all that she could through the memory of the Curse, irritated that some critical images were being kept from her, Ursina realized that it was time to move on to the task that she had been dreading but was essential to what she wanted to do.

Staring down at the roiling pool of black, Ursina sent several more streams of the Curse into the seething cauldron.

In seconds, a frigid mist floated up above the boiling, pitch-black fluid, touches of frost appearing on the rim of the cauldron. A cold settled within the cave shortly thereafter, making Ursina shiver uncontrollably, bringing to mind the time she spent in the Frozen Waste, the temperature dropping precipitously while a frosty wind blasted through the cavern.

Fighting to keep her teeth from chattering, frost beginning to work its way out from the base of the cauldron, along the stone floor, and then up the walls, she remained where she was. Enthralled by the roiling liquid and the billowing mist, unable to take her eyes away from it.

She was close, that thought frightening her and thrilling her both at the same time.

Ursina sent a final stream of the Curse into the bubbling ink. With that last effort, the swirling mist coalesced into a thicker cloud that began to spin slowly just above the surface of the liquid, then faster and faster, until finally it took shape.

A cloaked figure who stood slightly over six feet tall, grey mist seeping out from beneath the cowl, stared down at her, the pitch-black eyes freezing her in place. As the distorted figure gained greater substance, becoming more a part of the Natural World, the temperature in the chamber dropped to well below freezing. Ice thickening along the walls, icicles began to reach down from the ceiling.

"You have found it," whispered the spirit that hovered above the inky pool, the liquid now calm, flat. Frozen.

"No, Ancient One." Ursina's breath was frosty, her lips blue, the cold almost paralyzing. Yet the creature's voice made Ursina's entire body shiver worse than the frigid temperature ever could. "We have the one piece that I acquired for you but not the other." She made sure to remind him of her efforts on his behalf, not wanting him to forget the lengths to which she had gone to acquire the first artifact. "Have no fear, however. We will acquire the other artifact. It is only a matter of time."

"Then why have you requested my presence, Ursina? I have

other matters that require my attention. More important matters."

"The Protector, Master."

"What of him?" whispered the Ancient One, his voice quiet, glacial, insistent.

"There is a power in him, Master."

"He is a Magus," the Ancient One replied, a hint of annoyance in his tone. "Of course there is power within him."

"Yes, Master," Ursina acknowledged with a bow of her head. "Yet there is a power beyond even that of the Talent. I don't understand what it is. I fear that because of this power, the Protector might hinder my efforts to acquire the other artifact for you."

"What kind of power?" questioned the Ancient One, his curiosity piqued.

"A power stronger than I have ever encountered before, Master. Other than the power that you wield, of course."

Ursina's reply intrigued the Ancient One even more. He closed his eyes for several seconds, allowing his unique and singular perception to focus on the Protector.

As he did, his misty shape flickered. It took a great deal of effort for him to send a small portion of himself into the Natural World, only able to do so because of the liquid beneath him. If he lost his concentration, there was a risk that he would slide back into the Spirit World before he was ready to return.

The light in the chamber clouded as the Ancient One continued to fade, the green algae dimming in brightness as the Lord of the Spirit World pulled in the energy around him.

The black pool started to boil once again, demonstrating a mesmerizing violence. Another gust of frigid wind blasted through the chamber and threatened to douse the few torches set along the wall.

Then, with a violent flash, it all stopped, a strange calm settling within the cavern.

"The Seventh Stone," hissed the Ancient One. "I never thought it possible. I believed that repository of power was lost to me forever when Viktor Keldragan stole it from the Temple of the Ghoules."

A bolt of fear shot through Ursina upon hearing that. Why hadn't she thought of that possibility? That could explain why she couldn't see all the memories of the Protector, those images occluded by that ancient jewel.

She could only hope that her failure to identify that prized artifact so essential to building the Weir went unnoticed by her Master, because she knew from experience that he had little patience for incompetence.

"The Seventh Stone is a part of the Protector," whispered the Ancient One, nodding his head as he took in the ramifications of what that meant.

"The Seventh Stone? How is that even possible?"

"A good question," confirmed the Ancient One, "but that doesn't matter. You are right, Ursina. This Protector is more than he seems. Much more."

"That's why I thought I should bring him to your attention, Master."

"You were right to do so. I must have the Seventh Stone."

"You want me to kill him for you?"

"You cannot kill him, Ursina," the Ancient One chuckled in a bitter tone. "Although I admire your confidence, it is misplaced."

Ursina nodded, not bothering to say anything, not even annoyed by his condescending reply. She was simply pleased that she avoided a reprimand or worse from her Master.

"I want you to bring him here to me," the Ancient One continued. "I will kill him. And when I do, I will take the Seventh Stone."

"The Seventh Stone can free you from the Spirit World?"

"No. But its power will prove useful when I am free."

"I will do as you command, Master."

"I know you will, Ursina." The shadowy figure stared down at her, his deep black eyes swirling like the liquid over which he floated. "You understand the penalty if you fail?"

"Yes, Master."

"Good. Now what is it that you truly want from me? You did not ask me to come here just because of the Protector."

Ursina gulped, another bolt of fear shooting through her.

"I cannot find the Bearer of the Blood Ruby. My trace of him is gone. As is the Skath you sent to aid in the hunt. That is why I requested your presence and aid, Master. I acquired the Blood Dagger for you. And I can acquire the Blood Ruby as well. I just need some means to locate the Bearer."

She chose not to reveal to her Master that she needed the Bearer for another reason as well. Because only with the Bearer could she appease the Wraiths, or at least keep their focus off of Shadow's Reach for a time until she figured out how to deal with them with the power at the Protector's fingertips. Certain that even if she gave the Wraith Hunter and his Lord what they wanted, any agreement between them would only last so long as it served the purposes of the Wraiths.

Ursina thought that the Ancient One would be angry with her because of her admission, but he wasn't. Instead he appeared more thoughtful than anything else.

"It seems that we face several challenges, Ursina," he replied finally. "This Protector who could be useful to me and the Bearer of the Blood Ruby. Do you not know who the Bearer is? I gave you that trace only because I thought it would make it easier for you to find our prey."

Ursina didn't want to admit the truth, but she feared the consequence of deceiving her Master more than she already was. "No, Master. I do not. At least not with absolute certainty. I have only claims, not confirmation."

The misty figure shook his head in disappointment. "I am

surprised, Ursina. I expected so much more from you. Then again, I cannot blame you for your failure since the Skath returned to me without the prize I seek."

"The Skath returned to you, Master?" That revelation shocked her. Nothing could escape a Skath once that creature had been given the scent. "I wasn't aware."

"Yes, my Disciple lost the trail as well, Ursina. And that is why I will not punish you for your failure."

Ursina gave in to the terrifying fear that shivered through her body, unable to stop it. Grateful for the reprieve because she understood that with the Ancient One there were worse punishments than death.

"Thank you, Master," she mumbled, her teeth chattering from the bone-deep cold.

"Thank the Bearer of the Blood Ruby, Ursina. I cannot punish you if my Skath failed as well. The Bearer has disappeared just as you said, and somehow he is hiding himself from me."

"You cannot locate him?" Ursina was unable to control her natural curiosity. She didn't think that such a thing was possible, so she didn't know how to interpret what her Master revealed to her.

Her shivering subsided somewhat when she realized that she was not going to face the ultimate punishment that she feared. At least not on this day.

"Yes, he has, but there is one thing he could not hide from me, Ursina. His identity."

Using the power that he exercised as the ruler of the Spirit World, the Ancient One scoured through the memories of the Stalkers and the Wraiths who had fought and died in New Caledonia, piecing together their memories. Feeling what they felt. Thinking what they thought. Sensing the power contained by the individual who had sent so many of them to his domain.

The one named the Lord Kestrel by his peers.

Through the creatures touched by the Curse, the Ancient One put together an image of this Lord of the Highlands from their remembrances, a figure taking shape right next to him so that Ursina could see for herself.

The scar that was visible on his cheek. The minutest detail of the double-bladed dagger that he held in each hand revealed. The sharp green eyes that flashed in the Murk. And the power that pulsed from the jewel tied around his neck.

"Do you recognize him, Ursina?" asked the Ancient One.

"I do, Master." She had never met the young man before, but she had heard enough about him to know exactly who the figure that had taken shape right in front of her was. The claims now proven.

"I thought you might." However, the Ancient One was not yet done.

He pulled free from the Stalkers and the Wraiths their last memories of fighting the Lord Kestrel, all the while becoming more and more certain that this young man was indeed the Bearer of the Blood Ruby, the power within him unmistakable.

Confirmation came when the Ancient One watched one of the Wraiths die at the hands of the Lord Kestrel.

It was a hard fight. A good fight. The young man quite skilled in the use of the haladie that he had taken as his own.

When the combat was done, the Wraith slumped on the ground, the thick mist of the Murk playing around the dying creature as his blood seeped out from the slice across his throat, the young man sheathed one of his daggers.

The Ancient One saw the mark on the palm of his hand then. The burn that told him that this young man had to be the Bearer of the Blood Ruby. It could be no one else.

And somehow the young man who had evaded the Skath he had sent to Caledonia in search of the Blood Ruby had learned to shield himself from him.

A potentially frustrating reality. However, the Ancient One

chose not to see it as such. Because he knew that the Bearer of the Blood Ruby would be drawn to the Blood Dagger.

The Bearer would be drawn here.

To the Shadow Keep.

It was inevitable.

The Bearer would have no choice, the urge to join the two artifacts into one too much for him to resist.

So the Ancient One didn't need to hunt the Bearer. He simply needed to be ready for when he appeared.

"Leave the Bearer to me," the Ancient One said with a quiet finality. "I will finish him when the time is right."

"You do not want me to find this Lord of the Highlands for you, Master? I promise you, Master, I can. I will. I will take the Blood Ruby for ..."

"You will do as I command, Ursina," the Ancient One hissed, the sharpness of his tone bringing the Dark Magus up short. "You will leave this Lord Kestrel to me."

Ursina nodded. She would not disobey her Master, at least not openly. "And the Protector, Master?"

"You will bring the Protector to me, Ursina. And to do that, I will gift you a few tools that should help you in that endeavor."

27

A FIRST STEP

"That was quite a display you put on." A vein of irritation trickled out from Lycia's voice. "Very final."

Jakob closed his eyes for just a few heartbeats, taking a deep breath, seeking to keep his temper in check.

He was tired. He was hungry. Every part of his body ached. He had more minor wounds and scrapes than he could count.

And ever since he and Lycia slipped through the crevice that allowed them to exit the mountain, she had been needling him about what he had done.

Standing against the Stalkers on his own. Waiting to act until the very last heartbeat before the Stalker closest to him sank its claws into his flesh.

Lycia hadn't liked him doing that. She hadn't liked it at all.

She had a lot to say about the risk that he had taken. About why he should never have done as he did. Placing himself in such grave danger.

Even so, Jakob believed that Lycia understood his decision. Why he allowed the Stalkers to get so close to him in order to ensure that he could remove them from the fight with a single strike.

That it was her concern for him that made her keep pecking at him.

That she was frightened for him.

Because she couldn't hide everything that she was feeling behind those dark eyes of hers.

He understood as well that part of her irritation came from the fact that he hadn't allowed her to stand by his side.

He had taken her agency from her, and she hadn't forgiven him for it.

For Lycia, it came down to choice, and he hadn't given her one.

At least that's how she viewed what he had done. While he viewed his decision as trying to make sure she got out of the mountain even if he didn't.

She hadn't said as much, but he saw it there written all over her face.

Lycia believed that she should have been standing right by his side when the Stalkers attacked. Thinking back on it now, perhaps she should have. Perhaps she was right.

But he didn't want to raise all those issues with her now. He wasn't in the mood to have such an intense conversation, and she clearly wasn't either.

"I was just doing what I thought I needed to do." Jakob attempted to hide his own vexation with a smile. "That's it. Nothing more than that."

"Put yourself at such a great risk knowing how much depends upon you?" scoffed Lycia. "That's what you were trying to do?"

"It was a calculated risk. No more than that."

"I disagree. It was a risk that you didn't need to take."

"Even though it paid off?" Jakob challenged, his eyes flashing. Revealing just how close he was to losing his temper.

"Yes, what you did worked, but that's not the point. Not everything will work out for you if you continue to place yourself in such dangerous situations. All it takes is a tiny mistake or a bit of bad luck and ..."

"I didn't have a choice," Jakob cut her off, perhaps a bit too sharply.

"You always have a choice," Lycia responded, her voice containing more heat to match his. Her tone and posture confirming that she wasn't going to let this go.

"Then we can agree to disagree," Jakob replied.

He didn't want to continue on this track. He knew what would happen if he did.

Jakob closed his eyes, struggling to calm himself. This conversation with Lycia reminded him of Senna. She had challenged him when she thought it was necessary. Which, thinking back on it, had been quite often.

Senna didn't do that just to be difficult. Rather she did it because she wanted Jakob to see all that was going on around him. She wanted him to see more than just his perspective. She wanted him to realize that the reality he constructed for his decisions and actions wasn't the only reality.

His was just one viewpoint, and a biased one at that.

It seemed that Lycia had the same desire in that regard as Senna. And, strangely, for the first time since losing Senna, he wasn't filled with a bottomless sadness and regret.

The guilt that he felt for her death had receded into the background. Still there, just not as intense and crippling.

For the next several minutes, Jakob and Lycia walked side by side in silence down the trail that curled back around the outside of the mountain. Eventually, the path would deposit them at the stockade, which, thanks to the Talent, Jakob already had confirmed now belonged to the Highlanders.

His gambit had paid off in the end.

He considered making that point to Lycia, but she was grumbling to herself under her breath, so he thought better of it.

Jakob grumbled to himself then. He should have been pleased by the outcome of their battle in the mountain. And he was.

Yet the woman walking beside him had a unique knack for tempering his satisfaction. It was much like throwing cold water on a flame.

If he tried to make his point, she would simply tell him that yes, his gambit had paid off in the end. They had achieved their objective.

She would agree that they had stuck a very large stick in Torstan Sharperson's eye, and thankfully not at too great a cost to the men and women fighting for him.

Even more important, from what Duff had said when Jakob connected to him with the Talent, they had rescued one hundred and thirty-three people forced to work in the mine.

Truly an impressive victory.

Yet even though he hadn't known Lycia for very long, he was absolutely certain that if he offered any of that as part of his argument, she would simply give him that hard-eyed stare she used so effectively and frequently, maybe even grunt, and then tell him once again that he was still a fool to do as he did. That the risk that he had taken hadn't been worth it.

"Do you think those cave dragons have any path that they can follow to come out of their den?"

"No, there's no way for them to leave the mountain," Jakob replied, grateful that Lycia was making an effort to move past the argument they had been having since walking back out into the light. "There's no crevice or tunnel that connects to their den that would allow them to reach the surface."

"Not even the main entrance to the mine?"

"Not even the main entrance, and even if it had, it doesn't any longer."

Lycia glanced at Jakob from the side, offering him a raised eyebrow. "You're proud of yourself, aren't you?"

Jakob frowned, eyes tightening, having lost patience with the gladiator. "I'm proud of the Highlanders. We came here for a specific purpose, and we achieved that purpose."

"Yes, and you have every right to be," Lycia replied, her voice quiet though still intense. "The Highlanders fought well. They also fought for you."

"The Highlanders fought for themselves. For this Territory that we want to make our own."

Lycia stepped in close to Jakob then, placing herself right in front of him. Her quick movement and her hand on his chest forced him to halt abruptly so that he didn't walk into her.

Even so, the gladiator moved so swiftly that there was less than a knuckle between them when she stopped.

"The Highlanders fought for you." Lycia's eyes blazed with a fire that was almost frightening, wanting Jakob to grasp her point. "Yes, they fought for the Highlands. They fought for themselves. But they wouldn't have done that, they wouldn't have had the chance to do that, if not for you."

"Yes, maybe so, but ..."

"There is no maybe, Lord Kestrel." Her use of his title stopped him cold, as was her intention. She never called him that. He didn't like it. That was fine with her. She hoped that Jakob getting a little angry would help him to better understand what she was communicating to him. "They fought for you." She tapped him not so gently on the chest with her finger each time she said a word to emphasize her point. "They. Fought. For. You."

Several replies were perched on the tip of his lips. None of them useful. None of them anything more than a useless complaint.

Jakob closed his mouth, realizing that it was open. At that very moment, another of his father's many sayings passed through his mind.

Why complain? Why not do?

His father was right. He didn't like the situation he was in. He wasn't comfortable with it. At least not yet. And he didn't know if he ever would be.

But that didn't matter.

What mattered was the doing and not the complaining.

He heard the truth in Lycia's words. And he couldn't ignore what she was telling him. No matter how much he might want to.

Yet even after being proclaimed the Lord of the Highlands at the Grove, he hesitated to acknowledge what accepting that title, what accepting that responsibility, truly meant.

He closed his eyes for just a second, taking another deep breath. He could continue to argue. There was no purpose in doing so, however.

Lycia was right. He hated that she was right. But she was.

He needed to accept who he was now. His title did have a meaning, a resonance, that somehow made him different from what he had been before he took up the mantle put on his shoulders by the Highlanders.

He needed to be who he was now. Because the future of the Highlanders rested with him.

Lycia reached up to him then, placing a dirty palm streaked with the blood of Stalkers on his cheek.

Jakob opened his eyes, surprised by her action. He had never before seen such sympathy on Lycia's face.

"This is hard for you, Jakob. I know that. It's quite obvious to those who see you for who you are."

Jakob smiled at that, spying a side of the gladiator that intrigued him. "And who am I?"

"You're much like a gladiator on the white sand, seeking the best path to ensure you live to fight another day. However, unlike combats in the Pit, you're making decisions about how you move, how you maneuver, based not on what you need, but on what the people who believe in you need. That's a much harder responsibility to manage."

Jakob closed his eyes again, taking another deep breath just as his father had taught him to do, seeking to center himself. To push away the stress that threatened to take hold.

When he opened them again, Lycia was smiling.

"It's a heavy burden."

"It is," Lycia agreed, "just as it should be."

"Sympathetic one moment, hard as steel the next," Jakob murmured.

"That's probably the nicest thing anyone has ever said to me."

"You're welcome," Jakob replied, giving Lycia a grin. "I will try to do as you suggest. I will *try* not to take any unnecessary risks."

Lycia heard how Jakob emphasized the word *try*. She chose to let it go. Feeling like she had made some progress with him, she would take that small victory.

"Good," Lycia replied, removing her dirty palm, but not before giving him a gentle pat on his cheek. "Because if you don't I'll be the first in line to give you the spanking that you deserve."

"Promises, promises."

28

FIENDISH EVENING

Aislinn walked up next to Bryen. He stood on the balcony, deep in thought.

With the Talent, she sensed the residue of the power that only minutes before Bryen had been using. That gentle sizzle in the air was fading slowly and reminding her of what it was like growing up in Battersea when the lightning storms flashed across the Silent Sea, the electricity in the air making her hair stand on end.

"It can't be good if you were talking to two of the Ten Magii." Aislinn said it in a lighthearted tone, giving him a nudge with her shoulder. "What did you do, Bryen?"

"Nothing that I didn't say that I was going to do," he replied softly, coming back to himself.

"Bryen?" Aislinn prodded, slightly worried by his response.

Still leaning over the railing, he explained briefly what had occurred during his interaction with Ursina. What they talked about. How she tested him. How he responded. How he left it between them.

"You're certain?" Aislinn asked.

"Absolutely certain."

She turned away from the deepening darkness, leaning back against the railing, the sun setting and leaving an orange hue to the clouds. "I can't really say that I'm surprised."

"Why not?"

"There's something wrong with my uncle."

"With Kendric? What do you mean?"

"He took me around the city today, showing me all the work that's being done," Aislinn explained. "More times than I'd care to remember, he wasn't there."

"Wasn't there?" Bryen didn't understand. "What do you mean by that?"

"He's sick, although he won't admit it. At least not to me." Aislinn sighed, frustrated and worried. "One moment he's talking nonstop. Voluble. Smiling. Making jokes just like he did when I was younger. Then that part of him disappears. His eyes glaze over. He just stands there, completely oblivious to what's going on around him."

"Is he lost in thought?"

"No, he's not. I'm certain of it. His mind has gone somewhere, and sometimes it takes several minutes to return. Then when he comes back to himself, he clearly doesn't know what happened. Or rather he does know but he doesn't know what to do about it."

"Did you talk to him about it?"

"I tried. Several times in fact. He shrugged it off when I did. First, he said that I was mistaken. Then he told me that it was just because there was so much that he was dealing with, his brain never turning off as he sought solutions to the many problems plaguing the work being done here. The last time I asked him, he admitted that he'd been feeling a bit under the weather for a while. That's as far as he was willing to go."

"Under the weather?"

"His words, not mine. But clearly, though he's trying to hide it, he knows what's going on. And it scares him. I can see it in his eyes. Whatever is afflicting him frustrates him as well, which suggests to me that it's been happening for longer than he's letting on."

"A natural ailment?"

Aislinn bit her lip, then she shook her head. "No, it's not. I used the Talent to try to get a better sense of what was ailing him when he faded out right before we began to make our way back here."

Bryen nodded, understanding dawning as he took in Aislinn's sorrowful look. "The Curse."

Aislinn nodded. "Based on what you just told me, it would make sense. It has to be Ursina. She's done this to him."

"To her own husband?"

"If she's a Dark Magus, she must have a good reason. Although for the life of me I can't understand what it could be."

Bryen turned and leaned back against the railing, the darkness over the city now complete, the pyres set atop the city walls coming to life. "It makes you wonder, doesn't it? When I spoke with Juliette earlier today, she said that the day Ursina arrived in Shadow's Reach, she paid her respects to your uncle. From that point forward they were inseparable."

"You don't think ..."

"I don't know what to think. I only suspect after what you just told me."

Aislinn considered what Bryen was suggesting. The conclusion she reached made her sick to her stomach. "It would make sense, wouldn't it? In the Southern Marches, my uncle was known for stringing several women along at one time. My father never thought that he would settle down. He said that Kendric didn't believe in committing himself to one person, and his actions and decisions confirmed that. At least back then. He didn't want to be tied down, always trying to keep his options open."

"Yet here, within a day, Ursina is on his arm. They're

married shortly thereafter. Now they exercise the power of the Governorship together."

"I would argue that Ursina exercises that power," challenged Aislinn. "She's using my uncle as a mouthpiece."

"A fair point with a great deal of truth to it."

"It would make sense as to why my uncle is acting strangely," Aislinn mused.

"It would. And as you know, even just a small application of the Curse will affect someone over time. It burrows into the heart and the soul. Once there, it's very hard if not impossible to excise. I can tell you that from personal experience."

Aislinn remembered what it had been like for Bryen when he battled the Curse that sought to consume him before the Seventh Stone gave him the ability to lock away that tainted power. It was a memory that she preferred to keep buried.

"Are you sure it was a good idea? To provoke Ursina? You've put us on perilous ground."

Bryen thought about her question, then gave her an apologetic grin. "Probably not. I'm sorry. When she revealed that she was a Dark Magus, I couldn't help myself."

Aislinn shrugged. "She will do what she believes she must regardless. We're even more of a threat to her now than we were before. It's just a matter of when she makes a play for us. You probably just pushed up her timetable, and that might help us. It might increase the chances of her making a mistake." She reached out with her hand, squeezing his forearm. "You know, sometimes you don't have to shake a beehive to see what's going to happen. Sometimes you can let events play out naturally."

"Yes, but where's the fun in that?"

"Bryen ..." Aislinn began, her scolding tone reminding him of Rafia, although he kept that to himself.

"Sorry, you're right. I'll try to be a little more patient and circumspect next time."

"Thank you."

"Now what would you like to do about all this?"

"You mean with respect to Ursina?"

"In part," Bryen said. "My speaking with her and then Viktor and Mikayla helped me to better understand why the essence of evil that lies on this city feels as it does."

Aislinn studied Bryen, a curious expression on her face. She had sensed it as well, having talked with Bryen about it. The Curse for certain. That certainly wasn't surprising now that she knew Ursina was a Dark Magus. But just like Bryen, she had no real understanding regarding the faint, unique strain that ran through the miasma of evil concentrated somewhere in the Shadow Keep.

"Also with respect to the Curse?"

"Yes," confirmed Bryen. "Perhaps we follow your suggestion and see what Ursina is going to do next. In the meantime, we hunt down the source of the Curse, because I'm certain it's not Ursina. She's using it for her own purposes, but it's not coming from her. She's just a vessel."

"Then where is it coming from?"

Before Bryen could reply, he pushed himself off the railing and reached for the Spear of the Magii, which was leaning against the door that led back into the room. Aislinn stepped up next to him, both of them watching as a black mist seeped into their apartment through the narrow gap at the bottom of the door.

"This can't be good."

"No, it can't," Bryen agreed.

The black mist swirled into a massive cloud that enveloped the foyer. Once all of the noxious haze entered the apartment, it split apart into four strands that spun and wove with a mesmerizing speed. In seconds, four creatures stood in front of them, born from the mist.

"What are they?" Aislinn held her sword in her hand.

The monsters were humanlike in appearance, although

there were some key differences. Their misshapen skulls were too large for their tall and thin bodies, the weight of their heads pushing their shoulders toward the ground and giving them a stooped appearance. Their teeth were sharpened to a fine point that matched their razor-sharp, three-digit claws. And their black eyes burned with an almost unquenchable hatred for the living.

"Fiends," Bryen replied quietly, never expecting to come across such creatures.

"How could you possibly know that?"

"Declan told me about them."

"How does he know about Fiends? I've never heard of them."

"That's a story for another day."

"All right. Then what are they?"

"Monsters from the Spirit World."

Aislinn shook her head, grimacing, then muttering a few curses softly under her breath. This day was only getting better and better. "What are monsters from the Spirit World doing here?"

"I don't know for sure, but I think we just got our answer as to what might be aiding your aunt."

"She's not my aunt," Aislinn replied through clenched teeth.

"According to the law she is."

"We're going to argue about this now?" challenged Aislinn.

"No, sorry. Just trying to get a better feel for our opponents." The four monsters stared at them, hissing, scratching at the air on occasion. Yet they made no move to attack.

"Any advice on how to fight them?"

"No, that never came up."

"Wonderful."

"One suggestion, though, based on what Declan told me."

"What was that?"

"Don't let them dig their claws into you. Because of where they come from, they're not seeking to feed on your body. Rather, they're seeking to feed on your spirit. Once they get a grip, even with just a single digit, you'll have a hard time escaping them. They'll drain you of your spirit and then your body will die shortly thereafter."

"Always the bearer of good tidings."

"I do my best," Bryen replied with a half-hearted grin.

Aislinn grinned as well, then gave Bryen a nod. There was no point in waiting to see what the Fiends were going to do. Better to seize the initiative right from the start.

Aislinn rushed forward, Bryen right behind her. Their steel cut through the air in front of them, forcing the Fiends back toward the doorway and deeper into the foyer.

A good strategy they believed. A necessary one as well.

If they allowed the Fiends to break free from the confining space of the entryway, the monsters could come at them from more than one direction, and neither wanted to deal with that challenge.

Now, only two of the Fiends could attack at one time, and Aislinn and Bryen took full advantage of that limitation. Still, it was a difficult fight. Because the Fiends were devilishly fast. They also learned the hard way that these monsters were impervious to steel.

Several times Aislinn slashed with her sword and Bryen sliced with his spear, both believing that they were about to deliver fatal blows, only to discover that their steel passed right through the Fiends' bodies. The creatures turned to mist before the blades struck and then regained substance just a heartbeat after Bryen and Aislinn pulled back their weapons.

"This isn't a good sign," grumbled Aislinn as she ducked a swipe from the Fiend standing before her, then lunged, knowing that her sword was going to pass right through the

Fiend's gut, doing no harm whatsoever. "Declan didn't tell you anything else that might be of use?"

Bryen didn't reply immediately. Instead, he brought the Spear of the Magii up lengthwise, catching a Fiend's claw on the haft, then kicking forward with his right foot. At least in that respect he could make contact with his adversary's body, the blow catching the monster in the chest and sending him tumbling back into the two Fiends behind him, giving Bryen a brief respite.

"No, but I do remember something that Rafia told me."

"What was that?" Aislinn slashed with her sword from shoulder to thigh and then swiftly brought the steel back around, thigh to shoulder. She did no harm to the one Fiend that was still standing, the other three struggling to their feet, but at least she kept the beast off her for a little while longer.

"When in doubt, use the Talent." To make his point, Bryen infused the two blades of the Spear of the Magii with the natural magic of the world.

Aislinn was quick to follow his lead, her sword glowing brightly.

The tenor of the clash changed in that instant.

Recognizing the danger, the Fiend to her front charged at her, slashing for her throat with his deadly claws. She got her sword up in time, although the monster's charge forced her back a few steps.

Aislinn shoved the creature backward and lunged, recognizing that the creature behind it was preparing to rush out of the foyer. She couldn't allow that to happen. She stood little chance against these creatures if they succeeded in coming at her from two directions at once.

Her thrust did the trick. The Fiend, overextended and off balance, couldn't get out of the way in time. The monster stumbled back into its brethren as Aislinn's Talent-infused steel slid into its side, the sickly smell of burning flesh that permeated the room joined by a shriek of agony.

Tangled with the Fiend behind it, the monster couldn't get out of the way when, with the speed of a scorpion's striking tail, Aislinn pulled her blade free and then stabbed again, this time right through the Fiend's throat.

With a sad gurgle, the creature collapsed onto the Fiend behind it. That beast attempted to throw his dying brethren to the side so that he could leap at Aislinn, the tight space of the foyer impeding his efforts.

That gave Aislinn a moment to watch Bryen, who was working hard to keep his adversary contained. The Fiend facing off against him clearly had little patience, and the beast had paid for it. A half-dozen oozing burns marked his body where Bryen's blades had struck true. And she believed that lack of patience was going to cost the Fiend his life.

Just then, shrieking in rage, the pain of his sizzling wounds driving the creature forward, the wounded Fiend dove toward Bryen, both claws outstretched.

Bryen stepped out of the way with a graceful ease and with a single swipe took the Fiend's head from his shoulders.

Aislinn turned back to take up the challenge of the Fiend who was now standing across from her.

Much to her surprise, the beast leapt to the side and away from her. Joining his brethren, the Fiend targeted Bryen's back.

Her Protector was exposed, having already brought his spear up to block the slash of the Fiend now opposing him. There was no way that he could defend against this second attack in time.

Aislinn didn't even think, raising her free hand toward the Fiend diving through the air. A blast of the Talent shot from her palm, the creature letting out a gurgling hiss that drifted away the instant the beast, a large hole where its chest used to be, slammed against the far wall of the foyer.

"Thank you," Bryen nodded to Aislinn.

"I do what I can to protect my Protector."

"Funny," Bryen replied, although he didn't smile. Instead, he and Aislinn turned to face the last Fiend, which they had backed up against the door, the bodies of its three dead brethren scattered around the floor.

The cornered Fiend screamed in rage. Several times he stepped threateningly toward them. But seeing the blazing weapons blocking his path, the creature always scurried backward, avoiding the touch of the Talent.

Realizing the dire nature of his circumstances, the Fiend shrieked one more time, then much to Bryen and Aislinn's astonishment, the creature transformed into a swirling black mist that shot back out beneath the door.

A strange silence settled around them as Bryen and Aislinn looked at the door and then at one another. Clearly, they were both thinking the same thing.

They knew who had sent the Fiends to kill them. The question now was whether they should take the risk that they were both contemplating.

Reaching the same decision at the very same time, with a nod that Aislinn returned Bryen tore open the door. They raced after the mist, catching a glimpse of it as it fled down the hallway and then disappeared around the corner.

All the while, Aislinn couldn't get the thought out of her head that something wasn't quite right.

Were they chasing the Fiend? Or were they being led by the nose to wherever the Fiend wanted them to go?

She didn't know, and that's what worried her. Because clearly Ursina exercised a great deal more power than Aislinn ever had imagined possible.

A power that she and Bryen needed to destroy. Just as they had done in Caledonia.

BONUS MATERIAL

If you really enjoyed this story, I need you to do me a HUGE favor – please follow me on Amazon and BookBub. And if you have a few minutes, consider writing a review.

Keep reading for two chapters from *Storm in the Darkness,* Book 8 in my series *The Tales of the Territories.* Order Book 8 from my author website PeterWachtBooks.com. Also available on Amazon.

PETER WACHT

STORM IN THE DARKNESS

Storm in the Darkness
By Peter Wacht

Book 8 of The Tales of the Territories

This book is a work of fiction. Names, characters, places, and incidents are the product of the author's imagination or are used fictitiously. Any resemblance to actual events, locales, or persons, living or dead, is coincidental.

Copyright 2025 © by Peter Wacht

Cover design by Ebooklaunch.com

All rights reserved. In accordance with the U.S. Copyright Act of 1976, the scanning, uploading, and electronic sharing of any part of this book without the permission of the publisher constitute unlawful piracy and theft of the author's intellectual property.

Published in the United States by Kestrel Media Group LLC.

ISBN: 978-1-950236-49-7

eBook ISBN: 978-1-950236-52-7

Library of Congress Control Number: 2024912750

❀ Created with Vellum

1. TIME TO ADVANCE

"It is as we thought it would be, Lord." The fog masked the Wraith Hunter's features but for the pure black of his eyes and the sense of tangible menace that radiated from his thin, emaciated frame.

The Wraith Lord stood silent in the Murk, the wispy tendrils of grey swirling around him. At first, he didn't bother to acknowledge his second in command. Lost in thought. Finally, he nodded.

The arrangement his Hunter had made with the Dark Magus had little chance of success to begin with. To learn that it had failed to bear any fruit didn't surprise him.

No matter.

That poor though expected result simply meant that the time had finally come.

That conclusion sent a spark of pleasure through him.

There would be no more poking and prodding. He would grasp with clawed hands what belonged to him and his Horde. He would remake the world into what it needed to be for his Wraiths to reign supreme.

"Where do our preparations stand?"

"Our Scouts are returning from the mountains of the Dragon Spine. They have finished their work there, ensuring that we have nothing to worry about to the north of the Wyld."

"How soon?"

"They will be here in a matter of days, Lord." The Wraith Hunter smiled, the flesh on his skeleton-like face drawn even more tightly across his skull, his sharp, fanglike teeth briefly revealed. "They are hungry, Lord. They are ready for the Hunt."

"They should be," rasped the Wraith Lord. "We have waited a long time for this. Centuries. So many centuries." He was silent for a time, considering his next steps. "We cannot allow anything to prevent us from achieving what we have dreamed of doing for so long. What we must do."

"Yes, Lord. We are excited, Lord. We are ready. The Scouts understand. The Hunt will allow us to make the world our own. We will make our history what it should be."

The Wraith Lord shifted his dead-eyed stare to his Hunter. They looked much the same in appearance. Yet there was a clear distinction with respect to the Wraith Lord.

All of the Wraiths were creatures of the Murk.

Born to it.

Bred in it.

Because of that, all of the Wraiths had been touched by the Curse, a residue of that ancient evil flowing through their veins.

However, the true source of the Curse in the Murk, the source of the Curse for all the Wraiths, resonated within the Wraith Lord. The reservoir of corrupt power that only the leader of the Wraith Horde could tap into was unimaginable. Almost uncontainable. And it was that tainted energy that the Wraith Lord would unleash on the vermin to the south.

An energy that contaminated everything and everyone it touched. An energy that twisted all that it kissed into a tool for its own use.

With his first step, so it would begin.

The end result?

The world of man would die, the Wraiths building right on top of it.

"I selected you as my Hunter for a reason. You know that. There were many candidates, but of them all I believed that you were the most driven. The most capable. The most willing to do whatever is necessary to achieve our ends."

"Yes, Lord." A trace of nervousness touched the back of the Wraith Hunter's throat. He didn't translate what his Master was telling him into a compliment. Instead, he perceived it as something else entirely. A warning. "I am grateful for that, Lord."

"You should be." With a flick of the Wraith Lord's clawed hand, the wispy grey tendrils that separated him from his lieutenant spread apart, clearing a space between them. A reminder of the power at the Wraith Lord's beck and call. "You should also be wary. Even frightened. You are cognizant of the cost of failure?"

The Wraith Hunter quietly cleared his throat, understanding that he needed to answer in a strong voice. "I do, Lord. You have nothing to worry about."

"I don't?" mused the Wraith Lord. "Despite the stories that I've heard?"

A flush of shame rushed through the Wraith Hunter. He had hoped that those stories would not reach the ears of his Master. Not until he had dealt with the one obstacle that threatened to slow their advance.

He really shouldn't have been surprised. He should have assumed that his encounter with the Wraith who is not a Wraith would come back to bite him.

There were a select few in the Horde jockeying for his position as the Hunter. Sowing the seeds of worry in the mind of their Lord was an expected and time-tested tactic. If he was in their position, seeking his place, he would have done the same.

"Yes, Lord. You have nothing to fear. I promise you that. All will go as planned. Nothing and no one will be able to stand against us." He made sure that he said the last with as much confidence as he could muster. Yet, as he did so, a hint of doubt took root in the back of his mind, growing slowly as he thought more about the cause of his Lord's discomfort and the source of his own angst.

Once again silence descended between them, the Wraith Lord deep in thought. The master of the Wraith Horde stared off into the swirling grey. Seeing all that was happening in the Murk. Seeing what was beyond as well, his gaze turning toward the southwest and the Bloody Steppe. Beyond that was their first target. The Northern Peaks and the city that was nestled within.

Shadow's Reach.

"We should not have trusted the woman to find the one we seek," the Wraith Lord finally said.

"We didn't, Lord. We gave the Dark Magus time to prove her worth. Nothing more than that." The Wraith Hunter shrugged. He was pleased to see that his Lord seemed to agree with his assessment, though he could sense his increasing impatience.

The Hunter understood from where that impatience came. It had taken the Wraith Lord an enervatingly long time to reach this point, and he wanted to make the most of what could be his brethren's only opportunity. The future success and survival of the Wraiths depended upon it.

"We did not believe that she would succeed, yet there was nothing lost in letting her try," the Hunter explained. "The one we seek is too elusive. Too much like a Wraith for her to do what we required of her."

The Wraith Lord remained quiet for a while longer, not even offering a grunt of acknowledgment. The Wraith Hunter continued, feeling the need to fill the silence. "It matters not, Lord. We were not ready then. With the trouble to the north, we could do nothing more than probe. We needed more time to prepare. With the trouble to the north no longer trouble, now we can do what is required of us."

"You are certain that we are ready?" The Wraith Lord wasn't nervous. He just wanted to be sure. "We cannot fail. You cannot fail. A chance like this will not come again."

"We are, Lord. I promise you. We can release the Horde on your command."

The Wraith Lord waited several heartbeats before replying, his eyes locked onto those of his Hunter. He had selected this Wraith for this task because he knew his qualities. What he could do. What he had done. What he would do to achieve what was demanded of him.

Yet for some reason that he did not quite understand, the Wraith Lord experienced a touch of unease. A wisp of uncertainty flowing through him.

Was it because the time had finally come after such a long, almost unbearable wait? Or was there more to it?

His eyes flashed when he realized what was needling him.

It was the boy. No more than vermin and having no place in the Murk, yet still he entered it with impunity. He hunted in it just like his Wraiths did.

The fact that he was concerned about a creature that should be beneath the notice of the Wraiths gave him pause. It also unsettled him, although he made sure that he did not reveal that to his second in command.

"You know our history?"

"I do, Lord," the Wraith Hunter replied quietly, respectfully. "We all do. Our history is who we are, Lord. We understand that. We revere it. We build upon it."

The Wraith Hunter didn't need to remind the Wraith Lord that every Wraith learned the history of their kind, imbued it, became one with it, because their history was more than just a history. It was a way of life. A way of moving through the world.

A map for gaining revenge on those who had wronged them.

A map for making the world their own.

The Wraiths had been oppressed long ago, forced down a path that was not of their choosing. Consumed by the Curse. Made into the image of the Curse against their will.

Yet that subjugation had proven to be a blessing as well.

Because having been touched by the Curse, the Wraiths became something different. Stronger. More dangerous. Deadlier. Something more rapacious.

Thanks to the Curse, the Wraiths became a threat, their maker no longer able to control them. No longer able to compel them.

With the power that only they could call upon, the Wraiths broke their bonds, accepting both the gifts and the limitations that the Murk granted them. Mastering them. Making them their own. Allowing those gifts and limitations to make them stronger. More resilient. More determined.

When they were ready, when they were certain that their maker could no longer stand against them, the Wraiths used the Murk to conquer Frisia. They made the ancient kingdom into their home.

Most essential to their success, they sent their maker – the Dread -- fleeing beyond the Murk. And those who tried to stand against them were sent to the other side. Painfully. Without a hint of remorse, and with a great deal of pleasure.

Since then, the Murk had remained in place for a thousand years and more, staked over that land of yore. A birthplace of heroes becoming a home to monsters.

From time to time, the Wraith Lord grew restless, using his power to push the Murk beyond what had been old Frisia. Testing what could be done with the thick blanket of grey. Learning. Mastering. Planning. Yet each time he did so, he always had to relent, the Murk settling back into place within its original boundaries.

But no more.

As the centuries passed the Wraith Lord became one with the Murk. So much so that he learned how to move the Murk where he wanted it to be. That meant that his Wraiths, inextricably linked to the Murk, could go with it.

And now it was time for the Murk and the Wraiths to travel beyond the boundaries of the ancient kingdom that they had claimed as their own.

For good.

Because now was the time to expand their lands. Their power.

It was time to make the world as the Wraiths believed that it should be. As they needed it to be.

"Then write our history as we know that it should be written. Let the world discover what happens to those who seek to oppose us."

"Yes, Lord," replied the Wraith Hunter, breathing a silent sigh of relief. For a few heartbeats, he feared that he wouldn't be going with his Scouts. That his service had come to an end and that his Master was prepared to select a new Hunter as payment for his failures. So few though they were. Yet still so important. Therefore, best to make the most of his reprieve. "I will do as you command."

The Wraith Hunter turned and faded into the Murk, not wanting to give his master the chance to rethink his decision.

The Wraith Lord had pulled the Murk back closer to the borders of their homeland to ensure that the problem in the north could be put to rest with little difficulty. That challenge resolved, now the Wraith Hunter could push his skirmishers farther to the south in preparation for the coming of the Horde.

He and his Scouts had a long way to travel, and they needed to move swiftly if they were to get into position in time. Nevertheless, he was certain that they would do what was required of them because the Wraith Lord already had begun to push the Murk toward their first target.

The grasping grey flowing beyond the Wyld and Old Frisia.

Toward the Bloody Steppe and beyond.

The Wraith Hunter would advance with the vanguard. The Wraith Lord would follow a few days behind.

Yet as he headed off to set the Wraith Horde in motion, the Hunter couldn't escape the gnawing feeling that ate at him.

The man he had fought on the street in Shadow's Reach. The one who had sliced across his thigh. He had been a challenge.

Yet the Wraith Hunter had little concern about that master of the blade. If he still lived, the Wraith Hunter had little doubt that he would kill him if they encountered one another again. The human had gotten lucky.

The Wraith Hunter had slipped on the cobblestones. It had been no more than a quirk of fate.

Not so the boy he had fought in the Murk what seemed ages ago yet was no more than a year.

The boy who had given the Hunter a permanent limp thanks to his driving a dagger through the top of his foot.

The Wraith Hunter knew that the boy was still alive. That the boy still moved within the Murk with a confidence that grated.

The Wraith who is not a Wraith.

His only true rival among the vermin he was charged with exterminating.

The one who had almost cost him his place beside the Wraith Lord.

For the Wraith Hunter to continue to lead, to continue to live, the Wraith who is not a Wraith needed to die.

It was as simple as that.

One for the other.

Because no matter how hard the Wraith Hunter tried to ignore the feeling that had settled into the base of his spine, he couldn't. That feeling refusing to leave him be.

In fact, the more he thought about the Wraith who is not a Wraith, the more that feeling festered. Expanded. Burrowed deeper within him. Distracted him.

The Wraith Hunter struggled to manage that feeling, because it was so unfamiliar to him.

It was a feeling that he thought he had conquered long before.

A feeling of fear.

Fear that not only would he fail to kill the Wraith who is not a Wraith, but also that this boy, who he should have killed so many times before, would prevent the Wraiths from achieving their primary objective.

Blanketing the Territories with the Murk.

Slaughtering the humans.

Claiming the lands of the vermin as their own.

Then moving on to the next Realm and then the next.

Until there was nothing but the Murk.

Nothing but the Wraiths.

The Wraith Hunter feared that this Wraith who is not a Wraith would be the reason that the Wraiths' thousand-year dream would be extinguished for good.

That the Wraith who is not a Wraith would write the history rather than the Wraiths themselves.

He couldn't allow that.

Death would be much preferred to the shame of that failure.

Yet to avoid that and to make his ilk's dream a reality, the Wraith Hunter needed to conquer his fear.

And he needed to kill the Wraith who is not a Wraith.

2. BLOOD ON THE STONE

"Now this is something that I can use," Davin murmured appreciatively, eyeing what lay at his feet.

After his latest fall, he pushed himself back up with a slight groan, his scraped knees and palms the least of his concerns, the insistent urge to keep moving sounding like an alarm bell in the back of his skull. Even so, he needed to take a brief rest first, enjoying the touch of the cool stone on his back as he leaned against the wall.

The gladiator took several deep breaths, calming himself, his eyes turned back toward the direction from which he had come, searching for any hint of movement.

Nothing.

At least not yet.

Then he smiled. He wasn't out of danger. Not by a long shot. Nevertheless, he felt good about what he had accomplished.

He had gotten farther than he ever thought possible. Just a half hour before, his captor was about to do her worst. Strapped down to a stone slab, Hakea Roosarian taunting him, promising him a future that was worse than death. Stalkers staring hungrily at him from the cages lining both sides of the torture chamber.

Funny how events could change so quickly and drastically. And all because he had gotten lucky with a few drops of blood.

He really wasn't surprised, however. It had been much the same way on the white sand. An unexpected slip. A lucky strike. The sun hitting his opponent's eyes at exactly the wrong time.

There was no point in thinking about why it happened. Better just to be pleased and thankful that it did.

And Davin was.

He would never forget Roosarian's malicious, almost seductive, grin as she held that vial of horrific black liquid just above his mouth, a single drop of that putrid concoction just a breath away from dripping down his throat. By the skin of his teeth, he had escaped from Roosarian before she could transform him into one of the monsters hunting him.

Declan had taught him and all the other gladiators sentenced to the Pit that in order for them to succeed, in order for them to survive, they needed to control as many variables as they possibly could despite the precariousness of their circumstances. And, inevitably, when they couldn't, they needed to be ready to act when fate smiled down upon them.

Davin had been ready, even though he never expected a Stalker to break free. He never anticipated that all the monsters would escape their cages in the ensuing chaos. He never believed that he would unstrap himself and get out of the killing ground before he joined the unlucky Captain Oselnik, who was gutted by a Stalker at the start of the clash.

Since then, Davin had stumbled down the darkened corridors beneath the Rock, turning left or right based on a whim rather than any real knowledge of where he was going.

All he wanted to do was put some distance between himself and the monsters that were hunting him. He would worry about where he was once he found a place safe from his pursuers. Assuming that he could.

Lost within the warren of corridors running beneath the citadel, he had yet to find a door that wasn't locked or, in fact, any location that would allow him to better defend himself. The only option that he had found so far was where he stood now. One corridor running into another at a right angle. Limiting the direction from which a Stalker could come at him.

Adding insult to injury, Davin couldn't remember how many times he had fallen. In part because of the darkness. He could barely see in the pitch black that only so often shifted to a dull grey when he walked beneath one of the few slit windows positioned far above him.

Primarily because he was having such a hard time staying on his feet. The injuries he had suffered before and then during his imprisonment slowed him down and forced him to nothing more than an awkward hobble and shuffle.

As he stumbled along, he had done his best to ignore the Stalkers' shrieks and screams that echoed down the narrow hallways. The sound, similar to steel scraping across stone, made his teeth hurt.

He had been hoping for more time, maybe even the chance to evade his hunters entirely, but it hadn't taken the monsters long to take up the chase. They had his scent, and one of them already had a taste of his blood.

Pushing his fears to the side, he concentrated on the monsters coming his way. He was moving more slowly than he would have preferred, but he was moving.

Now, with the Stalkers drawing closer, he needed to avoid another fall. Because he feared that if he went down hard again, he wouldn't be getting back up. Then he'd just be easy meat.

Rather than allow his fears to drive him, he decided that he would worry about his hunters when he saw their blood-red eyes in the darkness. Until then, he would look for the one feature in the tangle of corridors beneath the Rock that might help him stay alive.

And at least now he was in a slightly improved position to stand against the beasts when they appeared. He had found a new tool that should prove more effective against his hunters than the one that he never would have escaped without.

Sliding between his ragged breeches and the small of his back the bloody spade that had helped him get past the Stalkers in the torture chamber, he reached down, picking up two of the sharpened steel rods, each about three feet long, that he had tripped over just a moment before. He had only succeeded in keeping himself on his feet because he had come to another turn in the corridor, the unyielding wall to his front preventing another tumble, the price he had to pay for that kindness a bruised shoulder.

He didn't know who had left the steel spikes there or why. He really didn't care. He was grateful to his anonymous donor.

Fate was smiling down upon him, and Davin wanted to make the most of it while he could.

He held the two steel spikes up to the dim light that battled the darkness above him.

He nodded in satisfaction. Things were looking up.

He had a better chance of seeing his pursuers in the greyish gloom. And, although the spikes were a little rusty, they still held a keen edge. These would do nicely indeed.

Davin was about to continue on his way, hoping to find what he was looking for before the Stalkers found him. But it was too late.

He pushed himself off the wall and turned to face the darkness from which he had emerged just minutes before. Even though he knew what was coming, the shriek that blasted down the hallway sent a shiver through his entire body.

He didn't have to wait long. The twilight shifted, a massive figure disturbing it.

He couldn't make out much of the monster except for its dim, towering shape, the creature blending too well into the darkness, and those blood-red eyes that blazed with an insatiable hunger.

He was really getting tired of this.

The smart play was for Davin to run. There was more light in the direction that he was going, and there might be some space just a little farther down where he could better defend himself.

Davin shook his head slowly from side to side, biting his lip, as he considered that strategy for a few seconds then threw it away.

He really didn't care about making the smart decision now.

He was done running.

He refused to give the Stalker the satisfaction of chasing him down from behind.

If this Stalker was going to kill him, then Davin was going to make the monster do it looking him in the eyes.

Jumping over the pile of steel spikes that had almost taken him to the floor, Davin raced down the corridor in a stumbling gallop, screaming at the top of his lungs.

The Stalker's shriek died in the monster's throat, shocked to see his prey charging right at him.

That heartbeat of hesitation worked in the gladiator's favor.

Davin didn't even bother to swing. He knew how hard it would be to get in a good strike with the darkness hiding the Stalker so well. Instead, he focused solely on the monster's eyes. Where the eyes were, so was the Stalker.

He barreled right into the beast, at the very last second ducking and turning, his shoulder slamming into the Stalker's gut and sending the beast stumbling backward.

Using his momentum to his advantage, Davin went with the

monster. Staggering for a few steps and then falling right atop the Stalker's broad chest and forcing it to the floor.

Davin smiled maliciously, hearing the air escaping from the Stalker's lungs when the beast's back hit the unyielding stone of the hallway.

Grunting, struggling to breathe, the Stalker was slow to raise its arms to defend itself.

Davin didn't hesitate, swinging his makeshift spears with a wild abandon. Arm, chest, neck, groin, gut. It didn't matter what he hit so long as he hit some part of the Stalker's body.

Davin allowed his rage to take over. To drive him. His only concern was keeping the monster on the ground. Giving into a desperate need to hurt the beast as badly as he had been hurt himself.

When he began his assault, savoring the beating that he was administering to his hunter, Davin thought that he might succeed. In fact, he thought he detected a whimper as the Stalker thrashed about, struggling to evade his powerful blows.

Davin realized that he had misjudged the situation when he felt himself soaring backward through the air.

The Stalker, ignoring its injuries, surged up off the ground and howled in triumph.

Davin landed heavily on his back, lying there for just a moment, seeking to reclaim the air knocked from his lungs.

When he finally took a breath again, he realized that it might be his last one.

Those blood-red eyes were coming directly toward him. The monster soaring through the air, claws reaching for him.

Understanding that he had no chance of getting out of the way in time, Davin reacted instinctively. He lifted the steel spike in his right hand and angled it toward his target as best as he could in the hindering darkness.

Davin grunted in pain, the breath knocked from him again,

several ribs cracking, as he was crushed against the rough stone. The seconds that followed passed slowly.

He expected to feel one of the Stalker's razor-sharp claws digging into his gut or his throat or his chest, and when he didn't that fear was overwhelmed by his fight to fill his lungs with air.

Finally, black spots at the edge of his vision, he gasped, taking a much-needed breath.

Rather than the excruciating pain of his body being ripped open, he felt the heavy weight of the monster lying atop him. Then the touch of wetness as a liquid that was invisible in the dark trickled down over his forehead and face.

Turning to the side, he spit it out, wiping his eyes with the back of his free hand.

Blood.

He spat a few more times, attempting to get the metallic taste out of his mouth even though he knew that it was a lost cause.

Despite his new predicament, he smiled then sighed with relief.

Through a quirk of luck, the second touch of luck that he had experienced since sneaking into the Rock, the steel tip of the spike that he held out before him had hit its mark. Puncturing the Stalker's eye, punching all the way into its brain and killing the monster instantly.

For just a few seconds more, Davin lay there, the crushing weight of the dead Stalker pressing down on him. He was struggling for breath. Bruised and battered. Every part of his body hurt in some fashion. Covered in blood. But most of it wasn't his blood, so what did he care?

He did care that there were more Stalkers hunting for him in the warren of hallways beneath the Rock. That reality made clear as several more shrieks echoed down the corridor.

Davin judged these hunters to be no more than a few hundred yards away.

Understanding just how poor his chances of survival were, he thought about simply staying where he was. He could be done with it all. He could escape the pain. The terror.

Davin snorted softly in disbelief, disappointed that he had allowed that self-defeating concept to pop into his brain.

Giving in, no matter the poor odds, simply wasn't in him.

Taking as deep a breath as he could manage with the dead Stalker lying atop him, Davin tried to push the monster off him. The body wouldn't budge. The beast must have weighed four hundred pounds if not more.

Hearing more shrieks drifting down the corridor, the shrill noise once more setting his teeth on edge and filling him with a desperate urgency, Davin pushed with all the strength that he could muster. Which, to his regret, wasn't all that much after all that he had suffered through during the last few days.

No success.

He barely shifted the corpse lying atop him.

Worse, now it was pressing down even more on his chest, making it harder for him to take a breath.

Davin tried again, not only pushing against the monster's chest, but also trying at the same time to turn his hip so that he could roll the beast off him.

Grunting and groaning, after several seconds of strenuous effort, he was able to shift the Stalker an inch. Maybe two. But no more than that.

Davin cursed, not quite believing how his luck had changed for the worse so quickly. Then again, he should have expected as much.

It was no different than fighting in the Pit. And now, his exhaustion almost complete, his muscles were shaking from what had proven to be an almost useless attempt to escape the dead weight pressing down upon him.

Two more shrieks echoed down the corridor. Davin guessed that the Stalkers couldn't be more than a hundred yards away.

And he was trapped beneath the body of one of their dead brethren. How remarkably appropriate.

The thought that he could be done with it all again flickered through the back of his mind.

He could do it.

He could give in.

He could accept his fate.

He had fought the good fight.

And in the end, just as he had learned on the white sand, he could only fight so hard. He could only give so much.

Because no matter what he did, no matter how much he gave of himself, no matter how hard he tried, fate would come calling for him.

Eventually, like it or not, he would go to the other side.

No!

Davin refused to give in.

If he was to go to the other side, then it would be on his terms.

He would never give in.

He would not leave this world until he could no longer draw breath. Until every drop of blood had been drained from his body. Until he could no longer fight.

That's how Declan had trained him.

That's who he was.

That sense of urgency mixed with desperation allowed Davin to connect with a hidden reserve of strength within him. With a last gasp of effort, every muscle in his body straining, he heaved the dead Stalker far enough to the side so that he was able to scoot the rest of the way out and finally take a deep breath again.

Pushing himself back to his feet, wobbling a bit because of his shaky legs, with a steel spike in each hand, he began to hobble down the hallway, taking some comfort from the dim light of the early morning that streamed through the narrow windows thirty feet above his head.

If the Stalkers were going to kill him, he was going to make them work for it.

The end of the chapter.

To keep reading *Storm in the Darkness*, visit my author website at PeterWachtBooks.com or Amazon.

MORE FROM PETER WACHT

THE FALLEN KNIGHT SERIES

(Forthcoming)

The Death of the Dragon (short story)*

The Dragon Awakens

Duel With a Dragon

Beware the Dragon

The Dragon Returns

THE REALMS OF THE TALENT AND THE CURSE

THE LEGEND OF THE DRAGON LORD

The Painful Truth (short story)*

Stealing the Light (Forthcoming 2025)

THE TALES OF CALEDONIA

(Complete 7-Book Series)

Blood on the White Sand (short story)*

The Diamond Thief (short story)*

The Protector

The Protector's Quest

The Protector's Vengeance

The Protector's Sacrifice

The Protector's Reckoning

The Protector's Resolve

The Protector's Victory

THE TALES OF THE TERRITORIES

Stalking the Blood Ruby (short story)*

A Fate Worse Than Death (short story)*

Death on the Burnt Ocean

Monsters in the Mist

The Dance of the Daggers

Bloody Hunt for Freedom

A Spark of Rebellion

Shadows Made Real

Shadow's Reach

Storm in the Darkness (Forthcoming 2025)

THE SYLVAN CHRONICLES

(Complete 9-Book Series)

The Legend of the Kestrel

The Call of the Sylvana

The Raptor of the Highlands

The Makings of a Warrior

The Lord of the Highlands

The Lost Kestrel Found

The Claiming of the Highlands

The Fight Against the Dark

The Defender of the Light

THE RISE OF THE SYLVAN WARRIORS

Through the Knife's Edge (short story)*

* Free stories can be downloaded from my author website at
PeterWachtBooks.com. My books are also available on Amazon and
other online retailers.